Clare Nicol is the ps
highly successful TV
BALACLAVA STR

For Douglas and Jenne,
who have bullied me
unmercifully for years.

Clare Nicol

Blitz on Balaclava Street

Futura
Macdonald & Co
London & Sydney

A Futura Book

First published in Great Britain in 1983
by Futura Publications, a Division of
Macdonald & Co (Publishers) Ltd
London & Sydney

ISBN 0 7088 2283 5

Filmset, printed and bound in Great Britain by
Hazell Watson & Viney Ltd, Aylesbury, Bucks

Futura Publications
A Division of
Macdonald & Co (Publishers) Ltd
Maxwell House
74 Worship Street
London EC2A 2EN

1

The Day of the Party

It was Saturday at last. There was a slight haze over the town which promised heat later on, and Londoners woke up to another of those lovely Indian summer days they'd been enjoying that September.

Kathleen Johnson drew the curtains of the bedroom and smiled as she looked out over her tiny front garden. There was only ten feet of ground between the front door and the pavement of Balaclava Street, but Kath had always regarded it with pride. She gave a little sigh of contentment. The floribundas were coming to an end, but there'd be enough to fill a bowl for the party tonight.

'It's going to be a lovely night, Stan,' she said, turning to her husband. The only reply was a muffled snort as Stan buried his face deeper in the pillow. Kath smiled. Poor old Stan! He did like his lie-in, and these days he didn't often get the chance. She decided to leave him while she got the breakfast.

As Kath started her day at Number Seven, her only daughter, Patricia, was making her way home from the Ambulance Depot in Battersea Rise, her black tin helmet perched on the back of her head, swinging her gas mask gaily in time to the song she was humming. Patty radiated happiness that morning, and a little of it rubbed off on the people she passed as they began their dull daily routine. Some of the bolder ones whistled or called out. Patty grinned and waved back. Nothing was going to upset her today.

'*Love walked right in and brought my sunniest day . . .*' she sang.

For Patty, love had done just that: walked right in – to the Hammersmith Palais, on her seventeenth birthday, only two months ago. Love in the shape of Sub-Lieutenant Peter Quayle. At the time, Joe Loss and his band had been playing that number; now it had become *their* tune.

'One magic moment . . . and my heart seemed to know . . . That love said "Hallo" . . . though not a word was spoken . . .—'

Not quite true. Peter had said 'How do you do?' before he'd asked her to dance. He was very polite and correct – everything an officer should be. And so different from most of the other servicemen.

'Too few men and far too many girls,' Lesley had said. Lesley was her best friend. They lived a few doors apart, had been through school together, and left at the same time. That evening they had gone to the Palais together.

Patty felt bad about Lesley. She was the one who'd convinced Mum that it was all right for them to go on their own. Mum was a bit old-fashioned that way, but Lesley had persuaded her they'd be all right and that they'd stick together until they came home. If they waited to be asked out, they'd wait forever. Nearly all the local boys had been called up and those that were left, you could keep, thank you very much!

After that first outing, the two girls went regularly to the Palais, which was invariably crowded and noisy. They soon learned the score, noticing how the girls always made a concerted effort to catch the eye of any Canadian or Australian who came in – they were much better paid than the British boys and were flash with their money, which didn't help to keep the peace. Patty, though, refused to join in. Not that she was scared, as Lesley suggested – it just seemed rather undignified. In fact, she didn't need to be pushy: men automatically gravitated towards the pretty little girl sitting there so quietly in the background.

Patty had inherited her mother's brown eyes, but her hair was naturally blonde and she had creamy skin to go with it – unusual colouring, and Patty was still young and inexperienced enough to blush when she was complimented on it. The men adored that, so she got more compliments than ever. Patty liked the overseas servicemen. Maybe they did throw their money around, but Patty supposed it was only because they were so lonely and far from home – a sort of vain effort to buy friends, or at least a temporary companionship. One or two of them had called around to see her, and it was clear that they would have liked to further the relationship. But somehow when it came to the crunch Patty made a hasty retreat and the friendship cooled.

For some reason, she couldn't go further than the odd kiss and fumble, unlike Lesley, who openly admitted that she enjoyed a good petting session. Patty was worried. Was there something wrong with her? Lesley teased her. How could she possibly know until she tried?

'Les – what do you . . . I mean, well, how far do you actually *go*?' Patty asked one night, on the tram coming back from the pictures.

Lesley giggled. 'Well, Joy says' – Joy was Lesley's elder sister, considered very sophisticated by the other two – 'Joy says anything above the waist is all right, but watch it if they start getting fresh down below.'

Patty pondered this piece of advice. It wasn't something she could discuss with Mum, much as she loved her. Mum would probably get embarrassed, like when she'd told her about having periods. And Patty didn't have an elder sister like Joy. But perhaps once she was over the initial hurdle she wouldn't be quite so timid about sex . . .

Which was why she found herself on Wandsworth Common one night with a hefty Australian, pressed hard against a tree, with the bark cutting into her back. She wouldn't go all the way – she'd made that quite clear to Vince. She was a virgin and wanted to remain one. Vince had smiled. No problem. He probably thought she'd give in anyway. He was very sure of himself.

Patty felt a moment's panic. Suppose she couldn't stop

him? He was a powerful man. But suddenly there was no time for changing her mind, for Vince was kissing her – not gently on her lips, but thrusting his tongue into her mouth. She could taste his beery saliva, and a shudder of revulsion ran through her.

Vince mistook it for excitement. 'Baby – oh baby!' he murmured. Now his hands were roughly fondling her breasts. 'Oh, you little beaut!' He fumbled with the buttons of her dress, pulling it open, and then his hands were inside, forcing their way round to unhook her bra. He was working himself into a fever now, massaging, pulling, tweaking at her nipples. He bent his head and his mouth closed over one. Patty shut her eyes and suppressed another shiver of distaste. She preferred his mouth on her breast – at least it was soft, whereas his hands had been scratchy and rough. Then he bit her. The agony! Patty screamed.

Vince was immediately remorseful. 'Oh, honey, I'm sorry! I didn't mean to hurt you, honest! Just got carried away.'

Now he was back to kissing her mouth again, and she knew she was going to be sick. Vince took her hand and pushed it down between his legs to feel the swelling between them.

'See what you do to me?' He was panting now and rubbing himself against her. 'God, I want you so much!'

She shook her head, lips tightly closed.

'I'd be gentle – I swear it! You'd only have to say the word and I'd stop right away! Just let me feel you close . . .'

As he removed his hands to undo his fly buttons, Patty took her chance.

With all her strength she struggled free and fled. Vince was caught off balance and it was a moment or two before he recovered and set off in pursuit. Patty stumbled across the Common towards the road, her heart pounding in her ears. It was all her own fault. She'd been a – what was it Joy had called it? A prick tease. Just then she tripped and fell. As she lay, trying to fight off the tide of nausea, Vince was on her again.

'No! I'm going to be sick!' she just managed to gasp.

What a ridiculous situation! Hunched on her knees and heaving up her supper in the middle of Wandsworth Common, while the man who a moment before had been wild to ravish her, stood a little way off, shuffling from foot to foot in acute embarrassment, his ardour suddenly cooled.

Finally Patty wiped her mouth and got up from her knees. 'I'm sorry.'

'You should have told me you weren't feeling good. Are you okay now?'

She nodded. How did you explain to a man that *he* was the reason she'd been sick? You couldn't – you just said: 'Please take me home.'

Vince didn't argue, and Patty was grateful for that. At the gate, he simply shook her hand, muttered goodbye, then hurried off down Balaclava Street.

Just as Patty darted inside and up the stairs, her mother came out of the living room.

'Aren't you coming in for a cup of cocoa, darling?'

'No thanks. I'm not feeling too good.' She ran up the stairs, sensing rather than seeing her mother's eyes on her, puzzled and uneasy.

As soon as she was safe in bed that night, the tears came – hot, salty tears, trickling down her cheeks. Well, she'd tried, and she still didn't want to know about it. There *must* be something wrong with her!

But there wasn't. She'd just been waiting for the right person. She knew that now – had known it from the moment Peter started dancing with her.

The first time Peter had kissed her, she'd experienced a feeling of excitement quite new. She wouldn't have minded Peter caressing her breasts – to tell the truth, she wanted him to. But he didn't. He treated her with a sort of reverence – like a Dresden china doll.

Thinking about him made the long walk home pass

quickly, and soon she was turning into Balaclava Street, still singing to herself. She looked at Number Ten to see if there was any sign of Lesley, but the blackout curtains were still drawn. The Aynsworths were late this morning. She and Lesley hadn't been so close since Peter had come on the scene. It had been Lesley who's seen him first that night at the Palais. She'd nudged Patty.

'Look at that! Just like Van Johnson, isn't he?'

He was a bit, but Patty thought he was more rugged-looking. She had to admit Peter wasn't very tall, only about five foot nine and a bit at a guess; but then Patty was only five foot two herself, so it didn't matter. The two girls couldn't believe their luck when Peter made his way towards them, but it was Patty he asked to dance; she had the feeling Lesley had never quite forgiven her for that. It was a pity they didn't see so much of each other nowadays, but Peter came first. With her doing a different shift each week and Peter working on a course at the Admiralty, their off-duty moments didn't often coincide, so they were very precious.

Peter hadn't actually said he loved her, but she was sure he did – almost sure anyway. She couldn't be wrong about that look in his eyes. Perhaps he'd say something tonight at the party. It was her brother Roger's twenty-first, and Number Seven was pushing the boat out as Roger had got leave from the RAF. It would be the first time Peter and Roger had met. She hoped they'd hit it off.

Patty smiled as she imagined the flap at home as her mother prepared for the party. Dear old Mum! Well, forty-two wasn't *that* old really – and Mum was still an attractive woman, even if she was putting on a little weight. There was hardly any grey in her wavy brown hair, and the lines on her face were from laughter rather than strain. Mind you, she let herself be imposed on far too often. That was Mum – she just naturally seemed to attract people in trouble.

Little Joey Williams was swinging on the front gate of

Number Nine, next door to the Johnsons. The hinge was rusted through, and Patty was about to warn him to be careful when she was startled by a loud burst of imitation machine-gun fire from behind the hedge and dive-bombed by paper-dart aeroplanes aimed by Joey's older brother, Glen. Hands up in surrender, she ran laughing into her own house.

'Hi Ma!' she called, but the kitchen was empty. The kettle was boiling on the hob and the back door was open. A moment later, her mother came hurrying in from the outside toilet, her faded old quilted dressing gown flapping round her bare ankles.

Patty gave her a peck on the cheek. 'When are you going to throw that old rag out?' she asked, fingering the dressing gown.

'Can't waste my money on luxuries.'

'Now, Mum, that's not the spirit! Remember what Evelyn Home says? Always look glamorous for your husband!'

Kath gave a snort of contempt. 'I'd like to see her floating down the garden path in her négligée in the middle of the night.'

Patty pinched a piece of hot toast from under the grill.

Kath smacked her hand, smiling. 'You're worse than Tim. Can't you wait five minutes?'

Patty grinned at her. 'I'll be ready for another by then. Any chance of a bath this morning? I see you've lit the boiler.'

'All right – give it half an hour or so.' Kath walked to the bottom of the stairs and called up: 'If you two fellers don't get a move on, Patty will have eaten all the breakfast.'

There were various thumps and clatterings from upstairs. Stan Johnson was the first down, in shirt-sleeves and braces, carrying the stiff white collar he would put on after his morning ablutions. He dumped his shaving gear on the draining board.

'Like me to get this out of your way first, love?' he asked his wife.

'Stan, I've cooked you a sausage and fried bread,' she protested.

'Keep it warm for me. This won't take a second.'

He set up his shaving mirror and busily lathered his face.

Patty turned away with an expression of distaste. She hated the idea of people washing in the kitchen while other members of the family were eating. Old Perkins, the landlord, had promised them a bathroom this year – some of the other houses had them. But now it looked like they'd have to go on pigging it until the war ended, whenever that would be.

Stan looked down the back garden. 'Anyone let Gert and Daisy out?'

'I'll go,' Patty volunteered, glad to get out of the kitchen.

She walked down the paved path, which was flanked on either side by serried rows of vegetables. Dad was certainly taking to heart the call to 'Dig for Victory'. At the end of the vegetables was a small chicken run and coop which housed Gert and Daisy, their hens. They'd been ensconced for all of six months and had been marvellous value, augmenting the family egg ration splendidly all through the summer – at least, when those Williams kids didn't scramble over the fence and pinch them first. Last time Dad had caught Glen and Barry red-handed and threatened to tan their hides. Barry swore they'd only hopped over for their cricket ball, but the eggs had been squashed in his pocket and there was yolk running down his legs. In the end Mum had saved the day by getting another couple of hens which she gave to Madge Williams. It wasn't long before half the street followed suit and every morning there was a chorus of squawks as the chickens were let out into their respective runs.

Gert and Daisy greeted Patty with a lot of cackling and

fluttering of wings, then waited expectantly for their morning ration of grain. Patty duly obliged, and they set to frantically picking at the ground.

Next, Patty looked in the nesting boxes. The industrious Daisy had dutifully presented them with two large eggs, But nothing in the other box. Oh dear! Gert was definitely off lay. She'd have to pretend there was one egg from each of them. Kath and Patty shared this secret, because Stan had decreed that as soon as the hens went off lay, they were for the pot. But Gert was like part of the family now – you couldn't wring her neck, let alone contemplate *eating* her; Patty looked at the white hen affectionately as it scratched away at the ground, oblivious. She picked up some of the white feathers and put them in her pocket, remembering the chat at the Depot in last night's shift. There were quite a lot of Conscientious Objectors in the Civil Defence, and they came in for much vocal scorn from the women. The Commandant's wife, Old Maudie Harris, had suggested that they should send them all white feathers. It seemed a bit strange to Patty, but apparently it was what they'd done in the last war.

Just then there was a clank of a chain and the noisy gurgling of the flush. Someone was in next door's outside lavatory. There was a coughing spasm, definitely of masculine origin. It was Bert, father of the Williams gang and a local Bobby. Diplomatically, Patty ducked down into the Anderson shelter to allow him to get out unseen. The outside lavatories had been constructed in blocks of two, with only the thinnest of wooden partitions between them. The Johnsons shared with the Williams.

Back in the kitchen, Patty gave her mother a meaning look as she placed the eggs in the larder. 'Only two, I'm afraid.'

'Those blasted birds!' muttered her father with a mouthful of sausage. 'Not keeping up the production line. How do you fancy a nice chicken stew next week?'

'*Dad!*' It was a united chorus of outrage in which even

Tim, the fourteen-year-old youngest member of the family, joined.

'Don't tell me you're all getting sentimental over those dratted hens,' remarked Stan.

'Well, I bet you wouldn't find it easy to wring their necks when it came to the point,' replied Tim, finishing his porridge and starting on the toast.

There was a pause as Stan considered. 'Well, we'll see how they go in a week or two . . .' The others smiled in relief. Stan looked at the clock on the mantelpiece. 'Best be off, I suppose. At least it's only a half day.'

He kissed his wife and daughter and cuffed Tim playfully on the ear. It was a pity Tim still had a mouthful of tea. He spluttered and choked. 'Dad! You made me do the nose trick!'

'How am I ever going to teach him table manners?' complained Kath, but she was smiling. 'Oh, Stan, don't forget to pick up the extra glasses from the Windmill on your way home.'

Stan fixed his stiff white collar and put on his dark office jacket. 'No need for an umbrella today,' he smiled to himself as he set off to work.

Tim scuttled away about his own business after breakfast and as soon as he was out of the house, Patty set about filling the large tin bath. Kath sat down at last with a cup of tea while her daughter soaked. They were both in a relaxed mood.

'Did you warn the Colonel you might be late on duty tonight?' she asked.

Patty chuckled. 'I don't get to talk to the old "B" very often, unless he wants to tick me off for something. I'll try to sneak in without telling him. Anyway, I don't start till midnight. The party should be over by then.'

'Yes. We'll have to put Gran on the last tram. I tried to get her to stay the night, but she won't. She's so stubborn.'

'Well, you know you'd only squabble if she did. You and Gran can't be under the same roof for more than a couple of hours before you're at each other.'

Kath smiled to herself. It was perfectly true. She loved her mother dearly, but they did get on each other's nerves. It wasn't that they were particularly alike – Gran was much more down-to-earth; she and Stan got along famously. But Gran did like to do things her own way and in her own time. And, more than anything, she liked to sleep in her own bed. An uncomfortable thing it was, too; an old-fashioned brass bedstead with a hair mattress. She'd had most of her children in it; her husband had died in it and, God willing, she would, too.

The phone shrilled, rousing Patty from her private day-dream.

'All right, love, I'll get it.' Kath went into the hall. One benefit they'd derived from Stan volunteering to be an Air Raid Warden was that they'd had a phone installed, and at Government expense. Almost before she'd learned who was at the other end, a breathless and dripping Patty, swathed in a bath towel, was at her side.

'Is it Peter?' she asked, eyes shining.

Kath nodded and handed her the receiver. She returned to the kitchen and with an indulgent smile mopped up the trail of water left by her daughter. Stan said she spoilt the kids, and maybe she did. But she couldn't help remembering how the last war had blighted her own youth. This war might well do the same for her children, so she was determined to give them as much enjoyment as possible while she could. Thank God, last time Stan had come out of it all unscathed. Would she be so lucky this time? She thought of Roger, her first-born, and felt a tight spasm of pain in her heart. There'd been some severe raids on the airfield through the summer, and heavy casualties. So far Roger had escaped with nothing more than cuts from flying glass. Thank God, he wasn't a pilot – she couldn't have borne that. She'd read somewhere that a fighter pilot's life-expectancy was twenty minutes in the air. How could people carry on a normal life with that knowledge constantly on their mind? And yet they did, apparently.

Though, of course, no one knew what private hell they endured.

All at once, Patty was back in the kitchen and babbling excitedly that Peter would be round with the car at midday to take her out for lunch at a little riverside pub.

'But when are you going to get your sleep?'

'I'm not tired, honestly, Mum! And we do get a chance to kip on night duty. Except when the old bastard does an emergency exercise!'

'You shouldn't talk about the Colonel like that!' Kath tried to look shocked.

'Anyway, it's all right if I go out? I'll eat an enormous lunch so I won't be hungry tonight, and there'll be all the more to go round.'

Kath smiled. 'Don't be late back, will you?'

'No. We'll be home teatime. Promise. Then we'll both be here to help.'

Together they lugged the heavy bath through the kitchen door and tipped it carefully into the trough Stan had made for water for the garden. People with proper bathrooms had been asked not to take more than four inches of water. They said King George had given orders for a line to be painted round all the royal baths so that everyone would know how much water they were using.

'Mum . . .'

'Yes, dear?'

'You . . . *like* Peter, don't you?'

'Of course I do.'

As Kath regarded her daughter's face, she felt mixed emotions. She was happy that her child was happy, but Patty was so young, only seventeen. Peter was a nice enough boy from what she knew, which wasn't much. He'd always been very polite and respectful; but then he was clearly trying to make a good impression. Some people would say he was quite a catch – Enid Belling from next door for starters; she was a great snob. Kath could imagine how saccharine sweet she'd be to Peter tonight. A naval officer! She'd go on about her husband being at sea too, though omitting to mention that George was on a merchant ship or that he wasn't even a sailor, but an ack-ack gunner temporarily attached to the service. Not that it made him any less brave. Kath had a great admiration for George, a quiet, kindly if rather stolid individual. It must be one hell of a life on those convoys. Then she remembered: George would be present tonight. He'd got back yesterday for a few days' leave. That would stop Enid boasting! Still, she mustn't be unkind about her next-door neighbours, because George had brought home a ham from Aruba and Enid had promised half of it for the party. Such a pleasant change from spam!

A loud knock on the front door sent her running to open it. There stood George Belling, and the look of tragic dismay on his face almost made her giggle, until the putrid smell that reached her nostrils told her why. In his hands was a parcel wrapped in a dirty newspaper, and it stank to high heaven. The ham!

'Kath, I'm sorry! What are we going to do?'

'Throw it in the dustbin, quick!'

'Yes, but . . . Well, Enid was so angry. She's rushed off to buy some tins of spam, but it won't be the same . . .'

'She shouldn't have done that!' exclaimed Kath, and chuckled. 'Don't be so miserable, George. No one was expecting ham, so no one's going to be disappointed. Here – get shot of that stinking mess and I'll make you a nice cuppa.'

'No, I won't stop, thanks all the same. Enid'll be over later to help with the sandwiches. I've promised to nip round The Windmill and have a drink with the lads.'

Kath nodded. That figured. Soon as George was home, all the local layabouts would be on the cadge for free drinks.

'See you later then. But just tell me one thing. How did you travel with that thing in your kitbag and not smell it before?'

George looked sheepish. 'To tell the truth, the lads in

the mess were complaining. I thought it was me dirty socks – they were a bit high, too.'

Joey Williams was astride the gate. 'Hi, Mr Belling. Got any chockies?'

'I'll give you chockies, you young varmint,' growled George, but his smile belied his tone.

Joey pouted. His sister, Megan, reproved him. 'You shouldn't ask, Joey. You know what Mam says – them that asks doesn't get.'

'And them as doesn't ask doesn't get neither,' retorted Joey.

George laughed. 'All right – you'd better come along with me and I'll see what I can find in me bag. But it's for all of you to share, mind.'

Megan decided to tag along too. She didn't altogether trust Joey's honesty regarding shares.

Back in the kitchen, Kath reflected on her guest list. Gran would be over from Stepney, of course, but she'd be the only Bowden present. The rest were too far afield. Kath's eldest brother had emigrated to Canada and was doing well out there. He and his wife had offered to have the kids and they'd nearly let them go, but they'd decided against it at the last moment. She was glad now. The bombing scares of the early war days had come to nothing, and then there'd been that awful tragedy of the *Athenia*, sunk with all those hundreds of children on board. Besides, nobody could say how long the wretched war would last, and an indefinite separation was more than she could bear. Stan agreed with her. They'd all stick together. The Queen had refused to send the Princesses abroad, and what was good enough for her was good enough for them.

Kath's youngest brother had been killed in the fighting prior to Dunkirk, as had her eldest nephew. The family had already suffered its first losses. Pray God, there wouldn't be more.

Stan's family was quite small. His widowed mother lived just outside Leeds and had decided the journey would be too much for her. Aunt Mabel, who lived with her, had informed them that she couldn't get away either – her work being of supreme national importance. Nobody liked Aunt Mabel. Even Stan only just tolerated her. No wonder nobody had wanted to marry *her*!

But what they lacked in family tonight would be more than made up for by friends and neighbours. All of Balaclava Street was invited. The war had changed a lot of things, but not all for the bad. A year ago she'd hardly been on nodding terms with a lot of the neighbours, and now they were all like old friends. Of course, Stan being the street warden had helped. It meant he had to go into everyone's home to check the number of occupants, their safety equipment and blackouts and so on. But people were kinder and more helpful on the whole. There was hardly a household in the street which hadn't volunteered some rations towards the party. It was the accepted thing that everyone chipped in – and it was the accepted thing that everyone joined the party. Heaven knows, any excuse was welcome these days.

The doorbell went again as Kath was in the middle of icing the cake. It was Mr Hempstead from Number Two over the road. Kath still called him Mr Hempstead, although he was known to all and sundry as 'Harry the Horse'. He tipped his battered green trilby and forced his lugubrious face into the semblance of a smile, showing his ill-fitting, discoloured dentures.

'Morning, Mrs Johnson,' he wheezed. 'Just popped over with a little pressie for young Roger.' He held out a bottle-shaped parcel wrapped in brown paper.

'Mr Hempstead – how kind! Er – would you like to come in for—'

'No – ta all the same,' was the reply, much to Kath's relief. 'I'm on me way to the races.' He patted his old satchel meaningfully.

'Oh, have a good day, then.'

'I certainly hope so, Mrs Johnson. Business is terrible these days, you know.'

'I'm sorry to hear that,' she responded politely. Kath knew nothing about bookies or the racing world in general, nor did she particularly wish to. Some of the characters she'd seen going in and out of Number Two looked very strange – some little better than common crooks. 'I suppose people don't have much time for racing.'

'True,' agreed Harry, with a melancholy sigh, 'and they've cut the meetings down to forty a year – not even every Saturday, would you believe? Doesn't give a bloke a chance to recoup his losses.'

Kath made a sympathetic murmur, but she couldn't help wondering why Mr Hempstead kept on in this line if it was so unprofitable.

'Well, mustn't bore you with my problems, today of all days.' He indicated the bottle in Kath's hands. 'That's real Moet and Chandon by the way – not vintage, but a good year. Can't get it in the off-licences now, you know. Champagne,' he added, noticing Kath's bewildered expression.

'Champagne! Oh, Mr Hempstead, you really shouldn't have!'

'Special occasion, isn't it? Well, ta ta for now,' he said in a bad Tommy Handley impersonation, and made for the gate.

'See you later, then,' Kath called after him.

She hurried back to the kitchen to resume her icing. What an unexpected kindness!

Being a bookie must have been quite a lucrative business before the war, because Harry owned his house. The even numbers on the opposite side of Balaclava Street were nearly all owner-occupied. They were larger and slightly more modern than the row Fred Perkins had bought. Number Two was the only house in the street to have a cellar, as Stan had discovered on one of his warden's calls. Not that Harry had allowed him down there – nor had he agreed to use it for an air-raid shelter, preferring the Anderson in the garden. 'Probably stores all his Black Market stuff down there,' Stan had chuckled to Kath. They'd all had reason to be grateful to 'Harry the Horse'; everyone in the street had purchased something from him at one time or another, be it silk stockings, fruit, packets of tea – you name it, Harry could lay his hands on it. Even the policeman, Bert Williams, turned a blind eye to Harry's activities, since his family benefited as much as anyone.

While her mother was busy in the kitchen, Patty dressed quickly. She'd have time to pop down the road to see Lesley before Peter arrived. Once again, she felt slightly guilty about Lesley. She'd promised to go into the West End with her this morning, and now she'd have to cancel it. Lesley's elder sister, Joy, worked at Dickins and Jones and could get a discount on clothes and make-up. There was a little dress, reduced because it was a bit shop-soiled, which Joy had reserved; Lesley wanted to pick it up to wear at the party tonight. She'd told Patty that she could just afford it if her Dad let her off this week's one-pound contribution to the housekeeping. By all accounts Mr Aynsworth was a mean old so-and-so, and Patty wondered how Lesley had got on.

In fact, at that particular moment, Lesley hadn't even approached him. She was still in bed, revelling in the knowledge that she was alone in the house and that today was Saturday. *Bliss!* In about half an hour, she'd have her bath – a lovely hot, full one, and to hell with that four inches bit! Then she'd paint her nails and get her clothes ready for the party. She didn't want to be late.

She was especially looking forward to seeing Roger Johnson again. She'd always had a crush on Roger, but he'd always treated her like a kid sister, pulling her hair and calling her 'Gingerknob', teasing her about her freckles and skinny legs. Well, he hadn't seen her for over six months now and, boy, would he notice a difference! The skinny legs had filled out nicely; the freckles could be hidden under a liberal layer of pancake; the hair – yes, it was still ginger, but she'd curled it now. If she could only make him notice her. Tonight would be the night!

Lesley surrendered to pleasurable thoughts about Roger. She rolled over on to her face and shut her eyes. As she imagined him making love, she began to work herself up. Suddenly she stopped and opened her eyes. She'd heard the noise of a van in the road. Don't say her father had chosen *this* moment to come home! Cursing under her breath, she hurried across the room to peer out of the curtains. Yes, blast it! There was his little black van with tinted windows.

Lesley didn't wait a moment longer. Gathering up various toilet accessories, she dashed for the bathroom, turned the taps on full, locked the door and started to sing loudly in the slightly nasal tone that she fondly imagined was like Vera Lynn. She was determined to get her bath. Her father always wanted one when he came back from one of these early morning jobs. He had this funny sort of smell about him. No member of family liked to talk openly about Mr Aynsworth's work, he was an undertaker – or as he rather pompously described himself, a funeral director.

Patty arrived at the door just after Horace Aynsworth had let himself in. He was scowling as he greeted her. His face, lugubrious at the best of times, now looked positively unpleasant. Patty didn't rate her friend's chances too highly if he was in *this* sort of mood.

'Is Lesley in?' she asked hesitantly.

'Should've thought the whole street could hear her,' replied Horace sourly. 'Dratted girl! She knows I like my bath after an early collection, and there she is, hogging all the hot water. She does it deliberately to irritate me.'

Patty reflected that this was more than likely, knowing Lesley. She followed Horace along to the kitchen, where he grudgingly pulled out a chair for her.

'Mind waiting in here? The wife's out on day shift. Oh, of course, you know.' Mrs Aynsworth worked at the same Ambulance Depot as Patty. The complaints continued:

'It's too bad! Up this morning at five. Had to collect the car from the funeral parlour, so as to be at the deceased's residence before seven. Well, we like to get the body out before the household is up and about. It avoids causing distress to the lately bereaved.'

Patty nodded. She found the topic morbid in the extreme, but felt it wise to be polite to Mr Aynsworth.

'I'm supposed to be back there by midday to receive the widow, see. Good impressions are very important – that's why I want my bath before I change into my best suit!'

He stumped angrily to the foot of the stairs. 'Lesley! Hurry up and get out of there!'

'I've only just got in, Dad,' came the reply.

'Well, you can just get out again. You've no business lying in bed as late as this.'

'But it's Saturday.'

'Some of us have to work Saturdays – Sundays too, come to that! You get a move on, I'm telling you! Anyway, your friend Patricia is here!'

Horace pulled at his beard angrily. He was a small, thin man and had gone prematurely bald. Patty guessed that the beard was to compensate. Also, he probably felt it gave him added dignity in his striped trousers and morning coat.

Lesley climbed out of the bath and began to dry herself. Better not push Dad too far, especially as she had a favour to ask. Then she flung on her kimono and undulated down the stairs, doing her 'Lana Turner' walk.

'Just going to make breakfast, Dad,' she said. 'Would you like some? Hallo, Patty!'

Horace regarded his daughter suspiciously. She wanted something, that was for sure. 'I'll have some tea and toast,' he said sourly. 'Have to give the boiler a bit of time to heat up again, I suppose.'

'That bloody boiler, it's the bane of our lives,' commented Lesley. 'Impossible to get two baths out of it, and if Mum does a big family wash we really have trouble.'

'All the more selfish of you to go taking all the water.'

After that, Horace relapsed into a sullen silence and Patty was able to explain the reason for her visit. A warning look from Lesley told her not to go on about the shopping trip. Clearly she hadn't broached the subject with her father yet.

As Lesley poured the tea and served up the toast, Horace surveyed her critically.

'What on earth have you got in your hair?' he asked suddenly.

Lesley turned. 'Curlers, of course – well, they're pipe cleaners really, but they do a good job and they don't hurt so much to sleep on.' Lesley unrolled one to show her father, leaving a ginger frizz behind.

Horace snorted contemptuously. 'Pipe cleaners! What will they think of next?'

'Got to look my best for Roger's party,' Lesley prattled on, starting a line of thought in her father's mind.

'Of course, it's his birthday, isn't it? How's your brother getting on in the RAF?' he asked, turning to Patty and looking for once quite amiable.

'Fine. He's just been made a sergeant, you know.'

'That's splendid, really splendid. And him only twenty-one. Your parents must be very proud.'

'Well, yes, I think they are.'

'Lucky people having two steady youngsters like you and Roger. And there's Mrs Aynsworth and me with only two empty-headed sluts to call our own.'

'Mr Aynsworth! That's not fair,' protested Patty. 'Lesley works jolly hard at her job.'

'Then why's she always talking of giving it up? All that money training her for the Civil Service, and now she wants to go off and join the WAAF!'

'It'd be more exciting than those dreary old forms I have to cope with,' said Lesley with a pout. 'Anyway, Dad, you needn't worry. They won't let me go – I'm reserved.'

'Good thing too,' commented Horace. 'You only want

to join up because you'd meet more men in the service. Man-mad both my girls,' he told Patty.

He smiled. In spite of his criticisms of his daughters he was in a better humour now.

But Lesley had seen her opportunity, and as soon as Patty left, she took advantage of it. Horace had always wanted a son, so that when he finally took over the funeral parlour from old man Truefitt, he could put up the sign *Aynsworth and Son* over the door. But, unfortunately, after two difficult births, the usually mild and compliant Mrs Aynsworth had refused to have any more children. Now Horace's thoughts turned to the possibility of a son-in-law – a nice, steady young man who could be trusted to take over the business from him one day. A young man like Roger, reflected Lesley. So far her friendship with Roger existed mainly within her own imagination, but her father wasn't to know that.

Stan returned from his office at lunchtime via the local pub. The Windmill, in keeping with most of the surroundings, was solidly Victorian, with little concession made to modernity or comfort. But this was a pub where real drinking was done – and most of it in the standing position. For many of the local residents, it was the focal point of their social life. The landlord, Tommy Glover, an ex-boxer, was a good sort who could always be relied on for a little credit when the going was tough.

Stan spotted George Belling at the end of the crowded bar and sitting hunched next to him. Sid Raynes, another Balaclava Street resident. Trust that old layabout Sid to be cadging drinks off poor George, thought Stan. At least George would be able to give him a hand with the crates, though.

Preparations for the party were in full swing at Number Seven. George's wife, Enid, had brought the promised tins of spam and had stayed to help with the mountain of sandwiches, which Kath was now wrapping carefully in damp tea towels.

'That should keep them from drying up, I think. Thanks for your help, Enid, you're a brick.'

'Pleasure,' replied Enid, rinsing her fingers daintily under the kitchen tap.

Kath had been surprised at Enid's offer, since usually she was too vain and selfish to care much about others. Or was that being uncharitable? Perhaps Kath was just the tiniest bit jealous, too. There was no denying that Enid was an attractive woman. She was the helpless, feminine type – though perhaps a bit on the plump side, now she'd reached the forty mark. Kath suspected that her china-doll complexion was helped along with a touch of rouge. What she *didn't* know was that Enid's lovely 'natural' blonde hair now owed much of its glory to peroxide and frequent, and costly, visits to the hairdresser's – a fact that Enid kept secret even from her own husband. But then, George wasn't very observant at the best of times.

'Must be nearly closing time,' Enid remarked. 'I suppose George'll be staggering home, wanting something to eat. You know, Kath, I missed him dreadfully when he first went off, but I've sort of got used to being on my own. Can't think what it'll be like having him under my feet all day long once the war's over.'

'Oh, come on, you don't mean that! Look how he dotes on you!'

Enid preened herself. 'Darling George. Mind you, the war's done wonders for us in one way,' she said with a wink. 'He was lucky if he got it up a couple of times a month before – now he can't get enough when he's home.'

Kath turned away to hide the flush in her cheeks. She was no prude, but she still found it embarrassing to talk about sex in a personal way. 'They say absence makes the heart grow fonder.'

'It's not his heart I'm talking about,' giggled Enid.

Just then there was a clatter at the door. The two men had arrived.

Enid slipped her arm in George's. 'Come on, pet. Better sleep it off before the party.'

'What you mean is, you want a matinée, eh, sweetheart?' George gave what he imagined was a bawdy leer and winked at Stan as they walked off down the path.

'Not such a bad idea of Enid's,' puffed Stan, dumping the crate of beer bottles in the corner of the kitchen. 'Little bit of love in the afternoon . . .'

'Oh Stan, really! Today of all days! I've so much to do. Besides, Tim might come in at any moment.'

'Only joking. Oh well, I'll have to content myself with the weeding, then.' He kissed her lightly as she pulled a face at him and went upstairs to change out of his City clothes.

Kath flushed again, but she couldn't help feeling pleased at Stan's remarks, even if he was just teasing. Twice a month was about all the lovemaking they seemed to have time for these days, what with Stan being on night shift so often. Their only free day was Sunday, and then the family were around.

It was a glorious afternoon. All over England, people enjoyed the weekend, and every village green sported its cricket match. Holiday-makers at Margate and Ramsgate strolled along the sea front. Some looked up and pointed at the sky as the heavy drone of massed aircraft engines reached their ears, but the planes were too high for the markings to be distinguished and very few of those watching experienced any real alarm.

As the Dorniers neared the Thames Estuary, they altered course slightly and began their descent. London stretched in front of them, bathed in sunshine, serenely peaceful with its silver barrage balloons floating protectively above, totally unprepared for the holocaust about to envelop it.

At last a puff of high explosive smoke from Canvey Island – the first sign of opposition. It wasn't until the bombers were over Tilbury Docks that they came under attack from Spitfires, and then only a pathetic few; Goering's strafing of fighter bases in the Home Counties had taken its toll. The Dorniers' mission was to put the London Docks out of action and to bomb Clapham Junction, that vital bottleneck through which all trains had to pass from the Victoria or Waterloo Terminals. Their raid was all but unopposed. Londoners would learn next day that of the sixty bombers involved, only two had been damaged and those not seriously.

On the ground below, chaos and panic prevailed until people gathered their wits after the shock of the first onslaught.

Kath heard the report on the four o'clock news, and her cry of alarm brought Stan running from the back garden.

'What's up, love?'

'Oh, Stan! The news – they say they've been raiding the airfields in the South East again.'

His arm went round her comfortingly. 'Now don't start worrying. They've plenty of shelters at Biggin Hill.'

'But suppose Roger can't get away?' Kath looked with despair at all the party food, so lovingly prepared.

Stan hugged her close and put his cheek against hers. Poor Kath – after all her hard work. He'd like to wring that pig Goering's neck! 'Cheer up, love. Even if Roger doesn't get here, we'll have a bit of a do and drink his health. Then we'll have a good excuse for another binge when he can get home.'

She looked up and smiled at him. 'You're right. I'm sorry.'

The telephone rang. Stan winked at her and went to answer it. When he returned his face was serious. 'Kath, I've got to go on duty.' He held up his hand to quell her protest. 'They want extra help. They're copping it pretty bad in the East End, round the docks.'

'But Mother—'

'Yes. If she gets here, you'd better keep her here, no

matter what she says. Tell her it's an order! From your local warden.'

Kath looked at the crate of glasses borrowed from The Windmill. 'No point in unpacking them, I suppose,' she said forlornly.

'Not really. Good thing I got the booze on sale or return. Why not have people round to eat the grub? Then they can run home if anything starts up here.'

She watched Stan anxiously as he pulled on his ARP Warden's uniform. 'Do you think it will?'

'Dunno. But if it does you and Tim go down to the shelter, right? I'll try and look in on you.'

Patty and Peter arrived back just as Stan was leaving. They'd heard the news too. Patty called them out into the road.

'Look! Look at the sky. It's all red!' She was pointing eastward. It was true: the entire sky glowed a dull orange-red, and ack-ack guns were booming in the distance.

They looked at each other. Stan told them what he'd heard about the dock area. Again Kath experienced that same tight spasm in her chest. Was it really going to happen after all? Or was this yet another one-off scare? Her thoughts were torn so many ways. Roger – was he all right? And Gran? Had she set out from Stepney already, or was she caught in the middle of all those bombs and fires? And Tim – she'd let him go off for the afternoon on his bike with his friend. Suppose he got caught in the raid?

Patty was looking at the sky with slightly different emotions. A flutter of alarm, certainly, but also, it must be admitted, a sort of thrill. So far, the war had hardly touched her – except to bring her Peter. And so in a way she was excited by the prospect of danger and gave little thought to the heartbreak that would inevitably come with it.

News spread fast at times like these, and by now half the residents of Balaclava Street were out in their front gardens, talking earnestly and shouting enquiries at Stan as he made his way to the ARP post. Rumour was rife too. St Paul's had received a direct hit! No – it was the Bank of England!

Kath went back inside. One thing seemed certain: her party was a non-starter. Tenderly, she placed the birthday cake back in its tin. Then she put the kettle on and told Patty and Peter to tuck into the sandwiches.

Peter turned the gas off, laughing at her astonishment.

'You're going to drink to your son's twenty-first in something a bit stronger than tea, Mrs Johnson,' he told her. 'Patty, where do you keep the glasses?'

Patty got three glasses and Peter produced a bottle of sherry.

'My contribution to the feast,' he explained. 'I'm damn well not taking it back, so come on!'

As they raised their glasses, everything started to happen at once. The phone rang, the siren wailed, Tim came belting into the house chattering with excitement, and the first burst of nearby gunfire shook the house, making the windows rattle.

Kath gasped. 'Bombs? We ought to go to the shelter.'

'I think it was gunfire,' Peter reassured her. 'Sounded like the ack-ack in Battersea Park.'

'But that means they're getting closer.'

'Could be just an isolated bomber – got lost from the main bunch or something.'

Patty had been to answer the telephone. Now she returned, a little woebegone. 'They want me on duty early,' she informed them. 'I couldn't very well refuse.'

'Of course not,' said Peter. 'Never mind, we'll make up for it all tomorrow. Hurry and get changed, then I'll run you to the depot in the car.'

'Peter, do you want to stay with us?' asked Kath. 'There's room enough in the shelter.'

'Thanks, but I'd better report back, Mrs Johnson. They may need me.'

Patty hurried with her dressing, her heart pounding as the noise of guns – or was it bombs? – intensified. She'd been expecting so much of tonight. Peter had been sweet and attentive over lunch. Several times she'd felt he was on the brink of saying something, and then at the last moment he'd changed the subject. A few drinks and a party atmosphere could so easily have loosened his inhibitions . . . Oh well – as Peter said, there was always tomorrow. Her heart lightened, filled with the blithe optimism of youth, that has yet to learn that in war tomorrow is never certain. She ran down the stairs, cheeks flushed, black helmet perched jauntily on the back of her head.

Peter and Kath were in the hall. Kath swallowed, suddenly struck by the terrible realization that her only daughter, this radiant girl, scarcely more than a child, was actually going off to war. But Patty and Peter only had eyes for each other.

'I believe regulations state that helmets should be worn straight,' he teased her.

'Phooey! Don't you start! I have enough of that from Colonel Harris.'

She turned, aware at last of her mother's silent presence. She hugged Kath.

'Bye, Mum, see you in the morning.'

'Bye, bye, love. Take care!'

'Sorry about your party, Mrs Johnson,' said Peter. 'Is it all right if I come over tomorrow?'

'Of course, dear. Come and have lunch with us.'

'You sure?'

She smiled. 'We'll make it stretch. And maybe Roger will be able to join us too.'

'Okay. Thanks.'

As they were going out of the front door, she called after them: 'Not too early though, Peter. I expect Patty and Stan will want to get a bit of sleep. Say about two o'clock.' She waved them off, as Peter started up his MG sports car and they zoomed off down the road, watched with interest by several of the neighbours.

Returning to the kitchen, Kath discovered her youngest son making rapid inroads into the party feast.

'Tim, really!'

'Better'n wasting it. You wouldn't like that.'

'You'll make yourself sick.'

'Nah. Try some of this trifle! Smashing! How'd you make it?'

'If I told you you'd probably go right off it.'

The fact was, Kath's mind was already on the various items they'd need to take to the shelter at the bottom of the garden! Matches, something to read, the kettle for a cup of something hot, overcoats in case it got chilly . . .

There was a tremendous crash, and the blast literally raised the floor. Everything shook and rattled. Kath grabbed Tim roughly by the arm.

'Come on, quick!'

'Let me get my comics,' Tim pleaded, but he was hustled out into the garden. No time for arguments now.

Outside, they both looked up at the sky. It was criss-crossed with searchlights probing the gathering darkness, trying to pinpoint a target for the anti-aircraft gunners. Battersea had its own searchlight section, stationed in the nearby Recreation Ground.

'Ooh, Mum – look!' shouted Tim.

He nudged her and pointed. There was no need. She'd already seen it – a silvery gleam caught in the searchlight, dodging and weaving in a desperate bid to evade the giant beam. Her first sight of a Jerry plane!

Next door Enid Belling was in her garden too, staring up at the sky. 'Bloody devils!' she yelled, forgetting all her customary gentility in her fury.

'Hope they cop him!' Tim was jumping up and down in excitement.

The noise of the ack-ack barrage was deafening. Then, as they watched, the plane released its bomb load; five tiny little pellets, gleaming in the searchlights, plummeting earthwards with that whining, whistling that was to become so familiar in the months ahead. With one accord they dived for their respective shelters.

There was a shattering explosion and they felt the ground shake beneath their feet. The gunfire continued to bombard their eardrums.

After a moment, Kath could hear Enid calling. 'Kath! Kath! You all right?'

Cautiously she peered out of the Anderson shelter. A very shaken Enid was clinging onto the fence.

'That was bleeding close! Where do you think it was?'

Kath shook her head, mystified, disorientated by the shock of the first bombs.

'George went round the pub. Didn't wait for me, the idiot,' Enid went on. 'Serve him right if it got hit! Oh lor' – you don't think . . .?'

'I'm sure it was much further away than that,' Kath reassured her. 'I expect he'll be home shortly.'

'Should hope so too.'

'Do you want to come in here with us? There's enough room.'

At that moment a light flashed on in the Belling's house.

'Mind the lights, George!' screamed Enid. 'Didn't have time to put the blackouts up when the siren went,' she explained apologetically to Kath.

The light flicked off and the figure of George appeared in the back doorway, fumbling in the darkness.

'Sorry, luv,' he muttered. 'Look, I brought back a couple of bottles of stout for you.'

'Fancy a drink with us, Kath?' asked Enid.

'Thanks, but no. I'd better try to get Tim settled. Not that we'll get much sleep tonight.'

She went inside the Anderson shelter – that little punishment cell, as Kath called it, designed and issued on the orders of the Home Secretary, Sir John Anderson. Made of corrugated iron plates riveted together in the form of an elongated horseshoe, it had to be sunk into the ground several feet and was therefore always damp –

even in dry weather. Heaven knows what it would be like in the depths of winter! When the doors were shut against blast, it was unbearably stuffy, since there was no ventilation. It was supposed to hold four people in 'safety and comfort'. 'Comfort' was a joke. As for 'safety', that remained to be seen.

Kath lit the hurricane lamp and settled Tim down on his palliasse in one corner and herself in a deckchair next to him. Tim was far too excited to sleep, so to keep him quiet she lit a candle in a saucer to give a little more light for reading. Not that Kath could concentrate on her book; her mind was much too active.

The noise from the Williams' shelter could be heard above the barrage. The baby was wailing – probably hungry, thought Kath. Madge would have been interrupted in the middle of feeding him when the raid started. The three boys were adopting an attitude of loud bravado, running in and out of the shelter, and their mother was trying rather unsuccessfully to comfort and control them all. Bert was obviously on duty.

Kath wondered whether to offer to take a couple of the boys into her shelter to help out, then restrained the urge; *she* wouldn't want to be separated from her children at a moment like this. Also it might set a precedent. After all, Stan and Patty weren't always on night duty and when they were here, the shelter would be full to bursting. All the same she felt a bit mean.

'Oh, God,' she prayed – really prayed, although she'd never considered herself a particularly religious person. 'Oh God – let us all come through this night!'

Little did Kathleen Johnson know how many times she would repeat that prayer in the months to come.

2

The Night of the Big Fire

Peter parked the MG at the tail end of a long line of ambulances – at least, they were called ambulances, but most were simply large old limousines or vans converted for the purpose. The back had been removed from the chassis and in its place was mounted a tall canvas contraption, large enough to carry two racks of stretchers on either side and a First Aid box. Two canvas flaps at the back could be pulled down to close it.

Peter looked at the line of vehicles with an expression of amused contempt. 'I hope I never have to travel in one of those things! They look bloody dangerous to me. Top heavy.'

Patty giggled. 'Especially when you get old Maudie Harris in one. She's the wife of our Commandant. Talk about top heavy!' Her hands did an exaggerated curve over her bosom. 'They do sway about a lot when you go round corners.'

'I'm glad you're not in one.'

'I feel safer on my bike. Anyway, we're only supposed to back up the normal ambulance service in an emergency, so I guess they'll be all right.'

The word 'emergency' brought Peter back to reality with a jolt. He leaned over and drew Patty close, kissing her hard on her lips.

As Patty and Peter embraced, they little realized that the emergency was so near, or that it would be so long drawn out. All Patty was conscious of was the steering wheel sticking into her rib cage and the violent pounding of her heart. Peter was holding her in such a tight clinch, it was almost as if he felt he'd never see her again.

This thought had actually just occurred to Peter for the first time. He had no real idea what Patty's duties entailed, and hadn't been in the least bit interested until tonight. But now it was obvious it could be dangerous. Suppose she was injured? Suppose that pretty little face was badly scarred? He didn't even dare to dwell on the possibility that she might be killed . . .

Breathless, Peter leant back and looked at Patty, his eyes dwelling on every feature of her face. It was unbelievable to think that she might be taken from him at this moment, just when he'd realized what she meant to him. He'd been very attracted to her; he thought he loved her. But now he knew for sure. There'd be no point to life without Patty. To think he'd be spending the night in a bomb-proof cypher room at the Admiralty, when she was out in the streets facing . . . what? He had no idea. He only knew that he wanted to start up the car and drive with her through the night, just the two of them, getting the hell out of everything.

'I . . . I'd better go in,' whispered Patty at last.

He nodded and kissed her again. 'Take care, my sweet. Take great care!'

She looked at him wonderingly, making no move. He seemed on the brink of saying something more. She *willed* him to tell her he loved her – but no words came.

'Sorry about the party,' she said, resorting to banality.

He smiled. 'That's the least of my worries. I wish you didn't have to go on duty tonight.'

'Why?'

'Because . . .' He paused. This was hardly the place or time to tell her he loved her, and yet he sensed that those were the words she was waiting to hear. 'Oh Patty!' he said at last, and held her close again. She was quivering. Tears weren't far away. One great drop rolled down her cheek. That broke the tension. Laughing, he wiped it away with a finger.

'You're not going to cry, are you? Driven to tears because I love you?'

There, it was out! And Patty did cry and thought that she could never be as happy as this ever again.

Peter tweaked her nose playfully. 'Don't I get anything in return?'

All at once a feminine contrariness arose in her. It restrained her overwhelming urge to throw herself into Peter's arms, declaring undying devotion. She was sure of him now. She could afford to play the coquette for a little while. She grinned and kissed him lightly.

'That's on account,' she said, and extricated herself from the low car.

'What?'

'On account of I'll see you tomorrow!' Blowing him a kiss, she ran into the old church hall that served as the Ambulance post.

'What's up tonight?' she called to Dusty Miller, who was busy in the little kitchenette amidst a haze of oily smoke.

'Cheese fritters. *Bugger!*' exclaimed Dusty, as sputtering fat burnt his hand.

'I didn't mean supper, idiot,' laughed Patty. 'Why all the panic?'

'I'll have a little more respect from you, young lady,' said Miller with mock-severity, 'Otherwise you'll get no jam on your toast for breakfast.' Dusty was a small, grizzled, gnome-like figure, who acted as chief cook and bottle-washer for the Depot. He thoroughly enjoyed being flirted with and teased by the younger females in the service and revelled in being in charge of the store cupboard.

'His Lordship 'asn't favoured me with 'is confidence,' Dusty went on, jerking his head in the direction of the Commandant's office. 'Something nasty going on down the East End, I gather. Let me know if you find out.'

Patty nodded and went on into the main hall. On the stage itself was a line of mattresses ready for the night shift, who were sometimes able to grab some sleep while things were quiet. A couple of hunched figures were already curled up under the dark grey issue blankets – probably people off night shift the previous week. Patty found it very difficult to readjust her sleeping habits herself – a week was never long enough. The way their rota worked, they got a week in turn on the three different shifts – 8 a.m. to 4 p.m., 4 p.m. till midnight and midnight till 8 a.m.

Patty made her way down the hall and was greeted by one or two people she knew, but as this wasn't her own shift most of them were strangers. There was a feeling of suppressed excitement in the air, although nobody seemed too sure what was going on.

At the far end of the hall some of the younger members were playing an energetic game of ping pong. Another group was centred round the dartboard, and there was the inevitable gathering of middle-aged women, knitting and gossiping in a little circle. Patty passed them and went through a door leading to two small rooms. The inner one was Colonel Harris's office.

The Colonel was in his element. Battle stations at last, after all these months of inactivity! Harris had been a regular soldier, and the Army had been his entire life until a stupid accident on a training exercise had deprived him of an arm and an eye. A medical discharge was the result, and he couldn't even claim it had been due to enemy action. Not surprisingly, it had made him embittered and bad-tempered. At the outbreak of war, he'd volunteered for every kind of service and had been rewarded for his persistence by being placed in charge of the Civil Defence post at Battersea. Later, he'd tried to transfer to the Home Guard, feeling it was a more suitable area for his talent and experience, but the authorities had asked him to remain in his present position. Colonel Harris was never one to shirk his duty, however irksome, so at Battersea he remained.

As Patty knocked and entered, he turned round from

the huge maps and charts that covered his walls. He was a fearsome sight: the empty right sleeve of his black battledress was pinned across his chest, which sported his First War medals, and a black patch covered his right eye. Even after all these months Patty felt tongue-tied in his presence.

'Evening, sir,' she stammered. 'Patricia Johnson. You wanted me to report early.'

'Yes, yes. Good of you to come,' he replied gruffly. He had to keep reminding himself that all the women were volunteers. 'Sign in, will you?'

'The book wasn't in the outer office, sir,' Patty explained.

'Ah – *hm* . . . Yes, well, Mr Graves is busy.' The remark was superfluous, for it was plain that his deputy, Arthur Graves, was fully occupied with the three telephones on the desk. The Colonel extricated the Duty Book from under his deputy's elbow and Patty signed her name and the time.

'Is there something special happening tonight, sir?'

'The whole city's on emergency standby,' the Colonel replied. 'The situation in the dock area and East End is bad. I shall be making a general announcement shortly, and—'

'Colonel Harris, it's Divisional Super for you,' interrupted Graves.

The Colonel dismissed Patty with a nod and took the phone. As he answered, his voice immediately took on a brisk, military tone.

Arthur Graves moved back to the wallchart which the Colonel had been studying and began to mark up the stretcher bearer and ambulance crews available from the duty roster. He was in his late sixties and his movements were slow and deliberate, a fact which was apt to irritate his superior. But Arthur was a retired solicitor, and habitually careful and meticulous. The Colonel's Blimpish attitudes sometimes amused him, for he was a tolerant sort of person himself, but he respected his boss and did his best to please.

'Very nearly up to two shifts now, Colonel,' he reported, as soon as Harris put the phone down.

'We're going to need 'em, too. We've been asked to send as many crews as possible to the Whitechapel area.'

'What about vehicles?'

'What we can spare,' frowned the Colonel. 'Leave ourselves a skeleton complement in case things move this way, but it seems Jerry's concentrating on the docks tonight. The people down there are stretched to capacity, so we'll send personnel even if we can't send the transport.'

Arthur waved a list at him. 'These are people not on the phone, or who haven't answered.'

'Send the messengers out. Meanwhile put teams A,B,C and D on instant readiness.'

'Yes, sir.'

As Arthur moved to carry out the orders and the Colonel busied himself with sticking various little flags into the wallmaps, a large lady pushed her way into the office.

'Bernard, what's all this extra duty business?' she demanded. 'You know very well I'd asked the Bannisters for bridge tonight!'

Arthur removed himself quickly and the Colonel sighed.

'Maudie, how many times do I have to tell you to knock before bursting into my office? We're not at home now.'

His wife glared at him, and a lesser man might have quailed. The Colonel was an impressive figure, but there was no doubt who dominated. Mrs Harris was used to command, but in this instance she decided on strategic retreat.

'Well, I'm sorry, but—'

'It's essential to keep discipline in this place, and if we set a bad example ourselves, it'll be hopeless. There's an emergency on. You'll hear all about it shortly with the others.'

For a moment it seemed that Mrs Harris would argue,

but suddenly she turned on her heel and stalked out. The Colonel sighed again. It was most unfortunate that Maudie had volunteered as an ambulance driver. He'd tried his hardest to persuade her into another branch of service, but all to no avail. Maudie had won, as usual. Mind you, she was a good driver. And she was completely without fear. You had to give that to Maudie!

Patty set off on her bicycle towards Prince of Wales Drive. She was one of nine messengers employed at the Depot, and had been there almost exactly a year now, having volunteered soon after war broke out. She'd taken all her First Aid and nursing tests since then and was qualified to go on the ambulances, but there weren't any vacancies. Messengers were badly needed, though, since the women's services had started recruiting. Patty often wondered if she'd been wrong to volunteer so early on. The messengers were supposed to keep communications going if the telephone service broke down but, of course, nothing like that had ever happened. Instead, months of boredom, cleaning the bikes and lessons – whereas she'd visualized herself speeding through the bombardment with vital messages – even being decorated for gallantry. These days, it seemed she might have led a far more fascinating life as a Wren or Waaf. Tonight, however, she was happy. It was the first time she'd felt useful since the start of the war, and above all – she was in love!

With an effort Patty brought her thoughts back to the task in hand and consulted the list she'd been given by Mr Graves. Quite a lot of people who worked at the Depot lived in Prince of Wales Drive – part-time volunteers mostly, combining this duty with their permanent employment.

Stephen Broome was just putting away his cricket flannels when a breathless Patty arrived with the message from the Colonel. 'Report at once,' she gasped. 'There's a big raid on the docks and we've all got to be on standby.'

'I heard the sirens,' he said to Patty – whose name he'd

forgotten if he'd ever known it – 'but I thought it was another false alarm.'

'It's the East End – it's being flattened right now! You'd better hurry – I've got lots of other calls to make. Bye.' She rushed off again down the stairs.

Stephen went over to the bay window of his bedsitter. The pale blue of a perfect late summer sky hadn't yet completely surrendered to dusk, and the sun filtered through the oaks and elms that stood straight and proud on the edge of the park opposite. The trees obscured the casual passer-by's view of the ack-ack gun emplacements and the neat rows of tents put up to house the artillery company stationed there, but from Stephen's fourth-floor vantage point he could see right across the park to the Thames half a mile away.

At the moment Stephen could see little sign of activity from the soldiers under his gaze some hundred yards away, and there were no sounds of bombardment. Still, the Colonel must know what he was talking about. With that thought, he smiled wryly and crossed the spacious room to his wardrobe.

As he searched for his black siren suit, he wondered at the hand of fate which had dealt him crusty old Colonel Harris. The Colonel was notoriously ill-disposed to people he couldn't understand – people, for example, opposed to the Army and its standards of discipline and smartness. Anyone who was a Conscientious Objector, whatever their motives, he regarded as distinctly 'odd'. It was hardly surprising, then, that he was suspicious of Stephen.

At twenty-five, Stephen was in the prime of manhood. He was six feet tall, healthy, by all accounts intelligent, and perfectly well-equipped to serve his country in the fighting forces. All this twaddle about religion was well . . . er . . . twaddle. All Quakers were good for was making porridge.

That, Stephen knew, would have been the Colonel's

view. A man was either a coward or he wasn't. It was all black or white for the Colonel.

Stephen's religious convictions were solidly founded in a family tradition that went back over two hundred years. The first person to have discarded the Quaker faith was his father, who had volunteered for the War to End All Wars some two months before his son was born in 1915. Stephen's mother, widowed at twenty-one, saw to it that her son would appreciate the merits of the Quakers' pacifist convictions. After all, what had war achieved for her?

Stephen's mother wasn't left destitute – indeed, the family's engineering business in Birmingham had prospered during the inter-war period under the guidance of one of his uncles. There was enough money for him to go to Rugby school from where he won a scholarship to Oxford. A First in History merely wetted his appetite for an academic career and he'd had no difficulty in persuading the college to allow him to read for a D.Phil in anthropology.

Stephen's thesis, the product of three years' diligent research and thought was accepted in June 1939. He'd already made plans to join a team of anthropological researchers investigating several promising sites in Abyssinia when war was declared. And so Stephen, in his usual quiet and unobtrusive way, volunteered for Civil Defence, having notified the relevant authorities that he was a 'Conchie'.

After six months as a stretcher bearer, Stephen could hardly claim that the work was either stimulating or necessary. The 'Phoney war' had lulled many into believing that Hitler would never invade Britain. And Stephen himself profited from this belief by using the time to visit the British Museum and catch up on his research.

The family with whom he lodged were old friends of his mother's. Prince of Wales Drive was definitely one of the more salubrious parts of Battersea. In fact, the tall mansion blocks with their splendid views of the park were quite fashionable, and Stephen had met some interesting neighbours. Built in late Victorian times, the flats were spacious and elegant. He had no complaints about his room, and few worries about money; he paid a mere eight shillings a week rent, and for a further seventeen and sixpence, his landlady provided all his meals. He earned £3 2*s* 6*d* a week as a stretcher bearer, so in many ways he was quite well-off.

At that moment he heard the *crump* of ack-ack fire in the distance over to the east. With a surge of excitement, he buttoned up his suit and ran downstairs. He was a little ashamed of his excitement, but if war really was inevitable, it was as well to get it over with quickly. As he reached ground-level he realized he'd left behind his military-style gas mask and its canvas pack. As he re-entered his room, there was his black helmet too, with its white-painted CD on the front. He'd been day-dreaming – he'd get no medals for that from Colonel Harris.

In her buoyant mood, Patty got through her list in less than half an hour. She'd managed to reach most of the people, and those who weren't at home would find notes torn from her official Civil Defence notepad, asking them to contact the Depot immediately. Even the slog back up the hill seemed less exhausting than usual. She arrived in the hall just as general assembly was called.

The entire company lined up, men on one side, women on the other. As the Colonel entered, followed by Arthur, Mrs Harris came loudly to attention; a few women in her vicinity felt compelled to follow her example, though looking and feeling slightly ridiculous. The Colonel regarded the ramrod figure of his wife with inner exasperation, regretting his earlier attempt to impose military drill in the command. How could you tell someone with a 44-inch bust to stick her chest out and hold her stomach in?

'At ease, everyone,' he said wearily. It was a rhetorical command, since most of them – the men anyway – were already slouched, hands in pockets, and a few with cigarettes dangling from their mouths. At least the women were clean and tidy and polite – except for that absurd Miss Pelley standing to one side, her long grey hair straggling from under her tin hat. She was holding a knitting bag and from it was trailing a ball of khaki wool, the thread of which had somehow got entangled in her legs. The Colonel averted his gaze quickly.

'You've probably all heard that the East End of London is undergoing an extremely severe air-raid at this moment,' he began. 'The first attack was with incendiaries and created major damage. Our Fire Services have been unable to control the fires, which are still raging and presenting a perfect target for the bombers in the secondary attack now in progress. They're dropping high explosives. I'm afraid the casualties are—'

There was a stifled shriek from a woman at the back.

'Oh Gawd! My family live there – in Commercial Road . . .'

Another woman put her arm round the first, who sobbed quietly. The Colonel paused a moment, then continued.

'Our Civil Defence colleagues in the Whitechapel and Limehouse areas have been stretched beyond their capabilities and rescue work is now somewhat disorganized.' The Colonel's tone implied that no such eventuality could happen under *his* command.

There was quiet shuffling of feet. People were looking at each other uneasily.

'Now!' The sharp tone drew attention back to the Colonel immediately. 'We've been asked to send replacement crews to the area to assist. I can't order you to go. You're well aware that this is largely a voluntary force for the defence and relief of your own area. However, I know this call for help from our colleagues won't go unanswered. Unfortunately the authorities have forbidden me to leave this post. I had hoped to lead our group myself, but I'm confident you'll acquit yourselves admirably. Mr Graves tells me that with the extra people who've reported tonight, we should be able to supply two heavy-duty rescue squads, six stretcher cars and ten ambulances with several spare crews in each section. But we can't leave this post entirely unattended, so I'm afraid some of you will have to stay behind. Now, if the volunteers will line up in front of Mr Graves, he'll assign the duties.'

There was a moment of stunned silence as everyone digested the impact of the Colonel's statement. Then Mrs Harris squared her shoulders and marched over to stand in front of Arthur. She was accompanied by a solid phalanx of women. The Colonel permitted himself a little smile of satisfaction. Good old Maudie – for all her faults, she could be relied upon to come up trumps!

Patty found herself in the body of women waiting for instructions. She wasn't quite sure how she'd got there – she'd just allowed herself to be moved along with the others. And now she'd go through with it, because she hadn't the courage to change her mind. Her stomach heaved and for some incomprehensible reason she suddenly thought of Dusty's cheese fritters, which did nothing to help.

A large lady raised her hand. 'Excuse me, Mr Graves, but can you say what time we'll get back?'

Arthur regarded her patiently. 'I'm afraid I've no idea, Mrs Thorn,' he replied. 'We don't know what we'll find when we get there.'

'Well, it's the kids' breakfasts, see. I made no arrangements, coming out unexpected like this.'

'Of course not. Don't worry, Mrs Thorn, we'll put you in one of the depot teams – we're leaving three here. You'll be sure to get home on time.'

'Thanks, Mr Graves.'

'Good. Thank you, ladies,' the Colonel smiled benignly at them, then turned his attention to the men. A few had followed the women over, but were now hovering uneasily, not sure whether they had moved too soon.

'Right men, over there, please!'

Nobody moved. There was silence, broken only by a

nervous cough and more shuffling of feet. The Colonel stared, unable to believe his eyes. He held his breath in mute fury, his face a mottled purple, veins standing out on his forehead. Arthur was afraid he might have a stroke.

'Well?' he exploded at last. 'We can't wait all night.'

A thin youth with dark, greasy hair and a pimply face muttered almost inaudibly: 'You said we didn't 'ave to go.'

'That's right, you did,' agreed his mate.

'You *refuse* to volunteer?' bellowed Harris. More shufflings and mutterings; then a couple of older men in the front row ambled over to join the few who were with the women, unable to take the fury of the Colonel's glare any longer.

The Colonel drew himself up to his full height and fixed the male contingent with a withering gaze. 'I'm appalled,' he said at last. 'I can't believe it. When I look at these ladies, who bravely volunteered without a moment's hesitation, and then I see *you*—' he paused to let the contempt in his voice sink in – 'for the first time in my life, I feel ashamed of my own sex!' He turned on his heel and left the hall.

There was a momentary hush, and then some truculent murmurs broke out among the men. The women, who'd been embarrassed until now, turned on them angrily.

'If you won't do anything, then shut up and let us get on with it in peace!' bellowed an outraged Mrs Harris.

'Hush everyone, please!' interposed Arthur. 'You men, dismiss! Now, let's see if we can muster any full crews. I think the best plan is to have a rollcall.'

As Arthur called out the names, Patty stood at the back and looked over at the men, who'd now returned sullenly to their darts or poker games, some looking a little shamefaced. She'd been really shaken by the episode, almost as much as Colonel Harris. Things like that just didn't happen in Patty's book, her whole attitude to life being coloured by magazines, romantic fiction or films, where the heroes were always clean-cut and courageous. She'd heard contemptuous remarks from the older women in her section. They considered most of the men were skivers or 'conchies' and that there wasn't anything much to choose between the two. It seemed now that they were right. She suddenly remembered the white feathers she'd picked up that morning. In the excitement she'd forgotten to bring them along.

Then she gazed at the handful of men who had volunteered. Mostly they were part-timers, too old for active service and carrying on their professions or jobs during the day. Some were younger ones awaiting their call-up or working frustratedly in reserved occupations and therefore not allowed to join the forces. And then there were the really young ones: little Ben Levy from the pawnbroker's in his thick pebble glasses – he'd been turned down by every service because of his terrible eyesight, poor boy; that pale, fair boy who had asthma – she didn't know his name; finally, there was Stephen Broome. Patty remembered he'd been on her list this evening. He was on her shift too, but she didn't know much about him – he was a bit stand-offish and didn't mix much; spent most of his time in a corner, reading. He was one of the Conscientious Objectors. Strange, because he wasn't a bit like the other conchies at the Depot: lazy, shiftless little spivs, who'd try anything to get out of a day's work. Apparently Stephen belonged to some religious sect – Quakers, that was it! Anyway, he was a bit of a mystery.

Suddenly Patty realized the woman beside her was nudging her. 'Mr Graves wants you.' She moved forward, blushing. She'd been staring at Stephen so hard she hadn't even seen Mr Graves, who was right beside him.

'We won't be sending messengers to the East End, Patricia,' Arthur told her. 'You can go home till your regular shift, if you like.'

'Now I'm here, I might as well stay,' she replied. 'There must be something I can do.'

'Well, we needed to call the extra duty volunteers, but—'

'I've passed all my First Aid and Nursing Tests, Mr Graves.'

It was a strange sensation. She could hear her own voice, but it was as if she had no control over it. She didn't *really* want to go out on the raid – it was that other someone doing it.

'That's true,' murmured Arthur. 'How old are you?'

'Seventeen . . . and a half.' The 'half', was a slight exaggeration. Her birthday was June 30th.

Arthur looked at her carefully; she was barely more than a schoolgirl. But then, schoolboys went off to fight in the front line too. He was short on extra crews, and the only alternative was Miss Pelley twittering nervously beside her. Arthur had no hesitation in deciding which of the two would be most welcome to the overworked and harassed Civil Defence people in Whitechapel.

'Very well, Patricia. You go on Mrs Ackroyd's ambulance as extra nurse. Miss Pelley, will you be on reserve?'

Miss Pelley retreated with her knitting-bag to a corner, relieved, but determined not to show it.

Patty ran out into the night to find her ambulance. Several of them were already revving up, heavily-masked headlights on. There was a clanging noise as stretchers were clamped onto the roof of the stretcher cars, and a buzz of conversation as people checked equipment. Patty's ambulance was first in the line-up of 'B' team. She already knew Olive Ackroyd, the driver, a plump rosy-faced woman who was the wife of their local butcher. Olive greeted her cheerfully.

'Climb on, love. 'Fraid it won't be a very comfortable ride at the back – there's nothing to sit on.'

Patty was helped into the back of the ambulance by another woman, whose olive skin and strong accent declared her to be of foreign nationality. She explained that she and her husband had a small Greek restaurant, and apologized that she 'no speak too well English'.

Olive's regular nursing assistant, Edie Long, sat in the front with her. 'Two extra hands!' she laughed. 'There won't be any room for the patients at this rate!'

Olive frowned. 'I'm more worried if this effing crate'll carry the load,' she grunted.

Stephen's face appeared at the window. 'Okay, Mrs Ackroyd?'

She grinned at him. 'Much as I'll ever be! You leading tonight?'

'Yes. We'll go in convoy as far as we can, but things are pretty chaotic, so we may easily get separated. We're to report for instructions to the Depot at Commercial Road, if possible. If not, make ourselves useful wherever we can. Got your maps?'

'Yes.' Edie waved them at him.

'Good luck, then!'

'And to you!' called Olive, as Stephen moved on to the next ambulance. 'Nice young man,' she commented, when he was out of earshot, 'doesn't seem right somehow, him being a conchie.'

'Well, I'll say one thing for him – he's got more guts than them others,' said Edie.

'Yellow-livered sods! I'd give 'em all hard labour if I had me way.'

Only a few minutes later, the 'B' team convoy pulled out from the side of the road and headed for Chelsea Bridge. Stephen had decided to take his team north of the river to their destination, hoping that the route would be less congested and chaotic.

Patty heard the two women in front laughing and joking, and guessed they were keeping up the chatter to ease their own nervousness.

'Okay in the back?' shouted Olive.

'Yes, thanks,' replied Patty. 'We're lying on the stretchers. Luxury travel!'

Olive laughed. 'That's right, duck. Take the weight off your feet while you can. Don't suppose there'll be much chance later.'

And so they jolted on – on towards the red glow in the sky and the ever-increasing noise of bombardment.

As Stan hurried off down Balaclava Street, he soon forgot the party and the inevitable hurt poor Kath would feel. All his thoughts were concentrated on remembering the training he and the other wardens had been put through over the past year. Perhaps now all that painstaking preparation would be put to good use.

Now that it was getting dark, the red glow over the East End took on an appalling and ominous appearance. It was as if the docks had become a giant cauldron. 'Poor buggers,' Stan muttered under his breath.

As he paused for a moment, Bert Williams drew up alongside on his faithful Raleigh bicycle.

'Looks like they're copping it good and proper in the East End,' puffed the policeman.

Stan increased his pace to a jog-trot to keep up with him. 'You on duty tonight then, Bert?'

'Yeah, I'd only just got home, too – for your party. But we've all got orders to report if there's an alert. Got to be prepared for anything.'

'Right. Bad luck having to leave Madge and the kids, though.'

Bert looked distressed. 'I know, but what can I do? I hope she'll be able to cope.'

'Don't worry. I'll give an eye to them.'

'Thanks, mate. 'Course, they may send me home again if nothing happens thisaway.'

Bert tipped his helmet to Stan and pedalled off towards the police station in Battersea Bridge Road, while Stan turned off towards the Henry Bolton Elementary School, his local ARP Depot. As he jogged along, he felt a pang of sympathy for Bert, torn between duty and his young family. Should have had the lot evacuated when they had the chance, he thought; but then he remembered how reluctant he and Kath had been to let their children go at the beginning of the war. An indefinite separation wasn't a happy prospect, especially when the kids were as young as the Williams lot. Babies forget so quickly, and whatever one might think of Madge and Bert, they were devoted to their children.

The dark block of school buildings loomed up in front of Stan and he made his way quickly to the gymnasium, which had been assigned to the wardens as their HQ. With this first general alert, the full strength of the post had turned out. The Chief Warden was holding forth on tightening up blackout regulations. 'It wasn't so serious while the Germans concentrated on air-fields and the like, but if they're going to start bombing civilians, we'd better be prepared!'

There was a growl of assent from the wardens, and each went off to check individual houses in their particular areas. Stan was sure that everyone in Balaclava Street had their gas masks and stirrup pumps. He'd visited them many times and advised on papering up the windows against bomb blast and to have a bucket of earth or sand ready in case of incendiaries. However, his pitch included more than just his home street, and he made up his mind to call at every house in the morning just to be on the safe side. Overhead, the searchlights were still probing the sky and the air was loud with ack-ack fire.

'Think they're moving this way?' asked 'Windy' Windward, the retired postman who shared Stan's patch, looking up with a frown.

'Nah. That racket's from the guns. Anyway, why'd they want to bomb Battersea?'

'They might go for Clapham Junction. They could easily miss and hit us instead.'

Suddenly the ground rocked with a series of explosions, throwing the two men off balance. Windy stumbled and fell.

'That was bloody close,' he muttered.

'Should've kept your big mouth shut,' Stan joked, as he helped the older man to his feet. 'You all right, cock?'

'Yes thanks. Hey, Stan – look!'

Windy pointed in the direction of Battersea Bridge Road. They could see several fires raging on the rooftops, one much nearer and larger than the rest, the flames reaching hungrily into the sky.

'God Almighty . . . That must be near the Windmill—'

Stan set off down the street, at a run, with Windy in laboured pursuit, but long before they reached the scene, they could hear jangling bells announcing the arrival of the Fire Service. At least the blaze would have expert attention now, thought Stan. God knows how they were expected to fight a fire that size with only a stirrup pump. Those incendiaries must have been dropped before the bombs – the fire had obviously got a good hold. He wondered how long it had taken the fire engine to get there. It would have had to come all the way from Chelsea.

Even before he rounded the corner, Stan caught the acrid smell of burning paint and plaster.

'Blimey – it *is* the pub!' gasped Windy, tagging in the rear.

A crowd had gathered, and Bert Williams was trying to keep them back, both for their own safety and to give the firemen room to operate. Stan and Windy went to his aid. Luckily the solid old Victorian building had held up long enough for the customers to get out before the ceilings fell in.

There was a reverberating crash as huge rafters plummeted down and a thick cloud of dust billowed out, clearing to reveal the bizarre sight of a chintz-covered sofa straddling the bar. A shriek of dismay and misery came from a woman on the pavement. It was the landlord's wife. Stan felt a surge of sympathy as he hurried to her; what a terrible experience to see all your personal possessions, the lifetime's collection that goes to make a home, disappear in front of you and a crowd of spectators. There was a general murmur of concern, and Tommy

Glover put his arm around his wife, who was fighting back the tears.

'You two all right?' asked Stan.

Tommy nodded with a wry grin. 'It's just the shock, isn't it, old girl?' he said, giving his wife an encouraging squeeze. She was still shaking, but she managed a watery smile for Stan.

'Course! We were lucky no one got hurt,' she croaked. 'I was upstairs in the bedroom when the bombs fell. Never moved so fast in all me life – slid the last few stairs on me bottom!'

Stan was glad their sense of humour hadn't deserted them. 'Look, why don't you go round to the school? They're opening a rest centre there with mattresses and so on. The WVS will be dishing up tea and hot soup. It's only temporary, but it's somewhere to sleep till we get you sorted out in the morning.'

'Take a few weeks to get that lot sorted out,' sighed Tommy. It was a gross understatement, and they all knew it. Water was everywhere, almost six inches deep, but the roof was still alight. One fire engine was pumping endless gallons over it, while the men struggled to get the blaze under control. 'Still, I guess they're worse off over there.' He nodded towards the East. The red glow was even brighter now, spreading across the night sky like a warm coverlet.

'Poor sods,' muttered his wife. 'Well, Tom, are we going to the rest centre, then? Not much point standing here and upsetting ourselves.'

'I'm a bit nervous leaving everything. There's money in the till, Stan.'

'That's my responsibility,' Stan reassured him. 'I'll be around to make sure there's no pilfering. Soon as it's safe, I'll ask the Fire Chief to check the till.'

Stan watched them go and renewed his efforts to get the remaining spectators off the streets. Old Windy puffed up to him. 'Another house copped an incendiary in Edna

Street,' he wheezed. 'It's not too bad at the moment, but the place is empty and I need some help to break in.'

'Okay, get Bert on to that. I'll ask the Fire Chief to send for more help.'

'Fat chance of that, Warden,' was the surprising response from the fireman in the white helmet. 'Everything's out already. There's a whole row of houses in Parkgate Road to deal with.'

'But that's not our area—' began Stan, until he realized his own stupidity. The Fire Brigade had the entire district to cover, not just a few streets like old Windy and himself. It was still a bit of a shock that resources would be at such a premium.

The Chief grinned, reading his thoughts. 'I'll let you have an appliance as soon as we're finished here. Do your best till we arrive.'

Stan hurried off, and then had to double back, remembering his promise to Tommy Glover about the till. Suddenly the task in front of him and its attendant responsibilities assumed mammoth proportions. The safety and welfare of an entire neighbourhood rested on his shoulders – plain, ordinary Stan Johnson, clerk in an Inland Revenue office. He squared his shoulders and found to his surprise that he wasn't afraid. Instead he felt an exhilaration that he hadn't experienced before.

Back at Battersea Rise, Arthur saw the last of the teams on its way and returned to the Commandant's office. The Old Man had taken that confrontation badly. Funny how he always thought of him as the Old Man, even though he guessed he could give the Colonel a good twelve years or so.

He found Harris staring gloomily at the blotter. He'd been there for about half an hour, ever since he'd left the hall. Nothing like this had happened in his life; he'd always had strict discipline and unquestioning obedience.

Now he was at a loss. There was no punishment he could impose, or threats he could use. He was impotent.

Arthur looked at him compassionately. 'Four complete teams dispatched, sir,' he reported, knowing that the urgency of the situation would bring his chief back to himself. 'Three extra crews. We haven't even been able to muster one heavy-duty rescue squad though, I'm afraid.'

'Bastards!' was the Colonel's muttered comment.

'Yes,' Arthur agreed. He went to his briefcase, extracted a hip flask of brandy, filled the cap and offered it to Harris. 'I know it's against the rules, sir, but this *is* an emergency. I carry it for medicinal reasons, you know.'

The Colonel accepted the brandy and knocked it back. 'Exactly. Thank you, Graves.' His face was still quite straight, but now there was the faintest twinkle in the one eye. 'You'd better report the position to Divisional HQ.'

Suddenly Harris seemed to snap back into his normal brisk manner. He drew a fresh sheet of paper towards himself and deliberately dipped his pen in the inkwell. 'I'm going to make a report on what happened tonight,' he went on. 'Those buggers can't be allowed to get away scot-free.'

'Don't suppose they'd have been much use over there in their bloody-minded mood,' remarked Arthur, as he waited for HQ to answer.

The Colonel snorted. 'Damn right! But it leaves us in bad shape here. What happens if *we* have an emergency? We can't operate with a squad of snivelling schoolgirls – no, I take that back,' he corrected himself. 'The girls – and ladies – showed a lot of guts tonight.' He cleared his throat. It hurt his pride to admit it, but credit where credit was due.

There was a knock on the outer door, and since Arthur was now halfway into his report to HQ., the Colonel went to answer it himself. There stood the wizened figure of Dusty Miller.

'Sorry to bother you, sir,' the little cook apologized,

and his hand went up to his forehead in a half-salute. Ex-soldier, the Colonel noted with approval.

'Yes?'

'Hear you're a bit short on the rescue squad, sir. Like to volunteer.'

The Colonel's expression relaxed. 'Thank you, Miller. I'll tell Mr Graves. Er . . . you haven't passed any First Aid Tests, have you?'

'No, sir, but I can pull bodies out of the rubble along with the best of 'em. Leave the patching up to others.'

'Yes. Meanwhile can you rustle up some black coffee? I reckon we've got a heavy night ahead.'

'Coming up pronto, sir.'

Dusty limped off quickly, and the Colonel returned to the inner office, his chin a little higher and a gleam in his one eye. At least there were a few of the old guard left.

As he entered, the second telephone was shrilling and Arthur was still talking on the first. Harris hurried to answer it.

An emergency – on his own doorstep! Quickly, he noted down the details.

'One ambulance to Parkgate Road,' he said to Arthur, who'd just replaced his receiver. 'Direct incendiary hits on several houses. No severe casualties reported yet, but better be on the safe side . . .'

The Colonel was his old self again. He pulled various lists and charts towards him and started to make his dispositions.

Patty could feel and hear the fires before she actually saw them. Even through the canvas hood of the ambulance, the heat was scorching and the roar of the flames drowned the noise of bombs or guns.

'Jesus Christ!' exclaimed Olive, jamming on the brakes.

Patty and the Greek woman scrambled up and peered through the square window cut in the canvas above the driver's cab. Ahead was a solid wall of flame and, silhouetted against the glare, what seemed like tiny black figures running around like ants, carrying hoses and ladders. It was impossible, thought Patty – no power on earth could stop that blaze!

The scale of the conflagration was stunning – and it was spreading rapidly. Before long, they too would be enveloped.

'What do we do now?' asked Edie.

'Well, we can't go any further, that's for sure,' said Olive. She turned to Patty. 'Any sign of the others?'

They'd been separated from the other ambulances and the stretcher car of their convoy long ago. The journey itself had been perilous enough, but somehow they'd struggled through the explosions, diversions and blocked-off streets to find themselves in this inferno called East India Dock Road.

As if in answer to prayer, Stephen Broome materialized out of the swirling smoke.

'Thank God you're here,' he croaked, in a voice made hoarse by the fumes. 'Quick! We've got a load of stretcher cases and nobody to cart them away.'

The note of authority brought them back to earth, galvanizing them into a flurry of activity. Patty and the little Greek woman whom they called Poppy, got to work unloading the stretchers from the back. Once they were clear, Olive had the task of turning the ambulance – by no means an easy job in the surrounding chaos. Patty guided her round, since it was almost impossible to see where she was reversing; and meanwhile Edie Long and Poppy went hurrying off after Stephen.

'Okay – thanks, Pat,' shouted Olive. 'Find out if they're ready to take off straight away or whether they want me over there, will you?'

Patty nodded and hurried after the others. It was difficult to see more than a yard or two in front because of the smoke and dust, and breathing was difficult. Patty put a hand over her nose and mouth and then tried undoing the top of her battledress tunic, but it didn't really help. Her eyes were smarting and the heat was scorching her face. She stumbled over the rubble, blindly making her way forward; so intent was she on not tripping over that she blundered straight into a hunched figure directly in her path.

'Terribly sorry,' muttered the figure.

'My fault,' gasped Patty. She peered at the smoke-begrimed face. There was something familiar about it. 'Why it's Ben Levy, isn't it? Didn't recognize you without your glasses.'

'That's the trouble,' explained Ben, still scrabbling around at her feet. 'They got knocked off and I can't see a thing without 'em. Don't recognize you, I'm afraid.'

'It's Patty. Patty Johnson,' she told him. 'Hold on – let me see if I can find them for you.'

She went down on her knees and looked around with her torch. She soon spotted them, but as she picked them up, she saw that one of the thick lenses was cracked and the frame was bent. Ben had obviously trodden on them in his search.

'Oh, Benny!'

The despair in her voice told Ben what had happened.

'Broken, are they? Oh Gawd.' He put out a hand. She placed the glasses in it and he fumbled with them, re-bending the frame to fit.

'Only one lens—' she began, and then dissolved into giggles. 'Benny – if you could see yourself . . .' The boy looked a bit like something out of a Keystone Cops comedy: his face filthy, his bent spectacles now perched lopsided across his nose.

'Well, at least I can see you now,' he grinned back. 'Half of you, anyway. Thanks Patty. Felt so ruddy useless before.'

'Yeah.' Patty's response was barely a whisper. They both stood for a moment, silently gazing at the spectacle in front of them. How could either of them be of any use against this?

As they watched, there was an ear-splitting crack,

followed by a rumbling like thunder overhead. An entire wall of a warehouse collapsed before their eyes, taking with it the firemen, who'd been perched on turntable ladders, vainly trying to stem the blaze. There was another blinding explosion of flame as the fire engine went up too, and the monstrous inferno engulfed more victims. The piercing screams of dying firemen echoed in the youngsters' ears.

'*Bloody Hell!*' exclaimed Benny.

It seemed impossible that anyone could still be alive in there, but as they rushed to the scene they could see figures working away at rescue. Under Stephen's supervision, Edie and Poppy were helping the stretcher bearers to pull the casualties clear. Nine men were lying on stretchers, twitching and moaning in agony. A few walking cases staggered behind them and collapsed on the ground in hunched misery.

'Any sign of the other ambulances?' Stephen asked sharply.

'Not yet,' Patty told him.

'Blast!' He turned to Edie. 'Load up as many as you can and get them away fast.'

'Okay. Here, young Benny – give us a hand!'

Benny hurried forward and grabbed the back end of the stretcher as Edie ordered. Edie was a big woman and lifted the stretcher with ease, setting off at a purposeful trot with Benny struggling to keep pace behind. Two other stretcher bearers heaved up and quickly followed suit. Stephen started to move towards another stretcher, where the last of his helpers was waiting. Sudden shouts made him turn. A figure came stumbling out of the flaming wreckage, his clothes on fire – a human torch. Stephen moved fast. While the others stood, numb with horror, he snatched up a blanket and threw it over the burning man, then rolled him on the ground, beating at him with his hands. The other helper ran forward to help.

'It's all right,' gasped Stephen. 'You get on moving the injured.'

Patty moved to assist him, but was stopped by a call from Stephen.

'Hey – you, Miss – what's your name?'

Patty ran to him where he crouched by the blanket-shrouded figure. 'Patty – Patricia Johnson.'

'Got your First Aid Kit?'

'Yes.'

Patty put her box on the ground and opened it. She steeled herself to administer to the badly burned man on the ground, but to her amazement Stephen shoved his own right hand under her nose.

'Slap a bandage on that for me, Patty, there's a good girl.'

'But—' she stammered uncertainly, looking at the man on the ground.

'You can't do him any good with your little box of tricks. Doubt if even the hospital can save him.'

She stared at him, appalled by his callous tone. He waggled his hand at her again.

'Come *on!* You'll have to patch me up if I'm to be any use here.'

She set her mouth tightly and pulled back his charred sleeve to reveal a vivid purple burn covering his wrist and arm. Patty hacked away ruthlessly at the thick sleeve with her scissors.

'You ought to go to hospital with this,' she said.

'Later. Don't bother with the ointment – just stick a bandage over it. And don't worry about hurting me,' he told her, 'pull it tight! I don't want it to slip.'

She finished it off with a knot and tucked the ends in neatly. He moved his arm about and flexed his fingers while she packed her box up.

'Thanks,' he said. 'Can you get a couple of those chaps to the ambulance?' he pointed to the group of men sitting by the stretcher cases. 'Tell Mrs Ackroyd we're supposed to take our casualties to Bart's. When you've delivered them, come back here as quickly as you can.'

She nodded and made her way to the group. As she was helping the first man to his feet, the bearers came running back with more stretchers. One of them, an older man, was panting from his exertions but still carrying on gamely. They were followed by little Poppy leading the second and third ambulance crews.

'At last!' exclaimed Stephen. 'Over here!'

Patty guided her two charges carefully towards the ambulance. One had been badly burnt about his head, which was swathed in bandages. He couldn't see where he was going and clutched her in panic.

'Am I blinded, miss?' he groaned. 'Say I'm not blinded!'

'Don't worry – your eyes are bandaged,' she soothed, hoping to God she was right. 'You'll be all right when we get you to the hospital.'

The second man had said he could walk without help, but he was lagging badly. She waited a moment to let him catch up, glad of the rest – she was drenched with sweat, and her lungs were bursting. She tried to gulp some air, but it was thick and smoke-laden; it felt as if her throat were closing in on itself, suffocating her. A wave of self-pity flooded over her, until she remembered how very much worse her poor charges were.

'That's right, you're doing fine,' she encouraged the second man, as he stumbled up to them. 'Not much further now.'

The first man clutched her even tighter, leaning on her heavily. She could smell him even through the thick atmosphere, and turned her head away to avoid the stench, trying to stifle her revulsion. Poor fellow – but at least he couldn't see her. She'd never smelt anything like it before. Then the sickening reality dawned on her: it was the smell of frying human flesh.

Olive Ackroyd came hurrying up to help, and Patty

pulled herself together, passing on Stephen's instructions while they struggled to get the men aboard. They tried to be as gentle as possible with them, but even so there were heartrending groans of pain from time to time.

'Anyone know where Bart's Hospital is?' asked Olive. When there was no response, she gave a grunt of ironic laughter. 'Oh well, let's hope we find someone who knows the way. Bound to come across a hospital sooner or later.'

Olive went round the front and climbed in her cab, thinking what a mess it all was. None of the Colonel's carefully thought-out training exercises could have prepared them for this. She had a thorough knowledge of the routes and hospitals in her particular area, but no-one had ever taken her round the East End – it hadn't seemed necessary.

Olive's usually cheerful face was grim as they jolted off. It took all her concentration simply to keep the engine going and see her way. There was so much rubble in the road she could easily overturn the top-heavy vehicle, yet she didn't dare go too slowly because the bloody engine might stall. One thing was for sure: those poor buggers in the back were in for a bumpy ride.

In the crowded canvas back, the stench was overpowering. Edie was on her knees, gently swabbing the face of a badly burned man in the lower bunk. Every jolt and judder of the ambulance was agony for him. Patty crouched beside her, trying to fight down her nausea. Thank goodness Edie had once been a nursing sister in a hospital and knew what to do.

'Can I help?' she whispered.

'Yes – pray! Unless you know some magic way to procure a few shots of morphine.' Edie bent close to her so that the patients wouldn't hear. 'What the hell good do they think we can do with a few aspirin and a roll of elastoplast?' She almost kicked her First Aid box in disgust. 'Look at 'em, poor sods. Makes you sick!'

She glanced up at Patty, noticing for the first time the girl's distress. She was swallowing and retching alternately. Roughly, she yanked Patty to her feet. 'Stick your head out the back, love, and breathe deeply.'

Patty stuck her head out of the canvas flaps. 'I'm sorry,' she mumbled.

'Don't you worry. We got used to it gradually in hospital, but you've really been shoved in the deep end—'

Her sentence was cut short by the sudden jamming on of the brakes. The jolt overbalanced Patty and she was thrown out into the road, landing with a thud which winded her for a few seconds. No longer able to control her stomach muscles, she vomited where she lay. She couldn't help it. She was crying with shame, too.

A police car was blocking the road. The driver yelled at Olive. 'Can't go down there. We've got an unexploded bomb.'

'I'm trying to find Bart's Hospital,' she shouted back.

'Not that way, duck. Turn back and take the third on your left. That'll bring you to Guy's. They may be full up by now, but they'll direct you somewhere else.'

'Thanks.'

'Hang on, I'll see you round.'

At the back, the policeman found Patty coughing her life up and Edie beside her, patting her on the back. At last it was over. Still shuddering violently, Patty wiped her mouth with her handkerchief. She felt she'd disgraced herself and the Corps.

'I'm so sorry.'

'Turn it up, I told you!' said Edie, her eyes meeting the policeman's in compassion above Patty's head.

'Okay now, miss?' asked the constable gently. She nodded.

'You get in front with Olive,' Edie ordered. 'She needs help finding the way.'

The policeman's eyes followed Patty as she climbed silently into the cab. 'They shouldn't send 'em out young as that,' he said. 'She's only a kid.'

'Yeah,' Edie agreed. 'But she's seen enough to last a life-time tonight.'

To Patty the rest of the night seemed to pass in a haze. She felt like a robot, performing duties as ordered, answering questions, carrying on without any real sensation or feeling. Certain events stood out: gulping down draughts of refreshing tea from a hospital trolley; a nun singing '*Roll out the Barrel*' with a group of slightly injured, but terrified children; her surprise at hearing coarse expletives issuing from Olive's mouth; her dismay at being turned away from the hospital after fighting their way back for a third time – there was no more room.

Patty knew she'd never get used to that smell, but she managed not to give way to her revulsion. She couldn't help but be inspired by the bravery and cheerfulness of the men – and some women too – and gave them what little help and comfort she could. She soon learned that speed was the first essential, rather than amateur attempts at dressing the burns. Often she saw men die and was glad for them – glad to see them find relief from the searing agony they were experiencing, and which she could do nothing to allay.

September 8th dawned another bright, sunny day, and most people were at breakfast when Stephen's convoy struggled back to Battersea Rise.

Olive slumped over her steering wheel. 'I'm fucked!' was her only comment.

Stephen presented himself in Colonel Harris's office. 'Before I give you my report, sir, may I request transport to take the crews home? The women, anyway. They're absolutely knackered.'

The Colonel's eyes took in the drawn face, the red-rimmed eyes, the pallor under the grime, the soiled and sticky bandage covering the right hand. The lad looked pretty knackered himself. 'Sit down, Broome,' he said in an unusually mild tone. 'Mr Graves will arrange the cars. Good idea.' As his deputy left the room, he called after him. 'Oh Arthur, tell Dusty to put the kettle on. Daresay you could do with some tea or coffee, eh Broome? And get somebody to come in here and change that dressing of his. Don't want infection starting up.'

Stephen wished he'd shut up. He knew the old man meant well, but all he wanted was to make his report and get to bed. Still, they were the first kind words he'd ever heard from the Colonel, so he mustn't complain.

'Right now – let's have it.' The Colonel's brisk tone brought him back to earth, and he started his report.

Kath saw the car pull up. She'd been into the front room so many times looking out down the road. Stan had got in some hours back. He was dead beat, but had refused to go to bed till Patty returned safe and sound. He'd heard from Dora Aynsworth that she'd been sent into the East End.

'Stan – she's here! She's all right!' She shook the nodding figure in the armchair and then ran to the front door to open it.

Tim was already at the gate. As Patty got out of the back of the car, he stared at her for a moment and then hooted with laughter.

'What do you look like?' he choked. 'You'd be a marvellous Guy Fawkes for bonfire night.'

'Be quiet, Tim!' Kath rebuked him, and held out her arms to her dirty, dishevelled daughter who was walking up the path like a zombie. 'It's all right, lovie, you're home now. It's all right.'

'Oh Mum . . .' Patty couldn't even speak. Later perhaps, but not now – it was all too cataclysmic to put into words.

Stan stood helplessly at the foot of the stairs, realizing that the horrors he'd undergone were nothing compared to his daughter's. 'Let's both grab a bit of sleep,' he muttered, following them upstairs.

Patty allowed herself to be led into her bedroom by her mother, and stood numb while she was undressed and put to bed. Her mother pulled the curtains and kissed her forehead, just like she used to when she'd been a child. Only she knew she'd never be a child again.

3

The Morning After

Kath had hardly got her daughter into bed than her youngest son was tugging at her sleeve.

'Mum, what's for breakfast?'

'Heavens above, boy, don't you think of anything but your stomach? You'd better have some bread and marge to keep you going, while I get things ready.'

She followed Tim into the kitchen, wondering what on earth she could give him to eat. It was getting difficult to manage on the rations these days, especially when the family ate at different times. She inspected her larder with a sigh: it would have to be porridge.

She'd just put the pan on the stove and was turning round when she caught Tim ladling a generous spoonful of jam on to his plate.

'Watch it!' she snapped. 'That pot's got to last us until the end of the month!'

'Sorry.' Tim guiltily scooped half the jam back into the pot.

'I didn't mean to shout at you, love,' said Kath remorsefully. 'I'm a bit tired, that's all.'

The telephone rang *Roger?* Kath quickly turned the gas down and hurried past Tim into the hall, motioning to him to stir the porridge in case it burnt.

Tim got up, holding his paper, and stood by the stove, casually stirring the saucepan.

Kath picked up the receiver, her heart pounding. It *had* to be Roger! 'Yes?' she answered expectantly.

'That you, Kath?' croaked an old familiar voice.

'Mum dear!' It was difficult to keep the disappointment

out of her voice. 'How are you? We were so worried last night.'

'I'm all right, I s'pose. Bit shook up. Flat's gone, though.'

'Good, I'm glad you're—' Kath stopped in mid-sentence. 'What did you say?'

'I said the flat's gone. Kybosh! Direct hit.'

Behind the abrupt words, Kath sensed how deeply the old woman felt the loss of her home and all her possessions. Poor Mum! Kath felt choked. She'd been so bound up in her own worries she'd forgotten momentarily that her mother had been in the thick of the bombardment. 'But you're not hurt? That's the main thing. Where are you?'

'Stepney Town Hall. They're using it as a Rest Centre – or they were: that got hit, too. Twice in one night! Takes some beating, doesn't it?'

'Mum, how awful! Look, shall I get Stan to come over and fetch you? He's asleep at the moment, but as soon as he wakes up . . .'

'Think they want me out of here sooner'n that. Kath, the WVS lady is making signs to hurry up. Can I come over now?'

'Er – yes, of course!'

A cool, efficient voice cut in. 'Sorry, Mrs Johnson – we don't want to sound unfeeling, but we do have over three hundred people to get re-settled as quickly as possible.'

'I quite understand.' Kath tried to sound equally cool, but inwardly she was panicking. Where were they going to put her? How long would she be staying?

All the time the anonymous voice at the other end continued talking. ' . . . we'll bring Mrs Bowden over by car and she'll have emergency ration cards until you can get new ones issued in your own area.'

'I see. Thank you. Is she really all right? I mean – should we get the doctor?'

'Might be wise to have a check-up in a day or so. It's quite possible to have delayed reaction, but at the moment she's fine. Being very brave indeed. Just a moment, she wants another word with you.'

Mrs Bowden came on the line again. 'That all right, Kath?'

'Of course, Mum. Don't you worry about a thing. We'll see you shortly, then.'

Kath put down the receiver and stood in the hall, her mind racing. But before she could even contemplate reorganizing the family's sleeping arrangements, the 'phone rang again – and then again. Both her sisters were calling, anxious for news. The next to call was Peter, distraught because the line had been engaged so long. All in all, it was some time before Kath got her eagerly awaited call from Roger. He was cheerful but in a tearing hurry. All he had time to say was that all leave had been cancelled, so he didn't know when he'd get home. The station had taken a pasting and they had to get as many machines as possible operational before the next raid. He rang off before Kath even had the chance to wish him many happy returns.

Suddenly Kath swung round. Stan was coming slowly down the stairs.

'Oh Stan – you should be resting.'

'Fat chance, with that phone ringing all the time. Anyway, I didn't feel like sleep.'

He followed her into the kitchen, where Tim was greedily devouring the last remnants of porridge. Kath's hands trembled slightly as she lit the gas under the kettle, and Stan looked at her sharply.

'What's up, love?' he asked.

'Oh Stan, Mum's been bombed!' The tears came in a flood.

Stan put his arms round her. 'There now! Come and sit down.' He gently pushed her into a chair. 'Tim, make us a cup of tea, there's a good lad.'

'Has Gran been killed?' Tim's morbid curiosity was silenced by a stern glare from Stan.

'No. She's all right, but the flat's demolished. They're . . . they're bringing her over here now.'

'Holy Cow! Is she going to live with us?'

This time Tim wasn't rebuked. His parents were gazing at each other silently in shared understanding. 'Of course – till we see how things go on.' said Stan at last. 'Hurry up with that tea, Tim. We've got a lot to do.'

Afterwards, Kath was to look back on that morning through a kind of mist. It was hard to remember exactly what order things happened; the house seemed to be overflowing with people – friends and neighbours popping in, all with their own experiences to recount; the telephone kept ringing; Tim had the radio blaring. And in the middle of this confusion, Gran Bowden arrived.

Muriel Bowden was short and stocky, but what she lacked in height she more than made up for in spirit. She strode up the little path to the front door, shaking off the helping arm of the WVS driver. Behind her back, the lady in green uniform winked at Kath. Mrs Bowden kissed her daughter perfunctorily and immediately demanded Stan.

'He's got to see about me bed,' she announced. Without waiting, she stomped into the kitchen to issue her orders.

'Hey, Gran – what's happened to your teeth?' piped Tim.

'When a bomb drops, you've a lot more on your mind than your teeth, me boy.'

'Did they get knocked out then?'

'No. Silly man trod all over 'em, didn't he?'

'What man?'

'This boy and his questions! The man what pulled me out after the roof fell, stupid! Not his fault, I s'pose. He couldn't see what he was doing.' She gave a mirthless – and toothless – laugh.

'She'll get compensation, of course,' explained the WVS woman quietly. 'We went round to the flats and salvaged what we could for her—' She handed Kath a large canvas bag full of knick-knacks '—but she's very worried about her bed – wants it moved here somehow. It seems to be all right.'

Kath groaned. That damn bed! It *would* be all right. It was as indestructible as its owner. But where on earth would they put it? She looked at Stan desperately, hoping he'd have some sort of inspiration, but Gran was already into her stride. Stan simply gave her a minute but helpless shrug. It looked as if that bed was coming to stay.

The WVS lady laughed. 'She's incredible. How she survived we'll never know. If you could see the flats – just a heap of rubble.' She shook her head and sighed. 'They only got three people out alive, the other two are in hospital. Your mother was lucky.'

Kath nodded. What was one ugly old bed compared with that tragedy? If it'd help Mum get over the loss of so many friends and neighbours, they'd make room for the bloody thing somehow.

'We'd only just got them all settled at the Town Hall, when that got hit,' continued the WVS woman. 'Fortunately, it wasn't too badly damaged, but it gave us all a bit of a jolt.'

Kath suddenly realized that the WVS lady must have been on duty all night too – was *still* on duty, caring for the victims of the raid; there were signs of weariness and strain under the cheerful manner. Looking at her, Kath felt awful: all these women out doing their bit – even her own daughter – and all she'd done was sit in the shelter and worry about her family. It was at that precise moment that Kath decided to take a war job. She wasn't quite sure what yet, but she had to do something if she wasn't to feel totally useless.

'Can I make you a cup of tea or something?' she asked the woman with quick concern.

The WVS lady smiled. 'Bless you, but no thanks. I daren't stop. If I sat down, I'd probably never get up again.'

Kath accompanied the woman to the car. 'We've been months preparing for this, and yet when it came we were caught on the hop! Still, we'll know what to expect next time.'

Kath felt another stab in her heart. It didn't bear thinking about – that there was more horror to come.

'If there's anything your mother needs, get in touch with the local WVS. I'm sure they'll be able to help.'

Kath turned back into the house to find Patty coming downstairs. All the hullaballoo had woken her. She had dark shadows under her eyes and was still dirty from the previous night's work. Kath turned everyone out of the kitchen and into the front parlour. Patty wanted a wash, and she had to get cracking with the lunch.

All over London similar scenes were taking place.

People faced Sunday, September 8th, with a mixture of horror and relief – horror at the damage inflicted during the night, and relief that casualties had been so light. Few imagined that Hitler intended to repeat the dose that very night and continue for the next two months, in a campaign of bombs, fires and human devastation on a scale hitherto unknown to the world.

A feeling of solidarity pervaded a midday meeting of the neighbours of Balaclava Street that Sunday. Most of them had heard the broadcast by Winston Churchill earlier in the day, commending them for their heroic stand; after that, it seemed natural to gather outside and express their pride in survival and their new-found companionship in adversity.

Stan assumed the mantle of leadership, simply because he was the ARP Warden. He began by outlining some of the ideas he'd picked up during the night.

'One of the things they found up at Clapham where the bombing was bad was that the Wardens didn't know how many people to look for in each house,' he began. 'So they've suggested that each occupant chalks up the number of people in the house every night on the front door. Even if you've got someone staying with you, let me know.'

The discussion continued, and in the warm Indian-summer weather there was an artificial gaiety in the air, almost a party feeling – though not at all the sort of party the Johnsons had planned.

Patty made an effort to be sociable at lunch that day, but behind her smile she felt flat and disappointed. She'd been looking forward to telling her parents about Peter, but somehow with the arrival of Gran and all her troubles, it didn't seem right to talk about her own happiness.

Peter had managed to join them, as planned, but he too seemed ill-at-ease, almost as if he were an intruder in the family circle. After the meal he suggested a short drive, and Patty jumped at the idea; it would be lovely to be alone for a while.

They drove to Wimbledon, parked the car and strolled hand in hand across the Common. But there was a curious restraint between them. The cataclysmic experience of the previous night hadn't been a shared one, and somehow that had affected their relationship.

'Do you want to talk about it?' Peter asked.

Patty shook her head. 'Not really. Not now, anyway. Maybe later.'

He squeezed her hand, as if he understood. But he didn't. He felt remote and somehow inadequate, conscious that while Patty had been exposed to the full horror, he'd been working away safely in a bomb-proof basement.

'I meant what I said yesterday,' he murmured, after they'd walked a little further.

Patty looked at him blankly for a moment. Surely she couldn't have forgotten? Suddenly her face came alight. She stopped moving and put her arms round his neck.

'Sorry – I was miles away! It's difficult to explain, but somehow after last night it seems wrong to be happy – personally, I mean. It was all a bit shattering.'

'I expect it'll take you a while to get over it,' Peter reassured her.

She smiled at him. 'Tell me again!'

'It's your turn!'

She wrinkled her nose at him, then stood on tiptoe to whisper in his ear. 'I love you!'

'Oh Patty!' He hugged her close and then kissed her until she broke away, laughing and breathless.

The tension broken, Patty suddenly felt more relaxed, more in command again. There were several other people on the common that afternoon, walking their dogs, pushing prams with their babies, or riding their bicycles, but she was oblivious to them all.

'It'll be better next week,' she observed. 'I'm on days, so we'll be able to spend the evenings together.'

'We'll have a special celebration then. Go out somewhere for dinner and dance.'

'Like the Spider's Web?' This had seemed like the last word in sophistication to Patty when Peter had taken her there on their first date.

'Okay, if you like,' Peter agreed. 'I wondered if you'd rather go somewhere smart – up West, perhaps?'

'Another time, maybe. This'll be like a sort of anniversary.'

They returned to the house in time for tea, and Patty was glad of the family around for once. She felt strangely shy with Peter today. Probably it was all to do with the unreal atmosphere of this extraordinary day.

It wasn't long after they finished tea that the sirens went. They all looked at each other, each of them with their own remembrance of the previous night and an unspoken fear of something similar, or even worse, in store. Hardly had the sirens stopped wailing than the telephone went. It was for Stan.

'I'd better get changed too,' said Patty.

'But they haven't called you yet,' her mother protested.

'I'd better get to the Depot all the same. They'll probably need everyone they can get hold of if it's like last night.'

'I'll take you there,' Peter offered.

While Stan and Patty changed, Kath, Tim and Gran prepared to move to the shelter.

'Got something to read, Mum?' asked Kath, with an effort at cheerfulness.

'No, and I ain't got me glasses neither,' came the sharp retort. 'Can we take the wireless out? Don't want to miss Variety Bandbox.'

Kath was doubtful about the idea, but Tim, naturally, was all enthusiasm. In the end Peter helped cart the cumbersome radio set to the shelter, where Tim swivelled it on its revolving base to tune it to the right station.

There was a new intensity in the way they all kissed each other goodbye this time, although the spoken phrases were deliberately casual. Stan set off for his post at a brisk walk, and Patty and Peter climbed into the MG.

It was just five o'clock, and Hitler's bombers were on their way again. To many this was a worse shock than the night before, which they fondly imagined to be an isolated raid.

The residents of Balaclava Street grabbed their gas masks and made their way reluctantly to their garden shelters. In the East End there was near-panic as thousands of people converged on the tube stations, either to spend the night on the platform or to travel 'up West' to the large shelters in stores such as Dickins and Jones in Regent Street. Already on this second night, families were beginning to 'trek' away from their homes in the East End to escape the horrifying devastation that the Luftwaffe would rain down on them.

In Balaclava Street, there was a belief that the bomb which had damaged The Windmill was a 'mistake' unlikely to be repeated, and that it was not the Germans' intention to bomb the civilian population. That belief, however, was destined to be shortlived.

Outside the Ambulance Depot, Patty and Peter clung together in silent desperation, until Patty became conscious of the activity around her; people were hurrying in and out of the door and getting the ambulances ready.

'I must go,' she murmured.

Peter nodded. 'I'll ring you in the morning, early, before you go to sleep, right? Be careful, darling. Remember you're my property now!'

She kissed him again and ran inside, not daring to look back.

Colonel Harris was on duty alone when Patty went to sign in. 'I caught up with some sleep this afternoon,' he told her. 'Now it's Mr Graves' turn. We'll have to devise a new system if Jerry keeps up the pressure like this every night.'

'Is that possible?' she asked.

'Not only possible, but probable, I reckon. Good of you to turn up early again after what you went through last night,' he went on. 'Lot of your shift are here too. Admirable spirit.'

'I thought there might be an emergency.'

'Well, at the moment they've put another area on standby to go to the East End, but you never know. You'd better go and get a bit of rest while you can.'

'Yes, sir.'

But Patty found it impossible to sleep in the hall; it was far too busy. Instead she listened as the Colonel made a little speech thanking them for their gallant efforts and saying how proud he was of them all. They'd had their own casualties, too. One ambulance had been blown up with the loss of the three women on board; Mr Seagrave, the elderly stretcher-bearer she'd noticed yesterday, was in hospital after a heart attack brought on by his exertions in the raid, then there were numerous cases of cuts and burns. Patty's eyes went automatically to Stephen and she noticed that he had his arm in a sling, his hand covered in a clean white bandage. As if sensing that someone was staring at him, he turned his head suddenly. Their eyes met, and he grinned. Patty blushed and looked at the floor, while the Colonel boomed on about a funeral service for the victims at which a unit from the Depot would be in official attendance. There would be a collection for wreaths.

Patty had remembered the white feathers this time, and she handed them over to Mrs Harris, who gave a loud grunt of satisfaction.

'Good show, Patricia! Now we'll give them something to think about!'

Patty watched with curiosity as she bustled off to a corner with one of her cronies and set to work addressing envelopes amid much elaborate and totally unnecessary secrecy.

That night they weren't sent into the East End but were kept surprisingly busy in their own area. Once again Clapham Junction station was a key target, and the surrounding districts suffered heavily. Colonel Harris did his best to avoid assigning heavy duties to those who'd gone out the previous night, but in the end there were so many calls that most of them were called at least once anyway.

To his surprise, Stephen was summoned to the Commandant's office early on.

'How's the hand, Broome?' the Colonel asked brusquely.

'Not too bad, sir. I don't really need this sling . . .'

The Colonel frowned. 'Don't forget I saw that burn myself last night.'

Stephen nodded. Not much escaped the Old Man's eagle eye.

'Well, you can't drive or carry stretchers for a few days, that's for sure.'

'But, sir—'

The upraised hand brooked no argument, so Stephen subsided. 'We can use you here,' the Colonel continued.

'In this office?'

'Yes. You can man the telephones and send out the necessary units. It'll free Mr Graves to keep up with the admin. We can't let that slip.'

Hesitantly, Stephen sat at the desk, as indicated. The prospect of spending an entire night in close proximity with the Colonel, was somewhat daunting. But the old bugger was right in a way – he wouldn't be much use out with the stretcher party. He was the last to admit it, but his hand was extremely painful at the moment. Luckily for him, if not for the general public, things soon became frantically busy in the office and conversation between him and his superior was limited to urgent business.

Patty, however, found the night boring. She wasn't sent out as extra crew on any of the ambulances, nor was she used as a messenger. Instead she spent half the time helping Dusty wash up, and the rest lying on a narrow mattress in the hall, trying to grab some sleep. Again, it was impossible. She was far more conscious of the noise of the explosions than when she was occupied.

She was just passing the outer office on her way back to help Dusty, when she saw Arthur Graves hard at work through the open door. He looked up and spotted her.

'Patricia! You don't type, by any chance, do you?'

''Fraid not, Mr Graves.'

He sighed. 'Never mind. I've got so many lists here – it'd be much quicker if they could be typed.'

'Can I copy anything for you? I write quite neatly.'

'It would be a help,' he said hesitantly, 'but are you sure you won't be bored?'

'I'd be glad to have something to do,' replied Patty.

She sat down beside him and was soon hard at work. She could hear the activity in the inner office, the nerve centre of the Depot, and learnt more in a few hours than she had in her whole service so far.

'We're bloody short of drivers!' commented the Colonel during a lull. 'Must recruit some more.'

'Isn't there anyone here we could teach?' suggested Stephen.

'Maybe. Good idea, Broome. Damn good!'

The telephone cut the conversation short, but Patty had heard enough. If they were going to give driving lessons, then she'd be the first to volunteer. What a thrill! Peter would have to let her drive his precious MG then!

Later on, Stephen passed through the outer office and Patty noticed with horror that he had a envelope in his hand. She saw him open it, then freeze for a moment where he stood. His face grew taut, but he said nothing – just screwed up the envelope and shoved it in his pocket. Patty was scarlet with embarrassment and guilt, but luckily he didn't glance in her direction. She felt dreadful. It had never occurred to her that Mrs Harris would send one of her feathers to *him*. Patty knew he was no coward – but then old Maudie hadn't seen him at the fire the previous night. For a moment, she was tempted to run and tell him it had all been a ghastly mistake, but her courage failed her.

At Number Seven Balaclava Street, the atmosphere was distinctly tense. Kath stood in the hall, surrounded by a collection of odds and ends that she'd hurriedly removed from the cupboard under the stairs. Tired and irritable, she looked at her mother. Mrs Bowden sat in an upright dining-room chair in the space Kath had just cleared, clearly uncomfortable and cramped, but equally clearly determined not to budge. She clutched her knitting in her gnarled hands and scowled at her daughter.

'What are you standing there gawping for?' she asked.

'I don't like leaving you here alone,' sighed Kath.

'Nonsense! I'll be all right. You get back to Tim and that smelly hole in the ground.'

Halfway through the night, having grumbled incessantly about conditions in the shelter, Mrs Bowden had announced her intention of returning to the house. She'd been fine as long as there were interesting programmes on the wireless to listen to, but as soon as they finished, the complaints started. It had been impossible for either Tim or herself to sleep with Gran talking, so when Mrs Bowden finally heaved herself out of the chair and stumped off towards the back door, declaring that if she was going to be killed, she'd rather it was indoors than squashed in a tin can like a lot of sardines, Kath hadn't argued. She'd followed her into the house, torn between anxiety at leaving Tim alone and guilt at deserting her mother after her ghastly experience of the previous night. She reckoned the safest place was under the stairs – hence the hurried scramble to clear the cupboard as a hidey-hole for Mum. Not that Kath felt any conviction that the old lady would remain there one minute after her back was turned. Still, she'd done her best.

'Are you sure you won't be nervous on your own?' she asked again.

'Don't be daft! I'd be on me own in Stepney if I hadn't been bombed, wouldn't I?'

Unable to fault her mother's logic, Kath returned to the shelter – but it didn't stop her fretting about her during the long hours until three a.m., when the sirens finally wailed the All Clear and she was able to hustle the excitable Tim back to the house and up to his own bed. As she expected, the cupboard was bare, and she found her mother curled up on the sofa in the front parlour, toothless mouth open and snoring her head off. It wasn't a pretty picture, but Kath smiled as she fetched a blanket to lay gently over the old lady.

Only then did Kath crawl to bed herself. She fell asleep immediately, totally exhausted, and hardly stirred when Stan crept in beside her not long afterwards. It seemed just seconds later that the alarm clock shattered the silence. It was seven o'clock. Another day had begun.

4

Business as Usual

Stan Johnson shaved at the kitchen sink while a weary Kath got breakfast. In her view, it wouldn't matter if he was late for work just once in his life, but Stan was blowed if Hitler was going to keep him away from his job. This attitude was general. In spite of the bombs, absenteeism was almost non-existent and the vast proportion of working people clocked in on time. For Stan, it was the Inland Revenue offices in Kennington, where he was a junior inspector. For Horace Aynsworth, it was his funeral parlour in Battersea Park Road, where business would soon be brisker than usual. For Fred Perkins, the landlord of Balaclava Street, it was a visit to one of his building sites in Clapham, which had been partially devastated in the raid. This was followed by a visit to the Battersea Council offices, where he hoped to land a contract for repairs to bomb-damaged council property. He was looking forward to his day with relish.

Old Mrs Bowden was hunched in an easy chair by the fire, and Kath watched her with concern. Obviously, her mother was still a bit shaken up, and she couldn't make up her mind whether to leave her alone or jolly her along. She decided on the latter course.

'Come on, Mum, give me a hand hanging out the washing, there's a love.' Hitler or no Hitler, Monday was still washday at the Johnsons.

The sight of white sheets billowing on the line in the gentle summer breeze was restoring Kath's spirits, when the sound of the telephone brought her in from the back garden at a run.

The musical lilt of the voice on the line told her it was Sincerity Vale from across the road. 'Sorry to disturb you, my dear,' said the actress, 'but I wonder if you could spare a few minutes to pop over for a drink?'

Kath was taken aback. Drinks before lunch weren't the routine in the Johnson family, although Sincerity and her husband, being theatrical people, might indulge in such luxuries. 'Is it a special occasion or something?' she asked hesitantly.

'No, no. Just wanted a little chat with you.'

Kath's curiosity was aroused. Sincerity and her husband, Claude Windsor, weren't *quite* internationally known film stars, but they were celebrities, and Balaclava Street was proud of them. She wasn't going to pass up a chance like this. Pulling her apron off, she ran up the stairs to comb her hair and dab a bit of powder on her nose. She didn't look very smart, but she knew Sincerity would understand. The Windsors were a sweet couple and there was absolutely no side to them at all. On one occasion they'd both been in pantomime at Golders Green Hippodrome and had given her free tickets to take the children. It had been a memorable occasion with a special tea laid on in the stars' dressing room.

Calling out to her mother that she'd only be gone for about half an hour, Kath walked across the road, humming to herself. This would make a nice break to her morning.

Kath looked round the sitting room as Sincerity poured the drinks, gazing at the piano with its lace cloth, crowned with autographed photos of famous personalities; at the mantelpiece and various occasional tables, similarly adorned. Maybe some would say it was too cluttered, but it was a warm, homely room, full of mementoes of past glory. Over the fireplace hung an oil painting of a beautiful girl in period dress – unmistakably the young Sincerity Vale in one of her musical comedy roles.

Kath looked over to the original. Age and excessive drinking had taken their toll on the once-ravishing

Sincerity Vale, yet there were still traces of beauty behind her puffy eyelids and mottled face. Her auburn hair was as luxuriant as ever, although the colour was now a hard, unnatural red, but her smile was unchanged – the sweet, genuine, happy smile of a woman who knows she is loved. The great showbiz love story, lapped up by the public, was no publicity gimmick: after thirty-odd years of marriage, Claude and Sincerity still adored one another.

'Here you are, dear – cheers!' Sincerity moved gracefully over with the glasses and raised hers in a little toast. 'What a shame about your party. Everyone was looking forward to it so much.'

Kath nodded. 'I suppose we must just thank Heaven we all came through all right.'

'You know, I used to think it was a great tragedy that Claude and I never had any children, but now . . .' Sincerity paused and gave a little sigh. 'Maybe it was a blessing after all. The worries you mothers have to go through these days – I'm not sure I could take it.'

'Sometimes I wonder if I can,' said Kath. 'The only thing to do is keep busy.' She wondered what it was Sincerity wanted to talk to her about, but her hostess seemed in no hurry. She was enjoying the chat.

'By the way, it was so kind of your husband to look in on me the other night. He must be so busy, poor dear. I don't know what the street would do without him.'

Kath felt a glow of pride. 'Stan is good that way,' she agreed. 'But I don't know how long he can go without sleep if this bombing continues.'

'Don't, my dear! They can't keep it up at this rate, surely?' She walked to the window and opened it wider. 'You're not in a draught, are you? I like to let the sunlight in when possible. This sticky tape over the windows makes the rooms so dark.'

Kath glanced at the clock. Time was passing, and she really ought to get back. 'Er, Miss Vale, I don't want to seem rude, but I don't like leaving my mother alone too long. You did say you wanted to talk to me . . .'

'Well, yes – it's about your mother, actually. You see, I know she'll get compensation for the bomb damage, but I'm sure it won't be anything like enough to replace what she's lost. Besides, it takes such ages. I've been sorting through my things and I've got a few bits and pieces here that might come in handy.' She fetched a large bag from beside the piano and handed it to Kath. It was full of clothes. 'You don't think she'll be offended?'

'No, no – but really, it's too much! You shouldn't!'

'Of course I should! I don't need them. And I kept thinking all yesterday how heart-breaking it must have been for her to lose *everything* – all the little things one treasures so much.'

Kath suddenly felt overcome. The tears welled up, impulsively she hugged the older woman. 'You're so kind. I can't ever thank you.'

Sincerity was touched. 'It's nothing, dear. You can always tell her you found them in a jumble sale.'

Kath hurried home, wondering how to tell her mother. Sincerity was quite right: the old lady was far too proud to accept anything that smacked of charity.

It was too late for subterfuge, however; Gran had been watching from the front window and tackled her the moment she was inside the door.

'What you got there?' The gnarled fingers scrabbled away inside the bag and pulled out a stone marten tippet. 'This belong to that actress lady over the road?'

Kath began stammering out an explanation, but her voice tailed off as she saw her mother drape the fur round her shoulders and parade in front of the hall mirror. The temptation to show off to her cronies in Stepney was irresistible; Mrs Bowden decided she would accept the gift graciously. 'Nice bit of rabbit. What do you think, Kath?'

Later, Gran went upstairs for an afternoon nap, and Kath decided to follow suit. Within minutes she fell into a deep exhausted sleep and was only woken by Tim returning from school, hungry as always. Shortly afterwards, Patty returned from her day shift and Kath was surprised to find her putting on her best dress.

'You're not going *out?*'

'Yes. Peter's taking me to dinner.'

'But Patty, supposing there's a raid?'

'Supposing there is? I've been out in them two nights running, why should tonight be any different? Besides, we're going out of London. We'll probably be safer than here.'

Kath could hardly deny her logic, although it worried her not to have the whole family under her wing.

That Monday night the sirens wailed their warning just before dusk, and the Balaclava Street residents crept out to their shelters for a third uncomfortable night. The noise seemed, if anything, worse than on the two previous nights, with the ack-ack in Battersea Park becoming noticeably more active. At ten o'clock a bomb crashed down on an allotment immediately to the rear of Number Eight, the blast shattering every window in the house and several others in Balaclava Street as it swept through the air.

The prefabricated corrugated-iron sides of Raynes's shelter caved in and fell on the family as they lay on their mattresses. Miraculously, nobody was hurt, but they were all very shaken up. Many of the neighbours had hurried out after the explosion and helped Stan extricate the family from the wreckage. It was clear that Sid Raynes, in his usual slovenly fashion, hadn't dug the foundations deep enough and that that was why the shelter had collapsed so easily. Stan, however, decided this was hardly the moment to point it out.

Stan was surprising himself with his increasing confidence and authority, traits he'd never previously revealed to the world. Before, it had troubled him to be in a safe little reserved job, while others put their lives at risk. But now he felt a surge of pride in his work as a Warden which more than compensated for the fact that he wasn't serving with His Majesty's Forces.

He was glad, he had to confess, that his duties took him out and about at night. Because even though the work was dangerous, he was stimulated by the drama he faced – and it was infinitely preferable to being cooped up in a shelter, waiting for a bomb to fall. Instantly he thought about poor Kath and realized what she had to go through on these long, lonely nights.

The restaurant was packed, the lights were low and the music soft and smoochy. Patty felt as if she were floating as Peter danced her round the floor. It was a combination of happiness and gin. She'd drunk much more than ever before but, as Peter said, it was a celebration. There was a raid in progress, but no one was taking the slightest notice. It was funny how blasé everyone was becoming about the bombs, now they were a nightly occurrence. Of course, they were some way out of the centre of London, near Watford, so the bombardment was nothing like so intense. They'd meet it on their way home, unless the All Clear had sounded. It was possible. For once, they weren't in any hurry, and she could forget about duty and devote herself to enjoyment.

Peter had sent a note to the leader of the little combo and they were playing *Love Walked In*, especially for her. At the end, Peter kissed her in front of everyone, and the applause from the rest of the dancers was as much for this demonstration as for the band.

There were many young couples present, most of the men in uniform. Patty wondered how many others had just discovered they were in love. She knew there were some newly-weds here because the band had played the wedding march earlier on and a cake had been brought to a big table in the corner.

Peter offered the boys in the combo a drink and then guided her back to their table at the side, his arm round her waist in a proprietorial manner. He was very conscious of the envious glances from some of the other men and was determined to stake his claim publicly. They sat down and gazed at each other, feeling no need to talk. A waitress hovered. Peter ordered a beer for himself, but Patty shook her head. He grinned and put his hand over hers.

'Don't tell me I'm going to marry an old soak?'

Patty's heart missed a beat. Had he really said that?

'Is that meant to be a proposal?' she giggled.

'Well, it sort of slipped out. I didn't exactly mean to say it like that.'

'I should hope not! I expect you to go down on your knees and do it properly.'

'Right!' With that, Peter leapt out of his chair and went on one knee in a histrionic pose, still clasping her hand. 'Dearest Miss Johnson, will you do me the favour of bestowing this tiny hand on me in marriage?'

'*Peter!*' Patty was laughing and trying to restrain him and blushing all at once.

'Your answer! Or I shall remain here indefinitely.'

'You'll get terrible cramp!'

'Your answer!'

'Yes, yes,' cried Patty, 'if you'll just get up!'

By now they'd created quite a sensation at the surrounding tables and when Peter hauled himself up, there were cheers and another round of applause. Patty blushed again, and Peter bent over and kissed her.

'How does it feel to be engaged?' he asked with a grin.

'Fantastic! How does it feel to you?'

'Can't quite take it in yet!'

'Trying to get out of it already?' teased Patty. 'I shall sue for breach of promise.'

Soon they were back on the dance floor, and Peter was holding her close again. 'I don't think long engagements are a good idea, do you?' he murmured into her ear.

'I've never thought about it before,' replied Patty. 'I'd like a white wedding, though. With bridesmaids.'

'What'll your parents say, do you think?'

'They like you – I know that!'

'Good. But will they think you're old enough to get married?'

'Do you mind!' She remonstrated indignantly. 'If I'm old enough to be in Civil Defence, I'm old enough to get married. Anyway, you're not so ancient yourself!'

'Twenty-three in March.'

'When's your birthday? Anywhere near Easter? That would be a gorgeous time to get married. If it was your birthday too, you'd never forget our anniversary, could you?'

'But you'd have to buy me two presents each year!'

'Mercenary!'

As the badinage flowed back and forth, Patty realized with something of a shock how little she knew about the man she had just promised to marry. Not even the date of his birthday! She didn't know anything about his family or his background. He at least had met hers.

As if reading her thoughts, Peter said suddenly, 'Can you get a whole day off sometime soon?'

'I think so – why?'

'We could take a run down to Lymington and you could meet my parents. I'll ring them up tomorrow and tell them the news, but they'll be dying to see you in person.'

The thought of meeting prospective in-laws made her quake inwardly. Would they think her good enough for their son? Peter was an officer; Patty's background and upbringing were working-class. Would it matter that there was a difference between them? It had never occurred to her to think about it before. Peter had always been perfectly natural with her family; but would she feel equally at ease in a higher social stratum? She'd hate to feel she was letting Peter down.

Questioning him about his home and family, she learned that his father had a small boatyard and hired out sailing and fishing boats. Peter had spent his entire life by the sea. He'd been a sea cadet, and so when war broke out he'd naturally wanted to join the Navy. They lived in a small house right by the yard. Not much of a garden, but a marvellous view across to the Isle of Wight. Seeing the way Peter's eyes lit up when he talked about it, Patty had a momentary twitch of nerves. He'd probably want to live down there when they were married. How would she fit in? Her, a Londoner born and bred. Oh well, she'd get used to it – and they'd be together, that was the main thing.

'Hey, this is worse than the Spanish Inquisition,' he laughed, when her spate of questions dried up temporarily.

'Well, at least you've met my family,' she explained.

'Only a few! You've got so many relations.'

Patty had to admit this was true. And of course, they'd all have to come to the wedding. Mum would have a fit trying to cater for that lot. She began to wonder how much it would all cost, and if they'd be able to afford it. Maybe she was being a bit rash wanting a white wedding, but it *was* the 'Once in a Lifetime' day. It ought to be something to remember. She'd have to talk it over with Mum.

Peter asked her what sort of ring, she'd like. She didn't know what to say. Sapphires were beautiful, but weren't they dreadfully expensive? She had no idea what Peter could afford – or how much he earned.

Peter laughed suddenly. Patty looked so comical in her worry, her thoughts were easy to read. 'Okay, we'll go together to choose,' he grinned. 'It won't be the Koh-i-noor, but we should be able to get something nice. Maybe a second-hand one would be a good idea.'

Patty's face fell somewhat. Peter laughed again and patted her hand. 'You have what you want, darling. You'll be the one to wear it.'

They were the last couple on the floor, and the band were playing *Goodnight Sweetheart*. When they left the restaurant, Patty looked back to impress the scene on her memory. It was a very special occasion.

They drove slowly and after a while, Peter pulled into an open gateway leading to a field. They were on a hilltop looking down on London to the south east. It was a brilliant starlit night.

'What a lovely evening,' Patty murmured.

'Lovely for the Luftwaffe, too,' agreed Peter. London was like some giant firework display spread before them.

'Yes, I've been trying not to think about the raid. It all seems so remote from here.'

'You're right. Don't let's spoil a perfect evening.'

He leant over and kissed her, long and hard. After a moment, he grunted. 'Blasted steering wheel! These cars weren't made for necking.'

'I'm glad of that,' chuckled Patty. 'At least you won't be tempted too much when you're away from me.'

He smiled and shook his head. 'You're the only girl I'll ever need, Patty.'

'Oh Peter.' She hugged him tight.

'Hey, mind my ribs! Let's get out of this wretched mousetrap.'

Peter spread his navy raincoat on the ground and they lay in a close embrace. Peter's hands wandered over her body, caressing but tentative. Patty stiffened, then trembled a little. Immediately, Peter desisted, frightened of putting her off. Patty wished he'd continue, but was too scared to say anything for fear of seeming forward. She could feel something hard as he pressed tightly against her, and realized with a thrill of excitement that Peter had an erection – and that she was the cause of it. She knew about erections, of course – mostly from lurid and inaccurate conversations with girls at school, but also from one hot summer afternoon, when Roger had been lying in the back garden sunbathing. The hard protuberance in his swimming trunks had been so pronounced that Dad had had to tell him gruffly to cover himself up. He hadn't been near a girl at the time, but she'd taken a look at the magazine he was reading. It was *Men Only*, and had some pretty saucy pictures of nude girls in it.

She'd discussed the matter with Lesley that evening and Lesley had told her categorically that unlike girls, men could get a hard-on even without touching anyone. Lesley was the oracle on those matters, though of course her only source was her sister, Joy. Patty longed to find out for herself, but was overwhelmed by embarrassment – her entire upbringing had conditioned her to precepts such as the importance of virginity, and the belief that nice girls let the man make the first move.

Patty felt Peter suddenly pull away from her. He lay on his back gazing up at the sky. She was hurt. Had she said or done something to upset him? Surely not. They hadn't said a word for ages and she hadn't stopped him kissing or touching her . . . The truth was that Peter, aroused to a point where he knew it would be difficult to control himself, had been reminded of Patty's youth and vulnerability. With a superhuman effort he'd wrenched himself away and lay, hardly daring to move or speak, concentrating on the stars until he'd calmed himself down. He was no saint, God knows; he was a normal, red-blooded young man. But he mustn't forget that Patty was little more than a child.

He lit a cigarette and puffed away determinedly. Patty glanced at him sideways, but could tell nothing from his profile. After what seemed like a lifetime, he stubbed out his cigarette and turned on his side to face her. She felt reassurance flooding through her: his expression was tenderness itself.

'Better take you home, I suppose.'

She nodded. They kissed again – a gentle, passionless kiss – then he sat up and held out a hand to help her. Suddenly, the air vibrated to the shrill whine of falling bombs and they both flung themselves down again, his arm across her back pressing her into the raincoat. The earth seemed to lift and shake with the force of the explosions, then, just as suddenly, all was still except for distant ack-ack fire. They sat up. Peter kept his arm round her as he peered into the sky, his eyes following the searchlights as they probed the night for the marauder.

'That was a bit close,' he muttered. 'Must have been off course, I suppose.' He turned and looked at her. 'Frightened?'

'A bit,' she admitted. 'I don't think I'd mind being killed if we both went together. It's the thought of something happening to you and being left here alone that's so frightening.'

'Exactly. Now you know how I feel when you go on duty. The sooner I get you out of London, the better I'll be pleased.'

He helped her up and they climbed back into the car. Patty was silent. His words had come as a bit of a shock. She hadn't really contemplated leaving home immediately – not till the war was over and Peter was demobbed.

'Do you think that's possible?' she asked.

'What?'

'For me to leave London?'

'Why ever not?'

'Well – I am in the Civil Defence. I can't just give notice like an ordinary job.'

It was Peter's turn to pause now. He frowned. 'I suppose not. Still, I'm sure you could get a transfer – on compassionate grounds. Once we know where I'm going to be posted, you can apply to the nearest Depot.'

'What happens if they move you around? I can't keep chopping and changing too.'

He grimaced and Patty laughed at his expression, which reminded her of a little boy refused his own way. Suddenly, his mood cleared and he smiled at her.

'You never know, we might have a baby. They'd *have* to let you go then. Have you thought about that?'

Patty hadn't. Events had already moved fast enough. She'd hardly got used to the idea of being engaged yet. But it was a nice feeling. Peter took his left hand off the steering wheel and put it over hers. She cuddled close to him. Not perhaps the safest way to drive, but there was virtually no traffic around, what with the bombing and the blackout. The little car sped through the night from Hertfordshire into the northern suburbs of London, where Peter was forced to devote both hands and all his attention towards steering them safely to Battersea.

5

The New Trekkers

Gran Bowden was better – there was no doubt about that. Kath was relieved but also somewhat exasperated, because now the old lady was showing her true colours. Keeping the peace in the small household was a full-time job. The bed was the main bone of contention, of course. Stan still hadn't had time to get over to Stepney to see about it. Gran had threatened to go by herself, but that was out of the question. In the end, Kath had promised to take her.

'All I want ter know is when,' growled the old lady yet again.

Kath sighed. 'Mum, *please!* As soon as I can find time. It'll take most of the day, I reckon. Maybe tomorrow.'

'And maybe never! This rate the war'll be over. 'Sides, I don't like the thought of it standing out there all by itself. Might get bombed.'

We should be so lucky, thought Kath, and then caught Patty grinning at her. Was her mind quite so transparent?

Just then Patty came to a sudden decision. 'Why don't I take you, Gran?'

'Yer mean it?'

Kath started to protest, but was cut short. 'I've got the day off,' announced her daughter. 'Why not?'

She helped Mrs Bowden up and the old woman disappeared with clucks of satisfaction to get herself ready.

'It's very good of you, Patty,' said Kath gratefully.

'It'll get her out of your hair for a day.' Patty smiled at her mother. It was the least she could do. Poor old Mum did look a bit tired and worn. Besides, until now she'd been in her own little world of happiness; it was time she spread some of it to others not so lucky.

'You'd think she was going to the Antarctic,' muttered Kath later as they watched Mrs Bowden surveying herself in the hall mirror. In spite of the heat of the day the fur was draped around her shoulders. At last she was ready, and tossing the tail of the stone marten over her shoulder, she stalked off down the path with Patty.

As they settled themselves on the tram, they were prepared for quite a long journey, but not for the interminable one it turned out to be. The nearer they got to the East End, the worse the sights that confronted them. Whole streets had been destroyed. Patty had never seen such wholesale devastation and was deeply affected by the sight.

'It's far worse than anything in Battersea,' she exclaimed, her eyes filling with tears. 'I don't see how anyone can survive.'

Mrs Bowden patted her hand. 'Lots of us got through all right. Look at me!'

'But why didn't they tell us on the news? It's practically half London flattened.'

'Well, the BBC wouldn't give out news like that, would they!' observed the old woman. 'No point in depressing everyone. Besides, why give old Hitler the satisfaction of knowing?'

But Patty refused to be consoled. 'All this . . . in only three nights,' was all she could murmur.

Slowly and fitfully, the tram made its way towards Stepney. Many of the passengers were returning home after spending the night in shelters 'up West' and didn't even know if they'd find a home still standing when they got there. And yet the traditional Cockney humour seemed to re-emerge with the September sunshine. Mrs Bowden quickly engaged in a cheerful badinage with a stout woman sitting behind them.

'Get these toffs!' she'd cracked, earlier, admiring Gran's fur. 'Must be the Queen on a State visit, I s'pose!'

Mrs Bowden soon informed her that she'd been left with only the clothes she'd been issued with by the WVS. Most of the women wore scarves on their heads and shabby overcoats which they'd slept in. They were unwashed and baggy-eyed, but still they smiled, grateful to be alive.

At last, after nearly three hours, the tram reached Stepney High Street.

'Soon be time to turn round and go back again,' observed Gran.

But Mrs Bowden seemed to have all the time in the world as she gossipped with her cronies and downed endless cups of tea. Then there was the blasted bed to locate. Patty felt her patience wearing as thin as her mother's. But the conclusion of the story made up for everything. They found the bed in all its glory at the local Rest Centre, and now Mrs Bowden faced a fearful dilemma: should she submit her bed to the outrage of being used by others, or risk being accused of selfishness if she removed it for herself? Charity triumphed in the end, but not without an obvious inner battle. Patty thought how relieved Kath would be at the news.

By now it was late afternoon and she realized with dismay that they'd never make it back to Battersea before the nightly air raid. One of Mrs Bowden's old friends suggested they should go to the Tilbury Shelter with her for the night. Gran seemed in favour of the idea, so Patty went off to call Kath and give her the news. Kath was very concerned, but there was nothing she could do about it.

Madge Williams had been in to see Kath earlier after returning from her job in Dolphin Square. Apparently Madge's employer, Mrs Hodges, had decided to move down to her country cottage in Wiltshire, leaving her husband to fend for himself. Madge had agreed to keep the flat tidy and do the shopping and laundry while Mrs Hodges was away. But there was an added bonus. Dolphin

Square had a vast underground shelter, and Mrs Hodges had reserved her particular corner for the Williams family. Madge was over the moon with joy. Her only problem now was how to carry some blankets and mattresses over to Chelsea. Kath immediately suggested the WVS. They were sure to have some transport available. Accordingly they went along to Number Three, where the Misses Wilkes resided.

Miss Mary and Miss Jessie Wilkes, both elderly spinsters and WVS members, had lived in Balaclava Street for as long as anyone could remember. Miss Mary liked to think of herself as the street's authority on most things and considered herself a cut above her neighbours socially, but Miss Jessie was a sweet soul and was generally liked and respected.

Miss Mary swung into action with a great show of authority and commandeered a car from their local depot. It was noticeable, though, that it was Miss Jessie who volunteered to go with Madge and help to get the family settled. So the Williams became the first of Balaclava Street's 'trekkers', people who made nightly journeys from their homes to large underground shelters where they felt reasonably safe from the Luftwaffe.

It was half-past five when the sirens began wailing.

'Just like a lot of banshees,' observed old Mrs Bowden, finishing off yet another cup of tea.

'We'll have to hurry,' her friend informed her. 'We usually reckon to have half an hour from the time the sirens go until the bombers get here.' She'd been busy making up packets of sandwiches and a thermos of tea for their supper. 'You'd better go to the toilet before we leave. There are only two lavatories in the whole shelter, and there's always long queues.'

'Bound to want to go after all them cups of tea,' cackled Mrs Bowden, and took herself off.

A few minutes later, the little party set out as fast as

they could for the Tilbury Shelter. Homes were emptying fast – most people making for the shelter, some taking their chances in the tube stations. Nobody in this district bothered with Anderson shelters. There'd been too many direct hits.

At last they arrived at the vast edifice. It lay in the heart of one of the poorest areas of London, between the blitzed streets of Cable Street and Commercial Road, two hundred yards from where Whitechapel Road merges with Aldgate: a massive structure, ten storeys high, with huge, thick walls of brick and concrete. The basement, now commandeered as a shelter, had been used in peacetime as a warehouse and goods depot and was still full of crates of margarine and bales of newspapers.

Once inside, they found themselves in a large stone courtyard sloping down into the earth in two directions. There were only two doors to the shelter which were still locked when they arrived. This caused some element of panic, as more people crushed against the ones in front. A couple of men started to beat a frenzied tattoo on the doors, while others shouted 'Kick it down! Kick it down!' One woman began screaming: 'They'll be here before we have a chance to get inside!'

Suddenly the doors were opened by two shelter wardens, and the crowd surged through. Mrs Bowden gripped Patty's arm tightly as she fought to keep her balance. It took a few minutes for their eyes to get accustomed to the darkness.

Their first impression was of an immense dimly-lit cavern. The roof was made of metal girders, held up by rows of arches, old and solid, giving the atmosphere of a church. The hall was oblong in shape, covering many acres. Between the lines of archways were wooden platforms raised about four feet from the ground and stretching the whole length of the shelter. Between them were wide gangways, and round three sides of the interior in almost total darkness, ran a narrow railway track.

They made their way to one of the platforms, where

the men were helping the women up. Mrs Bowden saw the funny side and nudged Patty in the ribs. 'Good job I wore me best bloomers!' she chuckled.

But Patty was speechless. She couldn't get over the numbers of people still pouring in through the doors. The place was already nearly full to bursting.

By seven o'clock every inch of floorspace in the vast cavern had been taken up. There were deckchairs, blankets and stools in profusion. People were lying on the railway track, between margarine crates – even under piles of newspapers. As the evening wore on, the floor became awash with urine from children and older people who simply weren't able to control themselves. The lighting was dim, and the passageways became littered with rubbish as the crowd discarded refuse from their evening meals. In one area some horses were stabled, and they contributed to the growing smell of filth and faeces.

Patty felt quite sick. She prayed the night would pass quickly, so that they could return to the comparative comfort of Battersea.

'Cheer up, girl,' said Mrs Bowden. 'Anything's better than being outside with them bombs.'

Nonetheless, conditions in the shelter were chaotic, and it was clear that the authorities hadn't bargained for this number of people. There were no rules, no penalties, no hierarchy of command and a totally insufficient number of wardens to control the crowd. Only gradually, as one squabble after another was settled, was some form of rough justice evolved.

6

The Greatest Target in the World

In Battersea the night started quietly enough, the bombardment being concentrated yet again in the East End. Stan Johnson stared up at the clear moonlit sky. Along with all Londoners, he'd come to loathe nights like these. They may have been romantic, but they also gave the Luftwaffe the clearest possible sight of their large and vulnerable target. Hitler's Blitzkrieg was being blessed by the gods, or so it seemed to the thousands below. Already by the fourth night there had been nine hundred killed, a further four thousand seriously injured, while another five thousand or so had been made homeless. And hard as they tried, the Civil Defence were virtually incapable of dealing with the crisis.

The East End had been the prime target from the onset, but there had been a fair degree of indiscriminate bombing as well, and by now every borough in Inner London, together with several of the outer boroughs, had been severely hit. Because of its proximity to Clapham Junction, Battersea got more than its fair share. Indeed, such was the accuracy of the German bombing that word had gone out among the residents of the area that a Fifth Columnist was directing bombers onto the station by means of a searchlight based on a rooftop nearby. However, frantic activity by both the police and the army failed to yield the identity of this Judas.

Neither the anti-aircraft gun emplacements nor the RAF fighter squadrons had yet mastered the intricate art of shooting down the opposition at night. And although the newspapers made claims such as 'Sixty-nine Huns bite the dust. We suffer two losses', Stan had an uncomfortable feeling that the reality was often nearer the reverse. He hadn't seen a single Jerry shot down yet. It was a testing time for the morale of the common people, and during those firsts nights it would be fair to say that panic and hysteria were widespread.

As Stan listened to the *crump-crump* of the ack-ack, both from Clapham Common and Battersea Park, he wondered how those army gunners could stand the noise night after night – it was bad enough from a range of half a mile or more. Periodically there would be a large explosion as a bomb landed – sometimes it would be a delayed action mine, one of the most devastating weapons in the Luftwaffe's arsenal. Stan could now distinguish between the various types of bombs, aircraft and guns. Thoughtfully, he made his way back to the Warden's Post.

As he turned into the building, standing tall and conspicuous in the moonlight, there was a terrific explosion which knocked him off his feet. The blast shattered windows for a radius of half a mile and tinkling glass fell all around him. Dazed but conscious, he picked himself up and saw a pall of smoke rising above Balaclava Street. His stomach clenched. Had there been a direct hit on one of the houses? Regaining his senses, he dashed inside the Post and quickly called the Fire Brigade and Ambulance Depot at Battersea Rise. Then he ran out and made his way back down the road, forcing himself to remain calm, although sick with fear at what he might find.

Gradually the dust was clearing, to reveal a house with a roof ablaze. It was at the far end of the road, that much he could make out – and it was beyond his own house. An involuntary surge of relief flooded his body, giving him renewed vigour.

As he reached the scene he could see straight away that the Perkins' house, Number One, had received a direct hit. Racing up to the front door, he saw that there were no chalk marks. But perhaps old Fred Perkins had forgotten his advice. As the fire was still largely in the roof, Stan decided to force the front door and have a look at the Anderson in the back garden, just in case.

Just then Bert Williams arrived on his bicycle and offered to help him force an entry. After three attempts they broke one of the small glass panes which surprisingly had failed to splinter in the blast, and Stan was able to put his hand through and unlatch the door. Inside the fire was beginning to rage, but Stan rushed through to the kitchen and out into the garden. The Anderson was unoccupied. Looking over the garden wall, he could see the two Wilkes sisters wandering about in a state of shock. But they seemed unhurt and acknowledged his enquiries with a cheerful wave.

'The Fire Brigade's coming,' he told them hurriedly. 'So's the ambulance. I think you should get out to the front of your house, just in case the fire takes hold.'

'It's all right, Mr Johnson,' said Miss Mary. 'We're just a bit shaken, that's all. What about Mr and Mrs Perkins?'

'As far as I can tell they're away, thank goodness,' he replied. 'Now do go out front. I'll see you later.'

Stan could hear the bells of the Fire Brigade as he edged his way to the front of the house again, past falling rafters and burning timbers. Seeking out the Fire Chief, he quickly told him: 'I don't think there's anyone in the house, but I could be wrong. Maybe in their bedroom upstairs. I've looked everywhere else.'

'OK, mate,' replied the Chief. 'I'll have the turntable up there in a jiffy. Where's your nearest hydrant?'

Stan pointed it out and then dashed to get his own stand pump. Already some of the other residents had hurried out on to the street to see what was happening. Stan urged them to return to their shelters, but to his surprise, the normally self-centred Horace Aynsworth insisted on helping. Stan reflected that it took a war to bring out the good in people.

In spite of all the firemen's efforts, it was fully three-quarters of an hour before the blaze was under control, by which time the entire ground floor lay under three inches of water and all the carpets were ruined, together with many pieces of furniture. The sickly smell of burnt rafters and charred material pervaded the house.

Stan saw the Fire Brigade off and turned to find Horace Aynsworth standing looking at the ruins with an expression of distaste.

'What a mess!' he said at last.

'Yes, I'm afraid it's going to be a dreadful shock to the Perkins when they come back and find this. At least no one was hurt, that's one blessing.'

'Yes. Mind you, with old Perkins in the building trade, he's bound to get himself on the priority list for repairs.'

There was a snide tone to the voice which caused Stan to reflect how quickly Horace had reverted to type. But at least he'd shown willing in the emergency.

'Thanks for your help, Mr Aynsworth,' he said.

'Glad to do something,' was the reply. 'I heard the explosion and I knew it had to be in this street, so I came out to have a look.'

And to see if there was any prospective business no doubt, Stan thought to himself. 'It's an ill wind', as the saying goes, and Horace must be prospering because of all the extra work. Not that it seemed to be improving his disposition. Stan found himself wondering, as many times before, how his wife Dora stood it. No wonder those two girls of his were so anxious to get away from home. There couldn't be much fun around Number Ten, Balaclava Street.

'Life's strange, isn't it?' said Horace thoughtfully. 'I've arranged so many funerals in my time, and yet I suddenly realized tonight that I've made no arrangements about my own. Have to see to that first thing tomorrow.'

He walked off down the street, lugubriously shaking his head.

Madge Williams felt more refreshed than she had for

ages. She'd managed a reasonable quota of sleep despite the noise. Probably sheer exhaustion had something to do with it, and certainly the large shelter gave her a feeling of security that she didn't get in the Anderson. The children had slept soundly too after the novelty of exploring and making new acquaintances had worn off. Now they were noisy and hungry as they made their way into the open air and home for breakfast.

Stan met her as she was shepherding them off the tram at the stop nearest Balaclava Street and offered to carry the baby. He was on his way home, too.

'My, you look tired, Mr Johnson!' she said, but refrained from mentioning his dirty face and dust-streaked uniform.

'Bit of a rough night, I'm afraid, Madge,' Stan told her. In fact, it had been the worst so far. Several houses on his patch had received direct hits or were badly damaged, and there'd been a number of casualties, some of them fatal. Stan had been deeply affected. Like Patty, it was his first experience of violent death, and although none of the dead were close friends, he'd known some of them by sight for a number of years. But it was more than that. He felt a personal involvement. These people had been in *his* charge. At the time, the horror of it all hadn't really sunk in – he'd been much too busy in organizing the rescue work, and he and his co-Warden, Windy, had been rushed off their feet trying to cope. Now he was suffering a kind of delayed reaction.

Madge was very shocked to hear about the disaster to the Perkins' house. It brought the Blitz that much closer to home. 'I'm glad I took the kids to Dolphin Square. It must have been frightening to be so near the explosion.'

'Yes. It shook everyone up a bit. How was it in the shelter?'

'Not too bad – at least we all got some sleep. It's certainly a lot better than that old Anderson.'

They'd arrived at Madge's gate and she retrieved the baby while the others pounded on the front door, calling to see if their father was back. Madge laughed at the racket. Somehow her good humour had returned with her first taste of sleep.

'I'll hardly have time to get them all washed and fed before I've got to go back to the flat to work,' she smiled. 'What a life! Still, mustn't grumble. Thanks, Mr Johnson.'

As Patty and Mrs Bowden turned into Balaclava Street they could see that there'd been an incident the previous night. The Perkins had just arrived back from spending the night in a tube station and they stood gazing in horror at what remained of their house. Rita was crying silently and Fred put his arm around her in a comforting squeeze. The end of the terrace had totally collapsed, leaving Rita's bedroom and part of the sitting room exposed to the world.

'Fred . . . Oh, Fred!' The sound was little more than a whisper.

'Hold on, love! It's only bricks and mortar,' replied her husband. 'We're both alive, and that's what counts.'

Rita felt a tug at her elbow. It was Mrs Bowden. 'I'll just go and get out of these best togs, then I'll come back and give you a hand clearing up some of this mess.'

'Oh, Mrs Bowden, that's kind, but I don't really know where to start.'

'We'll get things straight. Kath'll give a hand, too, I'm sure. Many hands make light work, remember.' And with that the old woman trotted off towards Number Seven, followed by Patty.

Before long Kath and Mrs Bowden were on the scene, armed with mops and pails, and as soon as they saw this, the Misses Wilkes volunteered to help as well. Rita was in the middle of the depressing job of trying to sort out her possessions.

'Looks as if half the Thames was poured in here,' she said gloomily.

'Let's hope this good weather keeps up,' remarked Kath. 'It'll help dry things out.'

'It was wonderful of your husband to get the fire under control so quickly. If I don't see him tonight, do thank him for me.'

'Oh, he was just doing his job,' said Kath. 'Anyway, it was the Fire Brigade mostly. Stan says everyone lent a hand – even Mr Aynsworth.'

'*What?*'

'I know,' chuckled Kath. 'He was quite worried about you. Even tried to get up the stairs to see if you were there.'

'Good God!' Rita felt a lump in her throat. The kindness of these people – these neighbours to whom she'd always felt superior, being their landlady. It was a humbling experience.

A little later, Miss Mary handed a tray over the back fence – tea and biscuits daintily served. Kath had to giggle to herself as she thought how incongruous they must all look in their overalls, squatting on boxes or kitchen chairs in the garden and sipping tea from exquisite china cups.

All of a sudden there was a shout from the road. It was Bert Williams, red-faced with excitement and pedalling hard. 'Winnie's coming!' he yelled. 'He's on his way now. You'll have to hurry if you want to see him!'

'*Winnie?*' exclaimed Miss Mary. 'You mean the Prime Minister?'

'Who do you think?' called Bert over his shoulder.

With one accord the ladies downed tools and hurried home to smarten themselves up. This was an occasion not to be missed! Kath could hear Miss Mary scolding Miss Jessie:

'You'll have to change out of those dreadful trousers! Why you wear such things – they're so unfeminine . . .'

'Mary, lots of women wear trousers now. They're practical.'

'Papa would turn in his grave if he could see you! I shall wear my WVS uniform and so should you.'

Trust Miss Mary to know best! Kath felt a pang of sympathy for easy-going Miss Jessie, but she also guessed, and rightly, that Jessie's outward subservience to her sister was due more to a cheerful nature and an abhorrence of rows, rather than to any weakness of spirit.

In no time at all, Kath found herself with her mother clutching her sleeve, in a cheering throng lining the road as the Prime Minister's car threaded its way through Battersea. The police attempted to form a cordon, but soon the enthusiastic crowd were pressing around the car and forcing it to a halt. It was all good-humoured and boisterous, though, and Churchill waved the anxious policemen away. Everyone was trying to shake his hand, and the old man was evidently enjoying every minute of his triumphant progress. He was standing up in the back of his open car, alternately waving his stick or giving his famous 'V' sign, the inevitable cigar clenched between his teeth.

Kath found the event extraordinarily moving and there were tears in her eyes as she cheered and waved along with the rest. No matter what disasters befell, they had a childlike trust that this one human being could bring them through. As they reached one particularly badly devastated street, Churchill descended from the car and picked his way amongst the rubble. Tears ran down his cheeks unashamedly and he wiped them away with his hand.

'Good old Winnie!' croaked Gran. She too had been moved by the scene. 'Nice to know he's human.'

'Yes,' agreed Kath. 'Goodness knows where we'd be without him.'

The great man was moving amongst the people now, stopping here and there to chat or crack jokes with them. Recognizing Sincerity Vale, he singled her out for special attention, and the other residents of Balaclava Street felt a surge of pride in their own particular celebrity. Sincerity asked him back to her house for a drink. He regretted that he didn't have the time, but winked at her and told her to have one for him.

And then it was over and Churchill went on to tour other badly blitzed areas. As the Balaclava Street residents walked back together in the summer sunshine, their conversation was animated and they were full of renewed vigour and determination. Sadly, the mood changed later on, when Rita resumed sorting out her possessions. Her jewellery case was found unscathed, but someone had forced the lock and stolen the contents. There'd been stories of widespread looting of bombed houses in the area, but it sickened everyone in Balaclava Street to think it had happened in their own neighbourhood. Everyone felt for Rita in her real distress.

That evening as she got ready to go to a shelter, Rita suggested to her husband that they might take the Johnsons and Mrs Bowden with them, seeing they'd shown such kindness. Fred was only too glad to agree. A bit of company might take Rita's mind off her troubles.

Rita found Kath already pre-conditioned to trying out a night in the deep shelter of a tube station. She'd had more than enough of the Anderson, and Stan had readily acceded.

'We thought of going to South Ken,' Rita told her. 'I'm told it's deeper than Clapham or Balham.'

'Oh yes – that's right. Mum, what do you say? Would you like to try the underground tonight?'

The old woman shook her head. 'I'll take my chances here,' she announced. 'I sleep better on the sofa than I do in any smelly shelter. You and Tim go along with Mr and Mrs Perkins. I'll be all right.'

Kath knew her mother well enough not to continue with a fruitless argument, so Tim was despatched to get two mattresses from the Anderson to load into Fred's van, while Kath got together some food and drink for their supper. Patty wasn't yet back from the Depot, but she was going out with Peter anyway.

Kath kissed Gran Bowden 'goodbye' with a last admonishment to take care, then followed the others out into the road. She squeezed into the front of the van with the Perkins, and Tim perched himself on the mattresses in the back.

But when they arrived at South Kensington station, it soon became apparent that they'd be lucky to find any room at all. The porter in the lift told them that children had been queueing since six o'clock that morning to book places for their families.

'Try it,' he said. 'But I'll bet you a pound to a penny you don't get a space.'

As they reached the platform, they heard a row in progress between the porters and the trekkers, the porters trying to keep a narrow strip of platforms free from bodies. The trains were still running until ten o'clock in the evenings and passengers had to be able to alight.

Tim had been wriggling his way through the crowds to the end of the platform and returned to report that there wasn't a space anywhere. There was only one thing for it: they squatted down right by the entrance, which was cold, draughty and therefore unoccupied. Even then, there was only room for two of their mattresses, so they'd have to share. Kath found herself wondering if she'd made the right decision after all – even the discomfort of the Anderson might be preferable to this.

By seven o'clock, there were at least four hundred people on each platform, and movement was virtually impossible. A painted white line a yard from the edge of the platform denoted the space reserved for alighting passengers. At the opposite end of each platform was a lavatory, one for men and one for women, consisting of a bucket situated behind a hessian screen, they were clearly inadequate for the volume of people who wanted to use them. Even more people were lying in the passageways leading to the platforms and this added to the strain on the limited resources. The late arrivals were nearly all men coming straight from work to join their families. Some were forced to sleep at the top of the emergency stairs right underneath a glass roof, which offered no protection whatsoever.

Kath noticed that there was a muted buzz of conversation, suggesting that many of the people in the station either knew one another or had met the previous night. Many had trekked from as far as the East End. But there was very little laughter, and few people read. Most simply stared into space.

At about eight o'clock some enterprising youths began selling spaces they'd booked, ostensibly for their families. Fred Perkins took up one offer and had to pay two shillings and sixpence for the privilege. He insisted that the women slept there, whilst he and Tim could at least have two mattresses spread in their original place. It wasn't until after the trains stopped running that they even contemplated sleep, but at last sheer exhaustion took over and Kath found her eyelids closing.

About three hours later, after a fitful sleep, she woke again to find herself stiff and sore all over. It was an effort to turn over, but when she did she was surprised to see Rita wide awake, sitting up and repairing her make-up.

'Hallo, love – get a bit of sleep, did you? Oh Lor – I do look a fright. Still, no worse than all the others, I suppose.' Rita looked around to reassure herself of this fact.

Kath struggled up. 'What's the time?'

'Gone four o'clock. You aching too?'

Kath nodded. She could hear the guns still firing outside. Obviously the 'All Clear' hadn't sounded, yet already people were beginning to move out.

Kath looked over at the entrance, where she could see the recumbent figures of Tim and Fred. It seemed they'd managed to sleep in spite of the discomfort. Maybe the feeling of security here helped people to relax. Still, it was a fairly dismal prospect if they had to spend the rest of the war in these surroundings.

Rita echoed her thoughts. 'We'll have to find somewhere else,' she declared. 'I couldn't take this every night. Feel like I'll never get clean again!'

'I know what you mean.' Kath suddenly remembered that Rita had no bathroom at the moment. 'You're welcome to a wash in our house,' she added.

'Ta, dear. It's sweet of you, but Miss Vale's already offered us the use of her bathroom till Fred can get our water going again.' There was a hint of superiority in her voice which Rita couldn't conceal, try as she might.

It was five o'clock before the All Clear rang out and Kath, Tim and the Perkins joined the queue of people leaving by the emergency exit. There was a box by the exit for contributions for the porters, who'd have the job of clearing up after everyone left, and Kath rummaged through her handbag for some loose coppers.

'Don't envy them their job,' she remarked, as she pushed her meagre offering through the slit in the box. 'Wish I'd got more on me.'

'It's all right. Fred'll put something in for all of us,' Rita told her. 'Heaven knows how they'll ever get it clean again – what with the kids being allowed to pee themselves where they sat.'

'Poor little mites! They couldn't do much else, could they?' replied Kath mildly.

Finally they emerged into the open and Fred strode off towards the street where he'd parked the van, calling back over his shoulder, 'You lot stay there. No point in lugging the mattresses around till I know if the van's still okay.'

But it was, and a few minutes later they were making their way back to Battersea, carefully skirting the numerous potholes in the road. As they crossed the bridge, they could see along the river to the East, where a great pall of smoke hung heavily in the early morning light.

'Cor! They must have copped it bad again last night,' exclaimed Tim, with the insensitivity of youth.

Kath felt a sudden tightness in her throat. She realized that she had no idea what she would find on her return. Would Number Seven still be standing? How about Gran, left alone all night? Most of all Stan – dear Stan. Was he quite safe and sound?

Stan's night was one he would always remember, but for none of the reasons he'd expected. In terms of incidents, it had been fairly uneventful, and for once it seemed the Luftwaffe had decided to give Clapham Junction a miss. Balaclava Street had seemed quiet as he made his rounds. Most of the residents had left for shelters, although Horace Aynsworth remained at home in solitary seclusion. The Windsors had gone to spend a couple of days with friends in the country, and the Wilkes sisters were on duty at the Rest Centre with the WVS. Stan noticed that Harry Hempstead had remembered to chalk up a '2' on his front door – perhaps the hit on the Perkins home had taught him a lesson. Then he called in to see Mrs Bowden and made her promise to retreat under the stairs if the bombing got worse in their area. He had very little conviction that she'd do it, though. She was a stubborn, tiresome old lady, but you had to admire her guts.

It was after midnight when he heard the familiar, uneven throbbing of a solitary German bomber overhead, separated from the rest of its flight. Stan looked up and saw it plainly as it ducked and dived in a vain effort to escape the searchlights. Stan felt a surge of pride: our boys are really getting the hang of it now. Puffs of smoke were exploding in the sky around the plane as the gunners bombarded their target. And then it happened! A blinding sheet of flame and a violent explosion in the sky, as the bomber was torn apart by a direct hit. Stan let out an involuntary cheer, but his exultation was short-lived: suddenly he had to duck his head as bits of débris began to rain down all around him. There were whistling noises and thumps as larger pieces of fuselage fell to earth – some sounded uncomfortably near. He straightened up and immediately made for Balaclava Street to check out his 'patch'. He knew he shouldn't put his own street first, but it was the one human weakness he'd been unable to conquer.

At first sight it seemed that all was well, although the air was thick with dust. Then he saw what had caused it. A large piece of aircraft fuselage had carved its way into the side of Number Two. It hadn't demolished the house and the structure looked in no imminent danger of collapse, but the great wedge of fuselage with its black cross was sticking out of the sitting room window like some gigantic price tag. Stan guessed that Harry and his mother were probably unharmed, safe in the Anderson at the back, but he had to check it out. All the windows in the front were broken, so he had no difficulty in climbing in.

'Anybody here?' he shouted. 'Anybody in the house?'

Silence. Only the creaking of the fuselage as it settled, and the scuttering of falling plaster. As he thought: they were out in the shelter. He started to move towards the back door when he heard a sound. He stood still – yes, there it was again. A groan – followed by a spluttering cough. Somebody was in the sitting room underneath all that mess. He hurried back to the door and tried to open it. The electricity was off, of course, so he had to work by torchlight, slowly scraping away the rubble.

'That you, Harry?' he called. 'Just stay still. If you struggle you may bring more of the ceiling down.' There was no reply, only more coughing. He tried again. 'Mrs Hempstead? It's Stan Johnson. I'll be with you in a minute or so. Don't worry.'

'Dad! Where are you?' called a voice. 'Can I help?'

Stan shone the torch up and saw his daughter framed in the broken window. She started to climb in.

'What are you doing here?' he asked.

'I just got home and heard you calling. Is the door stuck?'

This brought Stan back to the job in hand. 'Here – hold this!' He shoved the torch at Patty.

Gradually, he eased the door open until he could

squeeze through and then cleared the rubble from the inside. Patty played the torch around and the beam lit up a naked figure, propped on one elbow. Stan could see he was a young lad, about twenty or so, and his thin frame was trembling from shock or fear.

'It's okay, lad,' Stan reassured him. 'You'll be all right.'

'Harry – he's here – knocked out, I think . . ' muttered the boy, scraping the plaster from another figure lying beside him. The figure groaned.

Stan moved closer. The torchlight showed that Harry was stark naked also. The two had been lying on a double mattress on the floor. The full implication of the scene struck Stan like a blow to the solar plexus. Good God! Harry was one of *them*. Who'd have believed it? To Stan, brought up on working-class morality, homosexuals were simply not acceptable – they were beneath contempt.

His immediate reaction was to protect Patty. He stood, blocking her view. 'You'd best get out of here, love.'

'Don't be silly, Dad,' she replied and bending down, she started to clear the mess of rubble from Harry.

Smothering his feelings of revulsion, Stan helped her. A window frame had been smashed by the fuselage and a piece had fallen on Harry, momentarily stunning him, but he was fast coming round. It appeared that neither he nor his friend had sustained any other injury.

Hesitantly the young man handed shirt and trousers to Harry, who, though dazed, was now sitting up and looking at Stan in a shamefaced way. He opened his mouth as if to speak, but could find no words.

'Where's your mother, Harry?' Stan asked sharply.

'Oh . . . I made the old lady a bed in the cellar,' he wheezed. 'She'll be all right down there.'

'I'd better check. Come on, Patty.'

'No, no – I'll go—' said Harry, but Stan had disappeared before he could struggle to his feet. He was about to follow when he suddenly became aware of his nakedness. For a moment he stood there helpless, a slightly ridiculous figure in the wreckage of his sitting room. Then the boy bent down and started to help him into his trousers.

As Stan went cautiously down the old stone steps to the cellar, he was greeted by the sound of heavy snoring. No doubt about it – old Mrs Hempstead was all right. Clearly she'd slept through the entire episode. He located the sound of the snores and played the torch over the recumbent figure. No need to disturb her.

He shone the torch around the rest of the cellar and gave an involuntary gasp. No wonder Harry had been so reluctant to let him in to the cellar. The walls were stacked with cartons and crates, mostly with NAAFI markings. Tinned foods, cigarettes, silk stockings – you name it, Harry had it!

'Blimey!' gasped Patty, peering over his shoulder. 'He's got a proper Black Market all of his own!'

But Stan was already wondering where his duty lay. Should he inform the authorities? There were heavy penalties for this sort of profiteering. On the other hand, he'd never have known anything about it if he hadn't forced an entry – so wasn't it privileged information? Before he could come to any conclusion, he heard footsteps and turned to see Harry coming down the stairs. He was dressed now in shirt and trousers, but still looked very shaken.

'Your mother's fine, Harry. Fast asleep,' Stan reassured him.

'Yeah, well – she's pretty near stone deaf, you see. Doubt if she'd have heard anything even if she'd been awake.'

'You'd be much safer down here too, you know.'

'Yeah – well, I'll think about it, Stan, promise.' He shifted uncomfortably from foot to foot. 'About Rex—'

'Rex?' Harry jerked his head upwards and Stan caught on. 'Oh *Rex*.'

'The kid hadn't anywhere to stay. He's a sailor, see, on a forty-eight-hour pass. Not knowing his way around town—'

Stan's tone was curt. 'It's none of my business, Harry.'

'And you won't say anything about . . . all this?' He indicated the goods stacked around the cellar.

'It's against the law.'

'I know *that*. But times is hard, Stan. Racing business has all gone to bloody pot. Got to make a crust or two . . .'

Stan bit his lip uncertainly. 'Look – I won't say anything now, but I can't promise to keep quiet if you go on at this rate. Try and off-load this lot, and don't get any more.'

'Okay, okay. Ta, Stan.' Harry's mouth creased into its habitual yellow grin. Impulsively, he grabbed two packets of tea. 'Here, give these to the wife, mate.'

'I didn't mean it that way, Harry.'

'Come on, Dad!' Patty was already halfway up the stairs.

Harry began ushering Stan up the stairs too, as if anxious to get him out of the cellar as quickly as possible.

Rex had tactfully removed himself from sight when they emerged upstairs, and nobody referred to him.

'You'd better have a check-up at the hospital in the morning,' said Stan. 'You may have a bit of concussion after that blow.'

Harry forced a weak smile and gingerly patted his head. 'Ah – my bonce has taken harder knocks than that in its time.'

'Goodnight then. Oh, Harry' – Stan paused in the front doorway – 'make sure you chalk up the *correct* number of occupants on your door next time. It could mean life or death.'

Stan left without a backward glance as Harry watched, a hunched and lonely figure. For once, it seemed his cheery bonhomie had completely deserted him.

As Stan accompanied Patty home, his mind was full of this unexpected revelation into Harry's private life. Back flowed the disgust that had overwhelmed him when he had first discovered the couple.

'Sorry you were let in for that . . . nasty business,' he muttered, embarrassed.

'Good Lord, I've seen people with worse injuries than that.' Patty seemed quite unconcerned.

'No, I – I meant . . .' It was no use. Stan dried up. He simply couldn't find the words.

Patty laughed lightly. 'Oh *that!* I never imagined old Harry was a pansy, did you, Dad? Doesn't seem the type somehow.'

Patty watched her father as he went off again on his round. Despite her outwardly blasé pose, she'd actually been quite startled by tonight's incident. Startled more than shocked, for the morality aspect hadn't really entered into it. Of course she'd heard about homosexuality at school – even giggled over some rude graffiti with the other kids. But she'd never come into contact with it before, not in the flesh. The aptness of this thought made her collapse into a fit of giggles as she shut the front door.

'Bloody guns,' observed Gran, sucking loudly on the biscuit she was dunking in her tea. 'They're worse than the Jerries.'

'The foreman at work says we get 'em specially bad because they're trying to protect Battersea Power Station,' Enid Belling told them. 'If that goes up, we've really had it.'

Kath nodded wearily in silent agreement. She was almost too tired to speak. Five nights now with little or no sleep. She wondered how long they could all carry on under this pressure. Supposing Hitler kept up the bombardment? If the newspapers were to be believed, his losses were considerable – but then so were his reserves. Who would weaken first? Oddly enough, Stan seemed to be standing up to the strain rather better than she was, yet she'd always thought that women were the tougher sex physically. Stan was out every night on his Warden's duties and still managed to go to work each day normally. He actually seemed to find the ARP work exhilarating. Certainly, he got a lift from it that more than compensated for any feeling of exhaustion or strain. Patty was the same, though she had youth on her side, of course.

Kath felt the silence. Both Enid and Gran were looking at her, and she realized guiltily that they were waiting for her answer.

'I'm sorry,' she apologized, 'I was half asleep. What did you say?'

'She asked if you'd heard Lord Haw-Haw,' prompted Gran.

'It's uncanny how he knows just where the bombs have fallen,' said Enid. 'Do you think it's true there's a Fifth Column at Clapham?'

'Is that what they're saying?'

'It was all the talk at The Windmill yesterday.'

'At The Windmill? But—'

'Oh, it's 'Business as Usual,' laughed Enid. 'They've got tarpaulins rigged up, and they're using empty barrels for tables and chairs. George was round there giving them a hand most of yesterday. He would be! His last day an' all.'

George had gone back to his ship this morning, and Enid had popped in for a chat to cheer herself up. At least she'd brought a bag of tea with her, for which Kath was grateful. She hadn't yet found Stan's 'surprise' – the two packets of tea from Harry the Horse – in the larder.

'Pub talk!' growled Mrs Bowden, sucking noisily.

'It isn't just gossip, Mum. Stan was telling me yesterday. Here, Enid, let me top up your cup.'

'Ta, love. What did Stan say then?'

'Well, seems there's been reports of someone signalling with a lamp from a rooftop near the cinema. The Wardens have been asked to keep a lookout.'

'Stuff and nonsense!' snorted the old lady. 'Them Jerries is much too busy dropping their bombs to look out for signals. 'Sides, Clapham Junction's easy enough to spot.'

'I suppose so, but it gives you a nasty feeling all the same,' murmured Enid.

'If there is someone, it would serve them right if the

bombs dropped right on them,' said Kath. 'Did you know Haw-Haw originally came from the Clapham area?'

'No! Really?'

'Bloody traitor! Ought to chop his head off!' sniffed Gran.

'Expect they will after the war – if they catch him,' remarked Enid. 'Any news from your Rog? We've got to have that party for him some time, you know.'

'Not much chance with these raids,' Kath told her. 'All their leave's been cancelled. Mind you, we'll make it a double celebration when the time comes. Patty's got herself engaged now.'

'Not much to celebrate there,' came the sour old voice from the easy chair.

'Now, Mother, don't be like that!'

'Well, you don't like the idea yourself! Heard you telling Stan so. She's much too young to know her own mind.'

Kath's eyes met Enid's in mutual understanding. Enid winked.

'Love will have its way, Mrs Bowden,' she said archly, and was rewarded by a scornful grunt. 'Who's the lucky fellow? That young naval officer?'

'Yes,' replied Kath. 'He's ever so nice. It's not that we disapprove of him – but Patty's only seventeen. Still, what can you say when there's a war on?'

'Exactly. When are they planning to get married?'

'Oh, not till the spring – if then. Peter's on this course at the Admiralty. They don't know where he'll be sent after that.'

'With a bit of luck, it'll all blow over by then,' muttered Mrs Bowden.

'Now, Gran, don't start again,' Kath pleaded. 'It'll only upset Patty if you keep on at her and we don't want squabbles every night.'

'Why not? Livens things up a bit!'

'Isn't she awful?' Kath protested to her neighbour. 'We can't get her down in the shelter, either.'

'Can't say I blame her! I hate the damn things myself,' said Enid. 'I go on a night shift for the next week, so I won't have to bother, but when I'm here on my own, I don't know what I'll do.'

'I suppose we could go over to the big shelter in Dolphin Square. They've opened it to the public now. But you have to be there early to get a place. 'I must say, after what happened to the Perkins' house and to poor old Harry last night, I'd feel safer there.' Enid nodded agreement. 'What do you think, Mum? Would you like that?'

'I'll think about it.' Mrs Bowden wasn't going to be disposed of *that* easily.

Kath gave a sigh of exasperation. Her patience with the old woman was fast running out. Another problem was Tim: he would answer back when Gran nagged him, and that only made her worse. She thought he was cheeky and needed a good clip over the ear. Kath often agreed privately, but she resented her mother ticking off her children when she was around. Her thoughts turned again to the idea of getting a job. Even a part-time job would get her out of the house and away from Gran for a little while each day.

'I've been meaning to ask you, Enid, do they want any extra hands at your factory?' she asked.

'Screaming for 'em all the time,' was the reply. 'You thinking of applying?'

'It did cross my mind. I don't feel I'm doing much to help the war effort.'

'Well, it's not a bad racket. You can earn quite a bit on a good shift.'

'That's one of the worries. Do you have to do a night shift? I don't see how I could manage nights with Tim here.'

Another growl issued from the easy chair. 'You just said he could go to the big shelter with me, so what's the problem?'

Kath turned to her mother. Perhaps that was one way to get her mother to the shelter. She decided to try it.

'Oh, Mum – if you'd be responsible for Tim, then I wouldn't have to worry. That's marvellous!'

'Only got to ask!' the old woman grunted and subsided again.

Enid was grinning at her. 'You can go along to the personnel office any time, Kath. Say I sent you, if you like.' She made a mental note to talk to the foreman to ensure Kath was put on a different shift. She wasn't going to have anyone spoiling her fun or reporting her antics to George. Not that Kath was the sneaky sort, but it wasn't worth taking the risk. Enid smiled sweetly. 'It'll be great having you at the works. Someone to have a giggle with.'

The week was flying past for Patty, and her days at the Depot were happy. She'd now been accepted for the driving course and had been allocated to Stephen Broome as a pupil, along with three other women. They had one hour a day learning maintenance and repair, all very technical and bewildering, and one hour's practical instruction, which she loved. There was an added bonus in the fact that she was excused the chore of cleaning out the ambulances after the previous night's work. This was sickening work even for a hardened stomach, and Patty couldn't lay claim to that at the best of times. The sight, and most of all the smell, of blood and vomit were things she'd never get used to.

Stephen had warned them that the test for ambulance drivers was tough, and that there were no short cuts. Patty wasn't of a mechanical bent, nor did she have the physical strength or stature to cope easily with some of the practical exercises, such as jacking up the heavy ambulances and changing tyres. Many of the vehicles were old and needed hand-cranking – a job even the men found hard enough. As for the technical pamphlets they were given to study, Patty found many of them completely incomprehensible and compromised by learning a lot of the jargon parrot-fashion. Fortunately she had a retentive memory and so was usually the first to answer Stephen's questions. This, however, didn't endear her to her fellow pupils, all older women who struggled laboriously through the engineering handbooks. Patty had a sneaking suspicion that Stephen guessed what she was at. Occasionally he'd catch her out with a rephrased question and she'd spot an amused twinkle in his eye. But he made no comment, even when they were out alone driving. Stephen was a stern task-master but a good teacher, and Patty had a natural aptitude for driving. She didn't have the nervousness and indecision of the older women, nor did she get flustered when she made the occasional mistake. By the end of the first week, she was driving around quite confidently.

'You've done very well, Patty,' Stephen told her as she drew up outside the depot. She flushed with pleasure. 'Next week, we'll get on to the difficult bits.' He laughed at the expression on her face. 'It's not all driving around like a duchess and tooting at your friends, you know!'

'Oh, I didn't think it was,' she answered him quickly. 'Will we still be able to have lessons on night shifts?'

'Depends how much time the Luftwaffe allow us. But you'll have to get used to driving in the blackout.'

'Yes, of course.'

'You probably won't find it as hard as I did, seeing you aren't accustomed to anything else.'

'That's what Peter says.'

'Peter?'

'My fiancé' she told him, unable to keep the pride out of her voice.

'I didn't know you were engaged.'

'Only just,' she explained. 'We haven't even had a chance to get a ring yet.'

'Congratulations.' Stephen's voice was strangely abrupt, but Patty was too happy to notice.

In fact, Stephen was rather surprised, not only at

Patty's revelation but at his own reaction to it. So this child beside him wasn't such a child after all! He had grown to like her frank, ingenuous manner, her sense of humour, and now felt none of his usual shyness in her company. In spite of himself, he found it somehow disturbing to think of her as being engaged to another man. As he shot a sideways glance at her, he felt a momentary stirring of attraction, but quickly subdued it. No earthly point in that! Brusquely, he told her to get out of the car and fetch his next pupil.

The next day, Stephen's manner was deliberately withdrawn, although to Patty it simply seemed stern and disapproving. She thought she must have done something wrong and tried all the harder at the tests he set. She reversed carefully, threading through the line of tins he'd set up in the quiet private road. Three times she did it without touching one of the tins and waited anxiously for the customary words of praise. But Stephen just nodded abstractedly.

'Okay. We'll try some hill starts,' he told her.

Patty slipped the car into gear and drove off, following his instructions. There was an unnatural silence between them: Stephen preoccupied with his own thoughts, Patty hurt and puzzled by the change from his normal friendly demeanour.

'Are you musical?' Stephen demanded suddenly, out of the blue.

Patty was taken aback. 'I don't know really. I always wanted to learn the piano, but we don't have one in the house and Dad said it was pointless having lessons if I couldn't practise.'

'I suppose so.'

'I like music, though,' she said, anxious to please. 'I mean, I like listening to it on the wireless.'

'Concerts?'

'Well – no.'

'Oh, popular stuff.'

Patty immediately started apologizing. 'I suppose it's

because I've never been to concerts or operas. I'm sure I *would* like them.'

'Probably.'

But Stephen wasn't forthcoming. She tried once more. 'Why did you ask?'

'Mmm?' He was abstracted again, then his face creased into a smile, the first that day. 'Oh yes. Well, to me a car engine is like a musical instrument. Listen to it – always listen! It can tell you when to change gear, like changing key. It becomes instinctive. You'll find it hurts you to hear other people do it wrong.'

As they drove on, Patty concentrated hard on listening to the engine. Stephen, watching her, smiled to himself. She looked like a little schoolgirl struggling with an algebra problem. If she'd had the stub end of a pencil, he was sure she'd have chewed it.

After a few miles, she turned to him in triumph.

'I *can* hear it! I see what you mean now.'

'Good. Always let your engine sing to you – if you listen, you won't go wrong.'

They completed the rest of the lesson almost in silence, but Patty felt she'd at last broken through his reserve, if only for a moment. His coldness hadn't been due to anything she'd done wrong, after all – she must have imagined it. Maybe he had other things on his mind. People did have private lives, for Heaven's sake! She'd been an idiot to get herself worked up about it. She blushed self-consciously, then grated the gears in a panic that he might notice.

'Sorry,' she mumbled. Oh God, she was making such a fool of herself!

'Calm down,' he told her. 'No need to get in a state over a bad gear-change. We all do it sometimes.'

They pulled up outside the Depot and sat in the car for a few minutes, while he tested her on the Highway Code.

'Is that him?' Stephen enquired suddenly

'Who?' Patty's mind was still on the complexities of traffic signs.

'The boyfriend.' Stephen nodded towards a uniformed figure who was waiting by the entrance and staring at them anxiously.

Patty's heart leapt. Peter there, and she'd been so absorbed she hadn't noticed. 'Yes – that's Peter! But what on earth is he doing here at this time of day?'

'You'd better go and ask him, hadn't you?'

'Oh – yes, but . . . Well, do you want me to get Mrs Watling for you?'

'No, I'll fetch her myself. You see what the impatient lover wants.'

Stephen got out of the car and hurried inside the Depot, preferring not to wait and be introduced. Not that Peter minded. The moment he saw Patty on her own, he raced to her and enfolded her in a tight embrace.

For some seconds he didn't speak. Finally, Patty pulled her head back and stared at him. 'Peter . . . darling, what is it? What's the matter?'

'I'm being posted overseas.'

The shock made her speechless. They clung together in mutual misery. Patty knew it had always been on the cards, but somehow they'd pushed it out of their minds. It wouldn't happen to them – not yet, not for a long time anyway.

'When?' she found the courage to ask at last.

'In a couple of weeks.'

'As soon as that?' She bit her lip to stop herself crying. She *must* be brave.

'I've got to finish the course next week, then I get a week's embarkation leave.'

'Do you know where you're going?'

He nodded. 'Got a rough idea. They've told me to draw tropical kit.'

Patty swallowed. That meant the Middle East, the Far East perhaps – a long way, at any rate. No chance of home leave from there. It could be years before they saw each other again.

Peter was speaking. 'Look, can you make some excuse? Get off-duty now?'

Her mind raced. What could she say? Surely this sort of crisis didn't happen every day.

'I don't know—' she began.

He interrupted her. 'We've so little time! I don't want to waste a second away from you.'

'Nor do I,' she agreed. 'But you couldn't get off your work, could you? Oh, Peter – what are we going to do?'

'We could get married. Right away – now!'

Stan looked at the young man standing in front of him and was struck by his extreme youth. Somehow the almost belligerent attitude he was adopting only emphasized it.

'How old are you, Peter?' he asked quietly.

'Twenty-two.' Peter stuck out his jaw determinedly. 'But you needn't worry, Mr Johnson, I'm quite able to look after Patty.'

Stan sighed. This was going to be a difficult interview. For Stan, it came as a shock to realize that Patty was no longer a child whose world revolved around a doting father; that another man had usurped his position in her life. He couldn't accept it. Patty was only seventeen, for Heaven's sake! How could she possibly know her own mind at that age? And how could he allow her to tie herself down to one man, before she'd even had the chance to meet any others? Peter, was a nice enough lad, granted; his well-pressed Navy uniform gave him an air of authority and reliability; his face was open, and his clear, grey eyes looked straight at you. But the fact remained: he and Patty were simply too young to take the irrevocable step of getting married.

'Why don't you sit down?' he said at last.

'No, thanks – I'd rather stand.'

'Look. We're not going to sort anything out by fighting,' Stan pointed out gently.

'I don't see that there's anything to sort out, sir,' came

the reply. 'Patty and I want to get married and that's all there is to it.'

'Not quite. She *is* under age, you know. She needs her parents' permission.'

'You wouldn't refuse?'

'I don't know. I'll have to talk it over with her mother. We need time to think about it.'

'But, Mr Johnson, we haven't *got* any time! I want to get a Special Licence tomorrow.'

Stan shook his head. 'We can't decide something as important as this in a couple of minutes. We're talking about your whole lives.'

'Yes, but I've only got two or three weeks before I go overseas. We must get married before I leave.'

Stan shot him a look. 'It's not a question of having to, is it?'

Peter flushed a dull red, and for a moment Stan thought he was going to hit him. 'Of course not! How could you think that?'

'Well, you must forgive a father's concern. As I said before, Patty's very young. Why not wait until you come home again before getting married?'

'But I might be gone for years!'

'Suppose you are? Do you think it's fair to tie down a seventeen-year-old girl for all that time?'

Peter was vehement. 'We love each other.'

'I don't doubt it, but all the more reason to prove it can last. Two years isn't all that long at your age.'

'Mr Johnson, please! Don't you want Patty to be happy? We've only got a couple of weeks and we want to spend it together.'

'Look, lad – I understand how you feel. Kath and I went through exactly the same thing during the last war. But I still think you're rushing things. You only got engaged a couple of days ago!'

'If I wasn't being posted, I'd agree with you. But that changes everything.'

'I don't agree. You're far more likely to make the

wrong decision under this sort of pressure. What do your folks think about it?'

'I haven't told them yet.'

'Well, don't you think you should? You may find they agree with me!'

'It's nothing to do with them. No – I don't mean that, but – oh God, Mr Johnson, please be reasonable!'

'I'm trying to be, Peter, but you're not making it easy. I certainly feel your parents should be told before anything else.'

'Patty and I want to drive down to Lymington straight away. If we stay overnight and leave first thing in the morning, we should be back in time to go on duty.'

'What – introduce Patty and give them the news at the same time, eh? Bit of a shock for them, don't you think?'

'What else can we do? Anyway, they'll love her – I know they will!'

Stan didn't doubt that but even so . . . he could imagine how Kath would react if Roger sprung the same surprise on them. That reminded him it was time they adjourned to the kitchen to join Kath and the others.

Peter remonstrated with him. 'But you haven't told me your decision yet, Mr Johnson.'

'No, lad, and you won't be getting it tonight, that's for sure.'

For all Stan's easy-going manner, he could be firm when he wanted to and there was a steely note in his voice that brooked no argument. Peter followed him out of the room with a despairing sigh.

The atmosphere in the kitchen was electric. Kath was ironing, but the flush in her cheeks was certainly not due to the heat of the iron. Gran was muttering to herself and clicking away angrily with her knitting needles. Tim sat in the corner reading *Boy's Own*. When his father came in he winked, then raised his eyes comically to the ceiling.

Stan frowned. 'Where's Patty?'

'Upstairs,' replied Kath. 'She's upset. And so am I, to

tell the truth.' The look she gave Peter was uncharacteristically harsh. *He* was to blame for all this!

'Deserves to have her bottom spanked, that girl,' interjected Mrs Bowden.

'Mum, *please!*' said Kath. She was very near to tears herself.

'Look here, Mrs Johnson—' Peter began, but Stan held up a hand.

'No. *You* look here, Peter – the fact is, everyone's had a shock and everyone's being emotional. I don't want anyone saying things they might regret later. Much better let it all calm down before we discuss it any further.'

'You're absolutely right, Stan.' Kath turned to Peter, and this time her usual smile had returned. 'Go on upstairs, love. See if you can get Patty to come down. She's in quite a state.'

'Best thing is to carry out your plan, Peter,' Stan told him. 'Take her down to meet your parents. But go easy with them. You can see what a shock it's been here.'

Peter nodded. He too, was in a more subdued mood now, and already he was beginning to wonder how his own parents would behave. Their approval might not necessarily be automatic either.

Patty lay on her bed, a damp handkerchief clutched tightly in her fist. She was no longer crying, but her body was shuddering as she tried to control the sobs. As she pressed her face into the pillow, she wondered how suddenly utter happiness could turn to total misery. Only a couple of hours ago life had seemed perfect. Then suddenly all her happiness had been swept away and the war had invaded her very being. Peter sent overseas! The dreadful possibilities paraded themselves in front of her mind: Peter wounded, crippled, maimed, blinded . . . Peter as a prisoner-of-war . . . Peter killed . . . She shivered violently. If they didn't get married before he went away, she might never know what real love was: the living together, becoming one person. She could never feel like this about anyone else but Peter. She'd be condemned to a solitary life, watching her friends get married and have children, with only these brief, unfulfilled memories to sustain her. It was no good. They *had* to get married.

When Peter had first suggested the idea outside the Ambulance Depot, Patty had been unsure. It seemed such a giant step, and as her mother had been quick to point out, they hadn't known each other for very long. Then the pain of imminent parting had taken over, and her only thought had been to do what would please Peter. It hadn't occurred to her then to think of her own danger, left there at the mercy of the Blitz. Peter had, though – that's why he'd been so determined.

The next shock had been her parents' reaction. She hadn't expected such opposition, and it had quite shattered her. Before, getting married had seemed like a mere extension of her present home life, with Peter becoming another, if much dearer, member of the family. Now, if she went against her parents' wishes, she faced the possibility of being cut off from her home – of being denied the love and security she'd always taken for granted. She and Peter would be on their own, separate, a family themselves. They could only turn to each other now.

She felt a hand gently shaking her shoulder. It was Peter, kneeling beside the bed. She turned and clung to him and the tears started again.

'Hey – you're drenching my clean shirt,' he said gently. He fished a large handkerchief from his pocket and began wiping her eyes. 'Can't take you down to Lymington looking like a red-eyed rabbit!'

Patty laughed. All at once the prospect of meeting his parents seemed less frightening. What did it matter if they didn't approve? The two of them would survive. They had each other.

Stan and Kath sat on the sofa in the front room, alone. Patty and Peter had departed for Lymington and they'd packed Gran and Tim off to the shelter at Dolphin Square, where Kath would join them later.

The quiet intimacy of this moment was wonderful. Stan seemed to feel it, too. He reached out and gave her hand a gentle squeeze. What a long time it was since they'd been alone – really alone for any length of time! Not since Roger was born. And what with the war and Gran living in the house, they got even less time together. These days they couldn't even have an argument without Gran sticking her oar in. Yes, moments like these were very precious.

Kath looked at Stan and a warm flood of affection swept over her. He'd been very firm with Gran tonight – and the old lady had taken it from him, too. She was about to start holding forth about Patty again, but Stan had shut her up. Told her it was their problem – Kath's and his – and they'd sort it out themselves in their own good time . . .

But what *were* they going to do about it?

As if reading her thoughts, Stan stubbed out his cigarette, he turned to her and said, 'What d'you reckon, love?'

'Oh, Stan, I don't know,' she replied. 'We can't allow it really, can we? Patty's so very young.'

'Yes. All the same . . . Remember how we felt when your Ma said the same to us?'

'But they've only known each other three months!'

'And how long had we known each other when I popped the question, eh?' Stan put an arm round her and drew her close. 'Our marriage hasn't turned out so bad, has it, sweetheart?'

'Of course it hasn't! Oh, Stan!' Kath found herself being soundly kissed. After a moment, she drew away, flushing and patting her hair. 'Stan! Suppose someone was looking in the window?'

'Then they'd be a bloody Nosey Parker! Can't a man kiss his own wife if he wants to?'

Kath giggled. She relaxed and nestled her cheek into

the rough cloth of Stan's battledress top. 'Are you changing your mind, then? Do you think we should give our permission?'

'Well, I still feel they're rushing into things, but I wonder if we've got the right to stop them?'

Kath looked at him puzzled. 'If it's for their own good—?'

'How do we know that, any more than they do? They're both old enough to fight a war, after all. They say they're in love and want to get married. Ought we to deny them that experience?'

'But, Stan – she's only *seventeen!*'

'Yes – and suppose she never makes eighteen?'

Kath was struck dumb by her husband's words, almost as if by voicing them he could bring the reality closer.

'We have to face that possiblity, Kath. Everybody who stays here in London has to! Maybe we should let Patty live her life to the full.'

Kath sighed. She knew Stan was talking sense and yet her doubts persisted. 'And if it's all a terrible mistake?'

'They're the only ones who can find that out. But at least they won't resent us for stopping them. That's what's going to happen, Kath – you know that. I'd risk anything rather than drive Patty away from us, wouldn't you?'

She nodded. 'So we let them go ahead?' She gasped as the enormity of all the practical problems hit her.

Stan laughed and kissed her lightly. 'That'll give you something to think about in the shelter tonight. Come on, I'll walk you to the tram.'

7

A Wedding in the Family

There followed two weeks of excitement, frayed tempers, rush, bustle, tears and joy for the Johnson household. Peter very soon found out that it wasn't as easy to get married in a hurry as he'd imagined. Before he could get a licence he had to get permission from his CO, and that didn't happen overnight. Patty, too, had to be granted leave if they were to have a honeymoon. This came as a surprise to Peter, who'd assumed that once she was married, Patty would be able to give up the Ambulance Service – or at least become a part-timer.

Patty persuaded him to go to Colonel Harris with her. 'You'll understand why when you see him,' she urged. 'I'll need someone to hold my hand.'

So there they were – literally hand in hand, standing in front of the old martinet in his private sanctum.

'A honeymoon, eh? *Hmmph* . . .' he grunted, making a great play of looking through the roster. 'How long do you want to take off, Patricia?'

Patty quailed, but forced herself to utter the words. 'A weekend, sir.'

'A *long* weekend,' added Peter, more firmly.

The Colonel turned his gaze on the young man and the hint of a smile crossed his face. He definitely approved of what he saw, and a chap going overseas did deserve some sort of reward.

'Well, it's inconvenient, I must admit,' he rasped. 'But the circumstances are exceptional. I think we can find a way.'

'Oh, thank you, sir!' Patty beamed, and only just restrained herself from hugging him.

Colonel Harris was touched, and his tone became almost paternal. 'Let's see – you'll need a couple of days to get ready, Patricia. You'd better take a whole week while you're at it. But don't go spreading it about, or I'll have the entire Depot asking for the same treatment.'

'Thank you very much, sir,' said Peter.

The Colonel hauled himself out of his chair and shook Peter's hand warmly. 'And best of British luck to you both!'

The visit to the Colonel brought another bonus. On discovering that they were still looking for a suitable church hall in which to hold the reception, Colonel Harris offered them the use of the Depot itself. Up till now, things had been quiet in the daytime, and the main hall could be used without causing too much disruption. The offer was a godsend to the Johnsons, both from a financial and a catering point of view, since Dusty Miller was able to help where normal rations would never stretch.

There was no time to send out proper invitations, so the entire family was roped in to notify the guests by phone. Stan dreaded to think what his bill would be like, but forgot it every time he looked at his daughter's face. Patty was radiant. Being in love had turned prettiness into beauty. She'd resolved not to think of the future, but was living every moment to the full. Even lack of sleep seemed not to bother her. By now she was back on nightshift again – much to her delight, as it left her days free for shopping.

The Great Day was finally set and the time fixed – midday on a Friday. That would give all those who lived outside London time to travel there and to get away before the raids started. By now the raids had come to be accepted as a nightly occurrence and everyone made their arrangements around them. Sadly, the young couple would only have a four-day honeymoon before Peter had to report back, but they consoled themselves with the thought that it was more than many others in their position had achieved. After three nights in a hotel, they'd spend the last night at Lymington with Peter's parents. Patty would have preferred not to have to share even one of their precious moments with anyone, but she realized that his parents did have a claim on his time and was wise enough to enthuse about the plan.

The trousseau caused few headaches. Patty decided to limit herself to clothes for the honeymoon, and met up with Lesley and Joy Aynsworth at Dickins and Jones during their lunch hour. Joy had offered to let Patty take advantage of her staff discount, which meant pretending that the purchases were for herself – not exactly easy, since Joy was a tall girl and generously proportioned. There was a lot of giggling in the cubicles, especially over the underwear. How could Joy possibly pretend she could squeeze into a bra *that* size? Eventually they managed to switch tickets, and further hysterics broke out when Joy mimed the dismay some poor woman would endure when she found herself with the wrong fitting.

When they finally emerged, they were dabbing their eyes and holding their sides. Lesley had to rush back to her office, but Patty stayed to have a quick coffee and sandwich with Joy during what was left of her lunch hour. She wanted to talk to the older girl.

Finally Patty plucked up her courage. 'Joy . . . I've – er, I've got a bit of a problem.'

Joy stopped munching her corned beef sandwhich and stared. 'Well?'

'I've just realized my periods are due at the weekend.'

'Oh Crikey! That's bad timing.'

'I know, but I didn't have any choice, did I? Joy, isn't there something one can take to stop it – or put it off?'

Joy was chewing away slowly and thoughtfully. 'I *think* so. Don't know what it is, though. Have you asked your mum?'

Patty shook her head dispairingly. 'She wouldn't know. Anyway, she'd probably say one shouldn't interfere with nature.'

'All very well, but there's a war on and if you've only got three or four days with your husband you don't want a tummy ache all the time.' Joy sighed sympathetically. 'What rotten luck!'

'I'll probably be early, just out of nerves,' said Patty, adding to the gloom.

'Look, I'll ask around the girls at work,' volunteered Joy. 'Maybe somebody knows.'

'Thanks, Joy, I'd be ever so grateful.'

'You could try old Dr Lake, too. He may be able to suggest something.'

But Patty was somewhat doubtful. She was rather in awe of the elderly GP, and it took some courage on her part to present herself in his surgery that evening. It turned out to be an unrewarding visit.

Dr Lake was overworked and suffering from serious lack of sleep. He'd known Patty since she was a baby and was not unsympathetic, but with so many urgent cases needing treatment, her problem didn't seem as all-important to him as it did to her.

'I fear you've left it too late, my dear,' he told her. 'There are some pills, but you need to take them over a period of time.'

'Couldn't you give me some – at least to try?' she pleaded.

He shook his head. 'Sorry, Patty. they aren't a hundred per cent successful anyway. Could do more harm than good.'

He ushered her to the door firmly, smiling down at her woebegone face. 'It's not the end of the world. After all, you'll have a lifetime together. It's not all honeymoon!' He opened the door on his crowded waiting room and nodded to the elderly woman next in the queue. 'Oh, by the way – good luck on Friday!' he called after Patty's disappearing back.

She walked home slowly on leaden feet. What was she to *do?* She decided she'd have to tell Peter. It wouldn't be fair not to.

Back home she found her mother in a state of high excitement. 'Aunt Lily's coming down for the wedding. She's just phoned. It's two whole years since we've seen her!' Kath was so pleased that she at first didn't notice her daughter's quietness. Upstairs she watched while Patty sorted out her new purchases.

'Oh, that's sweet, darling! Put it on and let's see you in it.' This was the reaction to the suit Patty had bought to go away in, a brown cord number, cut in military style, double-breasted with square shoulders and brass buttons.

Patty shook her head and hung it up in the little wardrobe. 'Not now, Mum.' She returned to the task of putting away her new garments.

Kath looked at her, hurt turning to concern as she took in the white, worried face. 'What's the matter, pet?' she asked.

'Nothing, Mum.'

'If there's anything wrong, do tell me. I mean, if you've changed your mind—'

'No.'

'Well, I only wanted to say, it wouldn't be too late. We'd understand . . .'

Patty turned irritably. 'I have *not* changed my mind.' Remorse crept in as she saw her mother's stricken expression. 'I'm sorry, Mum. I've got a bit of a headache.'

Kath smiled with relief. Of course – nerves! She'd had them herself just before her wedding. 'I've got some aspirin in the kitchen. Come down when you're ready and I'll make you a cup of tea.' She hurried off, thankful to be of use.

Patty stared at herself in the mirror. Lord! What a fright she looked! She picked up a hairbrush and started to brush her hair with sharp, violent strokes. After a while the vigorous action helped, and she both felt and looked much better. There – she really must stop behaving like a soppy kid – heaven knows, other girls must have faced this problem before. The best person to talk to would be Peter. He had a sister himself, so he was bound to understand.

Peter stared at her, conflicting emotions tumbling around in his breast. What a rotten stroke of fate! Patty stared back at him, troubled by his silence, not realizing that he was speechless simply because he couldn't think what to say.

'I just thought . . . Well, if you'd like to do it now – today,' she stammered at last, crimson with embarrassment.

Suddenly Peter gathered her in his arms and hugged her close, touched to the heart by her youth and vulnerability. How she must have had to nerve herself to suggest this! It was the answer, of course. What matter if they privately advanced their honeymoon a few days? Who would ever know? Then the practicalities began to hit him. Where? When?

For the first time that lovely autumn, there was a distinct chill of frost in the air. The night sky over London was clear and bright as usual, and the Luftwaffe were making the most of it. High up amongst the bracken and scrub of Box Hill, Patty shivered violently – but as much from nerves as from the cold. Peter inwardly cursed. This was hardly the romantic idyll he'd intended.

Things had been difficult enough to arrange as it was. There was no question of going to a hotel for the night – funds were simply too tight – so in a moment of inspiration he'd suggested a drive down to Surrey to see his Great Aunt Bess. After all, it was the first day of Patty's leave, so she didn't have to go to the Depot. And how were the Johnsons to know that Great Aunt Bess had been dead for five years?

Patty had been so open-mouthed at his inventiveness that she hadn't even been able to giggle and give the game away. The story had been accepted without question – Peter had assured the family that they'd spend the night with Aunt Bess, so there was no danger of returning during a raid.

Feeling Patty's shiver, Peter held her closer for warmth. He'd brought a rug for them to lie on, but, now he decided to exchange that for his raincoat and tucked the rug over and around them so they were wrapped up like a cocoon. It was a great improvement. Apart from the warmth, it also gave a feeling of privacy. Both of them relaxed a little and were able to laugh at their predicament.

But it was a disaster. Peter's only previous sexual encounters had been with girls considerably older and more experienced, and he'd never had to take the initiative before. He was nervous of frightening or hurting Patty, and yet desperate for relief. As a result, his caresses, far from being tender, were either tentative and fumbling or over-eager and rough. Patty for her part was terrified. She knew she should relax, but the more Peter kept telling her this, the more she tensed up.

'I can't help it,' she said at last. 'I'm trying – honestly.'

Peter suppressed a sigh. The pain in his balls was almost unbearable, yet every time he attempted a penetration, Patty pulled back with a moan, tightening her legs together. As if she wasn't tight enough already!

'Does it hurt that much?'

'Yes.' It was no more than a whisper. 'Peter . . . do you think . . . I mean, is there something wrong with me?'

'Course not! It's always supposed to be difficult the first time.'

Privately, though, Peter felt as ill-prepared and ignorant as Patty. Christ – he'd never had a virgin before. He'd heard a lot of bawdy talk in the Mess, but no one had recounted an experience similar to this. 'Do you want to give up?' he asked.

'No!' Patty was desperate. 'No – we must go through with it tonight.'

'I can't bear the thought of hurting you.'

'Never mind. It's probably only the first time, as you say. Peter, you must keep going even if I yell. Promise me!'

He looked down at the tragic little face, wishing fervently that things could have been different. He kissed away the tears, then closed his mouth over hers. Slowly he moved down until his lips found her nipples, teasing them with his tongue until he felt them harden into twin peaks. Then his hand slid between her legs to explore the soft recess with its covering of down. Oh *no* – she wasn't even moist yet! The damn French letter didn't help. Maybe things would be easier if he took it off. There'd be a risk, of course, but anything to make this occasion work for Patty!

Without giving himself time to think, he pulled if off and pressed himself against her.

'Don't worry, darling – I'll pull out before there's any danger,' he murmured. 'I think it'll be easier this way.' There was no answer from Patty. Just a silent acquiescence.

Seconds later, a scream was wrenched from her throat. She'd never known such pain. It was as if she were being torn in two. Peter stopped immediately.

'No – go on – I told you!' she muttered through clenched teeth.

She tried to stop herself crying out, but it was no good – the sounds were involuntary. In any case, Peter couldn't have stopped – he was too far gone, his limbs working like a powerful machine, pushing, probing further and further, Patty's cries seeming merely to spur him to more vigorous thrusts.

'Shit – I can't hold it!' he gasped. His body jerked and he collapsed over Patty with great shuddering sobs of relief, burying his face in her neck.

Patty felt the warm rush of his seed deep within her, but it aroused no answering response from her wracked and torn young body – only gratitude that the pain was finally over.

After a few moments, Peter raised himself on his elbows and looked down at her. 'Are you all right?' She smiled. 'Oh baby, I'm sorry I had to hurt you so,' he breathed, suddenly smothering her in kisses. 'Next time it'll be better, I'll make sure of that.' And then the reality hit him. 'Oh God, I hope I haven't made you pregnant! I meant to pull out at the last minute, but somehow I just couldn't stop . . .'

'I'm glad you didn't.'

He gazed at her with adoration. 'Mrs Quayle, I love you. You really belong to me now. That stupid old ceremony on Friday doesn't mean a thing beside this.'

They kissed and clung together for another moment. 'Oops, I'm coming out,' he laughed, heaving himself off her.

It was then Patty became conscious of the mess: blood everywhere, mixed with the sticky outpourings of passion. Both her handkerchief and Peter's proved inadequate and finally his underpants had to be sacrificed, amid some amusement, for mopping-up operations.

Patty woke late next morning, having climbed into bed in the early dawn and fallen into a deep sleep of exhaustion. She lay still for a few minutes, allowing her body to come painfully alive. She felt bruised and battered, and somehow unclean. Her vagina throbbed from Peter's onslaught, and judging by the sodden towel between her legs, her period had started. A ruptured hymen couldn't cause *that* much bleeding, surely – although it had taken some pretty violent treatment. They'd made a second attempt at lovemaking last night. Peter had taken it very slowly and gently, but she'd been so sore from the first time, she simply couldn't feel anything except the pain – although she hadn't told him so, of course. After a while Peter became carried away with his own passion and restraint had been thrown to the winds, just like before. Patty was surprised: for that brief moment he seemed oblivious to anything but his own ecstasy – she was just a receptacle for his overflow – yet afterwards, he was all concern, repeating again and again how much he adored her. So that was love! It was certainly a bit different from the romantic idylls of popular novelists. Patty couldn't help feeling cheated. There was no excitement or physical pleasure to remember on her side, just the pain and messiness of it all.

She dragged her stiff limbs from the bed and went downstairs to see if there was any chance of a bath. Kathleen was worried by her daughter's white face and hollow eyes, but was reassured to hear that it was only due to a period.

'What bad luck, pet,' she remarked. 'But at least the worst will be over by Friday.'

The day after tomorrow! They were nearly there! Too late to turn back, even if she wanted to. She couldn't anyway – not after last night. For all she knew she might be pregnant.

She did the last bits and pieces of shopping that morning and then Kath made her go upstairs and rest. Patty was only too glad to comply. She certainly didn't feel too marvellous. But she revived after a cup of tea and resolved to put on a cheerful face for Peter. They were going to risk the bombs and go up west to a nightclub with Peter's best man, a brother officer of his. Patty had never been to a nightclub before and was quite excited. As the club was in a basement relatively safe from the bombs, they could stay there all night – even have an early breakfast in Town!

The next day Peter went down to Lymington to spend his last night of bachelordom at home. Patty teased him, claiming that it was really to say goodbye to all his old girl-friends. He countered by begging her to accompany him, but Patty refused. There was far too much to do getting ready for the next day. Gran Bowden backed her up. There was no question of Patty going off for the night with Peter – that would mean they'd see each other on the morning of the wedding before the ceremony. Dreadfully unlucky!

8

The Big Day

Of her actual wedding, Patty found she could remember only jumbled incidents – rather like a jerky Gaumont-British newsreel. But at least she could remember it in colour, not the black-and-white of the 'flicks'.

In fact, it was the colour of the ceremony that stayed in her head, as she and Peter stood in line at the entrance to the Ambulance Depot Hall, welcoming all the guests.

They'd abandoned the idea of a white wedding, and Patty had compromised by choosing a simple cream dress gathered in at the waist. Though she wasn't aware of it, the simplicity of the dress made her look even younger, and Kath's eyes had brimmed with tears as she saw Patty that morning, coming down the stairs.

Patty knew nothing of her mother's feelings at that moment, or of Stan's, but she did remember the shock she had when standing with her father at the foot of the aisle, just before the organ struck up the Wedding March and all those familiar faces turned towards her. Her feet had scrunched on something gritty and she'd looked down to see little particles of coloured glass lying in the dust-strokes of a broom. It was only then that she realized how light it was inside the church, not the familiar gloom she recalled from Sunday school days. The glass fragments sparkled in the sun and she looked up to see great holes in the roof with sunbeams lancing down from them. To right and left the familiar stained-glass scenes were gone. But her heart lifted when she saw that her favourite window depicting St Francis of Assisi was still intact.

The church had lost much of its original colour, but

Balaclava Street had seen to it that as much as possible was restored. Where the flowers had come from it was best not to ask; homes that were now rubble had no need of flowers in their gardens. Like so much else in Blitz life, you brushed away the dust and carried on. But what a riot of colour there was in the congregation! While the men looked slightly uncomfortable in their Sunday best suits, their women had, with one mind, decided that cheerful colours were the order of the day. In every pew, great flower patterns strained across bosoms and bottoms, and hats that would have done credit to Petticoat Lane tilted at every conceivable angle. The street had turned out in force, determined to see that one of their own was married in style, Blitz or no Blitz! But there was little doubt who took first prize – Sincerity Vale, in a magnificent picture hat and veil that Patty guessed, quite rightly, was a souvenir of some past musical show. Claude stood erect beside her, his iron-grey hair matching his smart grey suit, resplendent with white carnation. Love and pride seemed to radiate from both of them. Patty was touched. She prayed that she and Peter would be as happy in their old age.

Patty shook hand after hand as she stood there next to Peter, but only Lesley's comment really penetrated her happy haze: 'Tonight's the night, eh, Mrs Quayle!' Patty blushed, and the blush stayed with her. Tonight should really have been the night. For a moment she regretted that early lovemaking on Box Hill. Damn the curse . . . they should have waited! The thought of her period made her glance around, trying to see the back of her dress. How awful if . . . Kath caught her daughter's anxious look, and gave her daughter a discreet 'thumbs up'. Patty looked at her mother in surprise. How could she have known exactly what she was thinking . . .? Mums were clever! She turned back to smile happily at Mr Aynsworth's stilted compliments.

Was she really happy? Course she was! What more could a girl ask? Here she was with her husband of five minutes by her side. Her Mum and Dad were welcoming people to *her* wedding reception. And next to them, Mr and Mrs Quayle – both of them brown-faced and country-looking, different somehow from Londoners, but really sweet. They'd made her feel so much at home on that first visit with Peter even though the news they'd brought must have been a shock. And she was wondering if she was *happy!*

Right on cue – or so it seemed to Patty – Peter turned and squeezed her hand very gently. Patty looked deep into his eyes and all she could see was love. Love pouring into her mind, washing away all doubts . . .

Kath Johnson saw that look pass between the young couple and was greatly comforted. To be honest, when she'd seen Patty coming down the stairs that morning, she'd almost called the whole thing off. Why, Patty looked like the little girl she'd reassured years ago, before going off to her first big party up the street! That time, it had been so simple to take her in her arms and reassure her. This morning she'd wanted to do the same thing. But something came between them. Something . . . Well, now she was a woman, an equal. And you couldn't cuddle another woman in quite the same way that you could a child.

Kath had been on the verge of tears, and then she'd looked at Stan. Stan saw, and understood. And he'd given her that tiny shake of the head which she'd recognized over the years as a warning. Seeing Patty and Peter gazing at each other now, as though there was no-one else in the world, Kath was glad she hadn't over-reacted and spoiled Patty's great day. Stan had been right, as usual.

Relieved, Kath looked around the hall. Some of the faces weren't immediately familiar and Kath realized with a start that they must belong to the stand-by ambulance crews. Please God, said Kath, please, *please* don't let there be a raid now. Let us at least see our daughter married in peace . . . It was the same prayer she'd repeated to herself all the time in the church and so far at least, it had been answered. For that Kath was thankful, though she knew that no prayers would hold back the Jerries tonight. They came every night. It was now a fact of life – or rather, death.

Suddenly Kath's thoughts returned to the present, and to the great hum of conversation and laughter that filled the hall.

'C'mon you two,' she said to Patty and Peter, 'enough of this star-gazing. You've got to get around and talk to people. It's your party.'

Most of the laughter seemed to be coming from the group standing by the beer barrels at the end of the buffet table. God knows how much all this is costing, thought Kath, but if Stan said it was all right – well, they'd manage. Mind you, the whole street had rallied round over the food. The tables positively sagged with sausage rolls and sandwiches, and someone had found a whole cheese, which for the moment no-one dared to cut. Kath reckoned that contained in that one barrel-shaped monster were more than the cheese rations of the whole of Balaclava Street put together – but she knew better than to ask where it had come from.

She found herself standing near to the stage which took up one end of the hall and which seemed to be almost entirely covered with sleeping kits. One mattress, she noticed with surprise, was occupied, and from the gentle snoring coming from a hump of blankets, whoever it was didn't intend to let a small thing like a wedding party deprive him of his shut-eye. Mind you, the noise was nothing to compare with the guns at night. If you could sleep through that, you could sleep through anything.

Kath sat on the stairs at one end of the stage and looked down over the party. It was certainly going with a swing. She could spot Patty's blonde head. Peter was still holding her hand and they were clinging together amid all the jollifications as though nothing could ever drag them apart. Kath frowned slightly as she thought how soon they'd be separated. Peter looked serious, but when he smiled his whole face lit up. All in all, Patty had done well to find such a sensible young man. She could have done much worse . . . especially going to that Palais dance-hall place!

Not far from Peter, Kath could see Sub-Lieutenant Ian Camp, Peter's best man. He was on the same course as Peter and would be going with him wherever it was they were sending them. Kath smiled at the way the two young men had dodged all her questions. The Silent Service!

Well, there was nothing silent about Ian Camp at this moment. He was chatting avidly with two girls, both of whom looked distinctly tarty. With something of a shock, Kath realized that it was the Aynsworth girls, Lesley and Joy. All that make-up! Kath couldn't help tutting. A touch of lipstick and powder was all right, but that pancake stuff made them look as though they were going on the stage – or something worse!

Kath would have been surprised if she could have known what was going through Lesley's mind at that moment, as she deliberately moistened her lips with the tip of her tongue. Gazing up at Ian Camp, Lesley saw this had produced the effect intended: Ian had flushed.

Lesley would have been even more surprised if she could have guessed her sister's thoughts. For, unknown to her, Joy was playing a waiting game. Lesley could get him all excited, the little cow, but when the moment came Joy would step in and nick the prize. Men appreciated an experienced woman. She waved her empty glass at Ian. 'Darling,' she said, 'it takes more than one glass to get me in the mood – would you mind?' Ian grabbed the glass with indecent haste and hurried in the direction of the bar, while Lesley looked daggers at her sister.

It was another blonde head that guided Kath to her husband. Enid Belling seemed to cling to Stan more and more these days. Kath surprised herself with a slight twinge of jealousy, then felt remorseful; Enid must be very lonely now that George had gone back to his ship. And besides what better man to turn to than her Stan?

He'd become a real tower of strength since the bombing started.

The laughter round the beer barrels grew, and as Kath moved through to the centre of the party, she wasn't surprised to see that Sid Raynes had established himself as dispenser of the pint pots. Some appeared to have ominous cracks in them, but no-one seemed to worry. Obviously the glasses were survivors from the bomb on The Windmill.

Matters around the beer supplies weren't helped by the Williams children, who were playing hide-and-seek among the guests' legs. Nobody really objected, though Bert gave Joey a clip round the ear when the boy careered into Miss Jessie by mistake.

Soft-hearted Miss Jessie tut-tutted at this swift punishment but Miss Mary thoroughly approved. 'Discipline, that's what children need. Why, when *I* was a governess . . .'

Sensing that her sister was about to embark on one of her monologues, Miss Jessie shut her ears and beamed happily around her. What a good time everyone seemed to be having!

In another corner of the room a most unlikely friendship was being formed, between the formidable figure of Colonel Harris and old Gran Bowden. It seemed Gran didn't find the Colonel in the least intimidating. 'You in charge, are yer?' she demanded, instantly putting the Colonel on the defensive.

'Er, yes . . . yes . . . I suppose I am . . '

'Well, then, yer can get me a drink!'

'Ah – er, not actually in charge of the wedding party, Madam,' the Colonel said stiffly, 'but delighted to oblige all the same.'

Harris set off towards the bar and returned some moments later with one replenished glass for Gran.

'Ain'tcher drinkin' yerself?' demanded Gran suspiciously.

'Can't,' said the Colonel, 'not on duty.' And he cast a

stern glance around to satisfy himself that the stand-by ambulance crews weren't drinking either.

The gin certainly loosened Gran's tongue, and she launched into a full account of how she'd been bombed and her subsequent rescue, to which the Colonel listened with deep interest.

'. . . Got some way of finding their way, those Jerries have . . .' Horace Aynsworth was saying to Madge Williams. 'My cousin works for the gas company – *he* says that they know where every one of those great gas holders is . . . that's what they aim at . . . Then when that goes up, they can see . . . can't they . . .?'

'Is that right?' Madge shivered at this new threat to her peace of mind. There were lots of those great gas things around Balaclava Street.

'Course,' said Horace, sensing a captive audience, 'my cousin says that's why the Jerries drop those great breadbasket things full of incendiaries – so they spread out over a big area. Bound to hit the gas works then.'

'Oh Lord!' breathed Madge. In the brief pause before Horace Aynsworth added more fuel to her anxieties, she thought she could hear a siren wailing far away in the distance. But no-one else seemed to take any notice, so perhaps she was imagining things.

'How do you know all this?' asked Fred Perkins suddenly, rounding on Horace.

'I told you,' said Horace irritably, 'my cousin in the gas company. He says that some of their lads are proper heroes . . . sitting up there on top of all that gas just waiting to explode and mending holes so it don't catch fire. Wouldn't stand much chance if it did, would they? Never recover the bodies . . .' This last fact seemed to be a direct threat to Horace's business and he pondered on it gloomily.

Just then a jocular Bert Williams joined the group, and was surprised to find his wife looking ashen-faced.

'Oh Bert,' she wailed, almost throwing herself into his arms, 'we're all going to be burned alive when those gas tanks go up. Mr Aynsworth says that the Germans know where they are, and . . .'

Horace Aynsworth suddenly found himself the target of Bert Williams' angry glare.

'What've you been saying?'

'N-nothing,' stuttered Horace. 'I was only repeating what my cousin told me—'

'Spreading rumours and defeatist talk,' said Bert in his best policeman's voice, 'is an offence!' And to Horace's horror, his hand moved towards his top uniform pocket as if to take out his notebook.

Whether Bert would have taken any action is open to doubt, for at that moment the whole conversation was drowned by the deafening roar of a motorbike outside.

Everyone turned to see where the sound had come from. More than one of the guests jumped. One dropped his glass. Noises like that meant trouble.

9

The Party's Over

For a moment everyone in the hall stared in silence at the strange figure entering through the double doors. He stopped in front of the blackout curtains and clouted himself once or twice to remove the dust from his Air Force uniform. He was wearing goggles over his eyes and an RAF forage cap, but instead of being cocked jauntily on the side of his head, it was pulled down, unbuttoned, with the ends tied roughly under his chin.

He was to all intents and purposes unrecognizable. But Kath knew – knew just an instant before he pushed up the goggles and pulled off his peculiar-looking headgear. Patty was only a fraction of a second later, but while Kath hesitated, Patty had no such inhibitions.

'Roger!' she yelled. 'Mum, it's Roger!'

With a collective sigh of relief, the wedding party relaxed and the hum of conversation resumed. The guests made a path for Roger and as he passed, they thumped him on the back, each friendly pat drawing forth yet another cloud of dust. Roger's strange looks didn't bother them. Balaclava Street today was used to surprises, and for once this was a pleasant one.

Finally Roger stood in front of his mother, with Patty hanging on to his arm and Peter just a pace or two behind.

'Hello, Mum,' he said, 'sorry I cut it a bit fine. Can't stop long, the Don R – that's the despatch rider – is going to pick me up on his way back.'

Kath found the tears trickling out of the corners of her eyes. In front of all these people too! Once again she was grateful for the comforting presence of Stan, who suddenly appeared at her shoulder.

'Well, aren't you going to kiss your mother, boy?' asked Stan gruffly. 'We've really been going through it, while you Brylcream boys live the life of Reilly out in the country.'

Roger was about to retort when he suddenly realized that Stan's remarks had been for Kath's benefit. 'Didn't want to cover you with dust, Mum,' he quipped and took her in his arms. He could see that she was trying desperately to control her sobs, and soon found tears pricking at his own eyelids.

'There, there, Mum,' he murmured 'I'm a big boy now. Dad's right – from what I saw on the way, I'd say I've had it easy.'

Kath murmured shakily: 'That's not what we heard.'

'Honestly Mum, that's all propaganda,' said Roger. 'Would I be here now if things were as bad as Lord Haw Haw says?'

'No,' replied Kath hesitantly, 'But you said you'd got to go back soon?'

'So I have. Sergeant's Mess are playing the Pilots, and I'm our demon bowler.'

The lie was so transparent that even Kath, who desperately wanted to believe, rejected it. 'You couldn't even throw a ball straight when you were little.' The tears brimmed again at the thought of Roger as a boy, but Kath bravely fought them back. 'Have you really got to go?'

''Fraid so,' said Roger, 'the Don R has to deliver some messages and then he'll be back. Nice of him to bring me.'

'Certainly was,' agreed Stan. 'Now, say hello to your married sister and her husband.'

'Dad! you sound like a bleeding Sergeant. Over here, over there!'

'I can see life in the RAF isn't doing you any good!' laughed Stan. 'And you watch your language, too!'

'Now then, Sis,' grinned Roger, 'who's the lucky man – don't tell me it's the same one as last week? Ah well, I suppose now all the real men are in the Raff, you girls have only got the sailors left to choose from!'

Peter had sensed Kath's unease and saw that his role was to carry on with Roger's light-hearted banter. While the two of them cross-traded insults, Stan was pleased to see Kath unwinding a little.

It was Roger who finally broke the tension. 'They say the Navy can drink, but I've been standing here all this time and no-one's even thought of asking me what the Raff would like!'

Stan took his cue. 'Come on! This way to the bar. And Patty, if you can spare the man in your life for just a few moments, we'd like to see what the Navy's made of!'

Stan carefully steered his son and son-in-law to a reasonably quiet spot near the bar. As soon as they all had drinks, the conversation changed tone immediately. Gone was the easy repartee that had calmed Kath.

'Well, son?' asked Stan.

'Not good, Dad,' Roger told him. 'They kept on thumping us so bad, we couldn't even get the kites off the ground. Thank God, they switched to London. No, I don't mean that . . .'

'I know,' nodded Stan. 'Go on.'

'Well, like I said, it was bad. The bloody runway at Biggin was so messed up with great holes everywhere that we had to switch to a grass runway. If you could have seen those pilots keep on plugging away – Dad, I've seen them cry like babies . . . and I've seen them throw up at the sound of another 'Scramble' . . . and . . .' To his obvious embarrassment, Roger realized that it was his turn to find tears welling up, but somehow he controlled them.' And those Waafs, only little tiny tarts really . . . seeing all their bodies spread out with only a groundsheet over 'em . . . well . . .' Roger broke off and took a great swig of neat whisky.

Stan looked at his son gravely, astonished by the change in him. 'You mustn't tell Mum any of this!'

'Course not – I'm not bloody daft.'

Peter felt totally out of place. 'Perhaps I'd better get back to Patty!' And was amazed at the hardness in Stan's eyes as he turned towards him.

'No, you bleeding don't! You're part of this family now. There's a time for women and there's a time for men.'

The truth was that Stan was still hesitant about dealing with the two young men. He felt more confident and able now than he'd ever felt in his life, but even so, his ARP duties paled into insignificance beside those of his son. Roger was getting planes into the air to fight the sods. All Stan could do was to cope with the mess caused by the ones that got through. And Peter, too – he was going to the front line, where he could hit back at the enemy, not just put out a few fires or cope with the damage caused by some stray bomb.

But hadn't Balaclava Street – and streets like it all over London – become, in a sense, the front line?

Well, sod you, Jerry! Stan said mentally, and then to Peter and Roger. 'Drink up, lads it's going to be a noisy night.'

Patty, finding herself alone for the first time at the reception, looked around at the flushed faces of the wedding guests – faces that grinned and grimaced, their chatter filling the hall with a great buzz of noise. In some strange way, she felt detached from it all, as though she were watching some giant Punch-and-Judy show.

Then she saw Stephen Broome. The crowd parted for a moment and there he was, sitting on a chair at the far end of the hall. For a moment, Patty felt an almost motherly wave of pity sweep over her. He looked so lost – almost abandoned. He appeared to be studying the party as though they were creatures from another world – a world in which he had no part. Patty pulled herself up. Too right. He did have no part of the world of Balaclava Street. He'd always kept himself aloof from the general life at the Depot, and he had no close friends, it seemed. Was that what being a Quaker did for you? If so, she was glad she wasn't one.

Stephen looked directly at her and gave a tiny wave of recognition which seemed to Patty almost dismissive. Up till then she'd wanted to go over and draw him into the wedding party, but that cold little wave made her think twice. Angrily, she turned away.

Stephen hadn't intended his gesture to be anything more than friendly. In fact, he'd deliberately tried to make his signal low-key, but now he could see he'd overdone it. Damn the girl, why should she upset him so? After all, this was her wedding day. She had no interest in him, not with that handsome Navy bloke around. Get a hold of yourself, man. Conscientious objector abducts Navy bride on wedding day? Fat chance. For a moment, Stephen remembered that sudden stirring of desire when she'd sat beside him during her driving lessons, but savagely he pushed the memory away.

Patty felt lost for only a moment, then Peter's hand slipped into hers and she turned to face him once again. Whatever had she been thinking about? Stephen Broome meant nothing to her, except that they shared the same dangers. *This* was the man she was going to share her whole life with.

'Come on,' said Peter, 'I think they want us to cut the cake,' and pulled Patty through the guests to the bar.

Without any announcement, the noise in the hall died away and Patty found herself gazing in astonishment at a real wedding cake, with 'Patty and Peter' in Ovaltine-brown letters, set in a heart-shaped outline and decorated with hundreds-and-thousands from the Farleys' corner shop. The icing looked a bit runny, but to Patty it was the most wonderful cake she'd ever seen.

'C'mon love,' said her mother's voice in her ear. 'Now you and Peter have got to cut it.'

'*Tra-la!*' announced Ian Camp, and to everyone's amazement produced from behind his back, not a knife, but a full-sized Naval sword. 'Nicked it from the cloakroom', confessed Ian, grinning with delight at the astonished look on Peter's face.

'You'll get court-martialled, you silly ass!'

'No, I shan't. I'll have it back there tonight and if anyone's missed it – well, it was mislaid somewhere, wasn't it?'

The rest of the reception was a bit of a blur to Patty. Everything seemed to happen so fast. One moment they were leaning on the sword trying to get its blunt edge to penetrate Dusty's gooey icing, the next her father was speaking and then Ian said something and everyone laughed and then Peter was guiding her to the door, where her mother and father both kissed her.

'Be happy, love,' said Stan. Kath, however, said nothing – she didn't trust herself to speak without bursting into tears again. And then they were in Peter's car and everything was sunshine, and Balaclava Street was left far behind . . .

Though the bride and groom had gone, the party in the Depot showed no signs of stopping. Stan refused another drink. He knew that a raid was bound to come before long, and he wanted to face the night in a reasonably sober condition. Looking round the hall, he saw several guests who'd be feeling no pain tonight, whatever the skies rained down on them. They'd drunk so much they'd have a job even finding their way back to their shelters! At least they'd be able to sleep through it all.

Peter's parents had a long return journey ahead of them, and explained that they'd like to get started before it got dark. Stan agreed. 'No point in staying around here now that the kids have gone.' At his words, Kath felt another pang of sadness. Kids – that's exactly what they were.

Stan seemed to read her thoughts. 'Never mind, love,' he whispered, 'she'll be back after the honeymoon.'

Sadly, they didn't have much longer to enjoy the celebrations, for already Colonel Harris was glancing apologetically at his watch. 'I'm afraid my four o'clock shift's due shortly, Mr Johnson. I'd like to get things cleared up before they arrive.'

'Course you would, Colonel. Leave it to me – I'll get rid of this lot. Drink all night, given half a chance!' Brushing aside the Colonel's apologies, Stan called for silence and reminded the guests that it would soon be time to get to the shelter. There was no dissent. Everyone rallied to help get the hall straight again, and Dusty had never had so many willing helpers with the washing-up. Half an hour later, Stan and Kath were shaking hands with Colonel Harris.

'We'll never be able to thank you enough,' said Kath.

Stan and Kath walked home arm in arm, Gran and Tim having gone ahead. Kath sniffed and Stan handed her his handkerchief. 'Have a good blow, love.'

'Don't know what's the matter with me,' she muttered. 'Can't stop weeping.'

'Bound to be a bit of an anti-climax, now it's all over. Never mind. I've got a surprise for you.'

She looked at him, eyes wide – a look that reminded him of Patty and caught at his heart. He hugged her close. 'C'mon – we'd best get a move on if we're going to Dolphin Square. I've saved us a bottle of champagne. We'll drink it there.'

The Johnsons had finally decided to follow Madge Williams' example and make a nightly trek to Dolphin Square. It was reasonably near to home and was one of the better-organized large shelters. Stan was excused his ARP duties for tonight, and it seemed strange to him as he herded his family onto the tram, laden with their blankets and packed suppers, to think that tonight for the first time he'd be at the mercy of the Luftwaffe just like all the other helpless Londoners, instead of being in charge of his own patch. He wasn't sure he liked the feeling too much.

They arrived at the Dolphin Square shelter quite early and were able to settle themselves near the Williams.

Madge had already got her brood bedded down, but Glen and Joey leapt up immediately when they saw Tim, whom they held in some awe, volunteering to show him around.

Looking around, Stan saw a number of scruffy schoolchildren minding places until their parents arrived later from work. There seemed little bonhomie amongst the growing throng. Most looked tired and listless from lack of sleep and worry over the bombing. Pockets of fighting broke out. Even Stan, who'd witnessed plenty of violent behaviour in the last war, was shocked to see the way the basic human decencies were being overthrown.

'Rough lot down here,' he remarked to his wife, watching two small boys squabbling over a place. 'Poor little blighters can't help it, I suppose. It's not fair putting kids in that position.'

People gradually settled, ate their sandwiches and struck up conversations with their immediate neighbours. A young couple embracing ardently, seemingly oblivious to their surroundings, occasioned some ribald comments and a lot of vocal disapproval.

'Disgusting, I call it,' growled Mrs Bowden, 'worse 'n animals, carrying on like that in public.'

Kath felt a surge of pity for the young couple. The man was wearing battledress. 'Gran, maybe he's on embarkation leave,' she murmured. 'Maybe they've nowhere else to go.'

'Ought to be prosecuted!' Gran wasn't giving an inch.

It could have been Patty and Peter, thought Kath to herself, if Peter hadn't been lucky enough to be able to stand them a hotel. Her mind turned to her daughter, and she felt a lump in her throat. She prayed desperately that Peter would be kind and gentle with her. Stan handed her a glass of champagne and toasted her with a wink, as if guessing her thoughts. Dear Stan. Where would she be without him?

10

A Weekend on the River

Patty made sure the lights were out and the door to the landing properly closed, then she opened the blackout curtains. The view was beautiful, but it did little to lift her depression.

Almost beneath her window, the Thames glided by in the moonlight. Away in the distance the first searchlights probed the sky. Patty shivered, though the autumn air was still warm. She knew only too well that those distant beams meant that Mum and Dad were in the thick of it again. She thought of the Ambulance Depot and felt guilty at being away from it all. She had a sudden impulse to ring home, but rejected the idea. Phones were for emergencies only while the Blitz was on. Besides, Peter would only tease her again about being a 'Mummy's girl' – teasing that was more than just fun and had the ring of irritation about it.

There was no doubt about it, their honeymoon had gone sadly wrong. A tear rolled down Patty's cheek as she remembered how she'd dreamed it would be. Where had they gone wrong?

Suddenly the sound of footsteps on the stairs made her grab for the blackout, but the steps went on past her room. She heaved a sigh of relief. For a moment she'd thought it was Peter coming up from the bar.

She couldn't complain about the place Peter had chosen. It must have cost a fortune. The Compleat Angler at Marlow was the perfect place for a honeymoon. And everything had gone so well that night – or rather, that evening. Supper and a bottle of champagne in their room.

Peter had thought of everything, and she'd glowed with happiness and love.

And then . . . well, that was where the trouble had started. At first Peter had been understanding about her problem; kind and gentle, just as she'd expected him to be. It was only a matter of two or three days, she'd told him. Then she'd seen a side of her husband that she'd never seen before.

'A few *days!*' he exploded. 'For God's sake, we've only got a few days! It's not fair!' Suddenly he was like a small boy who'd been told that he couldn't go out to play. And how he'd sulked! He'd even tried blackmail, saying that she'd regret it when he'd gone; that he was certain to be killed; that other women would have been different . . . Eventually Patty had burst into tears – the idea of his being killed was too much for her to bear – and seeing her, Peter had been full of remorse.

For a moment, held tightly in his arms, Patty had once again felt the joy and tenderness of their first love. Gently, he'd started to caress her, moving his head down to kiss and suck her nipples. Cuddling his head against her breast, she began to respond. Her cheeks flushed and she tingled with a gradual sexual awareness. This was how it should be, she realized; this was the feeling of delight she'd read about. But her moans of pleasure only increased the urgency of Peter's desire, and soon he was thrusting himself against her, groaning, trying to prise her legs apart with his own. Patty kept them tightly closed. How could he even contemplate such a thing? She shuddered in revulsion and the magic moment vanished.

'No Peter! No, we can't!'

'Don't be such a prude!'

'Peter, please!'

'I'm sorry, but people must do it at these times. I'll wear a French letter.'

Her resistance only made him even more passionate. Now he was kneeling over her and cupping her breasts roughly with his hands, thrusting himself between them, rubbing himself into a frenzy.

'Suck me!' he grunted between thrusts.

'No!' Patty felt shocked and sickened. Worse still, she was frightened that in his present violent mood, Peter might actually force her to do as he'd suggested.

'Jesus Christ!' he yelled in frustration. 'If you won't let me fuck you, at least toss me off! Christ – do I have to show you?'

The trouble was he *did* have to show her. Patty knew little of the make-up of the male, and was so overwhelmed by fear and abhorrence that she had no time to consider her husband's plight. Peter seized her hands, his own clamped tightly over them to prevent escape – then quite quickly it was over. He gave a long, shuddering groan and lay face down on the pillow.

Patty managed to extricate herself and hurried over to the basin and scrubbed her hands clean with a nailbrush, rubbing the skin almost raw in her determination to rid herself of the sticky, sickly-smelling mess. Then she crept back to bed, her cheeks burning with shame as she wondered how much had been heard in the adjoining bedrooms.

Peter was soon asleep, but she lay awake listening to his heavy breathing, afraid to move for fear of waking him and prompting a repeat performance. Was this what marriage was all about? Was sex always such a one-sided affair? Surely things had to get better somehow?

She woke early, feeling stiff and cramped from lying in the same position. Peter was still fast asleep, thank goodness. She had a sudden urge to go to the lavatory. Very carefully, she eased herself from the bed and slipped on her dressing gown, then grabbing her sponge bag and towel she tiptoed down the corridor to the bathroom. Her watch showed that it was a quarter to seven. Would she be terribly unpopular if she took a bath at that time? She decided to risk it.

Lying back in the unaccustomed luxury of the hot

water, she felt her spirits recover. Perhaps she'd been unfair to Peter. There was so little time left before he went overseas, and she so wanted to leave him with happy memories. Tonight, she determined to make an effort to be loving and responsive, whatever she felt inwardly. Really she was very lucky – she had nothing to complain about.

After her bath, she returned to the bedroom and was dressed before Peter woke up, roused by the arrival of early morning tea. Patty opened the door to receive the tray and encountered a curious stare from the elderly porter. It wasn't often honeymoon couples got dressed that early in the morning.

Peter was astonished too, once he'd rubbed the sleep from his eyes. 'Got to pee,' he muttered and pattered barefoot over to the basin, where he relieved himself. 'What on earth are you doing dressed at this hour?' he asked, returning to bed.

'Well, I had a bath and I thought I might as well. It's getting on for eight o'clock, you know. Here's your tea – mind you don't spill it.' She put the cup down beside him and bent to kiss him. He pulled her down and kissed her again.

'Mmm, you smell nice. Am I all scratchy?' He felt his bristly chin tentatively.

'I don't mind,' Patty smiled. 'Makes me feel married. I'll enjoy watching you shave.'

'I could make you feel more married if you'd come back to bed.'

She pulled away, chuckling. 'Drink your tea before it gets cold. By the time you get dressed, we can have breakfast. I'm starving!'

'There's romance for you!' He gave a mock grimace, then held out a hand. 'I love you, Mrs Quayle.'

'I love you too.' She held his hand to her cheek.

He sipped his tea in silence for a moment. 'Was it awful for you last night?' he asked quietly.

She shook her head. 'It's just . . . well, I didn't

expect . . . Oh, I don't know . . . I'm so ignorant about everything.'

Peter grinned at her. 'I'm not that experienced myself! We'll have to learn together. I'll try to take things more quietly next time. But if you only knew how I'd been longing to make love to you properly – and then—'

Patty loved him so much at that moment, she had to kiss him. She leaned across the double bed. Unfortunately, Peter still had his teacup in his hand – it went flying, and they ended up in fits of laughter, mopping up the bed and carpet.

So the first day started reasonably well. But it didn't carry on that way. Peter had got talking to some Naval officers in the bar at lunchtime, and what started out as just a few social drinks had developed into a heavy drinking session. Patty had soon become bored and suggested going for a walk, but Peter had protested loudly.

'I'm sorry,' she'd replied quietly, 'I just felt like some fresh air.'

But Peter had refused to leave the matter there. He'd taken to calling her 'spoilsport', and pressing her to give up the soft drinks and have 'a drop of the hard stuff' instead. Finally, he'd announced that he felt like going to bed – to sleep it off. This had occasioned a burst of bawdy laughter from the others, but she'd distinctly heard him mutter: 'No such luck, old man! She's got the bloody curse.' At this, Patty had fled to her room and after sobbing her heart out, had decided to ring her mother. Peter had found her on the telephone and accused her of being a 'Mummy's girl.'

'Either I'm a spoilsport or a Mummy's girl – make up your bloody mind!' she retorted, with a rare flash of anger.

He'd been remorseful again, of course, but the damage was done.

That evening the drinking routine started all over again. Patty left him to it in the bar and went to bed. As she lay waiting for him, she remembered her mother's misgivings about their marriage. 'You hardly know him, love,' she'd said. Mum had been dead right about that. Still, he was a Naval officer going off on a dangerous mission and she must try and make allowances.

Patty was still awake when Peter lurched into the room and undressed to the accompaniment of curses and grunts. He slumped on the bed and started to kiss her. All good intentions on both sides were completely forgotten. Peter was too drunk to remember his promise to take things gently; Patty, for her part, had been revolted by the stink of alcohol on his breath and had turned away in disgust. So much for her loving response. She just lay there, still and uncomplaining. Peter felt he was fucking a dummy and said as much, but even this didn't elicit a tear from Patty, who was too miserable even to cry. Deeply disillusioned, she was still staring wide-eyed into the darkness long after Peter was snoring.

It seemed only minutes when he woke again with an urgent desire to urinate. Finding her awake, he hoisted himself on top of her with no preliminaries and began working away like a mechanical drill until he achieved release. At last it was over. He rolled off her and was asleep in a moment.

Patty crept to the bathroom early the next morning, but this time the warmth of the water failed to soothe her pain. The hurt was as much in mind as body. She felt violated, used. How could Peter behave like this if he truly loved her?

It was their last day at Marlow, and Peter seemed to have reverted to his usual self again. The previous night was not discussed, and Patty managed to convince herself that the bad patch was over. They walked along the river in the sunlight; chatted happily over lunch; joked about the ancestry of the steak in the steak and kidney pie, which in reality contained very little of either, and all in all she felt loved and happy once again. But it didn't last. In the evening, Peter hurried her into changing and they went down to the bar, where the drinking started again. Before long Patty made her excuses and slipped away to their room, leaving Peter apparently intent on demonstrating the superiority of the Senior Service by drinking everyone under the table.

Patty was sitting at the bedroom window, looking with longing at the flashes and searchlights playing over London, when heavy footsteps sounded on the stairs. She just had time to pull the curtains back over the window before the door burst open and Peter switched on the light. He was swaying slightly, and when he spoke, it sounded as though he were trying to swallow his own tongue.

'C'mon,' he said thickly, 'this is our last night. Let's go to bed.'

Patty, fighting down her panic, tried to stall. 'It's not our last night, darling. We're going down to your parents tomorrow.'

'Well, it's our last night here, and we're bloody well going to celebrate it!'

'Now, Peter, don't be silly . . .' Patty started, and instantly regretted it.

Peter rounded on her furiously. 'Silly! Being silly, am I!'

'I didn't mean that . . .'

'Oh, yes, you did! You think it's silly for a man to want to make love to his wife!'

'Peter, do be quiet! The people in the next room—'

'The people in the next room, sweetie, have probably been rogering away for hours.'

Patty kept quiet. Anything she said only seemed to make him angrier, so she turned her back on him and started some unnecessary adjustments to her suitcase, which she'd already half packed.

'What the hell are you doing now?'

'Packing.'

'You can do that in the morning. Now's the time for bed!'

Patty took no notice – another mistake, as Peter took it as a sign of compliance. He stepped forward and grabbed her. She gave a little scream and tried to struggle. Peter's drunkenness made him unsteady and he fell heavily forward, pinning her face-down on the bed. So that she could hardly breathe.

Next moment she felt her nightdress being pulled up over her hips and the protective towel being ripped away. The buttons on Peter's uniform jacket cut into her back. Struggle as she might she knew that he'd never stop now . . .

During the drive to Lymington Patty was silent, though to her surprise, Peter whistled happily for much of the way. Patty tried to analyse her feelings. Strangely enough, she couldn't bring herself to hate him. She'd never forget the humiliation and hurt she'd received, but she felt oddly as though she were to blame for it all. Perhaps she'd unconsciously egged Peter on until he couldn't help himself? If so, she could only regret it. At least he'd have to control himself a bit better at his parents' home! Or would he? Patty didn't feel all that sure.

'Will there be anyone else at your parents?' she asked tentatively.

'Shouldn't think so, why?'

'I just wondered. What room will we be in – your old one?'

'Course not! Couldn't swing a cat in my old room. I expect Mum and Dad will give us their bed, seeing that it's just for tonight.'

Their bed! Patty felt an instant surge of relief. In that case, Peter would *have* to behave himself. She leant back and almost enjoyed the rest of the drive through the autumnal colours of the New Forest.

The Quayles couldn't have been more welcoming. The house was even tinier than Patty remembered it, and

Peter had guessed right – his parents had given up their room to the newly-weds.

Peter was quite his old self, showing her off with pride to his parents, and Patty found the traumas of the weekend beginning to recede. As they walked around Mr Quayle's boatyard, Patty admired the neat line-up of boats for hire.

'Do you still get people wanting to go for a sail?' she asked.

Mr Quayle frowned. 'I can't let them have a boat these days. Something to do with spies and suchlike nonsense,' he told her. 'As if any spy would be mad enough to go sailing to France!'

He sounded so sad that Patty tried to cheer him up. Surely the Navy were bound to need an experienced sailor like him?

'No, dear, not at my age, I'm afraid. This war's for young sailors like Peter, not the likes of me. Still, I'm helping out with a fishing boat. The shorter meat gets, the more people will have to turn to fish. But what's happening to you? Would you like to come down and stay with us?'

'That'd be lovely,' said Patty, and meant it, 'but I've got to get back to the Depot.'

'Course,' nodded Mr Quayle. 'I forgot. You've got to tend your ambulances. Peter's got his submarines. I feel quite left out.'

By the end of the evening Patty had lost the strangeness she'd felt at first with the Quayles. She might have known them for years. All too soon, it was time for bed.

The old feather-bed creaked loudly every time Patty shifted position, and she knew every sound must carry to the two little single rooms where Peter's parents would be sleeping. Peter had stayed down stairs talking to his father, and Patty settled down anxiously to wait for him.

She awoke with a start to see Peter holding a towel, and then realized with horror that he was spreading it out on the bed. 'Peter,' she whispered urgently, 'you *can't!* Not in your parents' bed. They'll hear . . .'

'No, they won't,' he whispered back. 'Anyway, they're both asleep. I heard them snoring.'

With tears trickling down on to the pillow, Patty lay immobile during the next five minutes, dreading the creak which came with each of Peter's thrusts. Finally he came with a great shudder which combined with the creaks into one great groan. When Peter propped himself up on his elbows and looked down at her, all he could see were her closed eyes and the twin tracks of her tears. 'Oh, God!' he exclaimed and rolling off, turned his back on her.

Patty's humiliation and rejection were complete. For the first time in her young life, she wished that she was dead.

Patty clung to Peter as if she were losing him forever as he said his final goodbye at the door of Number Seven; but curiously she felt a great sense of relief when he'd gone. It was a relief that covered a great aching emptiness and sadness, but neither of those two emotions had yet surfaced. All she really wanted was to be alone and think things out.

Kath at least understood, and didn't press her into rejoining their close family life at once. Her father, too, simply kissed her and said 'Welcome back, love.' It was as if they'd both decided that questions could come later.

In her room Patty carefully put away all the clothes that she had bought so happily for her honeymoon. The dream was over – at least *that* part of it – and now real life had to begin again. Real life meant reporting back to the Ambulance Depot, and she felt happier when she'd put on her battledress and slung her helmet over her shoulder.

In the few days she'd been away, the nightly trek to the Dolphin Square shelter had become a routine for the Johnsons and now they got ready with the minimum amount of fuss – apart from the statutory grumbles from Gran Bowden.

As Patty entered the Depot, she instantly felt on familiar ground – as if she'd never been away. 'There you are, young lady,' the Colonel greeted her. 'On time as usual.' For a moment Patty thought he was going to forget himself and add that they'd missed her, but of course he didn't.

It didn't take Patty long to find out just how much hell had been meted out by German bombers during her short honeymoon. While she was studying the duty rosters, Arthur Graves came up and greeted her. Patty smiled back. Despite his battledress, she could never think of him as anything else than a retired solicitor in pinstripe and bowler.

'Good evening, Patricia. I hope you enjoyed your honeymoon?'

'Yes,' said Patty. 'Well, that is – I felt guilty, really.' For some reason she suddenly felt she could confide in Arthur Graves.

'Guilty?' Arthur sounded surprised.

'Well, me away from it all – and you lot left here.'

'I see,' said Arthur, and Patty felt that he did.

'I watched the searchlights every night, but it all seemed so far away.'

'Well, I'm afraid we've really been in the thick of it here, my dear. They came every night, you know – sometimes nearly three hundred at a time; never less than fifty. Perhaps I shouldn't say this, but the crews are tired out. And the ambulances – well, we're doing our best with them, but some of them are finished already. If they hit our area hard – I really don't know what'll happen. Still, as the Colonel says, we must soldier on.'

Patty nodded. Evidently, for all their outward differences, there was a great deal of mutual respect between Arthur and the Colonel; in her absence, they seemed to have been welded into a real team.

All over London similar strange partnerships were

being forged under the hammer blows from the skies. At Patty's depot, it was between a disabled old soldier and a retired solicitor; in others, commoners were commanding Lords, thieves worked side by side with retired policemen, and all differences were suspended for the duration – however long that might be.

By the time Patty rejoined the Depot towards the end of September, some ten thousand high explosive bombs had fallen on London – more than one thousand tons in weight. Most of them fell on Stepney, Poplar, Bermondsey, Southwark, Lambeth, Deptford, Shoreditch, Bethnal Green, Holborn and the City, but the riverside areas as far west as Fulham also took a heavy share. In three areas, over a hundred bombs fell into every square mile – and that was in September alone.

Such attacks couldn't leave Londoners unscathed. In fact 5,730 people were killed and 10,000 badly injured. Railways and stations were hit, telephone exchanges put temporarily out of action, roads blocked by craters or fallen buildings; gas, water and electricity mains shattered. Scores of thousands of houses suffered damage, ranging from a few tiles off or broken windows to complete destruction. Hospitals, it seemed, were even more badly hit than other public buildings. For the truth was that the ack-ack barrage, although giving comfort to the Johnsons and thousands of other Londoners, also forced the German air-crews to dump their loads more or less haphazardly.

Patty at the time had no source from which to drew such statistics, but she could see the effect the bombing was having on the Depot. Though it was only early evening, the floor of the main hall was littered with sleeping figures, compared to the two or three she was accustomed to finding there before she went away. The constant vigil was taking its toll.

She had a bigger shock when she went out to see the ambulances themselves. They'd never been exactly elegant, but now there wasn't one that wasn't scorch-marked or scratched and pitted.

While she was looking disconsolately at this scene, Patty noticed two figures deep in discussion over one of the engines. Suddenly one straightened up. 'You'll have to nurse it along, that's all,' said a voice, 'and that wasn't meant to be a pun!' Patty knew the voice immediately. It was Stephen Broome. For some reason the sight of him pushed back the misery that she felt deep inside her.

'Ah! exclaimed Stephen. 'It's Patricia Johnson. Did the Colonel tell you? You're joining my team.'

11

The Longest Night

The telegram boy whistled what he imagined was a spirited rendering of Joe Loss's *In the Mood* as he urged the old red Post Office bike around the corner into Balaclava Street.

It would have surprised him to know that those still left in Balaclava Street heaved a sigh of relief as he passed the door. The simple fact was that ever since the end of the 'phoney war' telegrams meant bad news.

For one heart-stopping moment, Kath thought he was calling on Number Seven as he propped his bicycle against the kerb. But instead, still whistling, the boy turned into the broken tiled path leading up to Number Five and rat-tatted on the Bellings' door. Enid was a long time opening it. She hadn't been back from work long, and she never opened the door without making sure that her make-up was immaculate. After all, you never knew who might be calling, did you? Enid hoped it was a man. Men were much more interesting – in so many ways! As the boy rat-tatted once again, Enid walked in leisurely style towards the front door, preparing a bright smile . . .

It was neighbourly concern rather than plain old-fashioned curiosity that made Kath call on Enid shortly afterwards – or so she told herself. To her surprise there was no reply to her knock, and she was about to go away when she heard a sound from the front room. She peeped in through the half-drawn curtains.

The sight that confronted her was quite a shock. Enid Belling was sitting at the table with a bottle of gin in front of her, and judging by the state of her, she'd made heavy inroads into it. Kath knocked on the window. Enid looked up blearily and then came to open the front door. She moved unsteadily back to the sitting room and slumped in the chair again. Kath followed her.

'Enid! What is it?'

'Silly bugger!' said Enid slurrily.

'Well, really!' retorted Kath. 'I only came in to see if you were all right. I saw the telegram boy.'

'Not you – George!' choked Enid. 'Silly bugger's gone and got himself killed.'

Kath's heart missed a beat. 'Oh, Enid! Perhaps it's a mistake . . .'

'No mistake,' repeated Enid firmly. 'See for yourself. "*Regret to inform you, Gunner G. Belling killed in action.*" That's George. Told him . . . I *told* him . . . Mucking about on ships . . . Not right . . . Silly bugger!'

Incident Report No. 275. Battersea Central. 19.55 hrs. Heavy H.E. on Milton Street. Casualties. Believed trapped. M.1. report follows . . .

At the Depot, Arthur Graves took the call. Colonel Harris waited impatiently while he filled in the report form. It only took seconds, but to the Colonel it seemed that Graves was taking more than his usual care.

Arthur replaced the phone. 'Milton Street. Our patch. Casualties.'

'Right. Send Team A and a messenger. They can send her back if they need more.'

Stan Johnson was sure that Balaclava Street had copped it. The great swishing noise that he now associated with close ones seemed to pass right over the post. Seconds later, a great thud shook the ground and little bits of ceiling fell on to the desk which they were using as a planning table. Stan ran outside, risking the shrapnel, and looked around to locate the site of the bomb burst. For a moment he could see nothing. Then from over the rooftops of Balaclava Street a great cloud of dust welled up, rising higher and higher until it quite blotted out the moon. 'Christ,' said Stan to old Windy, 'that's a big one! Not far away, either. We'd better get over there.'

'Hang on a sec,' muttered Windy. 'Let's call in first and make sure it's on our patch. Otherwise we'll be muckin' up the system – and you know how they hate that.'

Stan agreed reluctantly. All his instincts told him to go and help, but too many people merely caused confusion. Even now Stan could hear the ambulance bells getting nearer. Help was arriving.

Stan wasn't to know that the ambulance on its way to Milton Street was being driven by his own daughter.

Patty had been in the canteen, toying with one of Dusty Miller's less appealing offerings, when the call had come through. To her surprise, Stephen almost pushed her into the driving seat. She'd been gratified to find how well she could handle the ambulance, and had followed his directions with ease. Soon there was no need to tell her which way to go. As they turned a corner, a great cloud of dust rolled like a giant wave to meet them and the air was full of the choking smell that Londoners had come to know so well. It was a mixture of brick dust and the smell of high-explosive, and it hung over shattered buildings for hours after the bomb had struck.

Patty braked hard as visibility was blotted out. 'Go on, go on,' urged Stephen in her ear. 'You'll be able to see again in a minute.' Patty eased the ambulance slowly forward and just as sight returned, the ambulance wheels started lurching over bricks scattered in the road. Another second, and Patty could go no further. What seemed like the entire front of a house blocked the road.

In the cold moonlight, Patty could see that despite their speed, they weren't the first on the scene. A team of rescue workers in black helmets were already toiling at the mountain of rubble that had once been three houses.

Stephen hurried over and reported to the man in charge, Patty stumbling after.

'Good to see you,' replied the man, 'we're gonna need you.' As he turned, Patty stifled a gasp: what stared at her was the face of a clown. Then she saw that white dust plastered the man's face and the front of his battledress, leaving only his eyes and mouth clear.

The clown's face spoke again. 'According to the Warden here, there's a family in this one, but he thinks the others were empty.'

'That's right,' agreed the Warden. 'Only Mrs Jones and her four kids stayed behind.'

Four kids! Patty looked with horror at the mountain of rubble. Four kids under *that*. She felt sick. Suddenly a whistle shrilled nearby, and the men at work immediately froze. 'Quiet . . . Quiet!' Then a quick shout. 'Over here! I can hear someone!' The pattern of men on the rubble shifted, and shadows moved across to the other side of the pile. The whistle shrilled again and a silence fell over the scene.

'I can hear her!' shouted a triumphant voice. 'Keep still, love. We're coming!' And then, more quietly: 'Over here, Guvnor. She's in a right state. Says she's in the cellar, and so are the kids.'

'Right, show me,' said the clown's face. 'You'd be in a right state too, Charlie, if you were under this lot. Where's that bleedin' Warden?'

'Here,' muttered the Warden, clambering after him.

'No offence, mate, but I've got to know exactly where the cellar is. Voices get distorted under rubble. Sounds as though she's at the front and to the right. Is that it?'

'No,' replied the Warden firmly, 'I've been down there. She'll be at the back on the right. That's where all the mattresses were.'

'She bleeding well would be! Look at that lot! There's practically nothing holding it up.' Disregarding blackout regulations, the chief played his torch upwards to reveal the wall of the house next door, leaning at a crazy angle over the very spot where his men were digging.

It took nearly an hour for the men to work their way towards the cellar. They'd now constructed a trench through the jumbled brickwork – a trench that was open to the sky and overshadowed by the wall which seemed to lean at a crazier angle the more they dug into the rubble. Several times Patty noticed the chief of the rescue workers nervously playing his torch over it as the work progressed. Once he pulled all the men back as a cascade of dust showered down on them and the wall creaked ominously. But after a few minutes during which there was no further movement, the cigarettes were stubbed out and work began again.

The leaning wall now effectively screened the rescuers from view, and after due consultation, the chief was able to order in some big lamps to speed up the work without breaking the blackout. Patty, who'd never seen a heavy rescue squad at work at such close quarters, was enormously impressed with their skill. Here was no haphazard ripping at the rubble: no beam which blocked the way was removed until supports were in place around it to take the load. Then and only then was it eased out of the way, to be used in its turn to support some other part of the excavation. Patty could hear the woman quite clearly now, when the whistle shrilled for silence. Gentle words from the rescue men seemed to calm her down, and apparently she and the kids were coping reasonably well in their prison. Only once did she hear her scream, and that was when another bomb whistled down not far away. The impact must have moved something in the rubble, because she screamed out that the whole place was falling in.

'No it isn't, love,' shouted a reassuring voice. 'Hang on, won't be long now!'

And so they waited. Patty heard Stephen send the messenger back to report and was relieved when she returned with instructions to stay put. By now, Patty was determined to see the woman brought out safely, and she was therefore shocked when Stephen said bluntly that the only reason they were staying was because the chances of that weren't good. 'The chief says that wall's shifting. He may have to pull back if it gets any worse.'

'But he can't do that!' protested Patty. 'Not when we're so close!'

'If it shifts, he'll have to – no point in having another six men buried too . . .'

'But the woman and her children . . .'

'If that wall goes, he reckons the cellar will cave in with the extra weight. He knows what he's talking about, he's a construction engineer.'

Patty turned away. She felt choked. So close . . . All her own private miseries seemed to well up inside her, and she felt broken and defeated. She was walking back to the ambulance when a sudden shout stopped her and she hurried back to Stephen. 'What is it?'

One of the rescuers was calling to Stephen. 'Have you got anyone small?'

'*Small?*'

'Yes, small. Don't hang about! We've got a hole here and we reckon someone can get in if they're small enough.'

Suddenly Patty found herself stumbling forward to the rescue trench. 'I'm small,' she cried, 'let me try.'

'It's a girl,' said a voice.

'What difference does that make?' Patty replied angrily.

'All right, love,' soothed another voice. 'Don't shout, or you'll have the whole lot down on us!'

'Sorry,' muttered Patty, and found herself crouching beside the rescue chief. He turned his clown's face to her. 'Now look, kid, if you slide along there you'll drop down into the cellar. But I'm warning you – once you're in . . .'

Patty nodded. 'You can't promise to get me out.'

'Right,' said the chief. 'Now . . . what do you think?'

'I'm going in.'

In the glare from the big lamps, the clown's mouth

twisted into a grin. 'You'll do! Slither in feet first – try to hold on to the side of the hole. It's quite a drop. Then we'll lower anything you want down to you – OK?'

'It's not OK at all,' said a voice from behind her – the voice of Stephen Broome. 'She's not going in. I am. I'm just as thin as she is.'

'Make up your bleedin' minds.'

But Patty's mind *was* made up. Before Stephen could stop her, she slid into the hole, but in her haste, forgot to leave go of her First-Aid kit. As a result she could only cling to the sides of the hole with one hand. Suddenly there was nothing more to hold on to and she fell heavily down into the dark. Her ankle hit something hard and twisted, sending a shaft of agony right up to the back of her head. Somehow she got to her feet and in the faint glow from above saw five frightened faces staring at her. Suddenly, light blazed out in the cellar. A torch dangled down from the hole on a length of cord.

'Now then, Mrs Jones,' said Patty, with a brightness she didn't feel. 'Any of the children hurt?'

'Me,' quavered a small voice.

'That's Freddie,' said Mrs Jones, responding immediately to Patty's manner. 'He's always cutting himself.'

Mrs Jones spoke matter-of-factly but beneath the casual tones Patty heard the stirrings of hysteria. You couldn't blame the poor woman. 'Where's Mr Jones?' Patty asked, as she cleaned and bandaged a nasty cut on the small boy's leg.

'Army,' replied Mrs Jones. 'Catterick. Well out of this lot. He'll be livid when he hears.'

'Yes,' agreed Patty, 'yes, I expect he will. There, that's young Freddie fixed up. Anyone else?'

'I don't feel well,' whined an older girl who'd been sitting away from the others. 'I can smell gas. And I've been sick!'

Patty realized that she could smell gas too. Strongly.

From above a voice called, 'Are you all right? For God's sake, Patty, answer!'

Patty turned. 'Stephen? Stephen? Can you hear me? You've got to get them out now. There's gas down here!'

Stephen's voice was replaced by that of the rescue chief. 'Listen carefully, young lady. Can you hand the kids up to us?'

Patty looked at the height of the hole above her. It was way beyond her reach.

'Not a chance!'

'Hold on!'

'Hurry up! That smell's getting stronger.'

Without warning there was a sudden shower of dust and rubble and Stephen appeared feet first, landing in a heap on the floor. For a moment, he appeared dazed, but then came to his senses and scrambled to his feet.

'Now listen. We haven't got much time. Apart from the gas, that wall's shifting. We're going to have to hand the kids up. Stand on my back and pass them up.'

There was another shift of rubble and a beam creaked ominously as a pair of hands appeared at the hole. More dust fell, and the hands reached even further down from the cellar roof. The unseen owner of the hands said: 'Move it, or we'll all be goners!'

Patty and Stephen snapped into action. Little Freddie cried as Patty prised him loose from his mother. Stephen went down on his hands and knees, grunting as Patty stepped up with the child in her arms, then arched upwards on his hands for maximum height. Even so the rescuer stretching down from above could barely grasp hold of the child. Freddie screamed with pain as the man hoisted him up by one arm and slithered backwards as though being pulled by his ankles, dragging the child out after him. They could hear him screaming for his mother as he was carried off.

The same process was repeated with the two little girls, and they were just about to pass the fourth child up when they heard the sound of a major shift in the structure above them. A shower of broken brick fell through the hole. Directly in front of her, Patty saw dust falling like the sand in an egg-timer from another part of the cellar roof.

'Get the woman up next,' came an order from above. Patty started to protest. 'Why?'

'Don't argue,' hissed Stephen, 'they want the heaviest out now. The hole's closing up!'

Getting Mrs Jones out was easier than Patty had expected. Her added height enabled the man above to get a good double grasp on her wrists as she stood on Stephen's shoulders. She was gone in a moment. But it was a moment too long. Just as Patty turned to fetch little Jimmy Jones, there was a loud crack and a crash. It was clear that the wall above the hole had given way.

For a moment there was silence. Then a slow creaking and cracking of timber. Stephen looked at the roof of the cellar. Patty just had time to look up too. And then like some slow motion film, she saw it coming down towards her.

The next few seconds were chaos. Something hit her hard on the back of the neck and she was flung forward on to her face. Then darkness enveloped her and she could feel bricks and lumps of débris pummelling her legs and body. Then again silence. A funny kind of squealing noise was the next thing. It was as though her brain had gone into slow motion too, and it took her a long time to realize that the noise was coming from her own throat. She stopped instantly; she was only allowing more dust into her mouth. To her surprise, she found that she could raise herself a little and by twisting round on to her back she could push off most of the objects which pinned her down.

Somewhere close by there was a glow, and as Patty poked and pushed away the gritty things that covered it, she saw that she was looking at the torch – more important, the torch was still working, though its beam was being pressed down to the floor. Please God, thought Patty, let me get it free! Let it go on working!

It took her a long time to claw the torch out from its

little tomb, but finally she managed it and was able to swing the beam around. It was like looking through a London fog. The air was full of dust and the space left them was very small. Left *them?* Where was Stephen? Patty whimpered as she shone the torch wildly, trying to penetrate the fog. Then she saw an arm and a leg almost touching her right side. Somehow she heaved herself to her knees and began the task of scrabbling away at the débris that covered Stephen. At first, she thought he was dead. Then by the movement of dust near his mouth she could see that he was still breathing. Desperately, she pulled away the lumps of rubble that still pinned him down, and to her great relief he stirred. He opened his eyes, but it was almost a full minute before he really knew where he was and what had happened.

'Don't worry,' he choked, as more dust cascaded down. 'They'll find us . . .' The fact that he thought it necessary to reassure her was a shock. Until now she'd never doubted that the rescue men would get them all out in the end. Now she wasn't so sure. She glanced up anxiously to see if the roof, such as it was, was about to give way again. Then she remembered Jimmy.

'Stephen!' she almost screamed. 'Where is he?'

'Who?'

'The boy – the little boy – he was down here with us!'

They both stared around and the torch beam swung with them. All at once it lit up the face of Jimmy Jones. He sat facing them, eyes closed as though asleep. Patty scrabbled her way across the dividing pile of rubble. It was only when she got close that she saw why he was sitting so awkwardly – lying back at an angle from his waist. Right across his stomach and the lower part of his ribs was a huge wooden beam.

'He – he's asleep?' Patty wondered.

''Fraid not,' replied Stephen, as he bent over the boy.

'He's not dead!' cried Patty. 'He can't be – he was with us only a moment ago!'

'No,' Stephen's tone was grim, 'he's not dead. Unconscious. But he'll be dead very soon unless they get us out of here!'

Back on the surface, the rescue crew toiled on at the new mountain of bricks and rubble, as the sky lightened and the steady note of the All Clear was heard over London.

12

The Casualties were Small

Patty was late, but Kath decided to hurry on with her chores and not to wait for her. It was nothing new for Patty to be late back, and all she'd want to do when she came in was eat and go straight to bed. Still, it was a pity Kath wouldn't see her, this morning of all mornings.

Kath felt – though she wouldn't like to admit it – slightly nervous about going out to work after all these years. Enid had introduced her to the foreman and he seemed nice enough. He certainly seemed to have no doubts about her ability to do the work. But would she get on with the other women? Oh well, at least it was helping the war effort. And surely, if Enid could do it, helpless, fluffy Enid – well, not so helpless really, but fluffy, yes – if Enid could make parts for aeroplanes, so could Kath Johnson. It was a pity she couldn't have got on the same shift as her, but it couldn't be helped. She'd had a sneaking suspicion that Enid didn't exactly want her on the same shift, but maybe she was just being silly. Enid said she'd tried, but the foreman wouldn't have it.

'Stan!' Kath shouted up the stairs, 'I'm off. Your sandwiches are on the table. See you later! Tim, time to get up!'

'Mum?'

'Yes, love?'

'Bring me back a Spitfire!' Tim had been beside himself with excitement ever since she'd told him that she was going to make parts for fighters.

Grinning, Kath closed the door and hurried off down the road.

Stan Johnson poured himself a cup of tea and was debating whether or not to kill one of the hens, when someone rang the front doorbell. His resolve to kill poor Gert had been strengthened on finding that there was only one egg in the larder.

Stan opened the door, expecting to see Kath there, having forgotten something in her excitement. He was quite unprepared to come face to face with Colonel Harris. For a moment Stan didn't know what to say. The Colonel seemed to bristle with ferocity, and the empty sleeve, the black battledress and the black patch created a sombre figure. Stan recovered himself. 'Morning, Colonel. Did you want Patty? 'Fraid she's not back yet.' That's odd, he thought. It's not like the Colonel to come calling – he usually telephones.

'It's about Patty,' said the Colonel. He cleared his throat.

'She's not done anything wrong?'

'No, no,' declared the Colonel emphatically, 'quite the opposite. But there's been a bit of a hitch.'

Stan felt a sudden yawning sense of dread. 'What do you mean? An accident?'

The Colonel took a deep breath and decided that the best thing was to come straight out with it. 'Your daughter, Mr Johnson, was sent to an incident last night in Milton Street – mother and four children trapped in a cellar. The heavy Rescue Squad broke through, and Patricia volunteered to go down and administer First Aid. Another one of the team went with her. A Mr Stephen Broome. Very brave, both of them.'

'Yes, yes—!'

'They got the woman, a Mrs Jones, and three of the children out, thanks to your daughter, but before they could recover the fourth, a wall that was leaning over the site collapsed and trapped them. They're still down there.'

'You mean they're all right? Just trapped?'

'Well, to be honest, we don't know. There's a great deal of rubble to be cleared before we can make contact. But we've every reason to hope they're unharmed.'

'You're saying that my daughter's trapped under a great pile of rubble and you don't know if she's alive or dead?'

'I came to tell you—'

'I'm sorry, Colonel. Thank you. Where'd you say – Milton Street? Tim!' He called his son as the Colonel saluted and strode off.

Tim emerged from the kitchen, and Stan saw that he'd heard every word. 'Tim! Now listen, son. You know where your mother is. Go and tell her to come to Milton Street – Milton Street, got it? Tell her Patty's all right, but there's a bit of a delay in getting her out. Understand?'

'But, Dad, the Colonel said—'

'Tim, you've got to be a man now. Don't frighten your mother. Just tell her that it'll take a little time. She'll want to be there. Now run along!'

Tim needed no second urging. Now there was nothing else Stan could do. Milton Street was where he had to be, too.

As Stan pushed through the crowds of onlookers behind the tapes, he couldn't help wondering where they all came from. But come they always did. Realizing that they were waiting to see if his daughter lived or died, Stan felt a helpless rage against them, and in his fury barged one aside – a strong-looking man who in his judgment could have been better employed digging than watching. The man spluttered some protest, but Stan stepped swiftly over the tapes, heading towards the centre of operations. As he did so, a whistle sounded and Stan froze with the rest.

In the cellar, half-dozing, Patty heard that whistle as if from miles away. For a moment, struggling back to full consciousness, she wondered what it was. Then its meaning dawned on her.

'Stephen. I can hear them! I can hear them!'

'Hush! Listen.'

From his immediate response, Patty knew that Stephen hadn't been asleep. The torch was switched off – indeed, had been ever since they'd found young Jimmy, Stephen having judged best to save the light for when they might really need it. Patty had wondered then if he'd had it in mind for them to tunnel their way out; but then she'd remembered the great mass of the wall that must have fallen on top of them and knew that it was hopeless.

Patty reached out for the torch, but felt Stephen's restraining hand on it. 'We'll hear better in the dark.' He was right. They continued to strain their ears for voices, both picturing the scene just as they'd seen it before: the whistle for silence. Then the rescuers listening for signs of life.

'Stephen – we've got to call! They're listening for us!'

'Silly of me! You're right! Together then – *shout!*'

Patty shouted 'Help' and Stephen shouted 'Here . . . over here!' And then they stopped.

For a moment, Patty wondered if they'd been abandoned. Perhaps the whistle had been to call the men away for good. But then, almost as though from the next room, she heard a slightly muffled voice. *A voice!* To Patty it could have been the voice of God in Heaven, though in fact what it said was: 'We can hear you. Can you hear us?'

'Yes!' shrieked Patty. 'Oh, God, yes!'

'Right,' said the same muffled voice. 'Now listen carefully. You're not to move. No matter what happens – don't move. Understood?'

'Understood,' called Stephen, 'but hurry! I can't smell gas any more, but the air's getting foul. And the kid's seriously hurt.'

'Got you,' replied the speaker. 'Are you all right?'

'Patty and I are. The boy's got a beam across his ribs. I daren't move it. He's bad.'

Stephen went on to describe their position at the back of the cellar; how the beams slanted downwards, holding back a great slide of rubble; how he'd heard the rubble shift twice during the past hour. With a start Patty realized that she must have been asleep while Stephen kept vigil over her and the little boy.

Then it came back to her. They'd been speaking in the darkness just before she dozed off. He'd been talking about himself – probably so as to keep her from thinking about their desperate plight.

She remembered him saying quite simply that he was a Quaker, and that Quakers didn't believe in fighting. From one or two remarks, she could tell that he'd suffered for his pacifist convictions. Remembering the white feather incident, Patty burned with shame in the darkness. She'd been among his tormentors. Suddenly she had an urge to confess, but while she hesitated, trying to find the words, Stephen started to speak again and the moment passed.

'At least they didn't send me to prison,' he observed.

Patty gasped. 'Surely they couldn't do that?'

'Oh yes – it's against the law to refuse call-up, you know. Every case has to go in front of a special tribunal.'

'Did you have to appear?'

'Of course. It was rather like appearing in a Magistrates' Court. One of the panel was a woman – very fierce. Much worse than the others.' He gave a short laugh.

'Was it awful?'

'Well, it wasn't a pleasant experience, that's for sure, being a Quaker helped – one's principles are well known; but they had to be sure I wasn't just using it as an excuse. My poor mother was cross-examined, and my tutor from Oxford too.'

'Heavens! I'd no idea it was that complicated.'

'They make it like that to weed out the phoneys. Mind you, the fact that I'd already joined the Civil Defence was in my favour. In the end they gave me the choice of staying where I was or going down the mines.' He chuckled. 'Not much difference, as things turned out, was there?'

Patty joined in his laughter. The more she learnt about Stephen, the more she was drawn to him. Paradoxically, she felt safe with him – illogically certain that no harm could befall her while he was around. For a moment she compared him with Peter, but shoved the thought quickly away.

They could hear the rescuers quite clearly now – even the clink as bricks were tossed aside. Then one of the beams over their heads shifted and the rubble ran down, filling a quarter of the remaining space. They heard somebody say: 'Get this fuckin' beam out of my way, Charlie!' Then another of the roof beams quivered, and Stephen shouted: 'No! Don't touch it!' His voice must have reached them through the débris, for Patty distinctly heard the man say: 'Hold it, Charlie. I fink I heard them.' And then the whistle shrilled again and this time the voice was clearer. Stephen explained about the beams holding back the rubble. The voice understood and said in that case they'd have to tunnel in sideways. And that it was going to take a long time.

In the street above, Kath clung to Stan, feeling utterly helpless. Patty under all that! The Heavy Rescue Chief had told her what was happening and how brave Patty was being, but Kath didn't care: she just wanted her out – out here in the open air with her mother and father. Then she and Stan had learnt that it was going to take longer because of the danger of the rubble shifting. At that moment Kath came close to screaming.

In the cellar, every few moments Patty could feel, though not see, Stephen taking the little boy's pulse. But young Jimmy never regained consciousness.

Patty knew that Stephen was holding the boy's hand. She'd seen this in the one brief moment when Stephen had put the torch on, and Stephen knew she'd seen it, because he'd said: 'I don't think he can feel anything, but you never know. I liked someone holding my hand when I was ill.' Later, in the darkness, Patty felt her eyes fill with tears, and because no one could see, she let them run down her face without bothering to wipe them away.

It was when the noise of the rescuers seemed only feet away, that Jimmy gave a deep sigh as though he was coming round. Stephen switched the light on at once, but Patty knew what it meant even before the beam fell on the little boy's face. Somehow in the confined space, Stephen struggled out of his battledress top and placed it gently over the little boy's face. Patty no longer bothered to stifle her tears. 'Easy, my dear,' murmured Stephen. He put his arm around her and pulled her head down on to his shoulder, as the sobs racked her body.

They were huddled together like that when the first rescuer reached them.

Patty tried to go on duty that night, but the Colonel would have none of it.

'Appreciate your spirit, my dear, but you're no good to me in your present state. Go home and get some sleep.' Patty had meekly obeyed. But the Colonel wasn't so gentle with Stephen Broome. Stephen didn't expect to be treated like a hero, but he was unprepared for the lambasting he got from the old man.

'Risking your life like that! Not your job. Leave it to the Rescue Services. Don't do it again.'

'Yes, sir,' said Stephen, taken aback by the Colonel's

vehemence – although Arthur Graves toned down the reprimand by giving Stephen a most uncharacteristic wink from behind the Colonel's back.

Certainly, few of the other crews at the Depot shared the Colonel's disapproval of Stephen and Patty's action. 'Should get a medal,' was the view held by everyone from Dusty Miller right up to Arthur Graves.

Arriving home, Patty found that most of the street had called to offer congratulations on her safe return. She kept out of the way as much as she could, and it wasn't until the weekend that she found a chance to talk to Lesley.

Patty found Lesley fascinating. Not because she hadn't seen her since before her honeymoon, but because her friend was able to fill in all the spicy details of her wedding which Patty hadn't noticed. As Lesley prattled on, Patty saw for the first time what her mother objected to about the Aynsworth girls. 'Tarty' was how she described them, and watching Lesley, Patty knew what she meant.

Lesley seemed a different person. Her make-up was too thick – so thick that Patty found herself wondering if her face would crack if she laughed. As it was, there were lines running down from her nose to the corners of her mouth. The mouth itself was heavy with lipstick, and some of it was smeared on her teeth.

Lesley poured out an apparently endless stream of scandalous stories concerning the people of Balaclava Street. But at the same time, Patty had the impression that she was holding something back. When it finally came, it caught her off-guard.

'What's it like?' asked Lesley suddenly.

'What's what like?'

'Oh, come on!' said Lesley, leering at her. '*You* know . . .'

The question hung in the air and in the warmth of her bedroom, Lesley's sweating face seemed to loom forward at Patty. 'Do I have to spell it out? What was *it* like?'

'All right,' replied Patty almost desperately. 'It was all right.'

But Lesley wasn't satisfied. 'Did it hurt? Did you feel anything? Was it good?'

Patty hesitated. Was she going to tell Lesley that she hadn't been a virgin when she married? Or that Peter had forced himself on her? She suddenly realized that she was cast in the rôle of the experienced married woman and that Lesley was really anxious to know. Maybe if she told her some of it, it wouldn't be such a shock when the time came.

'Yes,' she said simply, 'it hurt a little.'

'Not really big pain? Not like cutting yourself?'

'No. Not like that.'

Lesley was relentlessly curious. 'And his thing – was it big? Is it difficult to get it in?'

'Honestly, Lesley – it isn't like that.'

'Come on – you can tell your Auntie Lesley!'

Patty fenced. Clearly Lesley suspected there was a secret. 'Is it,' she asked finally, 'like they say? Does some great orchestra start up inside you and waves pound on a moonlit shore?'

'You've seen too many films! It isn't like that at all!' For a moment Patty was tempted to tell of the misery and degradation that she'd gone through, but managed to hold her tongue.

Surprisingly, it was Lesley who switched the conversation at that point. It was a good thing she did, for the memories of the gritty pain of Peter's penetration during her period were so much in the forefront of Patty's mind that one more question might have opened the floodgates.

'Do you know what that cow of a sister of mine did to me at your wedding party?' She launched into the tale of Joy and Ian Camp. 'Nicked him from under my nose! Took over all my hard work and shot off somewhere with him. She comes back in his car, looking like a cat that's just swallowed the cream! Well, that's the last time she'll do that, I can tell you!'

'The last time?'

'Too right!' Lesley exuded malicious glee. 'The letter she got today will put a stop to all that! A Government letter, it was – and it wasn't properly sealed, so I had a look. Guess what?'

'Lesley! You mean you opened Joy's letter?'

'It was worth it! Do you know what that cow's gotta do?'

Patty said nothing. Lesley was going to tell her anyway. 'She's been called up!' she announced triumphantly. 'Land Army. Backs to the land! That'll suit her!'

13

A New Threat

PC Williams sighed wearily when he saw that the door of the Farleys' shop was half-open. Day was already breaking; the 'tea-leaf' will be long gone, Bert thought, but there was no point in taking chances. He drew his truncheon and made for the doorway.

From inside the shop there came a distinct sound of movement. Bert's grip on his truncheon tightened and he crept slowly forward. With one heave, he flung the door back and yelled at the top of his voice: 'Police! Stay where you are!'

The figure in the shop had its back to him. Bert kept his distance and said, 'Don't move!' in his most imposing voice. But the figure *did* move. It dropped the box it was lifting down from one of the shelves behind the counter.

The crash of the box hitting the floor startled Bert, and he began to swing his truncheon. He stopped just in time. A blow from a truncheon could kill, especially if it was delivered with full force. He tried to make his voice sound calm and collected. 'Turn around! Let's have a look at you!'

The figure turned slowly, and to Bert's embarrassment, he found himself looking into the frightened face of Peter Farley, the owner.

'Bloody hell! You put the fear of God into me, Bert.'

'Strewth!' breathed Bert, with equal relief. 'What are you doing 'ere at this hour?'

'Look for yourself,' said Farley, waving a hand at the disorder all around him. 'They've done me again!'

'Oh, no!' Bert's groan wasn't really one of sympathy

with the Farleys; it was at the thought of all the forms he'd have to fill in when he got back to the station. Gloomily he drew out his notebook.

'Did they get anything?'

'Some chocolate and a box of gob-stoppers. This is the third time in three weeks!'

'You don't have to tell me,' sighed Bert. 'Is that all?'

'That's all I left here,' Farley told him. 'After the last time, I reckoned it was the cigarettes they were after, so Susan and I take everything home after we've closed up.'

'The whole stock?'

'Stock!' Farley laughed mirthlessly. 'Can't get any bloody stock these days. Don't know why I bother to stay open really. Papers sell quite well, but that's about all that keeps us going.'

'How come you got down here so early?'

'Couldn't sleep for worrying. My deferral won't last for ever, and Sue's got the jitters about carrying on here alone. Can't blame her really. Anyway, got to get the papers ready.'

'What about the old lady upstairs? Did she hear anything?'

'Mrs Grainger? Haven't asked her. She's as deaf as a post, anyway. I heard her snoring when I came in.'

Bert hesitated. His Sergeant might ask him if he'd questioned the old lady. He decided to take a chance and wrote carefully in his notebook: '*Upstairs occupant slept through entry*.'

'Reckon they ought to do what they said in the papers,' said Farley suddenly.

'What's that?'

'Hang 'em! Didn't you read it? People are looting bombed houses – even dead people have been robbed. Paper reckoned the only thing to do was hang one of 'em as an example.'

'That right?' Bert didn't care for the idea. If thieves were going to be hung once they were caught, well – they wouldn't come quietly.

'Yes,' Farley went on, 'they can do it, you know. Under the Defence Regulations.'

Bert looked gloomy. 'They can do practically anything under those new regulations. Requisition your house and furniture for people who've been bombed out. Unlimited powers, the Sergeant calls 'em.'

He finished his writing and then closed his notebook with a snap. 'Well, I'd better be moving along. Anything I can do to help?'

'No,' replied Farley. 'Getting used to it by now. Here . . .' He slipped Bert a packet of twenty Players. 'Take 'em,' he said as Bert hesitated, 'they're like gold-dust. Won't be any left soon, if this goes on.'

Bert fumbled in his trouser pocket for some money, but Farley told him to have them on the house. Bert knew he ought to insist on paying, but then he thought of Madge and the kids and how he was trying to save money to get them all away to the country.

'Ta, very much, Mr Farley, very gentlemanly of you.' The packet of cigarettes made a comforting bulge in his pocket as he walked on towards the end of his beat.

Patty called out a cheery 'Hello' to Harry Hempstead as she passed him on her way to the Depot. She felt fine. A good night and day of solid sleep had worked wonders, and also her relationships with both Peter and Stephen at last seemed to be sorting themselves out.

Her new-found confidence made her quicken her pace. The long hours of blissful sleep had blurred those terrible hours in the cellar. Forgotten, too, were the painful memories of her honeymoon. In fact, when the phone had rung that morning and she'd heard Peter's voice at the other end, she could have forgiven him anything. Well, almost anything. Peter had been sweet: sweet because he sounded repentant; sweet because he'd been kind. He'd been calling from Glasgow – he couldn't say where exactly, but apparently there'd been some sort of delay in his plans and he'd try to ring her again before he left. He'd finished by begging her to wait for him – whatever happened. Patty had almost cried at that, but Peter had only time to say he loved her before he had to ring off.

At that moment Patty was sure she loved him too. But then she rounded the corner of the road and there was the Ambulance Depot. And, suddenly the thought of Stephen Broome dominated everything.

Those hours in the cellar had brought her closer to him than anyone she'd ever known, except her parents. Closer than Peter? Patty was appalled at herself. Surely that was unthinkable? Yet somewhere inside her, she knew that she loved Stephen.

She told herself that it was a different kind of love from her love for Peter. Stephen was more like a brother to her really. But, even so, was it possible to love two people at once? Well, she loved her parents, didn't she? A faint voice inside sounded a warning, but Patty ignored it. Her plan was to avoid Stephen as much as possible – although the very fact that she considered this necessary should have shown her that her feelings weren't exactly of the sisterly kind. And anyway, all her good intentions came to nothing as soon as she entered the Depot. Stephen leaped across the hall to greet her – and Patty made no attempt at all to avoid him.

Surprisingly, after the eagerness of their meeting, both felt a bit shy and awkward. Suddenly the hall started filling with new faces.

People were now pouring in a seemingly endless stream. Police mingled with Wardens, Heavy Rescue mixed with Firewatchers in civilian clothes. There was even an odd army uniform or two, which Patty rightly guessed came from the nearby ack-ack gun site.

'What's all this?' she asked, turning a puzzled face up to Stephen.

'It's a special meeting,' he said. 'Of course, you wouldn't know. It was arranged yesterday while you were getting all that beauty sleep. Dunno what it's about, really. It's for all the Civil Defence in the area.'

'There's Dad!' exclaimed Patty. She waved until Stan spotted her and squeezed his way over to them.

'You might have waited for me!' complained Stan. 'You shot off before I had a chance to tell you I was coming here.'

'What's it all about?'

Stan knew little more than Stephen. 'Something to do with new precautions. Oh, there's old Harry The Horse.' 'Harry?' Patty was incredulous. Stan grinned. 'He's just volunteered as a Warden and I'm to nursemaid him for a few weeks.'

Promptly at 5 pm the Area Controller brought the meeting to order with several short blasts on a police whistle. His first words dropped incisively into the resulting hush. 'Not going to keep you long, ladies and gentlemen, first of all because Jerry will be here soon, and secondly because these gentlemen can't spare the time.'

Everyone's gaze switched to a small group of men sitting almost dejectedly at the back of the stage. Dejected was the wrong word, Patty decided, after studying the men more closely. She knew how they felt. They were tired – dog-tired. And it showed.

'Let's get on with it then,' continued the AC. 'Jerry's up to some new tricks, so listen carefully . . . Major Watkins!'

Major Watkins hardly seemed old enough for a major. His battledress was open at the neck and something like an old spotted handkerchief poked out of it. Yet despite his youth, he had the attention of everyone in the hall.

'I expect you're wondering what right I have to talk to you about Jerry and his bombs. Well, I'm from Bomb Disposal. That's just a fancy way of saying that we try to stop the bloody things going off. I'm here to try to save you a lot of grief.'

Patty had seen the Bomb Disposal lorries and had read

how these men squatted at the foot of some shaft dug under or into the foundations of buildings, patiently disconnecting fuses from enormous bombs. Frequently they failed in their task. She shivered as she realized why this young man was already a major.

'... Up to now, Jerry hasn't been putting too much delayed action stuff down on us. But that pattern's changing. So if you hear a bomb coming down and there's no explosion, just a dull thud, note carefully where it fell, report it, and the boys and I are in business! And if by any chance you see the fins sticking out of a hole, leave it alone! Keep away and keep everyone else away. Don't try and be heroes – leave that to us!' He grinned and gazed round the hall as though to make sure his point had been taken.

'So much for the standard stuff. Now for one or two other nasty little tricks that Adolf's trying out. Let's have it, Bert!'

Bert, an army sergeant, who stood up and casually tossed a complete incendiary bomb across to the waiting hands of the major. Instinctively, most of those sitting at the front of the hall ducked. The major grinned again. 'Getting to be proper veterans, aren't we?' he teased. 'You all know what this is, don't you?'

There was a murmur of assent from the packed rows.

'*Well*,' the smile disappeared from the major's face, 'you're dead wrong. And I mean *dead!*'

Patty saw her father lean forward for a better view. Almost as though confirming Stan's thoughts, Watkins said: 'Yes, it's an incendiary bomb, but there's something different about it. You've got too good at putting them out, so they've added a little refinement. What's the difference? It's longer – not much, but it is longer. And that's because it's got a lump of high explosive in it. Oh, it'll burn like billy-o, just like the old ones. But there's a second fuse in it. And that'll be working away all the time you're fetching your sandbags and your stirrup pumps, and then—' As if by accident, the bomb slipped from the major's fingers and an explosion cracked against Patty's eardrums as the bomb struck the floor. She suddenly found Stephen's fingers entwined round hers reassuringly.

For a moment there was uproar. Then everyone realized that the major was bending down to pick up the bomb. 'That was just the detonator,' he told them. 'Imagine what would happen if the whole lot went up as you were dropping a sandbag on it!'

There was a stunned silence; then near the front a hand shot up. 'Don't bother to ask,' said the major. 'I know! I'm sorry, but I can't tell you how long you're going to have to wait, but wait you must. The fuse isn't all that long. Give it a minute, and I reckon that if it hasn't gone up by then, it's one of the old type.'

Stan thought of the damage an incendiary bomb could do in a minute. Saw again all those residents of Balaclava Street happily dropping sandbags on incendiaries in the road, as they'd done so often before . . .

Patty, too, felt the tension in the hall. Glancing surreptitiously at her watch, she noted that the major had only been talking for a few minutes. But he hadn't finished yet.

'. . . Now that shows you that Adolf's getting upset – and very nasty. He's flinging in the lot and hoping you'll pack it all in and leave London to him. We know he isn't going to succeed in doing that, but there's no point in getting killed to prove it. Which brings me to his next trick. Bert!'

This time the sergeant walked forward, pulling yards and yards of green material behind him. 'Look at this!' grinned the major. 'Pure silk. I'll bet you ladies would give your eye teeth for this!' His glance located Patty and he seemed to speak directly to her. 'But Bert's not going to give it to you, are you, Bert?' Bert grinned, and Patty blushed despite herself. Suddenly she felt very aware of the fact that Stephen was still holding her hand. She pulled it away, embarrassed.

'This, ladies and gentlemen,' continued the major,

taking his eyes away from Patty and letting his gaze sweep the whole hall, 'this is the top part of Adolf's latest trick. It's pure silk because it has to be strong. It has to float a bloody great mine down on top of you – silently. Those of you who served in the last war will remember the land mines, great chunks of metal stuffed full of explosives. Well, Jerry's making new ones – especially for us!' He paused for effect. 'The damage they can cause is enormous. A whole block of flats reduced to rubble in seconds. You can't hear them. At night you can't see them. So why am I telling you about them? Because sometimes they don't go off. They get hooked up on trees. Or hang down the sides of buildings. I've seen one hanging on a church spire. What I'm saying is you've got to clear everyone away – for at least a thousand yards, more if you can. Then report it! Tell us! And Bert'll have some more silk for the ladies.'

The lesson was going home. But the major rammed it in even further: 'The other day one of my men found a young lady heaving at yards of green silk draped over a wall. It looked like a dress that had floated down from Heaven. But when he peered over the wall and told her that there was a bloody great mine on the other end, she fainted clean away!'

The next speaker, who wore the uniform of a Royal Artillery Colonel, came as a bit of an anti-climax after that. But the Gunner Colonel also had important things to say. The guns, he warned them, might well fall completely silent at times. This was to enable British night fighters to try to find the bombers. The silence didn't mean that the guns had run out of ammunition, though the Colonel did suggest that they'd come pretty close to it at times. The Wardens in particular were to reassure anyone who panicked at the silence. For a moment it struck Stan as rather ironical, but the fact was that everyone was now so used to the continuous thunder of the guns that a raid without their background noise might well cause civilian upset. Rumours flew fast, after all.

Then the meeting was over. As Stan heaved himself wearily to his feet, Patty noted the lines of strain on his face. The sleeplessness was taking its toll on him, every bit as much as on the men who'd just been addressing them. Quickly she introduced Stephen and explained that he'd been her companion in the cellar. Stan looked at the tall young man appraisingly and shook his hand. He liked what he saw, but at the same time he couldn't help wondering why this seemingly ordinary young chap should be a 'Conchie'.

Patty walked with her father as far as the blackout curtains of the Depot's entrance. 'Look after yourself, love,' said Stan. 'And don't go taking any silly risks again!'

Patty was about to protest, but saw the anxiety in her father's eyes. 'Don't *you* go doing anything silly either,' she replied. 'You heard what the man said!'

He kissed her on the cheek and then ducking under the hessian, he was gone.

As Stan walked away from the Depot, Harry Hempstead fell into step beside him. Almost on cue, the sirens wailed out. 'Here we go again!' muttered Harry. 'You'd think the bastards'd let us have just one night off, wouldn't you?'

14

The Bomb on the Street

The bomb which fell on Balaclava Street wasn't part of the night Blitz at all. Nor was it a big one, being scarcely larger than the type dropped by the Zeppelin crews of 1915. But it was the best that could be fitted to the Messerschmidt 110 long-range fighter without impeding its speed and performance.

Londoners had become too used to all the attacks at night to take daytime warnings very seriously. For the most part, that sort of thing was well behind them now.

Unfortunately, the same attitude prevailed among some of London's defences. By the time the alarm had reached most of the fighter aerodromes in the southern area, Hauptman Weber was already screaming low under the radar over the New Forest and hedgehopping up to Windsor. When he turned east towards London, there was nothing except the guns to stop him. At this time most of the guns were well into their maintenance routine in preparation for the night's work. But even so Weber's Me 110 didn't come through totally unscathed. A lone Home Guard on Dulwich Common, firing more by instinct than anything, managed to get off half a magazine from a Bren before it jammed, and his aim was true, with just the right amount of allowance for the target's speed.

The German knew that he'd been hit, but it wasn't until he pulled out of the bank and shoved the nose down that he realized that most of the impact had been taken by his observer. It only needed the slightest twist of his position for him to see why his companion wasn't answering his repeated calls. Now all he wanted to do was to get home in one piece – home being Lille North airfield.

Weber had no desire to die, gloriously or otherwise. So he put the twin-engined fighter right down to the deck and jinked around the buildings which seemed to block his path in every direction. As soon as he could see the Thames, he tripped the toggle switches for the bomb release. Only one of the two small bombs he carried fell away; the other one had stuck. At last, after desperate aerobatics, Weber felt a sudden lift and knew that the second bomb had fallen free.

It was this bomb that curved in a low arc down towards Balaclava Street, but Weber didn't even bother to look. He banked tightly over the river and sped down it with nought on the clock, pulling up every now and then to jump the bridges. It was as he pulled up to clear Tower Bridge that the gun barge moored almost in midstream let him have it with everything they'd got. Weber knew nothing. He was dead before his plane broke up in the air and cartwheeled across the surface, to sink in a hundred pieces right in front of a burnt-out warehouse.

The bomb didn't make a loud noise, but it was enough to wake Patty. In spite of her fatigue, she was instantly awake. She knew enough about bombs to realize that this one was close. She scrambled out of bed and into her clothes.

'*Mum! Dad!*' No reply. The house was empty. She grabbed her watch. Just gone nine! Of course – they'd both gone to work. Tim was at school, and Gran was doubtless driving Dusty frantic down at the Depot. No wonder she felt tired. She'd only been asleep for three hours. The Colonel had instituted a new shift system recently, the old changeover at midnight having proved impractical with the raids at full swing. Nowadays the nightshift was from 5pm till 5am; then they had two weeks on days, working from 5am till 11am the first week and 11am till 5pm the second. There'd been a certain amount of grumbling to begin with, but soon everyone got accustomed to the new arrangement and most people admitted it was an improvement under the circumstances. Patty had found it difficult to sleep in the daytime at first, but after a while sheer exhaustion took over – as it had this morning, when she'd dragged herself up the stairs just before six, flopped into bed and gone out like a light.

She peered out of the front door. At first glance, Balaclava Street looked much as usual. Then she noticed a small flurry of activity outside Number Four. As she headed towards it, one of the Depot's ambulances drew up, and Dora Aynsworth and her attendant, Mrs Hoskins, got out. Patty quickened her pace. She could see an elderly warden ushering them inside. It was the vicar, but without his dog collar for once. Harry Hempstead and Sid Raynes were hovering, but he was urging them to return home, there was nothing to be done. *Nothing?* Patty's heart missed a beat – did that mean the occupants were dead? Sincerity Vale and Claude Windsor? Surely not. Patty looked at the house. The front windows were shattered, true, but otherwise there was no apparent damage. The vicar greeted her as she approached.

'Morning, Patricia. Your colleagues are inside.' He sighed. 'I'm afraid it's too late, though.'

In the sitting room, Sincerity Vale sat in her chair beside the chiffonier, the morning paper on her lap and not a mark on her body. For a moment Patty felt an upsurge of hope, but then she saw Dora Aynsworth look up and shake her head.

Patty was used to the sight of death by now, but this was the first time she'd been confronted by the death of someone she knew. She felt the tears welling up. She'd known Sincerity all her life; had idolized her, basked in her reflected glory at school and had often received little acts of kindness from her.

Mrs Hoskins broke in on her reverie. 'No sign of the old man,' she announced.

'Maybe he had a broadcast,' volunteered Patty.

'Yes. Well, the vicar'll have to break the news when we

find him,' said Dora. 'Going to be a dreadful shock, though. They worshipped each other.'

Poor old Claude! Dora was right – he'd be absolutely lost. Patty looked round the room. It was a mess. The bomb had entered through the roof and must have exploded right beside Sincerity. At least she'd have known nothing about it. The blast had blown outwards, shattering all the windows in the front but, remarkably, leaving the framework of the building intact. The chiffonier was unmarked too, and even the glass door and the drink bottles behind it were unbroken.

It wasn't true, however, as later gossip in the street had it, that Sincerity had a full glass of gin in her hand. The blast hadn't been that gentle. The piano was flattened, and the room was full of fragments of coloured glass from her prized collection. The dolls she'd amassed in her travels with Claude were reduced to matchwood, and in parts, the walls were stripped bare of plaster, exposing the scarred red brick. Yet some small objects cluttering every shelf and table in the room had survived. Blast, as many Londoners now knew, could play extraordinary tricks.

There were many tales of people who'd been within a few feet of a massive bomb and survived the blast with little more than cuts and bruises to show for it. But, of course, the lucky ones were few and far between; usually, close contact with a bomb blast brought instant death. The bodies might *appear* unmarked, but a post mortem would reveal massive internal ruptures, collapsed lungs and a displaced heart.

Londoners revelled in their own personal bomb stories. And so the story of the sudden death of Sincerity Vale was absorbed into the folklore of Balaclava Street. But that was later. Now Patty was brought back to the present by Dora's voice.

'You've got a phone, haven't you, Patty?'

Patty nodded. 'Where's Mrs Hoskins?' She hadn't noticed the other woman's departure.

'She's gone off with the vicar to try to get hold of Mr Windsor. We found his address book with his agent's number. I wonder if you'd give my husband a ring and tell him to get round here? No point in taking her to the mortuary – they're full up anyway, and we'd only have to move her again later to Horace's Chapel of Rest. I know that's what they wanted.'

'Yes, of course,' Patty agreed. 'Shall I report in to the Depot for you?'

'Thanks. Tell 'em we'll be back as soon as Horace arrives. Might as well tidy up a bit here.'

'I'll come back and give you a hand,' offered Patty.

'You'll do nothing of the kind,' Dora told her with mock-severity. 'It's your day off, and you deserve it.'

That evening, all the papers carried the story, with big pictures of Sincerity at the height of her musical comedy career. The *News* included one of Sincerity and Claude on their wedding day, and it brought a quiet tear to Claude's eye as he gazed at it on the tube journey to the theatre that night. It had been no surprise when Claude had insisted on appearing in his West End show as usual. Everyone knew the old saying that the show must go on, and as the vicar had pointed out, it was a blessing he had something to keep his mind occupied.

Earlier on, when he'd first returned to the house from the BBC, Claude had been stunned, and had wandered from room to room in a daze. Fred Perkins had already got a makeshift tarpaulin on the roof and assured him he'd soon have the house in good order. Claude nodded dumbly, and then went off to see Horace Aynsworth.

Horace was in his element, his spirits buoyed at the prospect of a big showbiz funeral. He followed Claude into the Chapel, wringing his hands in Uriah Heep fashion and murmuring platitudes of sympathy. Claude just wished Horace would shut up and leave him alone with his beloved. She looked so peaceful, so beautiful . . .

The little undertaker was still rambling on. Claude cut him short. He was certain that his wife wouldn't have wanted anything elaborate in these difficult times; just a small, quiet service somewhere . . . Kew, that was it! The little church where they'd been married. Somewhat crest-fallen, Horace had murmured his agreement and left to take care of the arrangements. Claude didn't want to be bothered with details – he left all that in the undertaker's capable hands.

As it later turned out, Horace almost got his wish for a big service. The entertainment profession turned out in force to show its respect for an old trooper, and the tiny church was packed to overflowing. Fortunately, those of Sincerity's neighbours who could attend had turned up early, otherwise they'd never have got a seat. The Press photographers were busy and Horace, presiding regally in black topper and tails, managed to get his picture in the papers at least twice. He returned home that afternoon, feeling he'd had the most satisfactory day of his life . . .

That day was still to come, however. Meanwhile, there was the show to get through. Claude, whose part was by no means the lead, stumbled once or twice over his lines but still received a standing ovation. As the applause faded, no-one backstage knew that in the privacy of his dressing-room, Claude sat in front of his make-up mirror, and groaned, 'Oh Christ! Oh, Sin darling, how am I going to live without you . . .' and burst into tears. Well, one person did know – the stage-door keeper, who, anxious to clear his theatre, knocked on Claude's dressing-room door and receiving no reply, softly opened it. Claude didn't hear or see him: his head was on his arms, and he was sobbing like a child. The door keeper waited for nearly an hour after everyone else had left, before Claude walked steadily past him, doffed his hat, said 'Goodnight,' then stepped out into London's shrapnel-scarred streets.

The day of Sincerity's death was memorable for another couple in Balaclava Street – the Farleys in Number Six. Returning home at lunchtime, Susan Farley gasped as she took in the mess that confronted her: plaster from walls and ceiling lay thick on the floor, and the air was heavy with dust. Susan's stomach heaved. Thank God, she'd been out when this happened – but what a task to clear it all up! That familiar reaction of panic engulfed her – that, and the urge to rush to her husband for help and comfort. Tears burned her eyes. Then came the second thought: where had the bomb fallen and what damage had it done there?

Her questions were soon answered. 'Are you all right, Mrs Farley?' She heard a voice calling. It was the vicar. He explained what had happened and told her he was waiting nextdoor for Claude Windsor to return from the BBC. Susan thought of the terrible shock in store for poor Mr Windsor, and flushed with shame and embarrassment at her moment of self-pity. The vicar, meanwhile, was tutting with sympathy. Apparently he hadn't noticed anything.

'Be careful here,' he said, 'There's a lot of broken glass mixed up in the plaster. Could give yourself a nasty cut.'

'Oh – my plates!' Suddenly Susan realized that her entire collection of old plates, lovingly accumulated from various junk shops, had been shattered by the blast. She was about to let out a wail of anguish, but caught herself just in time. She should be giving thanks that she was alive – not crying over a bit of old crockery! How selfish she must seem to the vicar. She laughed nervously. 'Oh, well, I can easily collect some more. They weren't really valuable.'

'Look what I've found! Your post.' The vicar was shaking the dust from a couple of letters. Susan put them in her shopping basket without even a cursory glance.

'I'd better hurry back to the shop,' she said, 'Peter'll be worrying himself sick.'

'At least your husband will be able to help clear up this mess.'

'Oh no!' Susan surprised herself with her own vehemence. 'Peter's got quite enough on his mind. I can manage this. I'll get it done by the time he gets home tonight.'

The vicar looked at Mrs Farley with new eyes. She'd always seemed such a painfully shy little soul before. 'I dare say the WVS would give you a hand if you asked.'

'What a good idea! Thank you, vicar.'

He smiled at her and returned nextdoor to await Claude Windsor, satisfied that she was in no need of his ministrations.

Susan went into the kitchen to cut sandwiches for Peter's lunch, and was relieved to find comparatively little damage. This wouldn't take long to clear. But first, she unpacked the shopping basket and inspected the two letters. One was fat and addressed in familiar writing – obviously from her mother and the children; she'd save that for later. Gazing at the other one in its official buff envelope, she froze momentarily. Peter's call-up papers!

The usual tide of panic began to surge up; but then just as suddenly, it receded. To her astonishment, she found herself in control. It wasn't as if the situation was unexpected – they'd known that his last deferment was only temporary. In fact, given that Peter was under forty, they were lucky he hadn't been required before. She'd cope somehow – well, she didn't have any alternative, did she? It was the loneliness that frightened her most, but maybe there was a way around that. A lodger perhaps? Someone to help in the shop? After all, their financial situation would improve with his Army pay and allowances, and they might be able to afford it. Susan's cheeks flushed, not with panic this time, but a feeling of excitement and determination. She'd show her husband that the woman he married wasn't quite the timid, useless object that he'd thought.'

'Amazing! You'd never believe it was the same girl,' Peter Farley confided in Stan, who'd called in for his evening paper and a packet of ten cigarettes.

'I've a feeling this war's changing a lot of things about our women,' replied Stan with a grin. 'There's my wife earning about as much money as me, and I can't see her wanting to go back on short rations again once this lot's over.'

'Too right she won't! Sue's even got some idea about selling second-hand clothes in the shop.' Seeing Stan's mouth drop open, Peter laughed. 'I'm telling you, she's full of ideas. She says if clothes rationing comes in, which seems likely, there'll be quite a market. Specially in kids' things.'

'She could be on to something.'

'I know! I'm not complaining. It's taken a weight off my mind, I can tell you – about going away, I mean.'

'I bet. Know where you're posted yet?'

'Catterick. Could be worse.'

'Yeah.' Stan gave the shopkeeper a friendly nod and started to walk home. He chuckled to himself as he thought over what Peter Farley had been telling him. It was true. The war was certainly changing people. After all, a few months ago who'd ever have thought of Kath building aeroplanes!

15

Saturday Off

Kath Johnson wasn't in the best of moods as she trudged to work early on Saturday morning. For one thing, she hadn't yet got used to working on a Saturday, and for another, it was one of those rare occasions when Stan had the day off. She wished she could have stayed home with him, but Stan would have disapproved – he had a stern conscience where work and duty were concerned. Ah well – he'd probably spend most of the morning in bed anyway, catching up on his sleep. Probably wouldn't even notice her absence. No – the real reason that Kath was dragging her feet was that she was bored with her job. It was so repetitive.

Kath's task was to fit together a nut, a bolt, and a split pin which went through the bolt. When she'd first started, she'd asked the foreman what it was all for and he'd told her it was a vital part of the control surfaces on the tail-plane of the aircraft. Once she knew that, Kath worked as though a pilot's life depended on each and every one – which it undoubtedly did. Everyone at the factory felt the same. If one of those young pilots was going to live or die because of their work, then it was going to be the best they could possibly do. But that didn't make the job itself any less monotonous.

At Number Seven, Stan was enjoying the fine autumn weather. He'd got up late – in fact, it was gone eleven when he awoke and dressed. Then he'd pottered around the house quietly so as not to wake Patty. Poor kid needed all the sleep she could get.

As he made a pot of tea, taking care not to fall into the

lifetime's habit of adding 'one for the pot' – tea was strictly rationed – Stan thought about Patty. Something had gone wrong on her honeymoon; he was certain about that – so was Kath. Stan had always found it difficult to talk to his daughter on the subject of sex – he'd always left that to Kath. But really, what did Kath herself know about sex? She'd been a virgin when they married, and he was pretty sure there'd been no one since. That didn't make her exactly experienced, did it? Mind you, he was no Don Juan himself. He grinned as he let his mind wander back over his own sexual exploits. There'd been that waitress from a Lyons cornerhouse – a 'Nippy'. She'd been nippy all right! Couldn't get enough of it. What was her name – Gloria, no – June – no – *Jean*, that was it! They'd never had it in bed, but she didn't seem to mind. Knee-tremblers against any old wall or tree. Stan smiled at the memory. Wonder whatever happened to her?

Stan had let his tea get almost cold. Finishing it hastily, he strolled out to the garden to see how his cabbages were surviving the Blitz. The cabbages were beginning to swell up nicely, and Stan stood admiring them. 'Dig for Victory' – well, he'd certainly done that, but he still missed the little patch of lawn that had been sacrified for the vegetables.

The sight of a sand-streaked area of earth near the corner of the cabbage patch started him reminiscing again, this time about the kids.

The sand was the remnants of the little sandpit he'd once made for Roger. Then he'd put in fresh sand for Patty when she tired of her dolls, and later still, another load for Tim. Funny how all the kids loved it. Pity they hadn't been able to take the kids to the seaside more often – just a day return now and then. Even that was expensive – something that had to be saved for. When this bleeding war's over, Stan vowed, we'll all go down to the seaside whenever we want!

His train of thought was broken by Enid calling from

the nextdoor kitchen. Stan cursed privately. He'd been enjoying his little interval of nostalgia.

'Do you think you could spare a moment to help me, Stan love?'

'What with?' asked Stan, trying to sound more agreeable. Poor helpless Enid! It was bound to be something anyone else could do in a trice.

'Come and see!' For a moment Stan thought again of Nippy Jean – there was something of the same sort of invitation in Enid's voice now.

Stan didn't bother to go all the way round – the fence was so low that you could step over. But when he pushed open the Belling kitchen door, Enid wasn't there. 'Enid?'

'In the sitting room, Stan.' Stan walked in. He hoped this little job of Enid's wouldn't take too long. He was looking forward to a quiet pint later on at The Windmill.

To Stan's surprise, Enid was standing on a table, still in her dressing-gown. As usual her hair was carefully combed and her make-up slightly overdone. But her stance was flagrantly erotic. It wasn't just the way she was standing on the table in high-heeled shoes; she was deliberately holding her dressing-gown so that Stan got a full view of her legs.

'What on earth? Come down off there, Enid! You'll fall and hurt yourself!'

'Don't be silly! I want you to help me.'

Stan choked. 'To get down? Well, really—'

'No! My legs,' Enid pouted. 'You haven't noticed!'

Stan tried to stay cool. 'Er – course I noticed! Very nice.'

'I've painted 'em. Fake stockings. It's the latest thing. See?'

Stan looked more closely, at the same time trying to keep his distance. Now he could see that her legs were unnaturally brown, almost yellow in places. They didn't look in the least like stockings to him.

'All the girls are doing this,' announced Enid triumphantly. 'Do you like it? You can't see properly from there. Have a closer look.'

Stan knew that he shouldn't, but he did. Enid's legs were good, there was no doubt about that. And looking up at her was good too. Stan suddenly thought again of that Lyons waitress. She'd had good legs. And when she wrapped them around you . . . Stan wondered what Enid's legs would be like wrapped around him. Which was precisely the effect that Enid had intended.

'What do you want me to do?' he muttered.

'Paint a seam on 'em! So they look like proper stockings!'

Stan stood, still looking at her legs, but not moving an inch nearer.

'I dunno,' he muttered, 'I don't think I ought . . .'

'Oh, you men!' Enid pretended to be exasperated with Stan's hesitance, but in reality she was delighted. She was pretty certain she'd got Stan where she wanted him. Now all she had to do was to get him to touch her and Enid knew from past experience that nature would take its course.

Stan felt guilty and excited all at once. He wasn't simple enough to believe that all Enid wanted was for him to paint the seam up the back of her legs. The little bottle and brush shook in his hands. As Enid slowly turned her back on him and hitched up the dressing-gown, he saw that she wasn't wearing any underwear, In fact, he could see a great deal of what a pair of knickers was meant to conceal. Stan could feel his erection rising and swelling and was glad that Enid's back was turned.

'Start at the top, love,' crooned Enid, as Stan made a timid start near her left ankle. 'Be sure to get it straight!'

Stan tried to paint the seam with only the tip of the brush touching Enid's flesh, but it was obvious, as Enid had foreseen, that he'd have to hold her with one hand and draw the seam with the other. As Stan's free hand steadied her on the thigh, Enid seemed to wobble and sank down a bit so his hand rode up into the cleft. Stan withdrew his hand as though Enid was red-hot – which she was – and somehow managed to complete one fairly straight imitation seam on her left leg. He was just about to start on the other – and Enid was figuring how she could accidentally fall off the table and into his arms – when they heard the telephone ring at Number Seven.

Stan tensed. 'That'll be for me.' Enid, sensing the collapse of all her schemes, made a desperate effort to keep the game going. 'They'll ring back, love, if it's important. Let it ring! I can't have a seam on one leg and not the other!'

But it didn't work. Suddenly Stan heard Patty pick up the phone. 'Christ!' he said, 'Patty's up! I'd best be getting back.' And despite Enid's entreaties, he hurried out.

Enid stared after him in fury. 'Oh, fuck!' she blurted out loud. Then, as she got down from the table, she allowed herself a little secret smile of satisfaction. There'll be another day, Stan Johnson, she promised herself. There'll be another day . . .

Nextdoor, Patty had awoken with that lovely feeling of being full of sleep and knowing that you didn't have anything to do for hours. The house was completely silent, and she let her thoughts drift lazily. Mum would be at the factory by now. Gran Bowden would be nagging the life out of Dusty Miller in the Depot kitchen. Patty grinned as she pictured it. Still, the food had improved, and Dusty didn't seem to mind being ordered around. Even winked at her when he'd caught her watching them.

Some time ago, Colonel Harris had caught Gran in the kitchen and demanded to know, in his most military tones, what she was doing there. A weaker woman would have left at once, but not Gran. 'I work here!' she'd told him indignantly, turning to Dusty. 'Ask him!'

The Colonel turned on Dusty, who positively quailed. 'Is that right, Miller? Have you employed this woman without seeking my permission?'

Dusty spluttered, but Gran leapt in quickly: 'Not so much of the "this woman" if you don't mind. Me name's

Bowden, and Patty, me grand-daughter, is one of your people. Anyway, you met me at her wedding.'

'I'm well aware of that, Mrs Bowden. But I'm afraid there's no room for an assistant cook here.'

'Assistant cook!' It was Gran's turn to splutter. 'Whod'yer think's been making the food eatable, eh?'

'Well,' the Colonel's tone became more conciliatory, 'it's true the food's been better lately. But that doesn't alter the fact that there are no vacancies.'

'Pooh!' snorted Gran. 'If I don't sort out this kitchen, you'll have vacancies soon enough. dead – from food poisoning! Worse than bombs some of 'is puddins are!' Dusty winced, but kept out of the fight.

'Perhaps, madam,' the Colonel remarked, conscious by now of a crowd of delighted onlookers, 'we'd better discuss this further in my office?'

'Righty-ho!' And with that, Gran swept out of the kitchen after him like a ship in full sail, to the vast amusement of those watching.

What the Colonel had said to Gran and what Gran had said to the Colonel, nobody but Arthur Graves would ever know; but it was clear who'd won, for Gran had gone straight back to the kitchen and given Dusty a dreadful going-over about his latest offerings. Clearly it would take a great deal more than the Colonel to defeat Gran Bowden.

The house was so quiet, Patty began to wonder if her father was still asleep. Normally, he worked a half-day on Saturdays, but she'd just remembered that he'd got today off. Tim was probably out with a mate from school.

On hearing the shrill tone of the telephone, Patty decided to let it ring a few times to see if anyone else answered. There wasn't the same urgency to get to it that there'd been when Peter was around. It went on ringing, so it seemed the house was empty. She reached for her dressing-gown with a grunt of irritation and pattered downstairs. But the moment she heard the voice at the other end, her bad humour melted away and a glow of pleasure took its place.

It was Stephen! He was offering to take her out for lunch in his uncle's car. There'd be time to go into the country and get back before they had to go on duty. He was brief on the telephone – he always was – but there was a warmth in his voice that belied any apparent curtness. They arranged that he'd pick her up in half an hour.

Just as Patty put down the receiver, her father came running into the house, looking flushed and somewhat breathless.

'Sorry,' he gasped. 'Didn't want it to wake you.'

'It was for me, Dad. Shame – you needn't have run all that way!'

'Only next door,' he mumbled. 'Well, now you're up, how about some breakfast?'

'Just a cup of tea, thanks. I'm going out shortly.'

As Patty ran upstairs to get dressed, she was far too preoccupied with her own feelings of guilt to notice her father's. She knew her parents would disapprove of her going out with Stephen. But what was she supposed to do? Live like a nun until Peter came back, whenever that might be? Stephen had already taken her to a couple of lunchtime concerts and Kath had voiced her disapproval then. Patty had insisted that there was nothing to it but companionship – had tried to explain the special bond of friendship they shared after the night they'd faced death together – but her mother had simply shut her mouth tightly as if unwilling to prolong the argument further. Gran, naturally had been more forthright. 'Playing with fire, that's what you're doing, me girl!'

Patty debated whether or not to tell Stan where she was going and decided she'd have to. He was bound to see the car when Stephen called for her. At least there wouldn't be any time on their return for the inevitable lecture from Mum.

It was a bit of luck Stephen getting the use of the car.

His uncle had an engineering works in the Midlands, though they'd probably switched to making armaments now. She wondered how the family squared that with their pacifist principles. She'd have to ask Stephen.

It was marvellous, the relationship they had. Sometimes she felt she'd known him all her life . . . She blushed. She'd no business to be thinking those kind of thoughts! Peter had only been gone a month. It would have been different if she'd heard from him, but so far, she'd only had one letter which he'd written the night before they sailed. She'd tried to write to him every day at first, but she'd run out of things to say. After all, there weren't that many ways to describe an air raid, and Peter didn't knew the people at the Depot, so she couldn't liven up the letters with little anecdotes about them. And that was her life, really – other than her trips with Stephen, which she only mentioned in the most general way. She blushed again and wished she didn't feel so guilty.

By the time she was dressed and downstairs, the telephone was ringing again. It was Lesley, asking her to go out to a tea-dance.

'I can't very well, Lesley.'

'Why not?'

'Well . . . I'm married.'

'What rot! You said you and Peter had agreed you wouldn't live like a hermit.'

'We did – but somehow I don't think he'd like to think of me going dancing.'

There was an explosion of scorn at the other end of the line. 'Do you imagine he'll stop in when the other lads go ashore?'

'I suppose not. But I can't go today anyway. I've been asked out to lunch.'

She knew Lesley was avid to hear more, but she cut short the conversation on the pretext that her father needed the phone. Poor Lesley. They used to be so close, and now she'd been ousted, first by Peter and then by Stephen. Patty knew she was hurt, and yet Lesley just wouldn't understand that their drawing apart was inevitable. If only Patty could help find her a boyfriend of her own.

Claude Windsor looked out on the traffic wending its way down Shaftesbury Avenue that Saturday morning and knew that he'd have to return to Balaclava Street: he couldn't put it off any longer. Immediately after Sincerity's death he couldn't bear to go near the house – it was too full of memories – and he'd gratefully accepted dear old Billy's invitation to share his little flat overlooking Shaftesbury Avenue. Claude's eyes suddenly filled with tears. How his darling Sin would have laughed at the idea of him shacked up with Billy. 'Nobody loves a fairy when he's forty, darling,' he could hear her saying. But she'd know it was nothing like that. Just two lonely old men living together with their memories.

Right now he didn't think he could ever live in Balaclava Street again – not alone. It was strange how sure he'd always been that *he'd* be the first to go – he'd pictured Sin living out her days quite contentedly in the little house. But maybe she would want him to carry on there. Had he any right to shut the door so firmly on their life together? Perhaps in time he wouldn't ache with longing for her every time he walked up the front path. Thanks to Billy, he didn't have to take an irrevocable decision all at once. He could shut up the house and live here for the time being. But that still meant going over to Battersea to sort things out. Sin wouldn't like the place to be left in a mess.

Claude straightened his shoulders and ventured out into the street. In front of him was an exceedingly rare object – a taxi. 'Where to, Mr Windsor?' asked a cheerful Cockney voice, and a vaguely familiar face grinned at him over the meter.

Almost automatically, Claude opened the door and

climbed in 'Home, James,' he said – and wasn't surprised when the cabbie set off unerringly for Battersea.

Stan saw the old actor arrive in the taxi, but decided to give him a little while on his own before popping over to welcome him back. Claude wasn't allowed much time to himself, however. He'd hardly stepped inside when there was a hesitant tap at the door. Opening it, he found Miss Jessie Wilkes bobbing about on the doorstep like a little sparrow. She was clutching a pot of yellow chrysanthemums.

'Please don't think I'm intruding, Mr Windsor,' she murmured softly, 'but I just thought I'd pop over with this little welcome home offering. I know Miss Vale always liked to have flowers around the house, and I hoped these might make you feel a bit better. Not that anything can really but – well—' Miss Jessie's voice trailed off in embarrassment as she found Claude staring at her with his eyes full of tears.

'How very kind – so sweet of you!' Claude felt choked with emotion. He took the pot and looked around vaguely for a place to put it. Miss Jessie indicated the mantelpiece, now rather bare with the broken bric-a-brac cleared away.

'So many of your lovely ornaments broken, I'm afraid,' she sighed.

'They were mostly Sin's. You know, Miss Jessie, I really shouldn't accept your flowers. I mean, I'm a bit of a fraud. I haven't come back to stay – just to try to sort things out.'

Her face fell momentarily, then she smiled. 'Of course. I should have thought. But you must take them with you!'

Further conversation was interrupted by another knock on the door. This time it was Harry Hempstead.

'Saw you got back, Squire,' he wheezed. 'I stopped your milk for you after the . . . you-know-what. But I get plenty myself, so I've brought a pint for you.'

Claude was about to embark on further explanation when Stan arrived on the scene, on the pretext of checking up on the repairs to the house.

Claude was suddenly like a lost child, overwhelmed by the unexpected kindess of his neighbours. It seemed appropriate to offer a drink. At least the bottles and decanters had escaped destruction. He managed to hide his emotion as he busied himself with pouring the drinks. He didn't want to make a fool of himself by bursting into tears.

Claude commented on how tidy the house was after the mess he remembered from last time.

'You can thank Miss Jessie for that,' Stan told him. 'She's been hard at work here every day.'

'Not just me,' she protested. 'All the WVS lent a hand – and my sister, of course.'

'You did the donkey work, though,' insisted Stan, 'even if your sister did the organizing.'

'My sister *is* very good at organizing,' replied Miss Jessie. Stan couldn't be sure, but he thought he detected a twinkle in her eye.

Claude sipped his Scotch and started to explain how he planned to shut up the house and live in Shaftesbury Avenue. But he was quite overwhelmed by a chorus of dismay from his listeners.

'Never sell it while the war's on,' said Harry.

'Doesn't do to leave a place empty,' added Stan. 'If the council don't commandeer it, you might get squatters in, and Heaven knows what they'd do to the place.'

'You just can't leave the street,' was Miss Jessie's contribution. 'Not after all these years.'

Claude was touched. He hadn't realized before the genuine affection in which he and Sincerity were held by the neighbours. Suddenly he glowed with a reciprocal warmth towards them all and began to feel he'd be guilty of desertion if he went ahead and left the street. The others saw him waver and pressed home their advantage.

'Course, you feel cut up about the place right now,'

Stan told him. 'But you don't want to rush into things. You might feel differently in a week or two.' There were nods of agreement from Harry and Miss Jessie.

Claude blew his nose and looked around the room, remembering the evenings he and Sin had spent there together; the little showbiz parties before the war, when old friends had gathered . . . Perhaps they were right – perhaps he should hang on.

'Well . . .' he began, 'I *was* going to ask Harry here to sell the furniture for me – lock, stock and barrel . . .'

Harry spluttered. Miss Jessie gasped. 'Bit drastic,' was Stan's terse comment.

There was a momentary silence, the three visitors staring at Claude as he wrestled with his feelings.

Harry reflected. There were some nice pieces, and no mistake. Make a tidy profit. On the other hand, he shared the street's affection for old Claude. After all, they were nextdoor neighbours, and you didn't make money out of a friend's grief, did you? You had to have some principles, even if you were Harry The Horse.

Eventually Claude spoke. 'It's Sin's things, though . . . must sort them out . . . don't know if I can bear it.' His voice broke and once again he blew his nose.

'Don't you worry, my dear.' Miss Jessie crossed the room and gently guided Claude to an armchair. 'You just sit there and drink up. I'll sort out her things and then you can tell me what you want done with them.'

After that, things went smoothly enough. Claude was only too grateful to be fussed over and sat in the chair, imbibing quantities of Scotch and directing operations, while Miss Jessie arranged Sincerity's clothes in a neat pile, ready for the WVS. All except the furs – Harry was to sell those. 'Should get you a few bob for these all right, Squire,' he breathed, stroking them reverently.

Claude waved a hand airily. 'Whatever you can, old boy.'

It was then the trouble started. Claude wanted to take something as a present for old Billy, his current host.

Eventually he settled on a little Meissen figure that Sin used to keep on the dressing table.

A few minutes later, Miss Jessie came down the stairs, shaking her head. The statuette had gone. 'I found this open too,' she added, handing a leather jewellery box to Claude. He clicked his teeth disapprovingly. 'Sin was so careless. I was always nagging her to lock it.' But even Claude's florid complexion paled when he looked inside and found it empty.

Stan felt a sickening tug at the pit of his stomach. Not again! He remembered how Rita Perkins' jewellery had been stolen after their bomb. He'd heard talk at the Warden's post of widespread looting in this area, but it hadn't really come home till now. It was disgusting!

'The poor old boy was quite stunned,' he told Kath later. 'Course, Claude didn't want to report it at first. Felt it might have put suspicion on people in the street. But we persuaded him in the end.'

'Quite right, too. It's – well, really horrible.' Kath grimaced. 'I suppose it was all insured?'

'I expect so, but it was the sentimental value, more than anything. I went nextdoor to see if Bert Williams was around. Walked right into a blazing family row, too.'

'Oh dear! What's it all about this time?'

'Money, I think. And the baby seems to be sick as well.'

'I know. Madge had to take him to the doctor's – he's got bronchitis. No wonder really. Germs spread like wildfire in that shelter.'

'Yes – and just you take care of yourself,' Stan told her. 'Don't want you cracking up.'

'Oh, I'm as tough as elephant hide,' Kath grinned. 'I feel sorry for poor Madge, though. I must see if I can help out a bit tomorrow so she can get some rest.'

'Old Bert was damn glad of an excuse to get out of the house, I can tell you.'

'Has he got any suspects?'

Stan shook his head. 'Nothing definite. First people on the scene were Harry Hempstead and Sid Raynes, but the vicar showed up soon after, so they wouldn't have had much time to pinch anything.'

'Might have marked things down for later?' suggested Kath.

'Maybe,' nodded Stan. 'Then Dora Aynsworth and Mrs Hoskins arrived, hotly followed by our Patty. Next was Horace Aynsworth, to take away the body. Then the vicar had a long time alone, waiting for poor Claude—'

'Surely you can't suspect the vicar,' interrupted Kath.

'Course not! I'm just telling you who had the opportunity. Last of all came Miss Jessie and her WVS ladies. Oh, and me, on my night patrol.'

'Stan!'

He laughed. 'Well, *I* know I didn't, and *you* know I didn't, but the police might think otherwise. Seems to me the whole neighbourhood's suspect.'

Kath looked at him gravely. 'Well, I just hope they find it's a stranger. It would be awful if it turned out to be someone we know.'

She looked so miserable, Stan gave her a hug. 'It's one of the bloodier things about war, love.'

She sighed. 'Everything about the war is bloody. Every bloody thing!'

16

'UXB'

At night, a flash of flame over twenty feet high spurts from the barrel of a heavy anti-aircraft gun every time it's fired. Stan Johnson had long ago learnt to distinguish these gun flashes from other deadlier lights in the sky. But this particular night, London was already brilliantly lit. A full, rich harvest moon floated over the city.

The gunners cursed the moon. It was no help to them. The firemen cursed the moon, knowing that no German navigator or bomb-aimer could wish for a better guide. Stan and Harry Hempstead looked out over the moonlit scene, and like thousands of other ARP wardens, they too cursed the moon.

It was one of those big moons that made you feel small and vulnerable, bathing you in its cold, white light.

'Bloody 'ell!' exclaimed Harry, 'I'll bet Jerry can even see the colour of our eyes!'

'Won't need flares tonight that's for sure,' agreed Stan. His voice sounded unnaturally loud, and it was a moment of two before he realized why. The guns had stopped. Stan glanced at his watch. It's only ten-thirty. Surely Jerry can't have finished yet?'

As if in reply, there came the steady throb-throb of German engines from high above their heads. A bomb whistled down somewhere far away.

Stan was alarmed. 'What's the matter with the guns?' The ack-ack guns might sling a lot of shrapnel down on them, but nobody minded so long as they kept thumping at Jerry. Suddenly, searchlights close by switched on and started waving back and forth as though beckoning. In the silence, they heard another engine note. It was different somehow. Faster. Harry was the first to cotton on.

'It's the fighters,' he shouted. 'They've put the bleedin' fighters up. See how you like *that*, you Jerry bastards!'

At that moment, one Jerry bastard was finding the moonlight and the lack of gunfire particularly unnerving. He knew perfectly well why the guns had stopped: it could only mean night fighters.

He put his aircraft into a slow diving turn, and as he did so, a searchlight beam flicked across him. Down in Battersea Park, the searchlight crew cheered as for a moment they spotlit the German bomber.

In the cockpit of his Hurricane, Squadron Leader Johnny Johnston from Biggin Hill also cheered at the sight. Suddenly out of the blackness ahead, there was the unmistakable sparkling silhouette of a Heinkel 111. From the leisurely bank of the raider, Johnston assumed he hadn't been seen. He slipped in behind, closing rapidly; soon he was only yards from the bulk of the Heinkel, which now filled his entire windscreen. He fired and broke away. For a few moments he thought he was going to ram the German, who continued his curving descent. Then flame bellied from the bomber and it roared on through the night, glowing redder and redder around the open bomb doors. Seconds later, fire bloomed in the sky.

'Christ!' shouted Stan into Harry's ear. They got one!'

As he spoke, the fire reached the bombs and there was a mushroom of white light as a hundred incendiaries all ignited at once and the bomber disintegrated in the sky above their heads. They dived for cover, but not before they heard the ominous sound of a whistle screeching above. Stan burrowed himself as deep as he could into the earth of the nearest front garden. The expected explosion never came. Nothing but a great thud, and then silence. Stan knew. And Harry knew. 'Unexploded,' muttered Stan, sitting up. 'Where'd you reckon?'

'The Farleys?'

'Further. Sid's or the Aynsworths, more like.'

The entry hole wasn't difficult to find. It was much bigger than Stan had expected, and it was bang in the middle of Horace Aynsworth's pocket-handkerchief-sized lawn. 'Strewth!' wheezed Harry. 'That's a whopper!'

By dawn on Sunday morning, Balaclava Street was roped off at both ends with 'Unexploded Bomb' notices planted squarely in the middle of each entrance to the street.

Bert Williams was posted at the Battersea Bridge Road end and a War Reserve policeman was on guard at the other. All the houses except Harry Hempstead's were empty. Harry had insisted on letting his aged mother stay put, claiming that his house was in no immediate danger. Stan could see the logic in this, but privately wondered if Harry's reluctance to move out had more to do with the goods hidden in his cellar than concern for his mother's welfare.

Soon after dawn, most of the residents of Balaclava Street had started to return home from the shelters. They'd protested at not being allowed to go past the ropes, and now gathered in a grumbling group on the side nearest Harry's house. Stan let them stay there, reasoning that the curve of the road would shelter them if the bomb did go off. Enid Belling had been one of the first to arrive, but though she'd fluttered her eyes at Stan, she hadn't made much of a fuss otherwise. 'If *you* say so, Stan, then we must do as you say.' She checked her make-up in her handbag mirror and dabbed a little extra Californian Poppy behind her ears.

As the rest of the Johnson family approached the street, they immediately feared the worst, but Bert quickly set their minds at rest. Kath's face lit up when she saw Stan, and she rushed to embrace him. He explained what had happened and the other residents listened attentively. After that, the grumbling stopped and they all stood around and waited. Harry suddenly appeared with a tray of cups and a pot of tea, and for a while the group had looked a bit like the street party they'd had for the Coronation, except, of course, that there was precious little to celebrate this time.

Soon after, Patty arrived from the Ambulance Depot and reported that Dora Aynsworth had gone straight to her shift from a night in the shelter. Poor Dora had no idea about the bomb in her front lawn.

It was Horace Aynsworth who was the biggest nuisance of all. He'd taken to spending the night at the funeral parlour and had popped back for a quick wash and change. Now he was indignantly demanding access to his house.

'I don't care where the bomb is,' he exclaimed furiously. 'I've a perfect right to go into my own house.'

Waving Stan away pompously, he made to step over the rope. Bert Williams moved forward.

'I'm warning you, if you cross that rope, I shall have to arrest you.'

'Arrest *me!* What for?'

'Obstructing a police officer in the execution of his duty!'

Horace hesitated. This was a side of Bert Williams that neither Horace nor anyone else in the street had seen before. What the outcome would have been it was impossible to say, for at that moment a three-ton army lorry with brilliant red mudguards roared round the corner and skidded to a halt right in front of the 'Unexploded Bomb' sign.

A head poked out of the nearside window. 'Morning, gentlemen. I believe you've got something for me?'

Stan found himself looking up into the face of the young major who'd lectured to them the other day. Major Watkins didn't look so young now. There were dark rings of fatigue around his eyes, and he seemed to have aged visibly as he climbed out of the cab and dropped to the ground.

'Up the road, sir,' Stan told him. 'Just round the bend.'

'Where we'll all be if we get much more of this.' The

major turned to someone in the tarpaulin-covered back of the lorry. 'Bert, let's go and have a look!' Stan wasn't surprised to see Bert, the sergeant, climb over the tailboard of the lorry. Obviously, where the major went, so did Bert.

'Who reported this one?'

'I did,' said Stan. 'I've found the entry hole too.'

'Good! Saves a lot of time. C'mon then, you'd better show us.'

The major and Bert set off calmly up the road. Stan only hesitated for one second, during which he could almost hear Kath say '*No, Stan*,' then hurried to catch them up. Bert Williams stayed behind – someone had to make sure that no-one else climbed over the rope. Horace Aynsworth had retreated into the group of residents and looked a little pale, the arrival of the Bomb Disposal Squad having brought home the reality of the situation.

'Any idea what direction it came from?' the major asked Stan.

'From over the Williams's house. That's almost directly opposite. We could see the aircraft burning. It wasn't very high by the time it exploded.' The major stopped him there and questioned him closely. By the time he'd finished, they were looking at the hole in the front garden of Number Ten.

Bert walked straight in through the gate, lay down and squinted down at the hole, then turned to the major. 'Well, Boss, the Warden's right – she wasn't very high when this baby fell out. The angle's low. I'd guess she's not in very deep either. There's clay under here. Roses like clay, did you know that?'

The major laughed. 'So you're always telling me! Question is, will I ever get the time to grow any? Is she a dud or a real DA?'

'No way of telling, Boss. Picks and shovels, the only answer.'

'Is it a big one?' ventured Stan.

'My guess is no,' replied the major, showing no inclination to move away from the hole, despite Stan's edginess. 'You can't tell a great deal from the entry point. I've seen really big ones make a tiny hole. Depends on the soil and the angle.'

To Stan's relief, the major at last moved out of the garden and strolled back towards the lorry.

'Why do you think it's a small one then?'

'By what you told us, sounds as thought she was carrying a whole load of incendiaries. Wouldn't have room for a really big one with that lot, eh, Bert?'

'Nah,' agreed Bert. 'A small one. And a dud, too.'

'A dud?'

'A dud as opposed to a delayed action. Sounds as though this one was blown out of the racks when she went up. May not have armed itself – may even have been damaged. We'll know soon enough.'

The more he heard, the more relieved Stan was not to be in Bomb Disposal himself. You'd have to be crazy to join that lot!

'Christ, Bert, look!' exclaimed the major. A crowd of mud-stained soldiers holding cups of tea were standing around the tailboard. In the middle of the circle, Stan saw a redhead and a blonde. By the look of it, the Bomb Disposal men had found the Aynsworth sisters.

'Trust them to find crumpet,' grinned Bert. 'That little red-head looks a likely candidate for a nice green silk dress.'

'Steady!' admonished the major. 'She's a bit young.'

'Never too young to learn,' cracked Bert. Stan felt there was another side to the sergeant that perhaps wasn't so heroic. The major's frown seemed to confirm this opinion.

A quiet command, and the soldiers were soon on their way with picks and shovels. It was noticeable, however, that the sergeant didn't accompany them, but lingered to talk to Lesley, who was obviously flattered by his attentions. Stan frowned. The sergeant was old enough to be Lesley's father! What was Horace Aynsworth thinking of, letting his daughter carry on like this?

'A penny for them,' said Kath's voice suddenly.

'Oh – er, I was just thinking about those soldiers. What a job!'

'I expect you get used to it,' said Kath. 'Wonder when we'll be allowed home?'

'I wonder if we'll *have* a home.'

The major had said there was no harm in using Numbers One and Two as shelter for the residents, so Harry took some and Rita Perkins the rest. Which was just as well, for the wind now carried more than a touch of winter with it. Soon the only sign of life in Balaclava Street were the solitary figures guarding the ropes and the group of men digging up Horace Aynsworth's front lawn.

It was mid-morning by the time the major and Bert returned to the lorry, but there was something about the way they walked that told Stan that they'd uncovered the bomb. As he moved towards them, the major answered his unspoken question. 'A hundred and fifty! Dud – thin casing – intended for the firemen after the incendiaries.'

'So what happens now?'

'We'll get it off your patch, then find ourselves another baby.' The sergeant grinned as he swung himself up into the lorry.

Stan thought for a moment that the grin was one of relief. But then he turned and saw that it was for Lesley, who was scurrying towards the lorry. 'Seven o'clock, love. Don't be late!' shouted the sergeant and let in the clutch. The lorry lurched forward up the road towards Number Ten.

The major looked after it, then at Lesley. In an offhand way, he muttered: 'Be careful of those lads of mine.'

Lesley giggled.

'You don't understand. They're a tough lot. Have to be in their job.'

'I can look after myself,' retorted Lesley, obviously offended at being treated as a child.

'You'll need to,' said the major grimly. It was his last word on the subject.

Very soon the red-painted lorry, bell ringing, roared back down the road, slowed to let the major jump up, and then disappeared round the corner at speed. Even as the bell died away in the distance, people were hurrying back to their own homes. Well in the lead was Horace Aynsworth.

Stan stayed long enough to undo the ropes and fold up the 'Unexploded Bomb' signs, and then headed homewards. As he climbed the stairs to bed, Kath called from the kitchen.

'I'll have lunch ready for four o'clock, okay?'

But Stan's reply was unintelligible. He was almost asleep on his feet.

It was mid-afternoon before he awoke. Down below, there were women talking. But it wasn't Kath's voice he could hear.

Kath had gone nextdoor to the Williams's to mind the children for a couple of hours while Madge had a lie-down. She'd been so grateful, but Kath had protested it was little enough

'You can't go on like this, love,' she'd told her, taking in the white face and darkly-shadowed eyes. 'You'll crack yourself up.'

Kath's sympathy had opened the floodgates, and all Madge's worries, tensions and fatigue had risen to one unbearable crescendo. Kath had bustled Bert out of the kitchen with the older children and told him to take them to play in the park. Even so it had taken some time to quieten Madge.

'I'm so sorry, Mrs Johnson. I don't know what came over me.'

'You're just dead tired, that's all,' Kath soothed.

'I'm frightened to drop off in case I don't wake up again,' sighed Madge. 'It's such a slog getting them all over to Dolphin Square, but I daren't not go.'

'I know. Madge, listen – we've been through this before, but don't you think you'll have to consider evacuation?' Madge stared back at her and mutely shook her head. 'It'll be forced on you if you get ill,' Kath went on. 'Surely it's better to arrange it in your own time?'

'It's the money, see,' explained Madge. 'I'd have to give up me job, and things are tight enough as it is.'

'Well, maybe you should send the children on their own. You're making yourself ill, love.'

Madge gave a deep, shuddering sigh and closed her eyes. Kath doubted if she'd sleep, but the rest would do her good. She crept down to the kitchen to look after the baby.

Back in the Johnsons' kitchen, Patty was listening to Lesley chatter away about her latest conquest. But it was some time before she realized exactly who was responsible for Lesley's euphoria. 'You don't mean the Bomb Disposal sergeant?'

'Course!' Lesley replied in surprise. 'Who'd you think I meant?'

'Well, it sounded like Clark Gable at least! Seriously, I thought you meant the major. You said he was in charge.'

'Oh, *him!*' Lesley said dismissively. 'He's just a boy. Bert's really in charge.'

'But isn't Bert a bit old for you, Lesley?'

'Not really. Anyway, you know I prefer the mature type.'

Patty didn't, but she let it pass.

'I'm meeting him at The Feathers just across the river at seven. He says he'll give me some parachute silk for a dress. He must be pretty keen on me, don't you think? Love at first sight!'

'You hardly know him!'

'Look who's talking! How long had you known Peter?'

As Lesley wittered on, Patty found herself reflecting her own life, and once more she was filled with doubts and uncertainty. It was becoming difficult to think about Peter with the love and the ache of loneliness she'd felt at first. She could hardly remember now the intense feeling of closeness and warmth they'd shared in those early days. But the last few nights driving for Stephen's team had been, despite the hell all around her, nights of great happiness. She felt wanted. She was doing a worthwhile job. And she was good at it – Stephen had told her so several times. Once, Stephen had almost kissed her. More, she'd *wanted* him to. He'd been leaning towards her when someone had rapped on the side of the ambulance and shouted: 'Tea up!'

Suddenly Patty was jerked back to reality. Lesley was accusing her. 'Patty! You're not listening! I said, will you come with me?'

'To the pub?'

'Where else, stupid! I don't much like the idea of walking in all by myself.'

'No . . . but – well, couldn't Joy go with you?'

'Joy? She can make her own dates, thanks very much.'

'The trouble is, I've already arranged something.' Patty felt overwhelmed by guilt as she saw Lesley's downcast expression; not only for the way she'd treated her old friend, but because the arrangement she'd made was to meet Stephen. She hesitated. 'All right! I'll go with you. But I'll have to leave when your boyfriend arrives, okay?'

'Thanks, Patty. Great. That's one in the eye for Joy!'

In fact, although Lesley was unaware of it, Joy had plans of her own. Plans which would have surprised her younger sister.

17

A Night to Remember

The siren wailed its warning almost at the same moment as Lesley pushed aside the blackout curtain and stepped inside The Feathers. Patty followed her. The sudden flood of light made them blink. The pub was surprisingly crowded, and for a moment they hesitated in the doorway as Lesley looked round for Bert. The two girls were the subject of a number of approving stares – but not from the landlord. He didn't encourage unaccompanied women in his pub. As the girls approached nervously, he fixed them with an icy glare. 'How old are you two?'

'Old enough to be married, so there!' retorted Lesley. 'Show him your ring, Patty.'

'All right, all right!' Satisfied, the landlord returned to his customer, a fat man thumbing open a roll of fivers.

The girls had never been in a pub on their own before. The truth was that Lesley's drinking was confined to a half of shandy with the girls after work, or a rare gin and orange at parties. Patty's was only a little more sophisticated thanks to her outings with Peter.

While they hesitated, the fat man didn't. 'Fancy a drink, lovies?'

'No thank you,' replied Lesley. 'we're meeting someone.'

'Can still have one while you're waiting,' laughed the fat man, once again flashing his roll of crackly white fivers. Patty decided she definitely didn't like the look of him. 'Come on. What's your poison?'

It was Lesley who relented. 'A half of lemonade shandy.'

'Shandy! You could handle more than a shandy!'

'A gin and orange then,' Lesley ventured.

'Same for me, please,' echoed Patty.

'No gin,' announced the landlord. 'Come on, Charlie, is that the lot? Can't stand here all day.'

'Give'em a rum and orange,' rasped the fat man, and slapped another fiver onto the counter.

'Christ, ain't you got nothin' smaller?'

Fat Charlie shrugged. Lesley took the proffered rum and orange. She didn't like the look of Charlie either, but at least he'd drawn them in to the bar. One or two of the men were now definitely leering at them. Thank goodness she'd persuaded Patty to come along!

'Cheers,' said Charlie.

'Cheers,' said Lesley, feeling suddenly quite a woman of the world – then choked on her rum.

'Too much orange?' asked Charlie, seeing her splutter. 'Here Fred, you've drowned it. Put another rum in there!'

'No, really!' Lesley's protest was to no avail.

'Cheers,' repeated Charlie.

Patty took only the smallest sip of her drink. She already regretted coming out on this adventure and was wondering how soon she could get away. Stephen would be waiting in Prince of Wales Drive. Surreptitiously, she glanced at her watch.

'Who you waiting for, darlings? Your husbands?'

Lesley was beginning to like the fat man. Fancy him thinking she had a husband! 'No,' she told him. 'Sergeant in Bomb Disposal. My friend's keeping me company till he arrives. He's late.'

'Oh,' grunted Fat Charlie, 'they're not usually in yet.'

'You know them?' Lesley was surprised.

'Course! They're often in here. Your sergeant – is he a big fellow?'

'Yes – yes, he is.'

'That's Bert.' Charlie winked knowingly. 'He's a one!'

Suddenly the curtain was yanked aside and a whole

stream of men in uniform poured into the pub. Finally Bert came into view, bringing up the rear.

'Hello, darling,' he grinned, coming straight to Lesley. 'Cor, you look gorgeous!' Lesley reeled with pleasure. Just like the films! She looked at Patty smugly. Now she'd see she wasn't the only one who could make a conquest.

'He's a one, our Bert,' laughed Fat Charlie. 'Evening, Bert.'

'Ev'nin', Charlie. What you going to buy us heroes, then?'

With a mock sigh, Charlie drew out his roll of notes and bought drinks all round. Lesley was a bit annoyed with Bert for bringing his mates with him; but maybe he couldn't get out of it. She thought about all those unexploded bombs, and Bert risking his life every day. He really was a hero. She glowed a little inwardly to think that he'd singled her out for his attentions. She leaned a little closer to him and was rewarded with a quick squeeze.

Patty rather spoilt the occasion by leaving almost the moment introductions had been made. Lesley had counted on her to talk to the others so that she could have the sergeant to herself.

Charlie suddenly announced: 'I'm orf,' and added in a loud aside to Bert, 'She'll look lovely in green silk. Go with *all* her hair,' There were sniggers from the others as Charlie swaggered out.

'I brought the silk,' Bert told her, and unbuttoning the front of his battledress jacket, showed her the green package underneath. 'Wraps up really small,' he whispered into her ear. 'You'd be surprised how much I've got here. Make nearly two dresses for a slim young thing like you.' And she didn't mind at all when his hands wandered appraisingly over her waist. 'Got a lovely sexy feel, it has. It'll cling to those little titties of yours a treat.'

Lesley giggled, suddenly feeling distinctly wobbly. She hadn't really noticed the amount of rum Bert had been pouring into her glass. ' 'Ere come on, love. You look as though you could do with a bit of air,' he whispered.

'Let's you an' me go out and see how the raid's getting on.'

With that, Bert put an arm around her and steered her to the door.

Once outside, she felt a lot better. She knew, of course, that Bert hadn't really taken her outside to see how the raid was getting on. In fact it was very quiet now, with only a few searchlights wavering away to the east – not that Lesley in her woozy state could have told east from west.

'Where are we going then?' She giggled, as Bert led her purposefully through the darkness.

Bert's answer surprised her. 'I'm gonna show you something that very few people are allowed to see.'

'Wassat?'

'The inside of our lorry! Here we are! Just a moment while I get up and help you over the tailboard.'

Lesley's memories of that scramble into the lorry were hazy, but somehow she made it. Inside, it was pitch dark.

'Here!' She could feel herself swaying. 'I can't see a thing! I'm going to trip over!'

'No, you won't, my little darlin',' said Bert. 'I've got you! There – now let's sit down all nice and comfy.'

Lesley did as she was told, and Bert was right: it *was* all nice and comfy. She closed her eyes and felt herself drifting away happily – but not so far away that she couldn't feel Bert's hands moving expertly over her breasts. He kissed her, and as if by magic she felt her blouse drop open. She melted in his arms and only started with surprise when she felt his teeth gently grip her left nipple. *Up top's all right*, she remembered Joy saying . . .

But soon Bert showed he didn't know Lesley's rules about top and bottom, and started moving his hand down well below her waist. Lesley found herself gasping as though short of breath. His embraces became more urgent and his fingers thrust their way into her soft cleft. She moaned, but any protests were smothered by his mouth over hers. Anyway, she didn't feel like protesting too much – it was quite a pleasurable sensation.

'Blimey,' she heard him mutter. 'You're already wet.'

Lesley was a bit puzzled. It was true – she was unusually moist between the legs.

Suddenly the sergeant shifted his position and Lesley found herself pinned down by his weight. She started to scream as one of his hands ripped away her knickers, but her cry was stifled as the sergeant jammed his other hand firmly over her mouth. 'Don't you start *that*, darlin'. You asked for this, and you're gonna get it! I don't stand for no prick-teasers.'

Lesley struggled, trying to clamp her knees tight together, but the Sergeant's leg forced them apart. Lesley felt sick. The only thought racing through her mind was that she was being raped. She bit the hand over her mouth as hard as she could. The sergeant grunted with pain and removing his hand from her mouth, gripped her painfully around her throat. Lesley stopped struggling. If Bert kept up the pressure on her throat much longer, she was sure she'd die.

'That's better,' he said quietly. Lesley felt the grip on her neck relax, but the hand stayed there, ready to be reapplied if need be.

She wasn't sure if it was before or after the Sergeant penetrated her that she heard the truck start up. But he was certainly in her before it drove off, because the sudden lurch forced the thing that was at the same time stiff and yet soft, so high that she thought it would come out of the top of her head.

After the initial shock of the rape, Lesley didn't much mind the sergeant thrusting and pushing away. But when she realized that he wasn't going to withdraw, she panicked. Christ! The girls had told her all about that! She'd be pregnant! Why had she ever come out with him? That young officer had warned her, hadn't he? Lesley started sobbing.

'You can cut that out too,' muttered Bert between

thrusts. 'Can't stand cry-babies.' Cry-baby! Lesley's sobs only increased in volume. God! What a fool she'd been. She suddenly felt her stomach heave. 'Lemme up!' she cried, 'I'm gonna be sick!'

The sergeant moved quickly, rolling off her, but Lesley was oblivious. All she was aware of was an unstoppable tide of vomit rising in her throat.

At last the retching stopped. 'Here,' said the sergeant, in something like his normal voice, 'wipe yourself up on this.' In the darkness, Lesley groped for the proffered handkerchief, and she did her best to clean herself up.

'Better?' said the sergeant. Lesley gulped and her nose seemed to fill with the stench of rum and vomit. She started crying again, silently this time.

'C'mon!' The sergeant's voice seemed more confident. 'I only did what you wanted! You was real 'ot for it.'

'My father'll kill you,' wailed Lesley.

'Oh, yeah?' the sergeant sounded cocky now. 'Then I'll tell him how you was flashin' yer tits and grinding yer arse into me in the pub. I got witnesses . . .'

'I never!'

'Anyway,' the sergeant shifted position, 'he'd have to kill a lot of fellers by now!'

For a moment his words didn't sink in. Then Lesley felt a mixture of anger and dismay. 'What d'you mean?'

'*What d'yer mean?*' The sergeant's voice mimicked hers. 'Well – what about the other fellers before me?'

Lesley was dumbfounded. For a second or two the words wouldn't come out. 'I never had anybody. Ever!'

'You mean you was a virgin! Hear that, lads? The lady says she was a virgin. Didn't feel like it to me!'

Lesley was about to reply when she realized that the sergeant hadn't spoken only to her: there were others huddled there in the darkness, even though she could see nothing. Suddenly a gun flash lit up the interior of the speeding lorry. And Lesley's horror became reality. There were at least four other men in the back. One face in particular was grinning, and it wasn't Bert's.

'Here!' Lesley's voice rose in a shriek. 'What's going on!' Before the flash died away Lesley could see that she was lying on a filthy tarpaulin and that her skirt was up round her waist. A crash of gunfire drowned her scream. She started to scrabble frantically towards the square of dark blue that must be the tail of the lorry.

She didn't make it. Strong hands grabbed hold of her and something soft was stuffed in her mouth. Struggle as much as she might, she was quickly spread-eagled back on the tarpaulin. 'C'mon lads,' said the sergeant, 'Who's next?'

Patty and Stephen sat in front of the gas fire in his bedsitter, listening to music on his gramophone. At least, Stephen was listening. Patty had only half a mind on Tchaikovsky; the other half was worrying. She felt bad about leaving Lesley on her own in that pub. A girl on her own was at a disadvantage, and those soldiers seemed a tough bunch. Though heaven knows what good she could have done if she'd stayed. Walking back over Albert Bridge, she'd almost asked Stephen if they could return to The Feathers. But Lesley probably wouldn't have thanked her, and for sure Stephen would be the subject of hurtful taunts and jibes. She decided not to say anything.

It was the first time she'd been to Stephen's place. It seemed like a palace compared to the poky little rooms of Balaclava Street, and some of the pieces of furniture were evidently genuine antiques despite their shabby appearance. Patty was somewhat overawed, but Stephen soon put her at ease. He ushered her into the kitchen with a joke about his culinary prowess.

'I've survived months of Dusty's cooking,' she quipped back. 'I don't suppose you can kill me off that easily.'

As it turned out, Stephen produced some very creditable omelettes made with dried eggs. In fact, Patty was ashamed to see that he was rather better in the kitchen than she was. 'More practice!' he explained. 'We bachelors have to learn to make do.'

Later they'd taken their mugs of tea into Stephen's room, which was smaller and cosier than the big drawing room. And here they were now, sitting on cushions on the floor, with Tchaikovsky drowning the sound of the desultory raid outside.

'Penny for them.' Stephen's voice cut across her reverie.

Patty was startled. The music had stopped, and Stephen was staring at her intently.

'What's worrying you?' he asked.

She stared back at him in silence. His eyes seemed to look right through her, yet somehow she didn't mind at all. They were kind eyes, and held a deep concern for her. All of a sudden she found herself explaining her fears for Lesley.

Stephen consulted his watch. 'We could go over there now, if you like. There's still time before the pub shuts.'

She shook her head. 'They're bound to have moved on, and then we'd have had that trek for nothing.'

'Okay. I must say I prefer it here to a pub.'

'So do I. That place was packed. We'd have had to stand.'

There was a comfortable silence; then Stephen chuckled.

'What's so funny?'

'You! All concerned about the moral welfare of your friend, and yet here you are, alone in a man's bedroom, totally at his mercy!'

Patty giggled. 'You're different.'

'How do you know, my dear?' Stephen twirled imaginary moustachios. 'I've got you in my power, wench!'

He grasped her in his arms and they were both laughing uncontrollably when in a flash the mood changed. Suddenly he bent his head and kissed her hard. Patty kissed him back. Her arms went round his neck and she held him as if she'd never let go. Then just as suddenly he released her and turned away.

'God – I'm sorry.'

'Don't be. It wasn't your fault.'

'I didn't mean to.' He turned back to look at her. 'Don't get me wrong – I *wanted* to kiss you, have done for ages, but—'

'I know.' Her eyes were full of tears.

He wiped them away gently. 'Don't cry, my darling, please. The last thing I want is to upset you. I was a fool to ask you here, but I thought I'd got things under control . . .'

'I wanted you to kiss me, too.'

'Patty, I'm not playing games,' he said hoarsely.

'Nor am I. Oh Stephen, I don't know what I'm going to do.' She buried her face in his chest. His arms went round her again, but this time he held her gently, almost paternally. After a few minutes, she looked up. 'Now it's my turn to be sorry,' she whispered.

'Don't you think it's about time you told me what's troubling you? Maybe I can help.'

And so she told him. All about Peter, about the honeymoon, about her disillusionment with love and marriage.

'It's a crying shame!' he muttered, after a long silence. 'It doesn't need to be like that, Patty, believe me! If only I could have been the one to teach you – to show you how wonderful it can be.'

She sighed. 'I should have listened to my parents. They said I was too young to get married. But at the time . . . Oh, this wretched war! I suppose we blame everything on that.'

'It has a lot to answer for. You wouldn't have got married so quickly if Peter hadn't been posted abroad.'

'We were so sure we were right . . . and now I'm afraid we've made a dreadful mistake.'

'You haven't given it much time. You'll work things out.'

But Patty heaved a deep sigh and looked more forlorn than ever.

He took her hand and kissed it. 'My poor little Patty. I wish I could help.'

'You do! If only you knew what it means to be able to talk to someone who understands.'

Once again he stared into her eyes in silence. Then he looked away. 'That's the trouble! I can't do it any more.'

'Why?' The cry came involuntarily from her lips, but whether it was a protest or a plea, she wasn't sure.

He turned towards her. 'I think I'm in love with you,' he said simply.

Patty felt herself trembling as emotion flooded through her. He'd actually said the words. Words that she'd longed to hear. Words that made her happy and proud. 'Oh Stephen.' She bent forward and kissed him on the lips.

His arms went round her and he kissed her hungrily; then just as suddenly he put her from him. 'That's what I'm afraid of, Patty. That's why we mustn't see each other any more.'

'I don't think I can bear it – not now we've just found each other.'

'It's no good. It can't come to anything, so it'd better stop now before anyone gets hurt.' He stood up and held out his hand. 'Come on, I'll take you home.'

They didn't speak much as they walked to Balaclava Street. Both of them felt flat, and it was all rather an anti-climax. Patty was glad they didn't meet her father on his nightly patrol. All she wanted was to slip quietly inside and be alone with her thoughts. They paused at the gate to Number Seven.

'Well, goodnight,' said Stephen awkwardly.

'Stephen,' Patty put a restraining hand on his arm. 'We can't just say goodbye like this. I mean, we'll be meeting at work all the time. Do you want us to avoid each other?'

'Of course I don't!' There was such obvious pain in his voice, that Patty had an overwhelming urge to kiss him again. 'You know what I want, but you're a married woman, so that's that. At work I'll try to act as normally as possible. It's when we're alone it's so difficult.'

'We can stay friends then? And still go to concerts and things?' she pleaded. 'I promise we'll behave ourselves.'

He smiled. She seemed so very young, like a little girl being denied a treat. 'Oh Patty! Have you any idea how difficult it's going to be? For me at any rate.'

He bent and kissed her lightly on the forehead, then hurried off as if fearful he might give way to further temptation if he lingered. Patty watched him out of sight, then went inside.

In her room she lay in bed for a long time, staring at the ceiling, trying to sort out the confusion in her mind. Was she in love with Stephen? Certainly she felt very different from the way she'd felt for Peter at the start – a feeling that she had to admit wasn't really standing the test of absence. Had that been just a passing infatuation? All she knew for certain was her joy when Stephen had told her of his love, and her longing to be in his arms again, to feel his lips on hers.

God, Patty – what a mess you've made of your life! She turned on her side facing the wall which reflected the occasional flashes of gunfire, but sleep didn't come easily.

It was Stan who found Lesley – found her staggering along Balaclava Street near the corner by the Perkins' house. He thought it was just a drunk at first. It was only when the figure got closer that he saw it was Lesley. It was her red hair that gave her away.

Seeing her dishevelled state, Stan's first reaction was disgust, particularly when he caught the smell of rum. It was only when she looked up into the moonlight that Stan saw the damage that had been done to her face. One eye was almost closed; her cheek was puffed up; and the whole area round her mouth was red, and her top lip was split. She wore no coat despite the frost in the air, her blouse hung open and there were black, smears of oil around her breasts.

'What the hell . . .!'

Lesley stepped back, alarmed. Stan took a grip on her arm, and she cowered as though to dodge a blow.

'It's all right, Lesley. It's me, Stan Johnson. You know me.'

Recognizing his voice, Lesley twisted her head to bring her good eye to bear on him, then dropped her head again as though it was too heavy for her neck to support it.

'Mr Johnson . . .' The voice was faint and pain-laden.

'Yes, love. It's me. What the hell happened?' Even as he asked the question, Stan had a vivid flashback of the sergeant grinning over his shoulder. He felt a great anger welling up inside him.

'They . . . they . . . all . . .'

'*They?*'

Lesley's mouth twisted as though it was an effort to get the words out. Stan pulled her towards him to catch the faint whisper. Even though he had a fair idea by now what had happened, the words shocked him. 'They all . . .' said the strange little girl voice, '*fucked me* . . .' And she collapsed into his arms.

For a moment he comforted her like a child, murmuring: 'There, there. You're all right now.' Then Lesley finally gave way to tears.

'There there, love. They'll pay for this. They won't get away with it.'

But as soon as he'd said the words, Stan felt helpless. Here he was in the middle of the road with Lesley Aynsworth, whom he'd known since she was a toddler, and he didn't know what the hell to do next. As if to remind him that the road wasn't the safest place to be, shrapnel suddenly fell like hailstones on to the roofs nearby. He'd have to get Lesley into shelter. But where? It was her mother she needed, but Dora would be down at the Ambulance Depot.

If only Kath were around! Who was left? He ran

through the names: the Williams family? No, Madge and the kids would be in Dolphin Square with Kath, Tim and Gran. Bert could be anywhere on this beat. Enid . . .? *No* – and anyway, she was on nightshift.

Stan half-carried Lesley into the shelter of the Perkins' porch. A neatly chalked 'O' on the door told him that Rita and Fred were sheltering elsewhere. At least someone followed his instructions!

Suddenly he remembered the Wilkes sisters. Every night, as soon as the siren sounded, they went into their Anderson shelter. And they were women. Miss Mary was a bit of a pain, but Miss Jessie would be a comfort to a girl in trouble. The Wilkes it would have to be.

'C'mon love,' he reassured Lesley, 'we'll get you sorted out.'

As it turned out, Stan had made the right choice. Miss Mary had kept up her usual nagging at Miss Jessie, but the two of them had been an excellent First-Aid team. One could almost believe that attending to young girls who'd been raped was something they coped with all the time. Stan's only real worry was that they'd abandoned the shelter and insisted on using the house for their good work.

In next to no time they had Lesley cleaned up, out of her tattered clothes and into a nightdress. Then they settled her down on a mattress and plied her with successive cups of strong tea. It was only then that Miss Mary started firing questions at Stan.

'Now Mr Johnson! Have you informed the police?'

'The police?'

'Of course! That girl has been savagely raped by at least four men. It's a matter for the authorities.'

Stan realized that Miss Mary was right. 'I'll see to it in the morning,' he replied. 'How is she?'

'As well as can be expected, given the way those brutes treated her. She's badly bruised, but not much worse. That cut on her lip should have at least one stitch in it, though.'

'What – right now?' I don't think any doctor would thank us for bothering them now.'

'Just then the door opened and Miss Jessie tiptoed in.

'Jessie!' breathed Miss Mary. 'You haven't left the patient . . .?

'It's all right, Mary.' Miss Jessie spoke with unusual firmness. 'She's sound asleep.'

'The best thing for her. I suppose the doctor can wait till the morning.'

Stan was about to speak, but found himself being firmly guided to the front door. 'Goodnight, Mr Johnson. Tell Mrs Aynsworth to come and see me. And don't alarm her. These things are better discussed woman to woman.'

As Stan started to walk back to the ARP Post, a small Army staff car passed him and stopped outside the Aynsworths. Stan saw Joy get out, and was about to go over and tell her about Lesley, but he stopped himself. Miss Mary was right. Some things are better left till morning, and woman to woman.

18

The Talk of the Street

The rape was the sensation of Balaclava Street, even taking precedence over bomb stories for a short while. The men, in general, tended to think that Lesley had brought it on herself and that she'd got no more than she deserved. Whereas the women were uniformly of the opinion that no matter what a girl did, there was no excuse for rape.

The subject was complicated, of course, by the fact that the men involved were in general regarded as heroes – so there was a bit of sympathy for them. At The Windmill, the more pints were devoted to the argument, the more confused the matter became. Stan got close to the crux of the matter when he said to Fred Perkins: 'It's like those Roman gladiators. 'Cos they might die the next day, they used to give them anything they liked. Women – wine. I read about it.'

And Fred Perkins got even nearer when he added: 'Right, Stan. But they *gave* them women. This lot went and helped themselves.'

Whatever the rights and wrongs, the street was united on the one thing: it was a matter for the police. There was no need to have beaten the girl up. Justice would have to be done.

Stan and Kath had discussed it at length. Kath had, of course, immediately translated the matter into the terms of her own family. 'Supposing it had been Patty.' The thought had shocked Stan and he'd tried to dismiss the idea.

'But our Patty wouldn't have egged them on like Lesley did. You saw her, Kath—'

'Six of one and half-a-dozen of the other,' replied Kath.

'What's that supposed to mean?'

'It means they got her stinking drunk and then took it in turns! Don't tell me it's not their fault as much hers!'

Stan decided to drop the subject. It was clearly liable to lead to a row, and he could do without that. Patty had acted strangely about the incident, too. Stan had been surprised to meet her getting up to go on early shift as he'd come home to bed. Most nights, she was either working or at Dolphin Square with the family, and they didn't see each other.

'Wish I'd known you were here last night,' he exclaimed. 'Could have done with your help.'

As he broke the news about Lesley, Patty turned quite pale with guilt.

Stan, however, couldn't understand why she held herself responsible. 'Don't be silly, love,' Stan he told her. 'It was damn good you left the pub when you did.'

He stumbled wearily into the bedroom, much to Patty's relief. If the discussion had gone further, she might have had to confess where she went on leaving The Feathers. It might also have explained the full extent of Patty's guilt, which wasn't all to do with leaving Lesley alone, if the truth were told.

It was some time before interest in the incident finally died down. Particularly as Bert Williams had to take a statement from Stan and the Wilkes sisters. He grumbled about it afterwards, complaining that everything seemed to happen on his patch. He was, however, strangely silent about Lesley's statement, which he'd taken shortly after she'd been seen by the doctor the next day.

Only Patty had some idea why Bert was so tight-lipped, because Patty was one of the few people to hear the full story at first hand.

Patty had been going the routine morning maintenance

tests on the ambulance, when Dora Aynsworth had appeared round the side of the bonnet.

Dora wasted no time: 'Lesley'd like to talk to you.'

'Oh – I was going to call round yesterday,' replied Patty, 'but I thought . . . Well, you know . . .'

'No, no,' Dora cut in quickly, 'she wants to talk to you.'

Patty hesitated. 'How is she?'

Dora sighed. 'Difficult to say. Her father didn't improve matters by blowing his top. But maybe she'll speak to you.'

Patty smiled. 'I'll do my best, Mrs Aynsworth. Poor Les – it must have been frightful.'

'As for Bert Williams!' Dora went on. 'He frightened her to death. Made it sound as though it was all her fault. The poor kid cried for hours afterwards. And now she's got to go to the station and tell it all over again.'

'Well, I'll be round later. Hope I can cheer her up a bit.'

Lesley was in her bedroom when Patty arrived – probably keeping out of her father's way, Patty suspected. She was surprised at how young Lesley looked without any make-up. But the biggest shock of all came when Lesley turned full-face towards her. A great purple bruise seemed to spread halfway down the side of her face, and the puffy upper lip made Patty wince.

'Right mess, aren't I?'

'You're no Betty Grable at the moment, but you'll look fine once that bruise has gone.'

'It's a shiner all right,' sighed Lesley. 'But at least it shows I tried to defend my honour!' Lesley gave a short laugh that had little mirth in it.

'Oh, Lesley.' Patty couldn't think of anything to say. She felt tears pricking at her eyelids.

'Now then!' Lesley's voice quivered. 'Can't have two of us blubbing over it. What's done is done. I expect they're all saying I got what I deserved, aren't they?'

'Of course they're not!'

'You can't kid me,' scoffed Lesley. 'You should have heard Bert Williams knocking on and on.'

'He had to ask you those questions. If they prosecute—'

'They won't! Not if PC bloody Williams is in charge. I saw the way he looked at me. He'd have been in the queue himself, given half a chance.'

'Lesley! Bert's a policeman!'

'They're all the same. *I* know!'

For a moment Patty was silent, remembering how Lesley had plagued her with questions after her honeymoon. Yes, poor Lesley certainly *did* know now.

Suddenly she remembered one of Lesley's earlier remarks. 'What do you mean they won't prosecute them? Surely they know who they are?'

'No, they don't!' announced Lesley. 'I haven't told them!'

Patty stared at Lesley's bruised face in disbelief, but her friend said nothing – just stared back in quiet defiance. Then, suddenly, she began to cry, the tears trickling down unchecked on to her dressing-gown.

Patty put an arm round her. 'That's it, love, it'll make you feel better.'

And so they sat together on the bed, until Lesley finally stopped sobbing and the light outside faded.

'Now,' said Patty firmly. 'What's all this nonsense about? You can tell me.'

'You won't tell Mum? Or the police?' Lesley sniffed.

'Lesley – you *must* say who's responsible. They might do it to some other girl. They might kill her!'

'I know.' Lesley seemed to make up her mind all of a sudden. 'I didn't say who they were 'cos I don't know. It was dark. I was pinned down. There were all these hands grabbing me and they kept sticking their things into me . . . I think I must have fainted!'

'But you know one of them!'

'No, I don't! I couldn't see. I told you, it was pitch black!'

'Lesley!' Patty's voice was stern. 'One of them was the sergeant, wasn't it?'

'Give over, Patty! You're as bad as the police!'

'All right. Then I'd better go.'

'No, don't!' Lesley pulled her back by the arm. 'Bert had me, yes – but that was before all the others.'

'That doesn't make any difference. He was there! How can you defend him! He must have planned the whole thing!'

'It wasn't Bert's fault!'

Patty knew Lesley was lying, but chose not to argue. For a moment she remembered Peter taking her during her period. That had been a kind of rape, too. Nothing like as bad as Lesley's ordeal, of course, but she too had been pinned down so that she couldn't struggle. Perhaps Lesley had egged the sergeant on, as so many people believed. Driven him so far that he couldn't help himself . . .

'Got to go to the police station tomorrow.'

'Tell them then. Lesley, you must!'

'Supposing something happens?'

Patty couldn't follow this train of thought.

'What do you mean?'

Lesley decided the only thing to do was to spell it out.

'Well, they all left their things in me!' She started to cry again. 'They say you always get pregnant the first time if the man leaves it in.'

'That's just an old wives' tale.'

'Mum and Dad think I will be. I heard them discussing it. Shouting about it, rather. They had the most god-awful row.'

'About you?'

Lesley nodded. 'Dad was all for turning me out of the house. Said I'd brought disgrace on the family.'

'How unfair! As if you could help it!'

'Fat lot he cares, miserable old bugger. But then Mum

turned on him. Gave him quite a shock! She really let him have it – said if I went, she and Joy went too! She told him she'd only been sticking around so's she could save enough money for her own home if he became impossible to live with. I wish I'd seen his face.' She gave a little chuckle. 'Course, he said he wasn't having any little bastards in the house.'

'I don't suppose you'll be pregnant,' said Patty, with a confidence she didn't feel. 'It doesn't always happen. I wasn't!'

'And did Peter . . .?'

Patty nodded, then hurriedly went on. '. . . But Lesley, it's vital for the police to know who's responsible.'

'So they can send him to prison? And the poor kid'll have a convict for a father?'

Patty stared at her. So that was why she refused to name the men.

'What good would that do now? Besides, Bert's not likely to want to see me again if I put the police onto him, is he?'

Patty couldn't believe her ears. 'You mean you *want* to see him – after what he did?'

Lesley put a hand up to her face. 'This wasn't him. It was the others. Bert was . . . sort of different – more sophisticated. I . . . I don't think I'd have minded so much if it had been just him.'

It didn't matter what Patty said, Lesley was adamant. Nothing was going to make her identify her attackers to the police.

When Patty left, Lesley was still sitting there in the dark.

That last night in October saw a raid on London that was officially described as 'light', with fewer than a hundred bombers pounding the capital. Even so, it brought the total of bombs dropped on London in that month up to ten thousand.

The nights of the full moon had brought the German bombers over in their hundreds. On one particular night, October 16th, more than four hundred bombers crossed the capital dropping over a thousand bombs. That night alone they killed four hundred and thirty civilians and wounded nine hundred. That one raid put five of London's mainline stations temporarily out of action, so no commuter needed to offer excuses for being late to work the next morning! But Londoners were made of stern stuff, and they got to work somehow – the Johnsons included.

When she reported for duty early the next morning, Patty found she had to go straight out on a call. With the rest of Stephen's team, she was to relieve the nightshift team, who'd been waiting on a site while the Heavy Rescue Squad toiled away, trying to reach some bomb victims. Arthur Graves drove them over in two lots in one of the Depot cars and returned the weary nightshift to their homes. It was still quite dark, and everyone had gathered gratefully round a WVS mobile canteen.

Patty edged her way nearer Stephen and caught his eye. 'Can you spare a moment?' she asked hesitantly.

'Something wrong?'

She nodded. He moved away from the group of stretcher bearers. 'Let's go and sit in the ambulance,' he suggested.

He settled back in the front seat and faced her. 'Okay. Shoot.'

She told him all about the rape, and then her meeting with Lesley that afternoon. 'Those men! They're just animals! I can't understand why she's protecting them.'

'I think I know what she's thinking,' he said slowly.

'Wish I did!' Patty gave a heavy sigh.

Stephen smiled at her. 'It'll sort itself out. These things always do. God moves in a mysterious way.'

Patty felt like saying that God didn't always seem to move in the nicest ways either, but she bit it back. At times, Stephen's simple faith seemed quite childlike to her. Sometimes, too, she felt like shaking him and saying:

'Look! Look at all the devastation around us. Is that what God does? But she knew that such arguments would never shake Stephen's belief. She knew his answer: it's men who are evil, not God. Men have free will. The fact that they choose wickedness isn't God's fault.

'Poor Lesley,' Stephen, went on. 'Perhaps she feels she can't report the rest of them without implicating the sergeant.

Dear Stephen. He spoke with such compassion. He was obviously going to say more when one of the rescuers beckoned towards the ambulance. Stephen got out and walked over to him, and there was a brief exchange of words which Patty couldn't catch. Then suddenly Stephen returned.

'Back to the Depot!'

'Aren't we going to wait?'

'No need. They got to them too late.'

Patty drove carefully back through the deserted streets. Shrapnel was the bane of the Blitz driver's life – the sharp edges caused puncture after puncture. And this trip was no exception. They were almost home, when an ominous bumping from the offside front wheel told her that she'd just collected her third puncture in a week. She pulled in to the kerb and sighed resignedly.

The heavy old ambulances were the devil to jack up. Patty's nursing assistant stood by, watching helplessly as Patty struggled. Just when it seemed Patty's patience would finally give out, she heard a familiar voice.

'You'd better let me have that before you do yourself an injury!'

It was Stephen, grinning at her oil-smeared appearance. He sent her assistant back with the others in the stretcher car, then knelt beside Patty, taking the jack from her firmly. 'You've got a big smudge of oil on your nose,' he told her. It was then he kissed her – for the second time.

Bert Williams sat in the semi-gloom of his front room

and glared balefully at the wall. He'd just returned from seeing his family on to the tram to Dolphin Square, and the sight of Madge's white face as she waved goodbye still tugged at his heartstrings. She'd been clutching their wheezing baby, bundled up like an eskimo papoose. Poor kid – she was in for a rough night. His conscience pricked him, too. He'd flared up at her when she'd asked him if he could find some extra money – not for herself, but to buy a tonic for the kids. Seeing her eyes fill with tears, he'd stormed out of the house – *had* to; he just couldn't bear it.

Madge didn't know, but she'd caught him on the raw, especially with the new station sergeant going on at him all the time. Before *he'd* come on the scene, Bert had felt hopeful of promotion, but not now. He smarted again as he remembered the sergeant's tirade about his report on Lesley Aynsworth.

'What's this, Williams? *Assault by person or persons unknown*. What kind of a report's that? What do you mean, she won't tell you? It's your job to *make* her tell you, my lad. Bring her in here. We'll soon get it out of her. And Williams – remember: I've got my eye on you, lad.'

Lad! How dare he! All very well for him – he didn't have a family to distract him from his duty. Course, they shouldn't have had so many kids. It wasn't all his fault, though. Only got to touch Madge and she was pregnant. Randy little thing she was, too!

Thinking about the old days with Madge raised Bert's spirits a little. Remembering also the sergeant's failure to extract anything further out of Lesley, raised them a little more. If it wasn't for the continual worry over money, things wouldn't seem so bad.

If he could just get himself in the sergeant's good books! Maybe if he could get Lesley to talk . . . He stared out of the window of Number Ten opposite. Was she going to the shelter with her sister, or was she staying at home? She'd probably want to stay at home, in her present state. Bert made up his mind and strode out of the house and across the street.

A tiny chink of light came from a side window. He could use that as an excuse: checking the blackout. Then he could get around to Lesley. Casual like.

There was no reply to his knocks on the front door, and when he walked down the side passage, it soon became clear why. The signature tune of *ITMA* filled his ears. Bert tapped on the kitchen door. No reply. 'Probably can't hear a bloody thing,' he muttered to himself, and turned the handle and stepped in, closing the door quickly behind him.

What he saw stopped him in his tracks. Horace Aynsworth was sitting at the kitchen table in his shirt-sleeves. At the sight of Bert, he blanched and his mouth dropped open in shock.

It was Joy Aynsworth who found the package on the doorstep as she came home in the early hours. She picked it up and examined it. It was soft. But her curiosity faded at the sight of the word LESLIE crudely scrawled on the brown paper wrapping. Couldn't even spell the name right! She left it on the hall table. No poing in waking her up just for that. Besides, she wanted a chance at the bathroom first.

Dora gave it to Lesley when she came down for breakfast.

Lesley tore at the wrapping, but stopped dead when she saw the contents. 'What is it?' asked her mother, 'a present?'

'No,' replied Lesley in a flat voice, 'just an old jumper I lent to Patty, that's all. I'll just put it upstairs.'

'All right, dear,' murmured Dora not noticing anything strange in her daughter's manner. 'I'll put the kettle on again and we'll have another cup.'

Once in her room, Lesley tore at the wrapping. She'd known what it was as soon as she'd broken it open downstairs. Once the string was cut, the parcel expanded and yards of green parachute silk sprang out over the bed.

Lesley ignored it and rummaged through the paper to see if there was a note with it. There wasn't. For a long moment she sat and stared at the silk, running her hand across it almost absent-mindedly.

Then she heard her mother calling out that tea was ready. With one violent movement, she scrunched the silk together and hurled it out of sight under the bed. As she got to her feet, she gasped. There in the doorway stood her sister.

'What are you doing – spying on me?' she shouted.

Joy sighed wearily. 'Don't be silly! I only came to see how you were. No message from lover-boy, I see. Take a tip from me – forget all about him.'

'It's all very well for you to talk! It's not so easy . . . after what happened.'

'Course it isn't! But it won't do any good mooning around over a bastard like him. He's married, anyway.'

Lesley swung round as if she'd been hit. 'Who told you that?'

'Douglas. Major Watkins, to you.' Joy paused, savouring her moment of triumph. 'I've been out with him a couple of times, didn't you know? He says Bert's been in trouble for this sort of thing before. He's grateful you haven't told the police, by the way.'

'You . . . you talked to him about it?' Lesley almost spat out the words and her face flamed with anger.

'Why not? They're his men, after all. Personally, I think you're mad to protect them, but it's up to you.'

Lesley's rage exploded into tears. She rushed back into her room, slamming the door. Joy shrugged and continued downstairs.

Madge Williams gaped at her husband, standing at the front door of the Dolphin Square flat where she was in the middle of her daily cleaning job. Her first thought was that something had happened to one of the kids. He quickly reassured her.

'Nothing like that, sweetheart. Wanted to see you. I'm sorry I blew my top with you – over the money. You're right. You don't have enough to manage.' He followed her into the kitchen. ' 'Ere,' he said, 'This'll make things easier.' And he tossed an envelope on to the table. 'Go on, open it!'

Madge did as she was told, and her fingers trembled as she looked at what she held in her hand. Pound notes. Twenty of them!

'Had a bet,' grinned Bert. 'On a horse.'

For a moment, fear rushed through Madge's mind. 'I thought you weren't supposed to bet, being a policeman?'

'We ain't! But a lot do. Anyway, this geezer gave me a tip and I put a quid on. Twenty to one. Walked it!'

'Oh, Bert!' Madge rushed round the table and flung her arms around him. 'Twenty quid'll make all the difference!'

' 'Ere steady on!' exclaimed her husband, recoiling. 'Don't you go kissing me, young Madge! You know what you're like – you'll be in the family way again!'

This possibility was only averted by the milk boiling over. Which was just as well for Bert's peace of mind, because Madge had been about to tell him the other thing which was worrying her. Her period was four days overdue.

19

'Remember, Remember'

Patty shivered and huddled deeper into her overcoat. It was so cold that she could almost see the frost forming on the privet hedges of Balaclava Street.

In the bright moonlight, her breath steamed away behind her as she made her way towards the Warden's Post. In fact, the cold was so bitter that for a moment she regretted leaving the house. But anything was better than trying to sleep and just tossing and turning.

Peter . . . Stephen . . . Her mind tugged her first one way and then the other. Finally, unable to settle, she'd dressed and set out to join her father on his nightly vigil over Balaclava Street. Not that she'd dream of discussing her problem with him. In Stan's world, Patty knew, marriage was marriage – for ever.

She was so engrossed in her thoughts that she nearly jumped out of her skin when her father emerged suddenly from the Warden's Post. Stan was startled too. 'What on earth . . .?'

'I couldn't sleep,' Patty explained. 'I thought I'd come over and see how you were getting on.'

'Couldn't sleep? But it's your first night off for ages. Something wrong?' Stan shot a worried glance at his daughter. 'Not ill, or anything?'

'No, Dad. Just can't get used to these new shifts, I suppose.'

That seemed to reassure Stan. A few aircraft droned in the distance and searchlight beams wavered in the same direction. 'The City again – poor beggars,' he observed, in a voice that managed to express relief and sympathy.

'Only hope the Jerries don't remember what day it is today.'

'How d'you mean?'

'Don't tell me you've forgotten?'

'Oh no, Dad! November the Fifth. Fireworks night!'

Whatever reply Stan made was smothered by the sudden crack of a nearby gun, its single round abnormally loud in the moonlit stillness. The echo had no sooner died away than Harry Hempstead appeared in the doorway and joined them outside the post. Patty grinned: he was wearing a tin-hat perched on top of a scarf which was wound round and round his head.

'What was that? Sounded close!'

Stan grinned too. 'Just one of the guns in the Park. You've got so much wool round your ears, they could drop one right on you and you'd never hear it!'

Harry pretended to be deaf and cocked a hand to his ear. 'Whassat?' Stan was about to make some sort of retort when there was a loud explosion that seemed to come from right above their heads. For a moment, they thought it was another gun, but the fluttery whistles all around immediately cancelled that idea.

Patty was rooted to the spot, but Stan reacted quickly. He literally flung his daughter into the shelter of the porch. For an instant Patty was stunned, but the crackling and crashing around left her in no doubt what was coming. Fire bombs! The incendiaries were actually bouncing in the road.

One in particular was rolling right up the path towards them. Before the long, grey cylinder had stopped moving, a great, dazzling glow erupted from it. As Patty scrambled to her feet, shrinking back from the white rain which came from the bomb, she saw her father grab a sandbag and slam it down over the blinding light.

Fireworks! Patty knew they shouldn't have mentioned them. Her father was now halfway down the path with another sandbag at the ready. Harry, too, had recovered his wits and was doing the same, holding the sandbag protectively in front of his face.

It was then that Patty remembered something she'd only noticed subconsciously when that first incendiary had rolled up the path. It was long! It was too long! It looked just like the one the major had shown them at the lecture at the Depot. Patty screamed: '*No! No! It's too long!*'

Whether Stan heard her, or whether he reached the same conclusion at the same time, Patty couldn't know, but she saw him run towards Harry, yelling something unintelligible above the din. Stan's hands were reaching out for Harry's shoulders as though to fling him aside, when the explosion came. For a moment, Harry's figure was outlined by red fire. In the same instant, Patty saw her father catapulted backward to lie in a crumpled heap on the pavement.

Patty raced towards him, her training in First Aid flashing through her mind. *Don't move the patient!* 'Keep still, Dad! Please! Where are you hurt?' It sounded so formal, Patty could have wept.

'Leg . . . nothing bad. Just my leg . . .' The fact that he could speak was a great relief. His clothes were badly scorched, but only his left leg appeared to be injured. Patty tore away the tattered trouser and found a jagged wound that didn't appear to be bleeding too much.

By now, the whole street was bathed in a fierce white light. 'Leave it, Patty!' ordered Stan. 'You must phone! Harry . . .'

Patty knew he was right. Lowering his head gently on to her rolled-up coat, she ran towards the Post. As she did so, she passed what was left of Harry Hempstead. She knew without examining him that he was dead. The worst thing was that smoke was pouring out of Harry's body as though he was on fire inside.

'I feel a proper fraud,' Stan smiled up at Kath. 'I'll be up and about in a week . . .'

'We'll see about that!' Kath tucked the blankets round him for the umpteenth time. 'Comfy now?'

'Couldn't be better. Mind you, I'd rather be upstairs in bed.'

'Typical!' laughed Kath. 'After we've gone to all the trouble of hauling a mattress downstairs!'

Stan became serious. 'Did you ring the office?'

'Yes. They all send their best wishes and say you're not to go back until you're completely well. I spoke to ever such a nice man.'

'That'd be Dickinson. He's the head of my section.'

'Well, he said you're not to worry about money, either. He'll get your wages to you somehow.'

Stan relaxed against the great pile of pillows. 'Where did all these cushions come from? They're never all ours!'

'Don't you worry about silly things like that,' soothed Kath. In fact, practically everyone in the street had offered something – things they could ill afford to part with, in some cases. The pillows had been a godsend. Mind you, there'd have to be a lot of washing done before she gave them back. Stan had already spilt some tea over the top one. Secretly Kath rather hoped it was the one that Enid Belling had pressed on her. Enid's habit of making up to Stan was getting beyond a joke.

'How's the patient?' Patty's cheerful voice cut into Kath's thoughts.

'Fine,' answered Stan, matching his daughter's tone.

Patty looked at her father carefully and was relieved to see that his face seemed to have filled out again. Stan's appearance immediately after the incident had been a great shock to her. He'd looked shrunken somehow, as if his face had caved in.

Stan looked back at his daughter just as steadily and reflected that Patty looked well, considering. Those brown eyes that she'd inherited from Kath. And the blonde hair. You'd think she'd be fragile somehow, but no, she was blooming. Looks as though she's in love. Well, of course, she is! – though God knows what was happening to Peter right now . . .

Kath bustled Patty out of the room. 'Come on, my girl, let your father rest.'

Stan protested, but once the kitchen door had closed he was quite pleased not to have to make conversation. Despite the strapping, his leg throbbed steadily. He tried to forget the pain and ran over the events of that night in his mind.

He'd known Harry was dead, even though nobody had mentioned it at the First Aid station where Patty had taken him. Stan shuddered at the thought of all that burning inside Harry. He hadn't been joking when he told Kath he felt a fraud. Compared with some of the other cases that had been brought in, his injuries were nothing. Mind you, the stitching had hurt like hell . . .

As he lay there, half-dozing, Stan's worries were more for the street than for himself. With Harry dead and him out of action, who was going to act as Warden? They'd got to have a Warden . . .

Stan's eyes were closed when Kath ushered the rest of the family quietly off to the shelter. There'd been little argument when Kath had announced her intention of remaining in the house with Stan. Tim had pulled a face at having to go to the shelter with Gran, but that was to be expected. Patty was now on the late afternoon shift and as she hadn't returned home, Kath assumed she must have gone straight to the shelter.

It was as well for Kath's peace of mind that she didn't know the truth. For when Patty came to the end of her shift, she'd lingered by her ambulance, giving it an unnecessary last-minute polish. This had become a regular routine with her. Stephen, being the team leader, was always the last to leave, since he had to hand over to the corresponding team leader on the next shift. Patty managed to delay her departure so that they could walk home together.

This, however, was something of a two-edged blade

to Patty – and, she suspected, to Stephen too. For the more they saw of each other, the deeper the attraction became. At times, the ache to feel his arms around her and his lips on hers was almost too much for Patty to bear. The previous evening as they'd said goodbye at the corner of Prince of Wales Drive, he'd looked at her with such longing that she'd very nearly given way to the impulse to fling her arms round his neck. She wasn't sure how much longer she could be strong. Even the prickings of her conscience were becoming less and less disquieting. The fact was, she'd begun to feel quite shameless.

She saw now that she should never have got married at seventeen – although at the time she'd fought tooth and nail to do so. Her feelings for Peter, she realized now, were an infatuation – a romantic calf-love, heightened by the drama of war and his imminent posting overseas. She'd let herself be persuaded by Peter's impetuosity, and hadn't heeded the little nagging doubts she'd felt. Their desire to get married had been born of fear: fear of losing each other. And the irony was that marriage hadn't prevented that – quite the opposite. The only memories she had of marriage were the miseries of the honeymoon, and those were quite enough to put her off married life for ever. They might have done so if Stephen hadn't happened along – quiet, gentle Stephen, who in his own way was so much stronger than Peter. Stephen, who'd given her the first inkling of what real love could mean. Stephen, whom she loved and wanted, yet who remained forever out of reach.

Out of the corner of her eye, Patty saw that Stephen was on his way over to the Depot. She gathered up her gasmask and tin helmet and unobtrusively headed in the same direction.

All of a sudden there was a warning shout. One of the heavy ambulances was lumbering backwards down the hill towards Stephen's unsuspecting back. Patty felt her heart miss a beat. Then she too was shouting and running towards him. Stephen turned, but was too late to dodge. The ambulance knocked him flat, trundling on until it smashed into another stationary vehicle parked just beyond. Stephen was completely hidden from view underneath.

People were running from all directions now, and Patty was overtaken by the leader of the nightshift who'd taken over from Stephen. He crouched in the road, peering underneath the vehicle. Patty knelt down beside him. Stephen looked very white and still. She felt her throat constrict in terror.

'Can't see much,' muttered the man beside her. 'Someone bring a torch over!'

But Patty didn't wait. She wriggled underneath the chassis, disregarding the dirt and oil. By the time she reached Stephen, she was flat on her stomach and there was barely room to raise her head. She felt his face. It was warm – but how long did it take before one grew cold after death? She tried to reach over to unbutton Stephen's tunic so that she could feel his heart, but there wasn't room to manoeuvre.

'Well?' demanded the impatient voice from the roadside.

'I . . . I don't know,' she replied.

'Come on out, then!'

Any argument was cut short as she was yanked roughly backwards by the ankles. She struggled up angrily, but the other leader gave her no time to protest.

'I'll drive forward so we can see what we're doing. You stay here and guide me.'

'Suppose the brake fails again?'

'Don't worry – we've got some bricks to shove under the back wheels.'

Slowly the ambulance was eased forward and the unconscious figure revealed. Patty rushed forward to cradle Stephen's head, smothering his face with kisses, oblivious to the curious stares of the onlookers.

'For a moment, I thought I was in heaven,' whispered a soft voice in her ear.

Patty gasped. To her incredulous delight she saw that Stephen's eyes were open. What's more, he was smiling.

'Oh, Stephen!' She bent her head and kissed him long and hard. 'I was so afraid you were dead.'

'Take more than that to do me in.' He winked at her, then murmured from the side of his mouth, 'Careful, sweetheart – we've got an audience.'

Patty became aware that the other leader was bending over them solicitously. 'Hullo mate,' he said, 'How d'you feel, then?'

By way of reply, Stephen struggled to his feet and flexed his legs and arms tentatively. 'Everything seems to work,' he announced.

'You were dead lucky. Wheels must have missed you by inches.' He watched Stephen feeling his head. 'Got a sore bonce, eh? You'd better come inside and we'll take a look at you in the light.'

Stephen tried to make light of things, but it was clear that he was badly shaken and bruised. He refused to go to the hospital for a check-up, but he was nonetheless glad to accept a lift home from Arthur Graves. Patty insisted on going too. She was determined to see him safely into bed and get him some supper.

The large mansion flat was empty, Stephen's landlady having gone to a groundfloor flat to be with friends if the siren went. Patty could tell that he was suffering more than he'd been prepared to admit. The aches and stiffness were beginning to override the numbing effect of shock, and it was quite an operation to ease him out of his uniform. Finally he stood there in his underpants, a great purple weal stretching across his midriff where the tailboard of the ambulance had caught him.

Patty drew a sharp breath. 'That's nasty,' she murmured, and gently ran a finger along the bruise.

Stephen winced, then smiled at her. 'Hand me my pyjamas, there's a love. I'd better cover up quickly. Your hands aren't having quite the soothing effect you intended.'

She stared, and then blushed scarlet as she saw what he meant. She threw his pyjamas at him and hurried out to the kitchen to see about food. He laughed and called out a moment later that he was quite decent and she could return. She was embarrassed, but he kissed her and made her feel relaxed again.

Patty moved to him and put her arms round his neck. 'I was so frightened – so terribly frightened,' she whispered. 'I thought I'd lost you for good.'

He looked down at her and gently kissed her forehead. 'It's going to be even more difficult now, you know.'

'Why?'

'It was bad enough when I thought I only had to keep myself under control. But tonight, when I came round and saw you so upset . . . I knew you cared, too.'

She nodded and kissed him again. 'I've been so muddled about things, but now I'm sure. Tonight clinched it for me.' She sighed and broke away gently. 'I don't know what I'm going to do. If only Peter and I had just been engaged – I could have broken that off. But a divorce . . .' It seemed a dreadful thing to contemplate.

Stephen frowned. 'I don't think you could get one, anyway. Not for a few years. You've only just got married.'

'Well, I know I can't go back to Peter, not loving you like this. I suppose I'll have to write and tell him.'

'No, Patty.' Stephen was quite definite. 'First you must wait and be quite, quite sure.' She opened her mouth to protest, but he put a finger to her lips. 'Besides, it would be cruel. The poor chap's been sent out east, and God knows what he's facing there. It could be a terrible blow to him.'

Stephen was right. Patty hadn't thought of that. 'But what are we going to do?'

'I suppose I could ask to be transferred to another Depot . . .'

'No!' She stared at him with agonized eyes. 'No, Stephen! I couldn't bear not to see you again – not now.'

She looked so miserable, he couldn't resist her. Soon they were in each others' arms again.

And so the evening went on, alternating between the excitement of their new-found love, the pleasure of touch and caress, and the painful moments of guilt and soul-searching. The raid was now at its height, and Stephen wouldn't hear of her walking home alone, so Patty decided to stay with him for the night.

They lay together on Stephen's bed, but the proximity imposed a strain. Patty thrilled and trembled under his hands, so gentle and caring where Peter's had been so rough. She felt aware of sensations she'd never experienced before. Yet each time it seemed that something would happen, Stephen somehow managed to stop.

'I . . . I can't do it, Patty. I feel such a louse.'

'But darling, I want it, too.' She paused a moment. 'It isn't only sex, though . . . is it?'

'No. Well, the truth is – of *course* I want to make love to you. But it's more than that. I love you – I want to be with you totally.'

She relaxed against him, happy for a brief moment. She could feel the firmness of him through his pyjamas and let her hand stray down in a tentative caress – something she'd never done or even wanted to with Peter. But immediately she felt Stephen tense.

'Don't! Darling, please – I can't take it.'

She drew back again, ashamed. 'I'm sorry.'

He smiled. 'I'm just not that strong, I'm afraid. Don't make me break all my good resolutions!'

In the end, Patty fetched cushions from the sitting room and made herself a makeshift bed on the floor beside him. She lay awake in the darkness listening to his even breathing long after he fell asleep. For the first time she was experiencing the physical pain of sexual frustration. Now, ironically, she was beginning to understand what Peter had talked of – beginning to know what a powerful feeling it was, once aroused. Oh yes, she understood now what it was all about, but oh Lord, it was too late.

20

The Uneasy Quiet

Kath went off to work feeling uneasy. She'd wanted to get leave of absence to stay and look after Stan, but Stan wouldn't hear of it. The truth was, however, that Kath wasn't so concerned about his welfare as to what Enid Belling might get up to when her back was turned. If she'd known that Enid was watching her departure with a calculating gleam in her eyes, she'd have been even more worried.

Enid waited a couple of hours – just long enough for Stan to get bored and lonely, and in need of a bit of company. And her strategy paid off, for when she arrived in the front room – by way of the garden fence and the Johnson's back door – Stan's face lit up.

'Just thought I'd pop in to see if you needed anything,' she cooed at him.

'Enid – your smile's a tonic in itself,' he grinned. He wasn't just flattering her, either. Enid *did* look particularly attractive – just the person to liven up a dull morning.

Enid was gratified by Stan's welcome. She moved closer and held up a half-bottle of gin. 'Brought a little something to brighten up your day,' she said. 'Nothing in doctor's orders against this, is there?'

Stan shook his head. He wasn't much of a drinker usually, but somehow the idea of a couple of gins in the middle of the morning seemed enormously exciting – along with everything else about Enid Belling. She fetched a couple of glasses from the kitchen and they toasted each other.

'Feel like a right old ponce,' he laughed. 'Lying here drinking while the rest of the world's hard at work.'

'You *need* spoiling, Stan. Especially with that injury.'

'It's not that bad!' he protested.

But Enid was determined to cosset him. What with her ministrations *and* the relaxing effect of a couple of large gins, Stan began to feel quite light-headed.

'Here, let me make you comfy,' she murmured, easing an arm behind him to plump up his pillows. Stan found his face pressed against Enid's voluptuous bosom. He made no objection – on the contrary, he enjoyed the sensation.

'Mmm, you smell nice,' he said.

It was all the encouragement Enid needed. Suddenly Stan found himself being kissed and caressed with an urgency that took his breath away. Her hands explored him beneath his pyjamas, and despite himself, Stan felt nature taking its course.

'Hey – watch it, Enid!' he protested, as her hands clasped his erection. 'I'm a sick man, remember.'

'Doesn't feel like it to me.'

'Please! Enid – no!' He pulled her hands away. 'We mustn't!'

She didn't fight him, just went back to soft, stroking caresses a little higher up. 'Relax, Stan – it's not doing anyone any harm. And I've been so lonely since poor George died.'

As she spoke, Enid's hands were creeping dangerously low again. Stan tried exerting mind over matter, but it didn't work. He knew it was wrong. He thought about Kath, how sweet and good and loving she was, and what a heel he was for cheating like this, but it was no use: Enid was arousing him, and there was no denying that he liked it.

Stan was saved by the bell – literally. The telephone in the hall shrilled.

'That damn phone,' pouted Enid. It wasn't the first time it had thwarted her plans.

'Answer it for me, there's a love,' gasped Stan, heaving a mental sigh of relief.

Enid disappeared, then moments later returned. 'It's the Head Warden. Can he come round and discuss a temporary replacement for you?'

'Course. Tell him right away! I'm not going anywhere.' He grinned at Enid, trying to dispel her irritated frown.

There was nothing for it but for Enid to admit defeat. After washing up the glasses, she scuttled back over the fence before Stan's visitor arrived. Still – there was always another day . . .

Stan, however, was shocked when he realized how close he'd come to falling, and made a firm resolve never to let himself be left at Enid's mercy again. He tried to compose himself before the Head Warden arrived, but nothing could remove the flush on his face caused by a mixture of gin and guilt.

It had been a mistake going into the pub. Patty knew that almost as soon as she and Stephen walked in.

The idea of going up West had been hers, and Stephen had agreed without any question. At first it seemed they'd chosen well – darkness had come and the sirens had stayed silent. As they'd walked hand in hand down the moonlit streets, even the shadows seemed to conspire in their happiness, covering the capital's scars. Laughter spilling out from behind darkened, boarded-up windows had drawn them to the pub and it had seemed natural to push aside the blackout curtains and walk in.

The bar was packed with soldiers. Patty suddenly realized how out of place Stephen looked in his civilian clothes, as he eased a way through to the bar.

Faced with the usual choice of rum or beer, they settled for two halves of extremely weak bitter – not that the troops around them seemed to find the beer all that weak: several were obviously well on the way to drunkenness. It was one of these flushed faces that started the trouble.

He lurched against Stephen, spilling some of his beer down Stephen's trousers. 'Steady,' said Stephen, mopping up with his handkerchief.

'Who're you saying steady to?' demanded the soldier truculently.

'Never mind.' Stephen turned back to Patty.

'But I *do* bleedin' mind – you spilled my beer! Reckon you oughta replace it.' There were murmurs of agreement from his drunken comrades.

'Forget it,' said Stephen. Perhaps the words came out a bit too much like a command. It was the sort of voice that Patty had heard him use before when the going got rough.

' 'Ere!' insisted the soldier, swaying slightly. 'Who you giving orders to? What are you? Some bleedin' officer or somethin'?' One of his mates, suspecting that he'd hit on the truth, tried to pull him away, but the drunk shrugged him off.

'No, I'm not,' Stephen cut in firmly. 'Please leave us alone. We came in for a quiet drink.'

'Stephen, let's go,' urged Patty.

'All right.' Stephen started to steer Patty towards the door.

The soldier gained more confidence as they retreated. 'Not a bleedin' officer, eh! Hold on! Which unit you with, then?' Annoyed at not getting a response, he shouted after them. 'Probably one of them bleedin' Conchies, that's what!'

The whole pub went deathly quiet. All faces were turned in their direction. Patty felt suddenly panicky as Stephen stopped in his tracks and swung round to face his accuser.

'Stephen, please . . .'

But Stephen wasn't to be deflected. 'If you mean that I don't approve of killing another human being, then you're absolutely right!'

It seemed the drunken squaddie could hardly believe his luck. 'You *are* a bleedin' Conchie!' He breathed the words with such venom, that Patty was afraid he was about to spit in Stephen's face.

Stephen said nothing, but stood his ground and gazed steadily at the man. It was the landlord who stopped what could obviously have developed into an ugly scene. He said pointedly to Stephen! 'Now then! I don't want no trouble. I'll have to ask you to leave.'

Stephen stared at him for a moment, then deliberately turned on his heel and followed Patty out of the pub.

Once outside, Patty found her legs quite weak, and it was some time before she could stop herself shaking. Finally she turned to face him. 'Oh, Stephen, wasn't it awful?'

'God forgive me,' Stephen whispered to himself, 'I nearly hit him.'

It was the night it stopped that Stan found most difficult to take. He could move about a bit now, and Kath watched him anxiously as he limped from room to room. 'Sit down, love. The doctor told you to take it easy.'

Stan sat down, but not for long. Finally he could no longer bear to be inside and despite Kath's protestations, he took his new greatcoat off the peg on the hall-stand, switched out the light and stepped out into the street.

The stillness outside disturbed him in a way he found impossible to explain. Nothing stirred. No searchlights, no guns – nothing. Just a great blanket of eerie silence.

Overhead the sky was clear. The stars glittered high above the frosty white of the rooftops. He stared up, as though willing something to happen. He felt rather than saw Kath come out beside him. Without a word, she slipped her arm through his and for a long moment they stood there in silence. Far away, a dog howled at the moon. It was that distant sound which somehow broke the spell.

'Where the hell *are* they?' demanded Stan. There was anger, not relief in his voice.

'Perhaps it's over?'

'Never! It's a trick!'

It sounded almost as though Stan were willing the bombers to come, but Kath knew he didn't mean it like that. Privately, she sent up a prayer that the bombers would never return. Already the thought that it might be over was growing in her mind.

Feeling her shiver, Stan led her back inside. Could the raids *really* have ended without anyone knowing? He twiddled the knobs of the wireless, and it was only when the voice of Lord Haw-Haw filled the room that he was convinced that nothing had changed.

All over London on that night of Thursday, November 14th, the inhabitants of the battered city felt the same: it was the silence that made them ill at ease.

The men of the rescue services also found the quiet difficult to cope with. The off-duty firemen sat up and smoked, whereas normally they'd be fast asleep despite the background thunder of the guns.

The on-duty ambulance crews sat and gazed into space, starting up at each solitary telephone ring and then slumping back in disbelief when no alarm came.

Stephen and Patty chatted quietly in a corner of the Depot, casting a questioning glance in the direction of the Colonel's office every time a door opened or closed.

In his office, the Colonel was telling Arthur Graves that the Germans had tried a similar trick near Arras in the First War.

'Just like this!' fumed the Colonel. 'Absolutely quiet. Everybody relaxed – couldn't believe it. Someone started a rumour that the war was over. Flew round amongst the men like wildfire. And then – all hell broke loose!'

At that moment the telephone on Arthur's desk rang. Arthur snatched at it, listened for a moment and passed it over to the Colonel. 'For you, sir.'

'Harris here.'

The Colonel listened intently. With a sinking heart,

Arthur saw the Colonel's good eye begin to sparkle. He was like a war-horse scenting blood. Something was up!

'Just a moment,' said the Colonel to the person on the other end of the line, then to Arthur: 'How many ambulances can we spare, Mr Graves?'

Arthur noted the 'Mr Graves' with deep unease. 'Depends,' he replied, 'We're up to strength. How long for?'

'A day at least,' growled his chief irritably. Why did Arthur Graves always answer one question with another! 'I'll ring straight back!' He slammed the earpiece back on the hook so hard that Arthur thought he'd broken it.

'That was Group. The attack's switched to Coventry. They need ambulances and crews to make up a flying column.'

Arthur was by nature and profession cautious. 'What if Jerry swings back to us?'

'Group thinks that's unlikely, judging by the number of aircraft they've got streaming up north. Can we spare six?'

'Give them three and a stretcher car,' suggested Arthur. 'It's a long run, and God knows when they'll get back. Going to ask for volunteers?'

The Colonel frowned, thinking back to the last time. 'Yes,' he grunted. 'But this time, ask the ones that you know will go anyway.'

It seemed to Patty that the drive would never end. First of all there was the muddle over the rendezvous point. Stephen was sure that he'd got his team to the right spot, but after half an hour no other ambulances had turned up. Eventually Stephen decided to push on to the outskirts of Coventry, where he'd been told they'd come under the command of the city's own emergency services.

They were sharing the driving with some of the men from the stretcher car. Stephen appointed himself Patty's co-driver, much to her relief. She'd never driven outside

London, and driving through unlit countryside wasn't easy. For one thing, all the signposts had been taken down to confuse the Germans if they invaded. But towards the end of the run there was no longer any doubt they were heading in the right direction. The red glow in the sky pointed the way, even as dawn paled the fields around them.

Now they could plainly hear the drone of planes and the thump of explosions ahead. Once Patty was forced to jam on the brakes to avoid running into the back of another ambulance, which had pulled up in the middle of the road in front of them. After a few minutes, they learned that there was a huge crater ahead, and that they'd have to make a detour.

As they moved in closer to the centre of the city, Patty could hardly believe what the full dawn revealed.

A faint All Clear sounded high but feeble over acres of rubble, débris, broken glass, charred timbers and brick-work. Smoke hung over everything. Twice Patty had to swerve suddenly to avoid lorries packed with women and children, intent on fleeing the stricken city.

Four hundred and forty-nine German bombers, more than had raided London on any one previous night, had rained over five hundred tons of high explosive and eight hundred and eighty-one cannisters of incendiaries on to middle-sized Coventry. They had smashed the heart out of it.

Flames still burst out of smouldering piles of débris, and exhausted firemen tried to keep up water-pressure through tangled hoses. Policemen, some barely recognizable in dust-covered uniforms and blackened faces, were the only real pillars of calm. One directed Patty to their position beside a badly-damaged hospital.

That Friday was, to Patty, a blur of toil as she ferried the badly-wounded to the nearest First Aid points and then to any hospital that could take them. As the day wore on, she learned to shut her mind to the horrors. Thank God, Stephen was beside her, encouraging her when it seemed the only thing to do was to sit down and weep.

In the midst of the haze of effort and agony, her brain retained isolated pictures: the police road-blocks at the entrance to the desolation; people leaning against railings, too exhausted to move further, unable to believe that they'd survived; the hiss and puff of steam as water sprayed on to red-hot metal.

In her mind she saw again a woman in rags, screaming and attacking a fireman who was fighting to save what was left of her shattered house. Saw the lines of still figures, their faces covered with blankets and tarpaulins. She knew that hundreds must have died, but couldn't know that the true account was 554, with 865 seriously injured.

Stuck in the city centre with yet another puncture – and fortunately an empty ambulance – she and Stephen were wrestling to replace the wheel with the multi-patched spare, when all at once she found herself working alone. Looking up, she saw that Stephen was crying. For a moment she couldn't see what had moved him so. Then she saw in front of them what was left of Coventry cathedral. At each end, the bare frames of the great windows were still standing, but in between all that remained was a jumble of bricks and pillars, girders and, poking out here and there, white memorial tablets – monuments to those long past feeling any pain.

As the afternoon drew to a close, Patty began to wonder if their task would ever end. The despair she saw on the faces of the survivors was beginning to infect her too.

'Tired?' asked Stephen.

'Yes. When do you think we can go back?'

'I wish I knew.'

Patty felt faint from lack of food and sleep. In one short rest-period, snatched as darkness started to creep in, she went soundly to sleep leaning against a wall, and was only awoken by an ugly scene in which two cars were attacked by a small mob hoping to flee the city before the bombers returned. There was no doubt in anyone's mind that the Germans would come back. By the time it was dark, the streets were deserted except for the police and small groups of rescue teams, who worked on under temporary lights.

By nine pm, it was clear that for reasons known only to them, the Germans weren't returning to deliver another blow, and Stephen's team was released to return to base along with the other London ambulances. The Coventry commandant was profuse with his thanks and praise.

Stephen saw their team on to the London road, then eased himself behind the wheel of Patty's ambulance. She was very grateful. She could hardly keep her eyes open and was wondering how on earth she'd cope with the drive.

'Mind if we take a short detour?' he asked. She looked at him in some surprise. 'My mother lives just out of town. I'd like to look in – make sure she's okay.'

Patty felt a little apprehensive. Naturally he wanted to see his mother, being so near; but how would she react to him bringing a strange girl home in these circumstances?

Stephen must have guessed her thoughts. 'Don't worry, sweetheart. We won't go into explanations. There won't be time.'

He was right. In the event, Mrs Broome's delight at Stephen's unexpected visit quite overcame any awkwardness. She bustled them into the kitchen, insisted on making them a snack supper and begged them to stay the night, but Stephen was firm: they must report back.

Patty caught Mrs Broome looking at her appraisingly, and blushed. The older woman laughed and apologized.

'You must forgive me, my dear. Stephen told me about you – about that terrible experience you both had in the cellar. I can't tell you how much I admire you. It's just that – well, I hadn't expected anyone quite so young!'

Patty was scarlet. Mrs Broome chuckled. 'There, I've embarrassed you! Take no notice, dear. I'm sorry.'

Stephen came to the rescue. 'We've really got to make a move, Mother. This child,' he grinned at Patty, 'needs some beauty sleep.'

He hugged his mother at the front door, and then Mrs Broome impulsively kissed Patty. 'Come and see me again, Patricia – and stay longer next time.'

Stephen led Patty out to the ambulance and insisted that she slept in the back. She was too exhausted to protest. In fact, she was asleep before he'd finished tucking in a blanket round her.

It was somewhere near Biggleswade that the much-patched spare tyre finally gave up the ghost. Stephen knew that he too must either sleep or crash. He bumped off the road and through an open gate-way into a field. The tyre could wait. Without even moving out of the driving seat, he put his head on his hands on the wheel and slept. In the distance, the low grumble of guns and flickers of light would have told him that the Germans had returned to their prime target – London. But in his state of total exhaustion, nothing could disturb him.

21

Playing Truant

It was nothing definite that woke Patty – not a noise, though as she lay there and wondered where she was, she did hear an owl hoot somewhere far away. She moved slightly to ease the dead feeling in one of her legs. God, it was cold! She stretched out a hand to try to pull more blanket over herself. With a start of pure terror she pulled her hand back. She'd felt someone else in the darkness! Had they left a body in the ambulance when they'd driven out of Coventry! Impossible! She started to shiver, and this time it wasn't just from the cold. It was several seconds before she plucked up enough courage to sit up and feel around for her torch.

When she did finally pull back the blanket and raise herself on one elbow, she saw that it wasn't dark at all. Not light enough to see much, but enough to ease the pounding of her heart. The figure on the opposite stretcher was Stephen, and her movement had obviously woken him; for the next moment she saw that his eyes were open and that he was looking right at her.

Back in Balaclava Street, Stan Johnson took some comfort from the background roar of the guns, though he fretted about Kath not being in a proper shelter. When he'd been on Warden duty, he'd been comforted by the thought that no matter what happened to Balaclava Street, at least he knew that Kath and Tim were relatively safe in Dolphin Square. But Kath had been unshakeable in her determination to stay with him until he was well again.

Stan flexed his leg tentatively. It was healing up nicely; wouldn't be long now before he could throw away his stick and put his full weight on the injured limb . . .

Kath watched him test his leg for the second time in five minutes. Worry flooded again into her mind. Damn him, why wouldn't he take it easy? Let the others cope for a change! Out loud, she said: 'All right, love?'

'Coming on fine,' replied Stan cheerfully. Kath smiled at him; she knew he couldn't wait to get back on duty.

As it happened, that night of November 15th was a busy one for the Wardens. London had its biggest raid of the month, and though Balaclava Street escaped unscathed, the destruction extended over the whole of the rest of London. Instead of concentrating on the centre of the city, the German pilots had spread their ill-will far and wide.

'Where are we?'

'Biggleswade – at least I think so. Gosh, it's cold!'

Patty watched a tendril of fog curl over the floor of the ambulance. Fog? Mist, more like.

'Are we in a lay-by?'

'No,' replied Stephen. 'I drove off the road into a field. Then I slept and woke up so cold I thought I'd see if I could find any blankets in the back here. We seem to have lost most of our quota. The Colonel won't like that!'

'Blow the Colonel!'

'Can't have that sort of talk from the ranks, my girl!' laughed Stephen. 'By the way, we've got another puncture.'

Patty groaned. 'Not again! Well, it'll just have to wait. Anyway, I doubt if we could see to do it in this fog.'

'That's probably what's making it so damn cold.'

'You know, we'd be much warmer if we were together. Then instead of having one blanket each, we'd have two.' The muddled logic of what she said didn't surprise Patty as much as the open invitation. She was quite brazenly asking Stephen to share her bed – or rather, stretcher.

To make matters worse, Stephen hesitated.

'I don't think we should.' His voice trembled slightly. Patty winced inside and decided to feign innocence.

'Oh, come on!' she said in an off-hand way. 'No point in catching cold if we can avoid it, is there?'

'No, of course not.' He was still hesitating.

'Oh, Stephen – I'm freezing!'

Stephen needed no further invitation, and moved on to the stretcher beside her. For a moment, he huddled up uncomfortably beside her, and it seemed only natural that Patty should lift her head to let his left arm go around her shoulders. For some moments, she fussed around with the blankets until they were both covered with a double layer. Then and only then did she relax against him. Stephen trembled. It was, she knew, a tremble and not a shiver. She felt herself trembling, too. Suddenly, Stephen pulled her close and kissed her, making no attempt to conceal his passion. A few moments later all thought of the cold completely left her.

Gran Bowden surveyed her kingdom: a small corner of the Dolphin Square shelter which others trespassed on at their peril.

Twice the shelter had been shaken by a particularly heavy explosion, and an audible moan had arisen each time. Gran looked round for Tim and wasn't unduly worried to see that his place was empty, the blankets thrown back carelessly. She tut-tutted to herself, and her false teeth gave a sort of delayed-action click. Playing with that unruly Williams lot again.

Gran eased herself out of the deckchair – the symbol of her authority since it put her in a position where she could look down on the sleepers round about – and pulled the blankets fussily back on to Tim's mattress. Fancy letting them get trodden on like that! Give that boy a piece of her mind, she would.

Clambering back into her deckchair, she dozed. The doze became deeper, and soon she dropped off to sleep. As she did so, her ill-fitting false teeth slipped forward, giving her a ferocious look – a sort of snarl that ensured that no-one, not even the official Shelter Marshal, dared approach her corner.

Not far off, Madge Williams couldn't sleep, no matter how hard she tried. It wasn't the two nearby explosions which had disturbed her, but a host of other worries. Baby David seemed better but he still wasn't really well. But another, more serious worry was where the money was coming from. For the third week running, Bert had given her an envelope with £20 in notes inside. Each time he said he'd got the money from a lucky tip, but Bert just wasn't a betting man.

If he was borrowing all that money, God knows when they'd ever be able to pay it back! Madge tried to shove the thought away. Perhaps she was worrying herself for nothing. But a small voice inside kept insisting that she wasn't.

In the shelter of Dickins & Jones, Lesley Aynsworth couldn't sleep either. Well, that was that then! She was pregnant. No doubt about it. Three weeks overdue. Next to her, Joy slept unconcerned. Lesley felt real rage. Why should her sister have all the luck? She'd a bloody good mind to wake Joy up and tell her! The moment passed. No good putting it off much longer. She'd have to tell Mum. Perhaps she could do something about it, but it seemed unlikely. Lesley looked around her at the sleeping shapes under the blankets. Better try one of the girls first. Perhaps that Marjorie in accounts knew something. From what Lesley had heard, she certainly should!

*

Stephen had made love to her in a way that Patty had never thought possible. Not that he was a very experienced lover. But somehow it had all been so different from the fumblings and gropings of Peter. She felt they belonged together. The mere physical act hadn't meant all that much to her, to be honest; but it had brought a feeling of closeness unlike anything she'd ever experienced before. Giving herself completely and with love had brought a happiness and peace that seemed perfect. Somehow she and Stephen had become one.

At first she'd revelled in that feeling; but with the daylight had come an awareness of all the difficulties that lay ahead. What had they done? How was she to break the news to Peter?

Out loud, she said: 'We'd better fix that puncture.' The matter-of-fact statement made everything seem worse – made it seem sordid. Just any old crew having it off in the back of the ambulance. But she knew – and Stephen knew – that it hadn't been like that at all.

22

A Rift in the Family

Patty found the month of December confusing. You couldn't be sure of anything – not even a nightly air-raid. Official records described the early days of the month as seeing 'light activity', but this certainly wasn't the case at the Depot. For on December 8th, the Germans came back with between three hundred and fifty and four hundred aircraft and bombed the city indiscriminately.

In a strange way, Patty welcomed the activity. It gave her less time to think. Ever since she'd seduced Stephen – for despite his protests, she insisted that she was to blame for what had happened – her mind had been in a turmoil. Here she was, newly married, her husband off risking his life God knows where, and she having an affair with the man she worked with! Her anguish wasn't eased by the fact that she and Stephen now made love wherever and whenever possible. And it got better each time. Both now felt only half-alive when they were apart.

Patty desperately tried to rationalize her behaviour. Surely in wartime a woman was entitled to snatch love and companionship where she could? But then the image from the woman's magazines, of the little wife waiting at home for the hero to return, would plague her. There was no escaping it. She *was* being unfaithful.

But what did she really owe Peter? Every time she asked herself that question, unbidden memories of that hateful honeymoon would return. Yet just when she was sure she didn't owe such a man anything, she'd remember Peter's sweetness and kindness to her on other occasions and she'd hate herself for deceiving him.

Patty's love for Stephen, however, was no magazine romance. It was a love born out of hardship and death and shared dangers. It was a deep, abiding feeling of desperate and passionate need. It was forever. Life without him was unthinkable. She knew she could never live an ordinary married life with Peter now.

Matters weren't helped by her growing awareness that her family guessed something of what she was going through. It was clear to Patty from the way her mother fussed over her, and from her obvious disapproval of her friendship with Stephen. Gran was awful, too. She voiced her feelings not in any direct attack on Stephen, but in veiled references to 'Conchies' in general. Patty tried to explain that Stephen's beliefs didn't allow him to kill his fellow man. But she soon gave up. It was obvious that such ideas would never be accepted in the Johnson household.

Matters came to a head when Patty asked her mother if she could bring Stephen to Sunday lunch. Gran overheard and immediately launched into a diatribe against pacifists. Patty was about to spring to Stephen's defence, but then thought better of it. No point in bringing her troubles home for Sunday lunch! No point in bringing Stephen either! She'd so hoped that her family would accept him, but it was obviously not to be.

The worst part was that Patty had no one to confide in. Once or twice she thought of talking to Lesley, but poor Lesley very definitely had troubles of her own.

'I've tried everything,' said Lesley, desperation in her voice. 'Hot baths . . . Gin . . . Nutmeg . . . Some pills one of the girls at work gave me . . . Jumping off chairs . . . I'm so bloody pregnant, nothing works!'

Patty's heart reached out to her. 'You poor dear! Have you told your mother?'

'I had to, didn't I? I mean, it'll soon be obvious.'

'What did she say?'

'Not much. You see, I thought she might know something, but when I asked her, she mumbled something about it being a sin.'

For a moment Patty pondered this unexpected side of Dora Aynsworth. She'd never thought of Dora as being a religious woman. 'But she's not angry with you?'

'No, just miserable, like me. Oh, I wish I was dead!' And Lesley burst into a flood of tears.

Patty put an arm round her friend and comforted her. 'I'll have a word with your mum, Lesley. We'll see if the doctor can do anything.'

'He won't,' groaned Lesley, 'I know he won't.'

'You can't be sure until you've asked him.'

'If I do – will you come with me?'

'All right,' agreed Patty, not at all sure that this was a good idea. 'But I'd better speak to your mum about it first.'

It was obvious from the way she brightened up that Lesley thought this was a step on the way to a solution of her problem. To Patty's surprise, she rummaged under the bed and pulled out a mass of green silk.

'What's that?'

'Bert sent it. It'd make a nice dress for the christening . . .'

Patty was suddenly furious. 'Does he think he can buy you off with a length of parachute silk!'

'I think it meant he was sorry for . . . for . . .'

'Rubbish! Have you told the police about him yet?'

'No!' Lesley was suddenly defiant, 'And I'm not going to!'

Patty looked at Lesley in amazement. The multiple rape must have disturbed her mind more than anyone had realized.

'Anyway, one of the girls at work knows a woman . . .'

Patty decided it was time to take a firm grip of the situation. 'You're *certainly* not going to a backstreet abortionist! Dirty knitting needle stuff is out. You could die!' Sulkily Lesley sank back into gloom. 'I'm going to talk to your mother right now!'

Patty's anger carried her down stairs and into the presence of Dora Aynsworth, whom she found alone in the kitchen.

'Mrs Aynsworth . . .' Patty began.

'She's told you?' asked Dora, nodding towards a chair and almost absent-mindedly taking down another teacup from the dresser.

'Yes,' said Patty, 'and she's saying all sorts of ridiculous things about illegal abortions and suchlike.'

'I know. I feel I've failed her somehow. She came to me for help – and I couldn't suggest anything.' A tear gleamed in Dora's eyes.

'What about the doctor?'

'I've spoken to him. No help at all.'

'But, surely . . .'

'I know! But he said it was God's will and that we must let events take their course.'

Patty noted the second reference to religious matters and decided to plunge in. 'Lesley says you said it was a sin.'

Mrs Aynsworth looked at Patty for a moment, then laughed. 'Silly girl! What I said was that she was more sinned against than sinning. I wanted to put her off trying anything silly.'

'So what's to be done?'

'Nothing.' Dora Aynsworth looked steadily at Patty. 'Look, love, she's nearly three months gone now. She's got to have the kid. When it's born, she'll have another decision to make: whether to keep it or not.'

'Adoption, you mean?'

'That's what her father's insisting on. But I've told him I won't have her bullied.'

It was Patty's turn to be quiet as she turned Dora's words over in her head.

'Commonsense, isn't it?' Dora went on. 'Lesley's got to realize that what happened wasn't her fault. It's up to us to show her that we love her and that we're gonna look after her. And the baby.'

For most of her way home Patty thought about Dora's words, and realized that she'd misjudged her. Patty, like most people in the street, had always considered her a rather cold woman. Now she was seeing a very different Dora.

She said as much to Stephen as they snatched a few moments alone together, returning from yet another ambulance call. 'It's what I keep telling you,' smiled Stephen. 'Basically, people are good – it's just that they rarely let it show.'

It was Stan who was more outraged than anyone by Sergeant Brown's call at Number Seven.

'Are you suggesting that my daughter would steal from a corpse?'

The CID sergeant sighed wearily. He had more than a suggestion of a hangover, but he was doing his best not to let it show. 'I'm not suggesting anything, sir. Just routine.'

'Well, I'm not waking her up just to answer some damn stupid questions. She's been up all night protecting people like you.'

Stan had gone too far. The sergeant reacted quite violently. 'Now, now. That'll be enough of that, sir!'

Stan fought back his first impulse to retaliate. 'Well . . . I meant . . . I didn't mean . . .'

'Quite so, sir. No offence meant, none taken. I have to take statements from everyone in the street about the missing jewellery. Now about the young lady?'

As Stan went upstairs for Patty, the sergeant's eyes roamed around the room, pausing for longer than necessary on the collection of bottles on the sideboard, which the Johnsons were saving for a Christmas celebration.

Bit of money around, thought the sergeant to himself. Wonder where he gets his Scotch from? He was just beginning to fancy a touch of the hair of the dog, when Patty entered.

'Sorry to disturb you, miss. I wonder if you'd be kind enough to help me with a few details?'

23

The Twelve Days of Christmas

Patty could hardly believe it was nearly Christmas – it seemed somehow so unreal in the midst of the horror of war. Oddly it was the rather pathetic paper chains and straggly pieces of holly decorating the Depot that brought it home to her. The Colonel had turned an apoplectic purple when he'd noticed them, but had been constrained by Maudie to grunt a reluctant approval to Miss Pelley and her cronies, the perpetrators of the outrage.

Stephen reported this with a grin to Patty, then emphasized the imminence of Christmas even further by asking her if she'd made any plans. She shook her head. It hadn't even occurred to her.

'Mother wants me to go home for a couple of days,' he said. 'Asked if I'd like to bring you along too.'

Patty looked up, startled. Stephen smiled a reassurance.

'I haven't told her anything. She's just guessing. Mothers tend to do that.'

'Don't I know it!' Patty laughed. 'Will you go?'

He shrugged helplessly. 'Don't see how. I might try to get up the week after, when we get the two-day break.' He looked at her searchingly. 'Wish I *could* take you, Patty. I don't want to be away from you even for that time.'

She sighed. 'What can we do? I hate all this deceit.'

'Me, too.'

'If only we could live together openly, without shame. Maybe I should write to Peter after all?'

There was no answer to this question. They'd discussed it endlessly and still had no solution. Patty had guessed that Peter was in Malta and everyone knew the hell that island was going through just now. They stared at each other in hopeless misery for a while.

'Perhaps he'll get transferred? They can't keep them in a place like that for ever, surely?' suggested Stephen.

Patty shook her head dumbly. Who could tell what the Admiralty would decide? She could only hope.

'You're not taking his money, are you? The marriage allowance, I mean?'

'Well, no I . . . I haven't really needed to,' she told him. 'I'm still living at home, and I've got my salary here.'

'Good! Leave it in the bank, then – in his name. I couldn't stand the thought of him supporting you while we're . . .' He left the sentence unfinished, and once again, Patty curled up inwardly with guilt. 'If you need anything, you just let me know. Understand?'

Just then, the large figure of Maudie Harris loomed up.

'I'm getting together a group for carol singing,' she announced. 'How about you two?'

Kath felt absolutely exhausted. She began to feel that Christmas ought to be abolished in wartime. She'd managed to procure a chicken, and the butcher had added a pound of sausages, though God knows what they were actually made of. Stan was supplying the vegetables from the patch where the lawn had been.

Kath gazed forlornly at her store cupboard. You could hardly call it a store, really – just a few tins. But she did take a pride in one thing: the Christmas pudding in its china bowl, with the cloth knotted neatly around it. Kath wondered what it would taste like. The sultanas and raisins would be scattered pretty thinly, but the Ministry of Food recipe had said you wouldn't be able to tell the difference. And besides, she'd made up for it with an extra ration of brandy, courtesy of Harry Hempstead before he'd been killed, poor old soul.

She heard a tentative knock on the front door and went to open it. It was an unexpected visitor: Madge Williams from next door, cradling baby David on her hip and bubbling with excitement.

Kath was pleased to see her. She put the kettle on and rifled her store of biscuits for the baby. Madge was in an unaccustomed mood of gaiety and it soon spread to Kath.

'Seems like everything's fallen into our laps for once,' said Madge. 'I still can't believe it. Two whole weeks in Wales! Me Mam's that thrilled. She's never seen young Davey here.'

'It'll be a wonderful break for you, Madge.'

'Course, Bert can't come for the whole time, but we'll be together Christmas Day. They put the names in a hat at the Station and he got lucky. We reckoned if we were spending all that money on fares, we might as well go for longer.'

'Quite right too.' Kath approved of Bert's suggestion. Once there, Madge might decide to stay on in the country – or at least leave the children there.

'Our luck's really changed,' Madge went on, 'what with that *and* Bert having his winning streak on the horses—'

'His *what?*' Kath's eyebrows shot up in amazement.

Madge gave her a self-conscious grin. 'Yes. That's what I thought at first. But I'm not complaining, mind.'

'I should think not.'

After Madge left, Kath felt a lot more cheerful. She was glad the Williams were going to have a happy Christmas. Now it was up to her to make sure the Johnsons had one too. Young Patty, for a start – her first married Christmas, and parted from her husband . . .

Upstairs, Patty was thinking about her husband, too. Sitting at her dressing table, she was trying hard to find words to put into a letter to Peter. So far, all she'd managed was the Admiralty box number. This was the third start she'd made. On the first she'd begun: 'Darling', on the second, 'My dear Peter', and this one seemed destined to be simply, 'Dear Peter'. As she wrote the words, they seemed to look back at her reproachfully. It was horribly like one of those 'Dear John' letters she'd heard one of the women talking about at the Depot; that was what servicemen called them – letters from their wives or sweethearts which told them that they had wives no longer, or that the heart back home wasn't so sweet after all.

Patty knew full well the sort of letter that circumstances demanded; it formed so easily in her mind!

'Dear Peter,

You must believe me when I say that this is the hardest letter I have ever had to write. What has happened is not our fault – perhaps we were too young, as Mum always said . . .'

But Patty couldn't bring herself to say that. *What has happened is not our fault* . . . Well, it certainly isn't *your* fault, Peter! It's all my fault – and yet . . . I didn't intend to get involved with Stephen. It just happened somehow . . . Perhaps we didn't know each other for long enough before we got married. It *was* my fault! I should have said no. A wartime romance – that's all that it was . . .

As the thoughts raced through her mind, Patty saw once again the dashing figure of Peter in his uniform, the dinner-dance, his proposal and then, with a shock, that bedroom at Marlow once again. Could she never get away from that? It seemed so long ago. Now Peter was out there somewhere, perhaps fighting for his life. And here she was composing a letter that would spell nothing but misery for him!

A glance at her watch told her that she hadn't got long before she went on duty. Resolutely, she filled the blank pages with trivia about Balaclava Street and her work at the Depot, playing down the horror of the raids, because she suspected that the Admiralty censor would take all that out anyway. She succeeded in writing four pages without mentioning Stephen once. When she'd finished, she realized she'd left 'Dear Peter' at the start, but decided to leave it as it was.

Kath Johnson was still thinking about her children and Patty in particular, when her daughter came down the stairs.

'I'm off, Mum,' she called brightly. 'Mind posting this letter for me?'

'Course not,' said Kath, 'now you be careful!'

'Okay! Bye.'

When Patty had left, Kath glanced at the letter and felt somewhat cheered. Well, at least she was still writing to him!

That Christmas should have been one of the happiest ever for the Johnsons. Roger managed to get two days' leave and brought extra rations with him. The chicken was just right too, nice and juicy. Even the Christmas pudding turned out well. What with that and the glass of port that Stan had pressed on her afterwards, Kath felt quite a glow of satisfaction with all her efforts.

She'd imbibed quite a lot today – a lot for her, anyway. They'd all been invited over for a pre-lunch Christmas drink with Claude Windsor, now happily back in his old home and beginning to build a new life for himself without his beloved Sin. Not all Balaclava Street had been there – some, like the Williams, were away. Fred Perkins had taken Rita and her elderly parents to a country hotel for a couple of days, and Susan Farley was spending the holiday with her children and parents. But the Misses Wilkes were there and Enid Belling, and it had been quite a festive occasion. Claude's funny little friend Billy had been especially charming and chatty. He'd invited Kath into the kitchen to ask her advice.

'I'm chief cook and bottle-washer, you see,' he confided. 'But I've never done a Christmas pudding before. Tell me, am I doing it right?'

'Well, you really can't overcook them,' Kath told him,

with an approving nod at the bubbling saucepan on the stove.

'I do want everything to be just so – it being poor old Claude's first Christmas without Sincerity.'

Kath sighed. 'Yes – he's bound to feel it.'

'I'm doing my damndest to keep him busy. I suggested asking the two old darlings opposite to dinner.'

'The Misses Wilkes?'

'That's it. The older one's a bit of a tartar, but I gave her such a whopping sherry, it should break the ice. We're having the blonde with the big boobies and the tiny mind too.'

Kath giggled at this description of Enid, and felt a surge of relief. Enid had been on her conscience. It was dreadful to think of her being on her own for Christmas, but when she'd suggested inviting her to join them, Stan had put his foot down very firmly. Surprising in a way. She'd always thought Stan rather fancied Enid – and certainly Enid made little attempt to hide her designs on him. Soon after, Kath had made her excuses to Claude and Billy and hurried back home to see to her own cooking.

Kath was having a quiet forty winks after lunch when the men trooped back into the front room, having finished the washing-up.

'We deserve a drink after that,' announced Stan. 'What do you fancy, Rog?'

'Hold on, Dad! You'll have me under the table!'

'But it's Christmas!'

'You'll be saying it's time for tea soon!'

'So it will be. Look – it's nearly four o'clock already!'

'Is it really?' Patty interjected. 'I'll have to be off.'

'Honestly,' sighed her mother, 'you'd think they'd let you off – tonight of all nights!'

'Anyway, thanks for a gorgeous meal, Mum,' Patty murmured, giving her mother an affectionate hug.

'I'll walk you to the Depot,' offered Roger. 'Do me digestion a world of good.'

Once outside, Roger expected Patty to set off at a brisk pace, but to his surprise she dawdled down the road. Though their breath steamed in the air, it was more muggy than cold, so the slow pace wasn't uncomfortable.

'What are you up to, then?' asked Patty suddenly.

'What do you mean?'

'Oh, come on, Rog, I know you. You're up to something.'

'It's not important—'

'Oh, yes it is! I can see you're absolutely fizzing inside! It *must* be a woman.'

'Well, there *is* rather a nice little Waaf corporal on the station . . .'

'I knew it!' Patty was triumphant.

'But it isn't her.'

'Well, what *is* it then?'

'If I tell you, promise you won't tell Mum and Dad?'

'Course! What have you been up to?'

He stared at her in silence for a moment. 'I'm going for air-crew.'

Patty looked at him. 'But – how can you? You don't mean flying – a pilot?'

'No. I couldn't do that. Remember, I tried at the beginning? No – they're asking for Flight Engineers. For bombers. And I know all about engines.'

Patty stopped and pondered. 'I see what you mean about Mum and Dad. They'd be worried sick!'

'That's why you mustn't tell them. Besides, they might be worried for nothing. I mightn't be selected.'

'But you think you will, don't you?'

Roger was quiet for a moment. Then he said slowly, 'Yes, I've got a good chance. And it'd be really hitting back, wouldn't it? Not just sitting on the ground, taking it!'

'Yes,' said Patty doubtfully, 'I suppose it would be that.'

They walked on in silence for some distance. Patty felt that Roger had grown up somehow since he'd joined up;

but maybe the war had that effect on everyone. It had on her. Suddenly thoughts of Peter and Stephen swamped her mind, and somewhat to her surprise, Patty found herself telling her brother all about her own troubles.

When she'd finished, Roger summed it up with one sentence: 'Seems to me you've got two wartime infatuations on your mind, not one, like most people!' For a moment Patty thought he was joking, and then she saw what he was thinking. Could it be true that she wasn't really in love with *either* of the men in her life? That both were just shallow wartime romances, as Roger was suggesting?

'It isn't like that!' she retorted defiantly.

'Listen,' Roger warned her. 'I'm not judging you. But please be very sure about what you do. My going into aircrew may worry Mum and Dad, but what you're up to will just about kill them.'

Patty knew he was right. In fact, she sensed Mum was worried already, but she wasn't sure about Dad. Did he know what was going on? She hoped not.

'We'll talk about it again,' said Roger. 'Here, what time are you on duty? You'll be late!'

Patty gave him a swift peck on the cheek. 'See you tomorrow!' And with that she hurried off.

But not to the Depot. Instead, when she was sure that Roger was out of sight, she set off in a completely different direction – towards Stephen's bedsitter in Prince of Wales Drive. They'd arranged to meet there on discovering that they were both off-duty on Christmas night.

Though Christmas night was comparatively peaceful, it made no difference to the trekkers; they couldn't afford to wait until the siren went before setting off, in case they were caught in a raid on their way to safety. Londoners still took as few chances as possible, though as the raids became less frequent more and more stayed at home, either in Anderson shelters in the garden, or Morrison shelters set up in the strongest room in the house.

Although the sky over the capital now remained clear of raiders for several nights at a time, most of the families in Balaclava Street who'd sought shelter away from their homes continued to do so. As some were to discover, however, the larger shelters housed another enemy, unseen and undetectable, though potentially just as deadly as the bombs themselves.

On Christmas night, Stan insisted that the family went to Dolphin Square as usual although there was little of the Christmas spirit about the resulting grumbles from his family, especially Gran.

The shelter was as crowded as ever, and there was a bit of a sing-song going on in one corner. People had done their best to cheer the place up: paper chains were strung from pillar to pillar: a couple of the wardens were wearing funny hats, and a WVS lady was presiding over a Christmas tree, handing out presents for the children. One little girl scrambling to get through the throng sneezed right over Kath. She wasn't the only one: the night brought forth an absolute cacophony of coughs, snuffles and wheezes. Kath would have cause to remember it vividly a few days later, when her temperature soared and she lay flat out in bed, one of the first victims of the virulent 'flu epidemic.

But that Christmas night, unaware of what was in store, Kath was inclined to count her blessings. At least the family had survived relatively unscathed. She couldn't help feeling worried about Patty, though. She sensed that she was hiding something, and that something was making her unhappy. She had an inkling the young man at the Depot had a lot to do with it, and prayed she was mistaken . . . Oh well, she was a level-headed girl – she'd probably sort things out for herself, even if it did mean heartache along the way. Reassured somewhat, Kath let her thoughts stray from her immediate family to her next door neighbours. Wonder how Madge and the kids are enjoying their holiday . . .

If Kath had but known it, Madge wasn't enjoying her Christmas all that much. In fact, she and Bert had had a blazing row, and he'd stormed out to the pub with his sister and brother-in-law. And the holiday had started so well, too. The children adored life on the farm, and it was marvellous seeing all the relations again after such a long time. It was when they'd got back to the farm after tea that the trouble began. Bert had started rummaging through her suitcase with a worried frown on his face.

'What are you looking for, love?' she asked.

'I put a little parcel in here.'

Madge blushed. 'Oh Bert – I opened it. I meant to tell you. You shouldn't have brought me such a lovely present.'

A strange look came over Bert's face and he grasped her arm quite roughly. 'You shouldn't have touched it! Where is it?'

'I'm sorry, Bert, I didn't mean no harm. It – it was for me, wasn't it?' Madge couldn't understand his anger. Maybe he'd wanted to keep it as a surprise, but even so . . .

'Where is it, I said?'

Madge swallowed nervously. 'Bert – please don't be angry . . . I sold it.'

'You did *what?*' For a moment she thought he was going to hit her. She'd never seen him so furious before.

'It was worth ever such a lot. I was going to tell you later, honestly – I never thought you'd be so upset. You see, I gave some of the money to Mary and Dai, to go towards our keep . . .'

'You'd no right to touch it!'

'Bert! Bert, listen, there's quite a bit of cash over. You can always buy me something else with it. That can be a surprise.'

But Bert hadn't answered, just stormed out.

Madge sat alone in the big farm kitchen. She huddled

over the stove, but even its warmth couldn't dispel the icy fear that pervaded her whole being.

Patty and Stephen lay entwined in the peaceful aftermath of passion. It had been perfect. Stephen had taken his time, gently kissing her all over, exploring her, rousing her to a pitch of excitement before moving inside her. Patty had experienced sensations she'd never known before. Locked in mutual ecstasy, they'd climaxed together in a glorious finale.

After a while, Stephen gave a deep sigh. 'Sometimes it worries me. Have we any right to be so happy? Will we have to pay for it somehow?'

'Don't say that, darling,' breathed Patty. But she knew what he meant. She shivered suddenly.

Stephen raised himself on one elbow. 'You're cold!'

'No, no. Someone must have walked over my grave.'

He stayed propped up, staring at her, as if memorizing every feature of her face. 'God forgive me – I love you so much,' he told her quietly.

If Christmas itself was relatively peaceful, the respite from the bombing was short-lived. On December 29th the Luftwaffe returned to its grim task with renewed ferocity.

The sirens wailed just before 7 pm. Soon afterwards the bombing markers flared over the City, and the most concentrated fire raid of the Blitz began. This time over a hundred planes poured incendiaries and high explosives into the City proper, and soon the whole area between St Paul's and Guildhall was engulfed in giant walls of flame. From Moorgate to Aldersgate Street and Old Street to Cannon Street, the firemen fought a losing battle. The great blaze around Fore Street was abandoned and left to burn itself out.

From Balaclava Street it seemed as though the whole

of London to the east was ablaze. Stan Johnson watched and shuddered as he thought of the hopeless task facing the firemen in that burning hell.

The material damage done in the City was staggering. Guildhall was badly damaged. Eight Wren churches would never be the same again. The Law Courts and the Tower were hit. But amid the giant inferno, the cross on St Paul's stood shining, intact, London's most unmistakable landmark survived the raid substantially undamaged.

That was one miracle. The next came at 10 pm, when exhausted firemen and civil defence workers suddenly found to their astonishment that the enemy was inexplicably deserting his target. With the greatest fires of the war raging beneath them and the entire City of London and neighbouring boroughs at their mercy, the attack was being called off.

The rescue workers couldn't believe it. Suddenly they were left in peace to cope with the appalling scenes of wreckage and devastation. In peace – if you discounted flames that swept a hundred yards at a time, acres of falling walls, and thousands of embers borne on the wind, which started new fires wherever they landed.

In fact, some of the ashes were still warm as London moved into the New Year.

24

'And the Consequences Were . . .

If Patty had told anyone that she felt sick when she awoke on New Year's Day 1941, they'd probably have laughed and put it down to a hangover. More than half of adult Londoners were suffering that crisp 1941 morning, for although drink was hard to come by, with rum the only spirit readily available, most landlords had let their regulars have enough to celebrate the New Year in style. 1941, most people reckoned, couldn't be any worse than the year before, and so they made as much of their parties as they could.

But Patty hadn't been to a party; she'd been on duty at the Depot that night. The most she'd managed was a surreptitious New Year kiss with Stephen behind a parked ambulance and a sticky glass of over-sweet sherry with Dusty Miller in the Depot kitchen.

The next morning, though, she couldn't shake off the feeling of nausea. Perhaps it was that terrible sherry. After a spoonful of Andrews in a glass of water, she eventually persuaded herself that she felt better. It was only when she remembered that she'd promised to go and see Lesley that the first nagging doubt crept into her mind.

Soon that doubt grew and grew until she found she could hardly concentrate on Lesley's troubles at all. Her friend looked the picture of health. Patty told her so, hoping to cheer her up, and Lesley gloomily agreed. 'But then you always do when you're pregnant, don't you?'

It was that word which did it as far as Patty was

concerned. *Pregnant!* Oh God, no. Was she pregnant too?

With a sinking feeling, she realized it was possible – even probable. They'd never taken any precautions. How could they have been so silly? Making some excuse to Lesley, she walked back to the house in a daze, thoughts whirling around in her brain.

For a moment she wondered if she was pregnant by Peter, but then she saw that it was impossible. They'd made love during her period on that horrible honeymoon. And she'd had another period after that.

Sitting in her bedroom, she did some frantic calculations. She'd just finished one period when they were despatched to help out at Coventry. Wait a minute! Was it before or after the Coventry raid?

It was before! And suddenly she remembered the scratchy feel of ambulance-issue blankets on her bare flesh. Remembered, too, being glad that her period was over and that she and Stephen could make love.

Well, that was November 15th. She'd always been as regular as clockwork. Now the full horror of the timing sank in. And today she felt sick!

Patty sat on her bed, staring at herself in the mirror, but not seeing the reflected image at all. Happy New Year? Patty saw nothing but trouble ahead.

If Londoners had hoped that their New Year would be better than the old, they were given some grounds for optimism during the early days of January. The pattern of raids was now unpredictable and the capital seemed to get off lightly. Then, as aid from the United States began to flow, the Germans concentrated their attacks on Britain's ports – Portsmouth, Bristol, Swansea, Cardiff, Liverpool. However, the lessons learned in London helped the local Civil Defence to cope with these attacks, and the American aid continued to roll in.

*

Shortly after the middle of January, Patty knew beyond doubt that she was going to have a child – Stephen's child. Strangely, now that the uncertainty was removed, she felt much happier.

Of course, she had several ordeals head of her, but at least now she could get down to some concrete planning. Her mother and father would have to be told, and she was fairly sure how they'd react. Horror and disapproval, certainly – but she doubted if they'd turn her out.

First, though, she'd have to tell Stephen, and much of her planning was devoted to the question of how to break the news. At first she had no doubt how he'd take it – after all, they were in love. Yet soon a dark cloud formed. Supposing he wasn't pleased?

The doubts over his reaction persisted. All right, supposing he did want her to have the child. What happened then? Should she try to get a divorce? How could she tell Peter? Would she really have to write him one of those 'Dear John' letters after all? The dark thoughts grew.

The days passed, and still the moment never seemed quite right to tell Stephen. She could see that he suspected something, but each time when she was about to tell him, she held back.

When the moment finally came, it was hardly what Patty intended. Stephen had taken her back to his room and they'd made love in front of the gas-fire. Patty found that in their tender love-making she could forget all her worries for a short while. But as they lay still, locked together, she started to cry.

Stephen raised himself up in surprise. 'What . . .?' And then she blurted it out. Stephen said nothing, but rolled off her and lay on his back. Patty suddenly felt naked and ashamed, and scrabbled at a loose corner of the eiderdown to cover herself. Her tears flowed freely. All this time she dared not look at Stephen.

Suddenly strong hands turned her round to face him, but still Patty kept her eyes shut. How could she have allowed herself to get into this mess! At least Lesley had the excuse that she was taken by force. But she'd willingly given herself to a man who wasn't her husband.

'Darling! Darling – listen to me.'

There was something in his voice that made her open her eyes in hope. She knew the moment she saw his face that it was going to be all right.

'Are you quite sure?' There was no rejection in his voice, nor in his eyes – only a quiet joy. Patty nodded.

'But that's wonderful!'

It was Patty's turn to ask him if he was sure.

'Of course I'm sure! It's the most wonderful thing in the world.' He couldn't disguise his happiness and pride.

Patty flung her arms around him and they clung together.

Patty and Stephen talked all that afternoon until darkness fell, and only the call of duty made them venture out into the snowy streets. Patty, however, was totally unaware of the cold, filled as she was with an inner warmth. Stephen had set all her fears at rest – and this in spite of the fact that she'd given him every opportunity to back out.

When she'd mentioned abortion, he'd been horrified, calling it murder. 'How could you even think of it? No, no, no!' She'd also suggested having the child in secret, then letting it be adopted. But this, too, Stephen had rejected out of hand. It was *their* baby, and they were going to bring it up – not hand it over to some unknown third party!

The thought of bringing up the baby had raised another problem in Patty's mind. Could she continue to live at home? Obviously she couldn't answer that until she'd told her parents and found out their reaction. But Stephen had put the alternative forward without hesitation: they'd take a flat or room, anything – and live together until Patty could get a divorce. Then they'd marry and live happily ever after – 'Just the three of us.'

At first, it sounded like a marvellous idea. But then Patty's Balaclava Street upbringing asserted itself.

'Whatever will people think?'

'I don't care! It's what we think that matters!'

'Oh, Stephen, that's all very well, but people will talk. My parents will be upset . . . and . . . and what about your mother?'

Stephen pondered. 'Well, she's always wanted me to get married and have children . . . but it's bound to come as a shock, I suppose.'

Patty nodded. 'She'll hate the business of divorce, too.'

'Well . . . she's not so out of touch, you know. Her main worry will be whether I'm happy, and when she sees I am, I think she'll get used to the idea. She already likes you, so we've got a head start.'

'When will you tell her?'

'I'll go up there as soon as possible. I can break it more gently in person.'

'Yes. I'll have to face my parents too. I'm dreading it.'

'Do you want me to come with you?'

'No, not yet. I'd best tackle Mum and Dad alone.'

'I'd like to come.'

'No, love. Leave it to me.'

Kath was shattered. She stared at her daughter, eyes large and troubled, her face white and drawn, struggling to take in the news. For a moment she swayed, and Patty rushed forward in alarm.

'Mum – I didn't mean to give you such a shock – I . . .'

But Kath had got a grip on herself now. On top of everything else, she knew that the 'flu was making her feel faint – she'd had a really bad go. Still, she wasn't prepared to admit that to Patty – and it didn't detract one jot from the anger she felt.

'How could you *do* this to us?' she blazed. 'Think of the disgrace! What's everybody going to say?'

Patty stared back miserably. 'I'm sorry,' was all she

could manage. Kath was generally so easy-going, it shocked Patty to see her so enraged.

'And I suppose you expect me to tell your father?'

'No, of course not, Mum. I'll tell him—'

'What? That you're going off to live with this . . . this man? A fine hero he's turned out to be! I tell you this, my girl, if you leave this house and go to him, then it's goodbye! We'll want no part of you!'

Patty fled from the kitchen, brushing past her father who was just coming in, and ran up to her room. Once there, she flung herself on her bed and sobbed her heart out. How could her mother say that! She'd counted on her to be sympathetic, understanding – but no: the rejection was total.

She was about to get off the bed and start packing, when she heard her father's footsteps coming up the stairs. They sounded heavy and tired. They sounded just as they used to sound long ago, when he'd come up to give her a spanking. For a moment Patty tensed like a little girl, dreading the coming punishment . . .

But when her father opened the door, she could see not anger, but concern and sadness in his eyes. He sat down awkwardly on the edge of the bed. 'Now c'mon, love! Perhaps you'd better tell me what this is all about. Your mother's so upset I can't get any real sense out of her.'

'Oh, Daddy! I'm in such a mess!'

'Well, straightening up messes is what fathers are for.'

Stan put his arm around her, and Patty suddenly felt safe. She told him everything, even about Peter and the honeymoon – it all came tumbling out. She could feel him tense angrily when she got to the bit about the honeymoon, but that passed and then she could feel him trying to understand as she told him about Stephen and Coventry and the baby. He listened in silence, and only spoke out once, when she said that she'd been thinking of packing right away because her mother had been so angry. 'We'll have none of that. Course your mother's upset. I'm upset. But there'll be no leaving this house until we've sorted it all out.' Then he left her. For a while Patty could hear raised voices from the kitchen, then the tones were lowered. Patty tried to catch the murmur of conversation until at last she fell into an exhausted doze.

The next thing she knew, her mother was calling her down for tea. But there was no note of forgiveness in Kath's voice. Clearly, Saturday tea at Number Seven wasn't going to be the happy affair it usually was.

Kath had managed to get a great rarity for the occasion, a tin of salmon, and it had cost her dear both in points and cash. Looking at the miserable faces of her husband and daughter, Kath could see it had been a waste of effort. Only Tim tucked in with any gusto. He was even allowed to wipe round the tin with his bread without reproach. Tim enjoyed his tea enormously.

No one else did. At one stage Kath found tears running down her face and had to turn back to the sink, ostensibly to fill the kettle. But both Patty and Stan had seen: Patty, knowing she was to blame, felt the tears brimming up behind her eyes and nearly choked on her piece of bread and margarine.

Most of the meal was eaten in silence, except for Tim, who chattered cheerily on, oblivious to the atmosphere. When the three adults exchanged words they were only requests, chillingly polite, for plates to be passed.

There was only one exchange that lasted more than a few words and that was when Patty got up from the table with the excuse that she had to go on duty. 'You'll be wanting to give your notice in there very shortly,' observed her father.

'Notice?'

The idea had never occurred to Patty. Of course – she couldn't go on driving an ambulance if she was pregnant.

'Not immediately,' she replied. 'I mean I'll be able to carry on for some time yet, I expect.'

'The sooner you pack it in, my girl, the better,' seid her mother, in a hard voice which made Patty wince. Kath's tone left room for no doubt: she meant that the sooner Patty was away from Stephen the better.

'I'm not leaving Stephen, if that's what you mean!' Patty retorted angrily.

'Steady!' Stan's tone had a cutting edge too.

Patty glanced from one parent to another and saw that they were now united in their disapproval. Clearly there'd be no chance of a reasonable discussion here – not yet, anyway.

'See you tomorrow,' she mumbled, and hurried out.

25

The Chickens Come Home

Kath had never seen Madge Williams look so pretty. Her face had lost its drawn, weary look and for once there was colour in her cheeks. She sat in the Johnsons' kitchen, while Baby David hauled himself unsteadily round the room on a voyage of curiosity.

'He's into everything now!' laughed Madge.

'He's certainly grown in the last few weeks. You're going to have your hands full,' Kath smiled in reply.

'The big problem's at work. They've got such nice things in the flat, and he hates it when I keep him strapped in his pushchair. Yells his head off.'

Kath could just imagine the racket. But now Madge seemed better able to cope with it – not like a few months ago, when the kids regularly reduced her to total despair.

'I suppose you couldn't have left him down in Wales with the others?' Kath asked, but she already knew the answer: Madge would never be parted from her baby. She'd only left the rest of the family because they so obviously loved the country life and because their health had improved so dramatically.

'It would have been too much for me Mam to cope with,' Madge was saying. 'Besides, she's only got a small cottage. Little Megan's no trouble, mind, and Mam's glad of the company now me Da's passed on.'

'She doesn't mind being separated from Glen and Joey?' Kath knew that the three boys had stayed on at Dai and Mary's farm.

'Love, you, no! Mam spoils her, see, and anyway, she goes out to the farm on Sundays. They're having the time of their lives.' Madge's voice was a little wistful; it was clear that even though the children were happy, she felt the wrench deeply.

Kath gave her arm a reassuring squeeze. 'You did the right thing, my dear.'

'Oh, I know that, Mrs Johnson. I wish I'd done it months ago!'

'You certainly look much better yourself.'

'I'm sleeping at night. Makes all the difference!'

Just then there was a loud knock on the front door, and both women looked at each other in surprise. In wartime, a sudden summons like that could mean bad news. Kath paled as she hurried to the door. Which one of the family was it?

She needn't have worried. The shape behind the glass-panelled door soon revealed itself as the familiar burly figure of Bert Williams. Kath smiled a welcome. 'Looking for Madge? She's here – we were just having a cup of . . .' Kath's voice tailed off as she took in Bert's haggard appearance. He was white as a ghost and shaking uncontrollably. 'Bert! Whatever's the matter?'

Madge appeared in the kitchen doorway with David on her hip. As she came forward to greet him, she too gasped at his woebegone appearance.

It was then Kath became aware of another figure behind him, a man in a shabby raincoat and trilby. It was Sergeant Brown, the plain clothes detective who'd been round before Christmas questioning everyone in the street.

'Mrs Williams!' The sergeant moved closer officiously. 'I'd like a few words with you.'

'Bert! What is it? What's it all about?' Madge's face had drained of colour and suddenly looked pinched and weary again.

'Better come home, love,' Bert muttered. 'We can talk private there.'

'Yes – yes, of course.' She started to follow Bert and

the sergeant down the path, then turned in the gateway. 'Sorry, Kath. Thanks for the tea . . . and everything.'

Kath stood on her doorstep until the front door of Number Nine closed behind them. Even then she lingered, consumed by curiosity . . .

As it turned out, she heard the story soon enough when she, Gran and Tim went nextdoor to collect Madge for their nightly trek to Dolphin Square. Madge didn't want to go and was clinging to Bert in a desperate fashion, while Gran and Tim looked on curiously from the garden path.

'No. I want to stay here with you, Bert. Please!'

'Won't do no good, sweetheart.'

'But what are we going to do?' The sobs started again – great, shuddering sobs that wracked her thin body.

'There now,' he comforted her. 'Calm down, love. You go along with Mrs Johnson – for Davey's sake.' His eyes met Kath's in a mute appeal.

'That's right. Where is that young rascal?' asked Kath matter-of-factly. 'Why don't I take him and go on ahead? I expect Bert's waiting to go back on duty.'

To Kath's dismay, this provoked another outburst of sobs. 'He's . . . he's not going back! He's been suspended!'

Bert gave his wife a little shake. 'Hush up, Madge, will you? Whatever will Mrs Johnson think? Now pull yourself together and go to Dolphin Square.'

'Why don't you come with us?' she quavered.

' 'Cos I need some peace and quiet to think straight,' he retorted, then in a gentler tone: 'Go on, lass, please. It's best – really. We'll sort things out in the morning.'

So eventually they all set off, and during the tram journey Kath managed to extract a somewhat incoherent explanation from Madge. It all began, apparently, with Bert's 'winning streak', which Madge suspected all along, but which she'd never questioned too closely.

'I wish I had now,' she moaned, 'But things were so bad with money, and I didn't know where to turn next.'

Kath nodded sympathetically. She'd seen Madge's

worry and the effect it had had on her. 'Are you saying that Bert stole the money, then?' she asked quietly, determined not to let her mother hear. Gran would know soon enough, but Kath wasn't going to give her the chance to spread the bad news first. Mrs Bowden was only knitting spasmodically and Kath knew that meant she was trying to listen to the conversation.

'Not exactly,' Madge explained. 'It was jewellery and stuff – from bombed homes. And it was all my fault it was discovered . . . only I didn't know! If only Bert had told me, maybe . . .' She shook her head and blew her nose again. 'Oh, I don't know what I'd have done. I just can't believe that Bert's done this. He's not like that really, Kath!'

'I know, Madge, I know,' Kath soothed her. 'He must have been under tremendous pressure.'

'That's it!' Madge grasped at the excuse eagerly. 'He just fell for the temptation of easy money. It was Christmas that did him in, though. He'd got this brooch, see – he was going to give it to Mary. A sort of thank you for having us all to stay. But I found it in his suitcase and thought it was a present for me. And I sold it and gave her the money instead. Bert was ever so angry with me at the time, but of course, I didn't know why.'

'I suppose the police traced the brooch to the shop you sold it to?'

'Yes. Bert was beginning to think things were all right and then this CID bloke turned up at the station. Now Bert's been suspended until the case comes up. He reckons he'll get sent down . . . Maybe five years, he thinks . . . I just don't know what we're going to do . . .' Madge dissolved into tears again, and Kath had her work cut out to quieten not only her, but David, who started bawling in sympathy. She was so busy that she didn't react fully to Madge's story until much later. Then it hit her full force: their own dependable local bobby had turned into a cheap sneak-thief; worse than that – a looter! Whatever the excuse, Kath was appalled.

So was Stan when he heard the story first-hand from Bert, whom he'd come across staggering back from the pub, clearly the worse for drink. Covering his astonishment, Stan helped him into the sitting room of Number Nine. There, to his embarrassment, Bert started to cry. Stan murmured something about getting back on his round and leaving him in peace, but Bert looked up in despair. 'No – please don't go, Stan. there's – there's something I want to get off my chest . . .'

Stan stared at him. Somehow Bert seemed to have shrunk in size; he was crushed, beaten, almost childlike. Bert blew his nose loudly and then motioned Stan to the armchair. Reluctantly, Stan seated himself.

'You and Kath, you've always been good to us,' began Bert. 'You've been real friends—'

'Anything we can do, Bert, you know that.'

'Don't reckon there's anything anyone can do now. I've been suspended from duty, see. Probably get five years hard.'

Stan's eyes were round with astonishment. 'Five years? Bert, what've you done?'

And so it all came out, with Stan listening, silent and horrified as the story unfolded.

'It started way before Christmas,' Bert told him. 'One night, I saw a chink in the Aynsworths' blackout. I knocked, but I couldn't make anyone hear, 'cos the wireless was on so loud. So I went round the back door.'

The sight that greeted him there was engraved in Bert's memory for ever. Facing him at the kitchen table was Horace Aynsworth in his shirt sleeves, spread out in front of him – in fact, one piece fell from his fingers when he saw Bert – was a whole spread of jewellery: strings of pearls, rings, clasps, earrings, pendants, sparkling in the light of the naked bulb hanging high above the table.

Bert's eyes turned from the table to Horace. It didn't need a trained policeman to recognize the expression on Horace's face; it shouted *guilty* as though he'd screamed it out loud.

'What're you doing here?' Horace's voice matched his face. It quivered with alarm.

'I came about the blackout,' said Bert automatically.

'Blackout?' Horace looked wildly round. 'There's nothing wrong with the blackout!' As he spoke, his hands scrabbled wildly at the jewellery, as though trying to sweep it into the table drawer.

'You're showing a light from that window,' repeated Bert, watching Horace with fixed fascination.

'I'll see to it,' said Horace, jumping to his feet. A string of pearls fell to the floor and broke free, rolling in all directions. Horace somehow avoided stepping on them and gave the kitchen curtain such a jerk that Bert was afraid he'd bring the whole lot down.

'There! Thank you . officer. Good night.' Horace moved towards Bert to usher him out of the back door.

'Hold on.' Bert stood his ground. 'Where did all this jewellery come from?'

Horace gabbled. 'It's mine. You haven't got a warrant.'

'I don't need one,' Bert told him. 'Not if I enter a premises to prevent a crime being committed.'

'What crime? There's no crime here. Just looking at Dora's jewellery – that's all. Now, if you'll excuse me.'

Bert was beginning to feel that his sergeant would be quite proud of him. All that jewellery! Reports of looting. Horace Aynsworth was an undertaker. Undertakers were often left alone with the dead . . .

'Your wife's jewellery, eh? I'd say there's about a dozen wedding rings there. Been married before, have you?'

It was Bert's attempt at sarcasm that really broke Horace. He collapsed back on to the chair and started crying and pleading at the same time.

'Bert – you know me. We don't have to make a big thing of this, do we? People couldn't pay for the laying out, so they gave me jewellery instead. Nothing wrong with that, is there?'

'No,' said Bert, very deliberately taking out his notebook and pencil. 'So long as you can give me their names and addresses.'

Horace said nothing; just looked at Bert in despair.

Just why Bert Williams didn't march Horace round to the station that night, he would have found it difficult to say.

Partly, it was to do with his own money worries. Partly it was to do with the fact that, as Horace explained, none of the people from whom he'd taken the jewellery had any more use for it; they were dead. Nobody would miss it. Anyone who did would assume it was buried in the rubble.

It had even more to do with the fact that Horace never actually tried to bribe him in so many words – simply suggested somehow that Bert would be doing more harm than good by reporting it. All those bereaved relatives having their grief rekindled . . . It was the performance of Horace's life.

Bert had suddenly realized he was weakening and had protested when Horace started tidying the jewellery away. Then Lesley had come down from upstairs and he couldn't continue the conversation in front of her.

It was only as he was leaving that Horace had said: 'See you tomorrow then, Bert?' and he'd said 'Yes.' And in that moment he'd known exactly what was in Horace's mind. Not that anything was said, but he knew.

'He gave me cash every week, Stan . . . for being co-operative, he called it.'

Bert looked at Stan appealingly, as if willing him to utter some words of comfort. But Stan couldn't speak. He was remembering the horror he'd felt when everyone had come under suspicion after Sincerity Vale's death. Looking at Bert, he could hardly believe this was really happening.

'Have you told your Inspector the whole story?' he asked.

Bert shook his head. 'What I done is bad enough. Didn't want to grass on anyone else.'

'You'll have to tell them, Bert. They're going to find out sooner or later. There was masses of stuff nicked. They'll know you couldn't have done it all on your own.'

Bert's next words shocked Stan even more. 'It'd mean getting Dora into trouble,' he muttered.

'Dora? What's she got to do with it?'

'She tipped Horace off, didn't she? About houses where there were valuables. Things she'd seen when she went with the ambulance.'

'Good God!' Stan was lost for words for a moment. 'Talk about shitting on your own doorstep! Bert, it's no good trying to protect the Aynsworths. Why should they be allowed to get away with it? They'll just go on doing it after you're sent to prison. They deserve everything that's coming to them!'

'S'pose you're right,' agreed Bert, and sank his head in his hands. 'I'll cop the worst, anyway.'

Stan couldn't help feeling he was right. There was scant sympathy for bent coppers. He got up and put a hand on Bert's shoulder. 'Come on, old son, you'd best get to bed. Try and sleep. Then you can go to the station first thing in the morning.'

Stan was a little afraid of leaving Bert alone. Would he do anything drastic? But the drink was taking effect, and Bert let himself be led to the bedroom and put to bed like a small child. He was almost asleep when Stan was removing his boots.

Stan let himself out into the street and took a deep breath of fresh air. Right opposite was Number Ten, the Aynsworths' house. It was shrouded in darkness, and looked somehow evil and menacing. Evil was certainly the word for Horace – taking advantage of the weakness and stupidity of a man like Bert at a time when he was under such pressure. It was too late to help Bert now but Horace must be made to pay himself whatever it took. Stan felt a shiver of revulsion run through him as he thought of the undertaker . . . and the ruin he'd brought on the unfortunate Williams family.

26

The End of an Era

What to do about Peter was very much on Patty's mind. Finally she pulled a pad of writing paper towards her and started to write the letter that she knew must be sent. After no less than five false starts, she settled for a simple 'Dear Peter' and then told him in straightforward terms what had happened. When she'd finished, she read the letter through and felt like tearing it all up, but instead, with a sudden resolve, she put the letter into an envelope, sealed it, addressed it and put it into her handbag ready for posting. No good putting it off any longer.

Gradually as the days passed, life at Number Seven returned to some semblance of normality. The barriers that Kath had erected between herself and Patty slowly crumbled, and Kath found that her love for her daughter gradually overcame her feelings of anger and shame.

One thing she couldn't do, however, was accept Stephen into the family. Stan seemed to find it easier than she did. Stephen had called and, somewhat to her surprise, Patty found herself excluded from the discussion with her parents in the front parlour. According to Stephen, it had been an uneasy occasion, although her parents had seemed to relax a little when he told them that he intended to marry Patty as soon as her divorce could be got through.

Kath's attitude was mirrored even more strongly by Gran. She was vocal in her disapproval of Patty, but Stephen she completely ignored. In vain, Patty pleaded and argued, the old woman was adamant.

Patty was surprised how equably Stephen took it all.

'It's her generation, darling. She won't accept me until she sets eyes on the baby. You'll be amazed how that child will change things.'

'But that's months away! I don't think I can stand this atmosphere much longer.'

In the event, she didn't have to. The chance to escape came sooner than expected. Patty had gone to the corner shop to see Susan Farley. Susan's second-hand clothes business was now flourishing – so much so that she'd advertised for help. It had occurred to Patty that before she handed in her notice at the Depot, she ought to fix herself up with another job. If it wasn't too heavy, she could work right up to the time the baby was due. Serving in a small shop seemed just what the doctor ordered – if Susan would have her. Of course, she'd have to tell Susan all about the baby. It was only fair.

As she turned into the main road, she hesitated for a moment. There was an ambulance outside the shop – not one from the Depot, but a hospital one. As she approached, two ambulance men eased out a stretcher, and Patty could see that lying on it was the old lady who lived above the shop, looking very grey and drawn. Susan Farley followed the little procession out onto the pavement and hovered anxiously as the stretcher was loaded. Then the ambulance driver shut the doors and with a reassuring wink to Susan, climbed in his cab and started up.

Susan suddenly became aware of Patty watching. 'Oh – hullo Patty. We've had quite a to-do, as you can see.'

Patty followed her inside the shop. 'Seems I arrived too late to be of any help.'

'Oh, yes, I forgot you were an ambulance driver.' Susan gave her a shy smile. 'I could certainly have done with you. I'm not much good in emergencies.'

'What happened to the old girl?'

'She fell down the stairs. I'm afraid she'd broken her hip.'

Patty drew a sharp breath. 'Nasty at her age!'

'Yes. Poor old dear – she really isn't safe on her own. She's deaf as a post and nearly blind too. We've been worried about her up there for ages. Lucky I was around when it happened.'

'Hasn't she any relatives to go to?'

'Only a niece. Lives out near Watford somewhere. Still, she'll be in hospital for a long time by the look of things, so she'll have to give up the flat.'

'Maybe they'll put her in an old people's home – if she survives. An accident like that can be a pretty massive shock.'

'Mm – well, I'll have to ring the niece and see what can be done.' Susan gave a sigh. 'Anyway, what can I do for you?'

'Oh – I've come about the job actually.' Susan stared at her, bewildered, and Patty could see she was preoccupied. 'Look, why don't you make that call? I'll explain afterwards. It's rather a long story.'

It didn't take all that long to tell, though. When it was all over, Susan gazed at the tea cup in her hands, then glanced nervously at Patty, her face bright scarlet.

Oh God, thought Patty, she's horror-struck. 'I'm sorry,' she muttered, and started to gather up her things.

'No – Patty! Don't go!' came the urgent response.

'But I . . . you're not shocked?'

'No. I can understand – I think. It's just such a strange coincidence, you coming here today of all days. My husband's been so worried about leaving me on my own. We've had several break-ins, you know. But if you and your . . . friend wanted to take the flat upstairs – well, there'd be a man about the place again.'

'That'd be marvellous! But it was the job I came about, really.'

'Yes, yes – but it'd be convenient for you to have the flat as well, wouldn't it? And we'd be delighted.'

Patty left the shop with a singing heart; she couldn't

wait to break the news to Stephen. Then it occurred to her that she ought to tell Lesley. News of her pregnancy would be round Balaclava Street like wildfire as soon as she handed in her notice, and Lesley was her friend – she should hear first. After all, they were more or less in the same boat now, weren't they?

Lesley received Patty's news with a curious mixture of envy and smugness: envy that Patty had managed two raging love affairs in the space of a year, and smugness that Patty had ended up no better off than herself, with an illegitimate child. Soon, however, she was chattering away excitedly, sensing a possible return to their old closeness. They exchanged details of their symptoms, discussed the question of children's names and generally made plans for the future.

Baby talk having been exhausted, they moved on to other things. Patty learnt that the atmosphere in the Aynsworth household had improved enormously. For one thing, Joy was now away in the Land Army.

'You should hear her carry on,' Lesley giggled. 'She has to get up every morning at five, all weathers, and it's non-stop all day. It's all she can do to crawl into bed every night about nine o'clock.'

'Poor Joy!'

'It's a hoot, isn't it?' crowed Lesley. 'She was looking forward to getting off with all those beefy country types, but the farmer she works for is over fifty and a real old prude, apparently. And the nearest village is ten miles away – she has to cycle there and back!'

The picture of the once-elegant Joy up to her knees in mud and turnips made both girls laugh, but they were brought up short by the unexpected arrival of Horace. To Patty's surprise, he gave her quite an affable smile, and she couldn't help raising an eyebrow as the door shut behind him. Lesley grinned.

'Told you! He's almost human!'

'What's brought this on? Not Joy leaving home, surely?'

'No. Old man Truefitt's retired at last, and Dad's King

of the Castle. He's loving every minute.' Lesley pulled a grimace. 'Can't say I enjoy *my* work, but I suppose I'll get used to it in time.'

Since she'd become pregnant Lesley had been working alongside her father, handling all the bookwork. It was probably this that had caused the improvement in Horace's attitude, thought Patty. Lesley was speedy and efficient in her work, and Mr Aynsworth would appreciate that. She was surprised by Horace's demeanour considering the enormity of the charge hanging over his head, then realized with a shock that quite possibly the Aynsworths were unaware of it. The police would move slowly and surely in a case like that. She wondered when the blow would fall and what effect it would have on the household. Should she give a hint of warning to her friend? She decided to keep out of it.

As Patty strolled back across the road, she pondered whether to tell her mother about the possible move to the flat above the corner shop. But she didn't get the chance. Awaiting her at home was another surprise. Kath called her into the front room, where a tea-party was in progress, and sitting on the sofa was Enid Belling – with a strange man! Enid was pink and sparkling with excitement, full of arch smiles and trilling laughter.

'Patty, dear, I want you to meet my new lodger,' she gushed. 'This is Fred Munday.'

Fred dutifully rose to his feet to shake hands, politely concealing a sigh of boredom. Patty guessed rightly that Enid had been parading him up and down Balaclava Street. He wasn't a bad-looking man; a bit on the shy side probably – although Enid was enough to daunt the bravest of souls. His eyes were intelligent, and Patty thought she detected a gleam of quiet amusement in them as he looked at his new landlady. Enid's designs on him were blatantly obvious, but Fred didn't appear to be put off.

'Fred's in the Auxiliary Fire Service,' Enid was explaining. 'He got bombed out when Clapham caught it that last time, poor love. Never mind, we'll make you nice and comfortable nextdoor, won't we?' She patted his knee proprietorially.

'I didn't know you were looking for a boarder,' interjected Kath.

'I wasn't really. But my Eddie and Fred's young lad Bill are together in the RASC, and when Eddie wrote me what had happened, it seemed like Fate was taking a hand. Fred's a widower, see? So we're both lonely people. Up till now, that is.' She flashed a winning smile at the hapless Fred.

The Colonel's reaction to Patty's resignation was predictable. Disappointment first, because he genuinely liked her and was sorry to see her go, but on hearing the full story, profound shock. He just managed to contain himself until Patty left the office, but then as usual, Arthur Graves bore the brunt of his outrage.

'I'd have believed anything of that Broome fellow,' he exploded. 'But that young girl . . . thought she was made of finer stuff. Husband in the Navy, you know. Just goes to prove you can't trust these Conchies.'

Arthur pointed out mildly that only the other day Colonel Harris had been praising Stephen's work, but it made no difference. All the Colonel's latent prejudice had been kindled by the news.

The Colonel's reaction was nothing to Kath's, however, when she heard that her daughter proposed to move in with Stephen to the flat over the corner shop. She came as near hysterics as Patty had ever seen. It took all Stan's tact and calm understanding to quieten her and make her accept the situation. There wasn't any alternative, after all.

And so the move was accomplished, and became the nine-day wonder of Balaclava Street. In the event, people weren't as hostile as Patty had feared; inquisitive, yes, but on the whole sympathetic. Not that she cared all that much what they said or thought. She was in a seventh heaven of her own: she and Stephen were more in love than ever, and now they were sharing their first home together.

Kath wasn't happy, though. To her, Patty's departure meant a break that was far more final even than her wedding. She had a feeling things would never be quite the same again.

27

The Cold Wind

Reactions to the news of Bert Williams' suspension varied. In the main, there was sympathy for the Williams, particularly Madge, who seemed to be wasting away with the strain and worry of it all. They'd now had to give in their notice to Fred Perkins, and tearfully Madge was packing their belongings to go down to Wales. Bert, meanwhile, had been suspended without pay until the trial, and they'd been forced to subsist solely on Madge's wage from her cleaning job. Financially, things were very tight for them.

'The waiting's the worst,' she told Kath. 'Not knowing when the case will come up and what'll happen.'

'You're staying here till then?' asked Kath.

'As long as I can. We have to be out of the house by May 1st, though. Mr Perkins is going to let it again. I hate to leave Bert on his own. He gets so down.'

Kath nodded. She'd seen him in the garden, looking morose and dejected, pottering around just for the sake of something to do.

'Can't he find some spare-time work?' asked Kath.

'Mr Perkins said he might be able to take him on to do some painting and decorating. Odd days, you know, but it'd be better than nothing.'

'Oh yes. I hope it works out for you.'

'People have been very kind,' said Madge. 'Miss Jessie gave me a jar of marmalade and some little cakes, and Mrs Farley gave Bert some fags. And you've been ever so good, too, what with the eggs and things. It's more'n we deserve.'

'Madge, don't say that! None of it was your fault,' remonstrated Kath.

'Well, even so . . .' she sighed. 'Do you know, I found a parcel on the step last night – full of all sorts of goodies. There wasn't a note or anything. I can't think who it can be . . . unless perhaps it was Claude Windsor. Oh dear, I wouldn't like them to think I wasn't grateful, whoever it was.'

'Don't worry, Madge. I'm sure they understand. You've got enough on your mind as it is.'

Madge smiled wanly. 'Well, I've given up worrying about the future now. God knows how we'll ever start again once Bert . . . when he comes out of prison. Something'll turn up, I expect. I'm just taking every day as it comes.'

'That's right, love.'

Madge turned to look at her little house and sighed again. 'We've had some happy times here. I wonder what your new neighbours will be like.'

Kath had been wondering about that, too. 'I'll write and let you know,' she told Madge. 'We won't lose touch.'

The attitude towards the Aynsworths was quite different, and ranged from coldness to downright hostility. Some of the younger elements even chucked bricks through the front windows.

Horace, however, kept on working. He was out on bail now, and as the business was more or less his own, there was nothing to stop him. He did listen to Lesley, though, when she suggested that perhaps it wasn't quite the moment to change the name, so Truefitt's it remained. Fortunately the scandal hadn't spread all round the district yet, though it probably would once the trial was on. Meanwhile there was still plenty of business, and Horace worked long hours, leaving home early and returning late so as to avoid contact with the neighbours.

Dora had taken the whole affair badly, and become listless and apathetic. She'd resigned from the Ambulance Service immediately on the grounds of ill-health – a relief to Colonel Harris, who would have felt bound to dismiss her otherwise. Joy came up from the farm and took her mother back to stay in the village for a few weeks, hoping to help her build up her strength before the ordeal of the trial. It wasn't a happy prospect.

Horace had been left in little doubt by his solicitor that he'd face a heavy penalty. Dora's case was doubtful, since there were mitigating circumstances if it could be shown that she acted out of fear of her husband. Horace wasn't keen on that, understandably, but the alternative was prison for Dora too, as an accomplice. She'd quite likely get a couple of years. No wonder the poor bitch was all to pieces.

The one who'd really been a surprise to Horace was his daughter, Lesley. Once the initial shock had passed, she'd been like a rock, coping with the housework and cooking after Dora went, and working long hours with Horace. He could hardly believe she was the same empty-headed little slut he'd always complained about so bitterly. She'd even set about learning how to run the business, so as to keep the firm going while he was inside. 'Don't worry, Dad,' she'd told him. 'You'll have something to come out to, or I'll know the reason why.' Hearing those words, Horace had felt the strange sensation of tears welling in his eyes.

Patty expressed surprise at her friend's behaviour towards Horace one afternoon when they went to the clinic together to collect their orange juice and cod liver oil.

'Well, he's my dad after all,' Lesley replied. 'We got to stick together.'

Patty forebore to remind her that Horace hadn't adopted that attitude himself when Lesley was in trouble.

One good thing about the Aynsworth affair from Patty's point of view was that it diverted the neighbourhood interest from Stephen and herself. For them, life improved enormously. For one thing, she now felt much better. The morning sickness had disappeared, and she hadn't yet begun to show as Lesley had, other than in an added plumpness to her breasts. Very attractive, Stephen told her, as he played with them teasingly one Sunday morning.

'You look prettier than ever – if that's possible,' he said tenderly. It was true – Patty looked radiant; in common with many pregnant women, her complexion was translucent, her hair shining.

'Make the most of it,' she grinned. 'Before you know it, I'll be like an apple dumpling.'

He stared at her for a few moments. 'Oh, Patty, I do love you. I must be the luckiest man in the whole world.' He bent his head to kiss her and gradually, as his hands caressed her, their passion erupted until their two bodies were welded into one moving rhythmic whole.

Patty felt she could never be happier. They were together, in their first home. Stephen had given the flat a lick of paint, and they'd now acquired a few bits and pieces of their own. It was really quite cosy: certainly it'd do until the baby was born, then maybe they'd look around for something larger. It would be nice to have a little garden but there was plenty of time to think about that. Only one thing disturbed her serenity – the lack of any response from Peter to her letter. Even with the uncertainty of overseas mail, she should have heard by now. There was new wartime legislation which allowed divorces to be hurried through in certain circumstances. If only Peter would agree, Stephen and she might be able to get married before the baby was born.

The rift with her parents was gradually healing. Kath popped in to see them quite often, Stan when he could find the time, though by unspoken agreement neither Patty nor Stephen ever went to Balaclava Street for fear of provoking a row with Gran. Patty refused to go without Stephen, so there the matter rested. But even Gran seemed to be coming round to the idea of the baby, according to Kath. Recently Gran's eternal knitting for the forces had been replaced by something white and fluffy. When Kath had questioned it, she got the gruff rejoinder: 'Little bastard's got to have something to wear, hasn't it!'

Kath missed not having the whole family around for Sunday dinner. It was particularly sad this particular Sunday, as Roger was back on leave. Kath sighed as she fussed over the stove. Roger and Stan had gone to The Windmill to meet Patty and Stephen for drinks, and sure as eggs were eggs they'd be late. She'd almost succumbed to the family's urging to go along too, but was frightened the meal might spoil if someone didn't watch over it.

Goodness knows when they'd see Roger again. It had been a dreadful shock when he broke the news that he'd been passed for air-crew training. It was only slightly tempered by the fact that he was being sent to Canada, well away from the fighting, to train. Roger himself – needless to say, was wildly excited.

Only one thing had marred Kath's joy at Roger being home – that was the amount of time and attention he'd devoted to Lesley Aynsworth. Of all the girls to be seen around with! She felt a hot prickle up the back of her spine just thinking about her. Roger said she was being uncharitable and that the poor kid had had a rough time; that she'd got a lot of guts and was facing up to things very well. She was only the same age as Patty, after all, and she didn't have Stephen to lean on. Maybe that was true, but Kath still pulled her mouth tight in disapproval. Perhaps it was a blessing Roger was being sent away, after all . . .

At that moment, she heard the key in the front door and all other thoughts were pushed from her mind as she concentrated on her cooking.

Patty made a conscious effort to throw off that Monday morning feeling, but from the moment she woke up, she'd felt somehow that it was going to be one of those days.

Stephen was late. Most times when he came back from

nightshift, he'd bring up tea for them to have in bed. It was a nice, gentle awakening from the ten hours' sleep she seemed to need these days. Stephen jokingly put it down to exhaustion after their love-making, but Patty knew that it was something to do with the baby. She needed that sleep to replenish her energy.

She felt distinctly tired that Monday morning, yet she couldn't put it down to an air-raid. Vaguely she remembered the siren going some time after Stephen had left for the Depot. Remembered, too, the grumble of far-away gunfire. But she hadn't really woken up, which must mean last night hadn't been anything like the heavy raids they'd had before. It was the sort of uneventful night they disliked at the Depot; usually it meant the Colonel would call a snap kit-inspection, just to be cussed.

She put the kettle on and wondered what had happened to Stephen. She only hoped he hadn't been sent off on a long trip, like the time they'd been sent to Coventry.

Night after night, as he went on duty, Patty wished she was going too. After all, she wasn't *that* pregnant; she could still drive. In her heart, she felt that she'd resigned from the ambulance service too early – largely because of pressure from her family. And perhaps also because she'd been laid low at the time with morning sickness.

She drained her tea, then washed and dressed quickly and set off down the stairs to the shop.

Early as she was, Susan was there before her. Patty pulled a face and said guiltily: 'Golly, am I late?'

Susan laughed. 'No, I'm early. It was so quiet last night that I slept like a log – I woke up even before the alarm.'

'Well, perhaps one day you'll oversleep and let me get here first. Dammit, I only live upstairs!'

'Who cares? I enjoy the shop. And you should make the most of being able to lie in bed! You won't get much chance once you've got a baby howling its head off!'

They both laughed and set about taking down the shutters and getting ready for the early morning trade. They'd hardly finished when the doorbell pinged loudly.

Susan and Patty stared silently at their customers, neither of whom had ever been to the shop before.

Patty was the first to recover. 'Why, Colonel . . . *and* Mr Graves. What a nice surprise! What can we do for you?' But despite her light tone, Patty was startled.

The Colonel seemed embarrassed, staring down past the buttons of his Service dress at his feet. Arthur Graves looked straight ahead at some spot on the wall.

'Yes . . .?' Susan prompted, but the silence seemed to stay unbroken.

'I'd like a word with you, Patricia,' said the Colonel at last, raising his head and staring with his one good eye directly at Patty.

'I'll go,' responded Susan quickly. 'I've got something to do at the back—'

'No, please! Stay!' pleaded Arthur Graves, equally quickly.

It was Arthur's tone that gave Patty her first inkling that something might be terribly wrong. A half-thought began forming in her mind, but she blotted it out with a quick flow of words: 'I know – you want me to come back driving – but after the quiet nights we've been having . . .' Her voice tailed away, and there was another pause before finally the Colonel spoke.

'It's about Mr Broome . . .er, Stephen . . . your . . .' For one fraction of a second Patty noted the Colonel's awkwardness and found it funny; but then horror welled up in her mind, and nothing was funny any more.

'Stephen . . . What about Stephen?'

It was Susan who realized what was coming. Instinctively she moved to Patty's side and put an arm round her.

'*No! No!*' Patty moaned the words, but to her it sounded like a great scream of anguish bursting forth from somewhere deep inside her. At the same time, she noted what had been strange about the Colonel: he was wearing his best uniform and peaked cap – not the tin helmet he normally sported. Then she knew. The

Colonel had dressed for this occasion. That could only mean one thing.

'I'm afraid Stephen was killed last night,' he told her.

Patty looked appealingly at Arthur Graves, but his face, the little shake of the head which he gave, told her everything. Suddenly she swayed on her feet, and Susan's arm tightened around her. As the colour drained from Patty's face, she grabbed at the counter and both the Colonel and Arthur Graves took a step forward.

'Help me get her into the back,' ordered Susan. 'There's a chair there!'

The next few moments were a blur, but Patty kept hold on one thought and as soon as she could, she voiced it.

'*How?* There wasn't much of a raid last night. You mean he was injured! That's it, isn't it?'

'I'm afraid not, my dear,' murmured the Colonel.

'But it was hardly anything! I slept through it!'

'They came,' sighed Arthur, and Patty suddenly realized that she was holding his hand so hard that the knuckles on her fist were white. The simple words somehow broke through her defences and she started to sob uncontrollably.

'There, there,' muttered the Colonel, but Susan said they were to let her cry and cry she did, until no more tears would come. Even then, she uttered sounds like a small child in pain. Finally she was quiet, and Susan forced some brandy down her – brandy that Arthur produced from his brief case.

The world seemed unreal. Part of Patty's brain still refused to accept that Stephen would never come home. Surely it had all been some terrible mistake? But part of her mind knew it was true, knew even before the Colonel told her the full story.

'It was one aircraft,' he began. 'It seemed to wander out of the main flightpath – at least that's what Control said. Got caught in the searchlights and then the ack-

ack got on to him and he ditched the lot. It was incendiaries mostly, but there was a DA amongst them – they told us that as soon as the call came. It was just on the edge of our sector. Caught a whole road alight. Big old Victorian houses. Five floors. Some damned silly woman had got her family up there instead of in a shelter. Been staying there since the big raids ended.'

The Colonel stopped, as though the complete stupidity of it was too much for words. Then, just as suddenly, he carried on again.

'They got them all down, or so they thought. It wasn't until Broome was trying to calm the woman that she started screaming that her baby was still up there.' He shook his head. 'Broome should have waited and left it to the firemen.'

'He wouldn't,' replied Patty, in such a calm voice that Susan and the men looked at her in surprise.

'No.' The Colonel glanced anxiously at Susan, but she nodded for him to go on. 'He got up all right – found the baby . . . but as he was coming down, the staircase went and he couldn't get further than the second floor. He shouted to the firemen to hold a blanket, and dropped the baby into it. He was going to jump too, but . . . well, the delayed-action . . . must have had a short fuse . . .'

'The baby?' asked Patty, in the same flat voice.

'The baby's fine,' answered Arthur. He understood the reasoning behind the question. It was a mother's question.

'Did he . . . could he?'

Once again it was Arthur who responded: 'No. The bomb must have been right underneath the house. He couldn't have felt a thing. It would have been instantaneous.'

There was silence for a long time. Finally the Colonel felt he had to break it. 'He was very brave. A fine young man. I'm recommending him for the new George Medal.'

Suddenly Patty seemed to shake herself. She had regained control now, and was quite cold. 'His mother? Does she know?'

'I'm writing to her this morning,' the Colonel told her. 'And of course there'll be the official telegram.'

'If you don't mind,' said Patty, 'I think I'll tell her myself before she gets the letter.' Once again, tears began to run silently down her cheeks. Susan motioned the two men to leave.

Two hours later, despite Susan's protests, Patty set off for Coventry. She'd reasoned it all out. It was her duty to tell Stephen's mother, not to let her receive the news through the official letter. She knew the Colonel would do his best, but the letter would end up like the sort of thing he'd written to parents of his men who'd been killed in the trenches of Flanders. She owed it to Stephen to see that his mother didn't learn that way. And Mrs Broome had been kind to her – had written a formal little note saying how pleased she was about the baby.

Patty had insisted that Susan rang the Depot, to persuade the Colonel not to send the telegram. There'd been a long conversation which Patty couldn't quite overhear, but in the end it seemed the Colonel had agreed. But he'd insisted on sending the letter. 'He says he has to,' reported Susan, and Patty didn't argue. The Colonel, she knew, had a set of rules to follow, and nothing would alter that.

The journey seemed endless. The train sat in Euston Station for an hour after it should have started, and Patty could only gaze out of the open window at the station's battered roof. She kept the window open despite the bitter wind, because if she shut it, the blackout paint made her feel as though she were sitting inside the tinted glass interior of a hearse.

The train crawled to Rugby, where once again she had to sit for what seemed like hours, waiting for her connection. Only later did Stephen's mother tell her how cold she's been when she'd arrived, and how she'd sat and shivered in front of the fire, on which Mrs Broome tipped most of what remained of her month's coal ration.

Finally the fire died down to a few glowing embers, and still the two women talked together, sharing their grief and their memories of Stephen. Mrs Broome kept urging Patty to move in with her and have the baby in what had once been Stephen's home. 'The baby's all I have left of my son,' she said, over and over again. But Patty gently refused. The baby was all *she* had left of Stephen, too. And besides, she had to return; anything else would feel like running away – running away from the raids, from her responsibilities to her family, from Susan and the shop. Above all, in the flat she felt that she was stil close to Stephen. It had been *their* home, and that was where she wanted to have the baby.

In the end Mrs Broome accepted her decision.

'You won't have to worry financially, you know,' the older woman assured her. 'We're quite comfortably off, fortunately, and I'll see that Stephen's money is sent to you each month.'

Patty demurred at first, but gave in eventually. She had to admit that it would have been Stephen's wish.

'There is one other thing,' said Mrs Broome hesitantly. 'He did so hope that you could be married before the baby was born. He wanted it to have our name. Now . . .' She spread her hands in a gesture of helplessness.

Patty stared at her. It was something she hadn't previously considered. 'Well, it certainly isn't entitled to be called Quayle. I don't know what we can do about that.'

'You could take the name Broome by deed poll. Think about it, Patty. It would make me very happy.'

Patty nodded. Clearly, it was not a decision that could be taken in a hurry. They went upstairs to bed, and Mrs Broome embraced her warmly. 'Please always feel that this is your home, my dear – and think of me as the mother-in-law I'd hoped to be.'

The train journey back wasn't so bad as it had been going up, and somehow it seemed fitting that as Patty opened the door and stepped down on to the platform, the siren wailed its warning. She felt that she was back home; and that she was bringing Stephen's child back home, too.

28

A New Life

Patty lay in the double bed that first night back from Coventry and stared unseeingly at the ceiling. She was wide awake, but in spite of the long journey, she didn't feel tired. She stretched out her arms and could feel the loneliness as a physical ache. It wasn't only that she'd never slept alone in the bed before; this was the first time that she knew for sure that Stephen wouldn't be coming back.

'Oh darling,' she whispered. 'Darling, how am I ever to go on without you?'

There was a sudden lull in the distant gunfire and a profound silence settled over the little room. Patty lay, all her senses tuned. It seemed as if the hush were specially meant. Then she felt it. A faint quiver inside herself! It was like a moth trapped inside a lampshade, fluttering its wings. There it was again! A great wave of happiness and comfort flooded over her. Stephen was there with her after all. His child had quickened in her womb. She would never feel lonely again.

Suddenly she felt relaxed. She was so very glad she'd remained here instead of going to Dolphin Square with the family. Naturally Kath had pleaded with her to go.

Having heard from Susan Farley what had happened, Kath had rushed round to the flat, only to find her daughter still in the Midlands. Kath had been a little hurt that Patty hadn't gone straight to her for comfort, and it had gone against all her maternal instincts to leave the girl alone so soon after the tragedy. But Patty had been adamant, and now she was grateful. The moment she'd just experienced had been a very private thing – just between herself and Stephen. Imagine if it had happened in that crowded, noisy shelter! She might not even have noticed. And she'd have missed the most important event in her whole life – something that would remain with her always, giving her the strength to go on: the knowledge that Stephen was still there, and would be whenever she needed him.

She drifted into a peaceful sleep and woke next morning quite refreshed. Susan noted the difference immediately she came into the shop. Overnight, Patty had come to terms with the situation, and was facing life with a new determination and courage.

Kath was aware of the change in her daughter, too. She'd suddenly grown up, become independent. She could see now how right she'd been when she'd thought Patty's decision to live with Stephen would alter their lives completely.

Kath had assumed Patty would return to Number Seven after Stephen's death, and had been quite shocked at her daughter's firm refusal. 'It's not right for her to be on her own,' she'd remarked to Stan.

'I don't know, love,' he replied. 'She's got to get used to it some time. We won't always be around to look after her.'

She stared at Stan, accepting the truth of his statement and hating it at the same time. Then Stan came over and gave her an affectionate hug. 'Don't be miserable, sweetheart. You may have lost your little girl, but think what fun you're going to have being a granny!'

'As long as she doesn't shut me out.'

'She won't do that. You'll see. That's when a girl needs her mother most – isn't that what they say?'

And Kath had to be content with that thought.

Patty saw a lot more of Lesley these days. Both of them had a horror of the big shelters, so with Susan's consent, they fixed up mattresses in the back of the shop, where they could sleep if the raids were severe. They got into a routine of spending most evenings together at one or other's home and they seemed to have reverted to the old intimacy of their schooldays. Any resentment Lesley had felt against Patty completely disappeared after the death of Stephen, and the two of them seemed to have more in common than ever.

'Have you thought what you'll do when the baby's born?' Lesley asked one night. 'I mean, where you're going to live?'

'Not really,' Patty replied. 'Stephen thought we might find a house, but now I don't know.'

'Would you think of sharing? With me?'

'Well . . . yes. But what about your parents' house . . . Aren't you going to stay on there?'

'It depends. It may have to be sold – we're not sure yet. But Dad's going to pay back everyone he took stuff from and if he can't trace the actual items then he'll have to give cash. It could add up to a lot of money.'

'I suppose so.'

'He didn't want to do it, mind,' chuckled Lesley in the dark. 'It was his lawyer's idea. Said it would look better to the judge. Mum never wants to come back here.'

'Not ever?'

'No. Apparently, she's been saving up for years so she could buy herself a little cottage in the country. That's why she went along with Dad on this business – 'cos it meant she could leave him all the sooner.'

'Lesley!'

'Yeah. Mad, isn't it? Mind you, he was a miserable old bugger to live with. Can't think why she ever married him!'

'How awful to think of her being unhappy all those years, though!'

'S'pose so. Might be better if Dad made a new start somewhere else when he gets out,' continued Lesley. 'So maybe it's better if the house is sold. He won't want such a big place anyway.'

'I wouldn't want to move away from this district altogether,' said Patty.

'No more would I. Wonder if old Fred Perkins has got a tenant for Number Nine yet? Or wouldn't you like to be so near your folks?'

'I wouldn't mind.'

'Be convenient for babysitting,' Lesley laughed again. 'Well, think about it and let me know. If we are going to share, the sooner we start looking, the better.'

'Guess you're right.'

There was silence for a while. Patty moved restlessly on her mattress, then seemed to make a decision: Lesley was the closest friend she had, and she was easier to confide in than Kath in some ways.

'Les – I'm a bit worried about something,' she said at last.

'What?'

'Well, I haven't heard anything from Peter. I wrote . . . oh, way back in January, telling him about the baby and asking for a divorce, but I never heard a thing.'

'Perhaps he never got the letter?'

'That's what I was wondering.'

'Or else he might have been so sick about it all, he didn't want any more to do with you.'

'But he'd have to give an answer some time – about the divorce, I mean.'

'Yeah. But if he was feeling really mean, he wouldn't be in any hurry, would he?'

Patty sighed. 'I suppose not. The difficult thing is not knowing whether he's told his parents. They're sweet people. They wrote the other day, asking me down to Lymington for a few days.'

'You'll have to get out of that. Say you're on a course or something. They'll never know.'

'No. They still think I'm working at the Depot. You don't think I should write to Peter again, do you?'

'Leave it a bit longer. You can't really tell about the

mail. It's not as if you're desperate for the divorce now, are you?'

'No.' Another sigh, and they relapsed into silence. Not long after that, Patty could tell from the deep breathing at her side that Lesley had fallen asleep.

In the chill air of the afternoon of March 19th, Sub-Lieutenant Peter Quayle huddled deeper into the folds of his Navy greatcoat and headed purposefully into the wind over Battersea Bridge. He looked neither to right nor left as he hurried along. A girl passing by gave the young Naval officer a cheery smile, but it faded as she caught sight of his face. True, he was tanned and handsome; but there was something about his eyes that dispelled the flirtatious thoughts from her mind. The young officer had a strangely grim expression, and unseen by anyone, his fingers were flexing and unflexing inside his greatcoat pockets.

As he turned to cross towards Balaclava Street, a heavy army lorry swept round the corner, and only the quick reaction of the corporal at the wheel saved Peter from being run down. The corporal was so shaken that he slowed right down and leant over to yell a stream of profanities at Peter. Then, suddenly conscious that he was abusing an officer, the corporal stamped on the bare steel arm of the accelerator and roared away. Peter, much to the corporal's ease of mind, didn't appear to have heard the oaths and continued on his way as though nothing had happened.

It was only when he was actually in Balaclava Street that Peter seemed to take any notice of his surroundings. He looked carefully at the numbers on the gates. When he got to Number Seven, he stopped for a moment to adjust his cap, then stepped purposefully up the little path to the front door.

It was Mrs Bowden who opened the door. For a

moment, she didn't recognize him, but when she did, she recoiled. For once, Gran was totally at a loss for words.

It was Peter who broke the silence: 'Is Patty in?'

'Patty . . .? Oh, my Gawd . . .'

'Mrs Bowden, it's me, Peter, her husband – you remember?'

'Course . . . Her husband . . .' Gran found herself mumbling nonsense, playing for time. 'Lovely weddin' . . . You don't half look brown . . .'

Peter struggled to control himself. It seemed as though the old lady had gone senile in his absence. He tried again: 'Patty? Where is she?'

'She ain't here! She moved. Didn't you get a letter?'

'Moved! What letter?'

His words confirmed the fear that had been growing in Gran's mind ever since she opened the door. He didn't know! What on earth was she to do?

Peter was obviously struggling to keep his temper. 'Look – do you mind telling me where Patty is?'

It was probably the tone of his voice that finally sent Gran into a complete state of panic. What a mess! For a moment she wondered if perhaps Patty hadn't written after all . . . She was about to explain, but decided not to; commonsense told her that it wasn't her job to do that. Let Patty tell him.

'You'll have to speak to Patty. She ain't here. Sorry, I can't stop. I got things to do. Nice to see you. Bye.' And with that, Gran ended the conversation by slamming the door in his face.

Bewildered, Peter stood in front of the door, as though it might re-open at any moment, to reveal Patty standing there. But no such thing happened, and slowly he turned away.

What did the old woman mean? Why had Patty moved? From what Gran said, the answers were in some letter Patty had written. But he'd certainly never received any letter. Perhaps it was rotting away in the hold of some sunken ship on the bottom of the Mediterranean, or waiting for him in some Naval Post Office. Perhaps it was in Valetta. But if it was, surely they'd have given it to him when he was in hospital in Malta? At the memory of that time, Peter's hands once again screwed up into white-knuckled balls in his greatcoat pockets.

Exactly how long he stood deep in thought, he had no idea. But it was some time before Gran, peeping from behind the curtains of the front room, finally heaved a sigh of relief as she saw the dark figure move slowly away down Balaclava Street and disappear into the deepening shadows.

Just as Peter turned the corner, the air-raid siren began its mournful wail, but he only heard the sound as a faint background to the thoughts whirling in his mind: memories he'd learned to suppress. All through his long trip by troopship from Suez to Capetown and then zig-zagging home, he'd been looking forward to the sanity that for him centred around Patty and their future life together. Only that could wipe out those other things – the things he *mustn't* think about. Not yet.

The distant thump of a gun made him jump, and he realized that he was almost at the Depot. He increased his pace at the thought that this would be where he'd find Patty, where life could start again. He pushed through the blackout curtains and found himself in the brightly-lit hall. Peter blinked at the sudden light. Immediately, faces turned to examine him curiously, but nobody spoke. He looked around desperately, hoping for a glimpse of Patty somewhere, but there was no sign of anyone he knew.

It was Dusty Miller who first spotted the lone figure; and even Dusty would have slipped away quickly if Peter hadn't recognized him.

Dusty wondered what Lieutenant Quayle was doing there. But his mind was quicker than Gran Bowden's and he had half an inkling of the truth even before Peter said 'Hello'.

'Wotcher!' replied Dusty. Peter's approach had cut Dusty off from the kitchens, into which he would have been only too delighted to make his escape. Peter's next words confirmed Dusty's suspicions.

'I'm looking for Patty – Patty Quayle. My wife, that is.'

'Just come 'ome, 'ave yer?' Dusty tried to strike a conversational note. Peter nodded, but said nothing. Dusty decided he didn't like the look of Peter Quayle. His eyes – well, they looked haunted. Nervously Dusty recalled stories he'd heard – stories of men coming home to find their wives had gone off with other men.

'I don't fink she's 'ere at the moment,' he muttered, then with a flash of brilliance, added: 'I'll just go and ask the Colonel if 'e knows where she is.'

'Thank you,' said Peter politely. Too politely, thought Dusty as he hurried away in the direction of Colonel Harris's office. Peter suddenly became conscious that he was still wearing his cap. He took it off quickly and twirled it round and round nervously on his fingers.

Dusty was gone a long time. When he finally headed back to Peter across the main floor, his steps were hurried.

'The Colonel says 'e'd like to see you in 'is office.'

'That's really not necessary,' murmured Peter. 'I just want a quick word with Patty.'

'She ain't around,' Dusty put in hastily, 'but the Colonel does want to see you. Got a bit of a flap on at the moment, but 'e thinks it's only a 'it-and-run basket trying to keep us on our toes.'

'All right.' Peter followed Dusty to the Colonel's office. At the entrance, Dusty knocked, stood aside to let Peter enter, then closed the door and stood listening outside, while he wiped the sweat off his forehead with a none-too-clean handkerchief.

Colonel Harris was on the telephone, but gestured Peter to a seat in front of his desk.

'. . . A bloody Blenheim!' the Colonel exploded with mock-anger into the mouthpiece. 'Can't Bomber command keep their blokes from giving us all a dose of the runs?'

He listened carefully to the voice at the other end. 'Yes,

all right, Training Command. Call it what you like, but it started a major alert.'

The Colonel laughed – a short cut-off laugh which almost sounded like a dog barking – and hung up.

'Good to see you, Quayle. Sorry about all that. Some blighter who got lost on a training flight has triggered off the whole of London's defences. Expect we'll get the All Clear soon now. How are things with you? Judging by the colour of your face, you've got your knees brown too, eh?'

Peter could only remember having met the Colonel briefly, but something about his joviality didn't ring true.

'I'm looking for Patty,' he said simply.

Colonel Harris's good eye searched Peter's face for some clue. He didn't find one.

'Ah, Patty . . .' He cleared his throat. 'Hrrmph . . . Yes. Splendid girl. She was one of the best drivers I had, you know.'

Alarm raced through Peter's mind. '*Was?* What do you mean "was?" Has something happened to her? I can't get any sense out of anyone!'

The Colonel cleared his throat again and looked distinctly unhappy about the turn the conversation was taking.

'Dammit, Patty's my wife!' Peter's voice rose in anger.

'Steady, old chap. Patty's quite all right. It's just that she doesn't drive for us any more. Resigned, y'know – the baby and all that . . .'

'Baby?'

'Ah . . . yes,' muttered the Colonel, and began to look even more unhappy. This wasn't going the way he intended at all. It wasn't his bloody job to go around telling young officers that their wives had run off with other fellers. Wait till he got his hands on that Dusty Miller, bursting in saying that young Quayle had come to murder his wife. Load of poppycock!

He studied young Quayle again. He certainly didn't look as though he had murder in mind. And suddenly, to his horror, the Colonel saw the change in Peter's face and recognized it for what it was – a great glow of happiness spreading through Peter's entire being.

'Now, just a second,' interjected the Colonel hastily, 'it isn't quite what you think—'

But Peter was no longer listening. 'A baby! We're going to have a baby. That's marvellous!'

'Yes, of course it is. In a way. That's why your wife had to give up driving. But—'

He was about to say more, when suddenly it seemed as if every phone in the room started ringing at once. The door behind Peter swung open and Arthur Graves hurried in, and with scarcely another glance at Peter, Arthur and the Colonel started answering phones and pressing buttons. Now messengers were arriving and being sent off with barked orders. Peter found himself edged out of the way until he was sitting with his back against the wall, unnoticed, and to his relief, unwanted.

Only once in the next twenty minutes did the Colonel speak to him. 'A big one, I'm afraid. Stick around – you may be able to help later.'

Peter was quite happy to be left alone as he thought over what the Colonel had said earlier. He still didn't know exactly where Patty was, but the mere fact that she was all right was enough. That, together with the news of the baby, was the first light in the gloom which had surrounded him for the past few months.

The Battersea Depot was only one of many all over London which were now on full alert. All fire and rescue services were put on stand by. Which was just as well, for that night, 479 German bombers droned their way from airfields in Northern France towards the capital, to claim the lives of 751 Londoners and leave a further 1,170 injured. It was to be the biggest attack in terms of damage and casualties that London had suffered so far, including the great attack of the previous October.

The Colonel was so busy that he had little time to look at, let alone talk to, the young man in his office. The noise outside the Depot grew in volume, so that at times the Colonel and Arthur had to yell down the telephone lines to make themselves heard. All non-essential personnel were ordered to the shelter area. A few minutes later, a large section of the ceiling at one end of the hall collapsed, showering the whole floor with plaster rubble and white powder, and Dusty Miller was left to clear it up virtually single-handed.

The attack went on and on. By midnight Colonel Harris knew there was little more he could do. Every single crew was out and until his messengers managed to get off-duty drivers back to the Depot to man the remaining few ambulances, they'd have to remain in the yard. He reported Fully Extended to Area HQ and the shrilling of telephones dropped noticeably in volume. Though the Colonel hated doing it, he had to refuse those calls for help that did come through.

It was just after one such call that the Colonel's eye fell on the figure of Peter Quayle. *He* could drive! The Colonel perked up. If Quayle drove and he rustled up an attendant from the off-duty crew members, then at least he could get one more ambulance on the road.

During a lull in the gunfire, the Colonel called across the room to Peter who was sitting opposite with his face in his hands. 'Quayle!' Peter didn't respond from his position in the shadows. The Colonel shouted this time, but still Peter didn't move. Perhaps he's got his hands over his ears, thought the Colonel, and moved out from behind his desk.

'*Quayle!*' He reached out a hand to Peter's shoulder, thinking that perhaps he'd gone to sleep; poor chap had probably been travelling for hours. To the Colonel's intense surprise, he saw that the young Naval officer was shaking like a leaf. The Colonel snatched his hand back quickly.

'Quayle,' he said sharply. 'Come on, man, we need your help!'

Peter looked up. As he did so, a violent burst of ack-

ack fire exploded in the sky above the Depot and before it had died away, a screeching whistle warned of a bomb on the way. Suddenly the room shook and small flakes from the ceiling fluttered to the floor. The Colonel looked down at Peter in amazement. In what light there was, he could see great spasms of fear ripple across the young man's face with each fresh explosion. Tears glistened on Peter's cheeks and a nervous twitch seemed to move each tear one stage closer to his mouth and chin. His mouth hung loose and his hands were clapped over his ears. His eyes were blank as though he saw nothing.

'Steady, man!' growled the Colonel. He didn't know what else to say. He remembered seeing faces like that before. Remembered using the same useless words.

The lights had been dimmer then, of course – just the odd oil lamp or two casting long shadows inside the big dugout. The noise had been worse. They'd been shelled for hours at a time. But the faces were the same. The mouth loose, as though the noise had forced it open. The hands over the ears. The trembling. And worst of all, the blank stares that saw nothing. By God, he'd almost cracked up himself. And all he'd been able to say then was the same thing: 'Steady, man!' It had sounded as inadequate then as it did now.

Yet the words cut into Peter's misery, and some sort of consciousness seemed to creep back into his eyes. He saw the Colonel staring down at him.

'I'm sorry, Colonel,' he apologized, and brushed the tears away with the sleeve of his greatcoat. God, he felt so ashamed. The slightest stress and he started crying like a bloody schoolgirl. 'I'd better go.'

The Colonel coughed gruffly. 'Nonsense. Happens to the best of us. I was just wondering if you'd feel up to driving for us?'

Peter said nothing, but held out his hands in front of him; they were shaking – badly. The Colonel doubted if he could even hold a driving wheel, let alone turn it.

'Hrrmph . . . I see.'

Though the Colonel hadn't meant to sound condescending, Peter reacted violently. In a flash, his mood changed to anger and the words surged out, as though driven from some white-hot source inside him.

'I don't think you see at all! All you see is me sitting here quivering like a ninny. A coward, that's all you see.'

'I assure you—' the Colonel began, but Peter cut him off.

'A bloody snivelling coward, that's what you think of me. Go on – say it! But say it to my face, not behind my back like everyone else!' Peter had gone white under his tan, leaving his complexion a ghastly pale yellow colour. And 'yellow' was the word that he used to continue his tirade as soon as he'd drawn breath.

'*Yellow!* That's what they call people like me. Other blokes seemed to be able to stand hearing those bloody great tin-cans bouncing off our hull. Everyone holding their breath in case the next second we were blown to Kingdom Come. But I couldn't! And I was meant to be Number Two. And . . . and . . . *I cracked!*' The last few words came out almost as a whisper. Much to the Colonel's embarrassment, Peter started to cry again.

When Peter finally managed to control himself, the Colonel spoke again – but this time in a voice quite unlike his usual clipped, military tones.

'Look, lad,' he murmured almost paternally, 'I know what it's like. Not your sort of shelling – don't think I could stand that. In a tin-can of a ship, hundreds of feet under water, with Jerry lobbing things down at you . . .? No, I couldn't stand that. You've got nothing to be ashamed of. But I do know what it's like. At Arras, they shelled us for ten hours; and afterwards I sat down and had a good cry myself . . . It's just taken longer to come out with you, that's all.'

A phone rang, and Arthur answered it quietly. He was looking at the Colonel with new eyes. He never knew the old man had it in him to be so human.

'Now then,' the Colonel was brusque again. 'Cheer up,

Quayle! You've got the rest of your life to look forward to.'

Peter managed a weak smile at the Colonel. 'Good try, sir, but it's not much of a life for me from now on. They shipped me home, you see. Lack of moral fibre, they call it. Given me a desk job. Just a clerk now.'

'A battle's never lost until it's won,' observed the Colonel. 'I expect they'll have you back in action as soon as the medics clear you.'

'I don't know about that,' replied Peter slowly. 'Once a coward . . .'

'Nonsense!' said the Colonel briskly. 'Never does to make snap judgments, you know. I've had to change some of my views over the last few months. And I take some shifting, I can tell you. Take this fellow I had here. Name of Stephen Broome. Conscientious objector! I gave him a bit of a rough time at the beginning . . .'

As Colonel Harris began to relate the story of the life and death of Stephen Broome, Arthur Graves listened too. And he decided to change his opinion of Colonel Harris once again.

29

Uncertain Future

The shop bell pinged, but in the back room, Patty didn't bother to look up. They really must do something about that door. Sometimes a tiny gust of wind was enough to make it open. At other times when someone came in, the bell didn't work at all.

This time someone *had* come in, because Patty distinctly heard footsteps; but as nobody spoke, she assumed it was Susan and returned to her task of checking the list of clothes.

As she worked, Patty mused over the change in Susan. Not long ago she wouldn't have hurt a fly. Now, running the shop and coping without her husband, she might almost be called bossy. Patty smiled to herself. Maybe that was unfair, but Susan was a prime example of the way the war could change a person. And then there was Lesley. Who'd even have imagined that Lesley could turn out to be such a businesswoman!

Poor Lesley had really been thrown in the deep end, with both her parents on trial and Joy away in the Land Army. But she hadn't given up. The way she'd taken over the undertaking business had been a revelation.

Suddenly Patty was aware of a stillness in the shop. But there *was* someone out there . . . With a sudden flash of fear, she remembered the visit of the policeman who'd taken over Bert Williams' beat, and his warning about the series of attacks on shopkeepers in the neighbourhood. Patty grasped the heavy round ruler she kept on the desk.

'Who's there?' she called, hearing the tremor in her own voice.

Still there was no sound. She stared at the curtain which divided the small back room from the counter area.

'Is anyone there?' There was no reply. Was she imagining things? All she had to do was to pull back the curtain. But she hesitated with the fear growing inside her.

Finally she took the plunge. She pulled it back with a great sweep of her left hand. The ruler in her right hand was poised for a blow. The sight that greeted her was such a shock that the ruler fell to the floor and Patty very nearly followed suit.

'*Peter!*'

On the other side of the counter, Peter stood as though frozen to the spot. Patty realized that he'd been standing in that same position ever since he'd come in. Her eyes ranged over him. Under his peaked cap, his face looked haggard. His eyes stared at her and past her, almost as though he was looking right through her into the little back room.

His arms hung at his sides, and Patty's immediate impression was that someone or something had dealt him a stunning blow. He said nothing. For an age they just stood like that and stared at each other.

'How are you?' Patty asked the question automatically. Peter didn't look well, and she wondered for one instant whether it was safe to be alone with him. He had a strange, wild look about him.

'All right,' replied Peter.

'You don't look too good,' she observed.

'I'm all right.' It was said as though to close any further argument about his state of health. Another long silence followed, but this time Peter forced himself to break it.

'I've been talking to Colonel Harris – at the Depot. He seems a nice man . . .'

'Yes,' said Patty. Her heart thumped violently. Had the Colonel told Peter? Was this the reason for his distraught appearance? She tried to maintain a calm exterior. 'Under all the spit-and-polish.'

'He knows what it's like . . .'

There was definitely something wrong with Peter. He was no longer the laughing young Naval lieutenant. He still wore the uniform, yes – but that was all.

'What it's like . . .?' Patty repeated.

'Being depth-charged for hours on end. That sort of thing . . .'

Some clue to Peter's haggard appearance seemed to lurk in those words, and Patty snatched at it.

'Was it awful? Are you ill? Have they sent you home for a rest?'

Peter gave the nearest thing to a laugh that he could manage. It came out as a mirthless grunt.

'Yes to Question One. No to Question Two. Yes to Question Three – well, if not for a rest, at least to get me out of the way while the heroes get on with the war.'

Patty stared at him, bewildered and unhappy. He gave her a twisted sort of smile.

'Never mind. I'll tell you all about that later. The Colonel told me . . . about . . . about the baby.'

Patty's throat seemed to close up, and she couldn't speak – not that she had any idea what to say to this stranger who stood in front of her, looking at her with that curious expression of desperation. She had been expecting anger, outrage, perhaps even violence. Instead there was sadness and a kind of pleading.

'It isn't mine, is it?' he asked softly.

She shook her head, still unable to speak. At that moment, Susan arrived. She flushed scarlet, aware that she'd walked into an awkward situation. Her arrival helped Patty find her voice.

'Peter, we can't talk here. Go upstairs to the flat and I'll join you in a minute. I just want a few words with Susan.'

Susan made a hesitant move of protest. 'It's all right, I—' But Peter strode, white-faced and tense, through to the stairs at the back. Susan turned to Patty with a look of concern. 'I'm so sorry.'

'No, *I'm* sorry. He just arrived – without any warning. It's awful, Susan! He obviously didn't get my letter telling him about . . . the baby and everything—'

'Oh, my dear – what a shock. The poor man!'

Patty sighed. 'Listen. Can you manage without me for a little while?'

'Yes, of course.' Susan bustled about, taking off her coat and getting ready for customers. 'Patty—'

Patty turned at the foot of the stairs.

'Will you be all right? Alone?'

Patty nodded and smiled her thanks, then headed upstairs.

Peter sat in the armchair in front of the unlit gas-fire. He still wore his greatcoat and was hunched up, as if suffering from the cold.

'I expect you'd like some coffee? I know I would,' Patty observed, and busied herself with the kettle and some cups. Occasionally she glanced across at the still figure, but Peter didn't react at all. Patty kept the chatter going. 'Why don't you take your coat off? I'll light the fire if you feel cold. Probably quite a difference from the Mediterranean – you're bound to feel it.'

Still no movement from the figure in the chair.

Patty put the mug of steaming coffee on the table beside him and pulled up the only other chair for herself.

Then she sat down in silence, wondering how to broach the subject as painlessly as possible. In the end there seemed no answer but to come straight out with it.

'Peter, about the baby,' she began, and then caught her breath. For he looked up at her then, and his eyes contained an indescribable agony.

'Don't tell me,' he muttered.

'I must. You've a right to know.' She hesitated, trying desperately to avoid staring into those tortured eyes. 'The baby's father was killed a little while ago. He was in the Ambulance Service with me and . . . and . . .' Once again she stopped. Her tongue seemed dry and too big for her mouth. 'His name was Stephen Broome . . .'

'I guessed as much. Colonel Harris told me what a splendid chap he was.'

'I did write, you know.'

'I never got the letter. Probably just as well. It would have been the last straw.'

She looked at him in a silent query, but he didn't elaborate. She went on: 'I haven't touched the marriage allowance. It's all in the bank, in your name.'

'I don't want it. You keep it.'

'No. I can't. Not after what happened.'

'Well, use it for the baby, then. I want you to, Patty.'

'It's very sweet of you, but it wouldn't be right. You never know what's going to happen. You might find you need it sometime – if you divorce me—'

'I don't want to do that,' he cut in sharply. 'Patty, it doesn't matter what happened. There's a war on; it makes people do funny things.'

'But—' He made an impatient gesture with his hand to forestall argument, and she fell silent. After a few minutes she tried again, this time confining herself to mundane conversation.

'How long have you been back?'

'Yesterday. I went to see you at the Depot. While I was there the raid started. 'Fraid I wasn't much use to him . . .'

'The Colonel?'

'Yes. He ran out of crews. Suggested I drive for him . . . But I couldn't help. I get the shakes, you see. Have done ever since . . . since Malta . . .'

Once the floodgates were opened, there was no stopping him. The words poured out and Patty listened, sharing the horror of that last depth-charge attack on the submarine, hearing the canister rolling over the metal hull, seeing Peter's tears as he relived it all.

Her eyes also glistened with tears. Tears for what might have been. But mostly tears for the living hell that Peter inhabited now.

'What are you going to do now you're home?'

He shrugged. 'They've given me leave while they make up their minds. I suppose they'll find me a harmless job in some backwater. Still, I mustn't complain. I'll be lucky if they keep me on at all.'

'Come on,' protested Patty. 'Course they're going to keep you. You'll get over it. You'll see.'

He shrugged again. Clearly he didn't care much either way.

'You'll go down to your parents, I suppose?'

Once more he stared at her in a desperate plea. 'Patty, don't turn me away – please!'

'But you can't stay here!' She was startled and at a loss. It was one eventuality she hadn't anticipated.

Peter clutched her hand, as if physical contact could somehow restore what had once been between them. 'Listen, Patty, can't we start all over again? Forget the past?'

Forget the past? Forget Stephen! Never! The thought was so shocking that Patty snapped out one word: '*No!*'

Peter was rocked by the vehemence in her tone. His face was white and drawn, but he made yet another offer.

'We could bring the baby up as ours. No one need ever know the truth.'

Patty's reaction was the same as before. But this time she softened the rebuff.

'No, Peter. I don't think that would be fair. To you. To the baby. To Stephen.'

'Well, one thing's for sure. Your Stephen will never know.'

Patty found she could ignore the bitterness in his voice. He was bound to feel like this. She gently eased her hand away from his. 'You'll think differently about it in time. We both will. I loved Stephen, and this is his child. It could never be anything else. I'm sorry.'

'But you loved me! You said so in Church, remember! Surely you have some feeling left for me?'

Patty searched her heart, but could find no answer. She

looked at him and felt compassion welling inside her. She had a sudden clear insight into Peter's mind. He was like a small child, searching for a prop to cling to. She was that prop – his only means of returning to sanity and self-esteem. No wonder he needed her so desperately. All at once, she felt quite old. Could she fail this man – her husband – at this moment? Surely she owed him this much, at least?

Peter seemed to sense the change in her attitude. 'Don't turn me away now. I couldn't bear it!'

'I couldn't sleep with you, Peter. You understand that?'

'Of course.' He nodded vigorously. 'Just give me the chance to be with you. I'll prove how much I care. Maybe after the baby is born—'

'No promises. Don't count on anything, please!'

He smothered her hand with kisses and started to cry again. His head dropped and she found herself stroking his hair and soothing him, as a mother might. All the time, her mind was racing. Everybody would get the wrong idea, that went without saying. But what did it matter as long as she knew the truth and those she loved knew too? Stephen had taught her not to care about people's gossip. All that mattered was to be honest with oneself. She didn't fool herself that it would be easy, but she felt she had the strength to manage.

Patty made Peter go to bed, and very soon he was enjoying the first trouble-free sleep he'd enjoyed for weeks, while she went downstairs to resume her normal day's activity in the shop. There were many practical arrangements to be made.

First, she telephoned Lesley and asked her not to come round tonight. The first evening with Peter would be difficult enough without company. Lesley was avid with curiosity, but Patty told her she'd have to contain it until they met. Next she explained matters to the family. She could see they didn't understand, and once again felt their disapproval; but never mind – in time she'd be able to make them see the true state of affairs. Then there was extra shopping. Once more she had a man's appetite to cater for.

On the airfields of Northern France, the engines of the Heinkels and Dorniers spluttered into life. Not long after, the sirens wailed over Battersea. Lying on the mattresses at the back of the shop, Patty felt Peter shudder. His hand reached out and grasped hers. She gave it a reassuring squeeze. It seemed a fitting way to face an uncertain future – hand in hand.

FIELDS OF BATTLE

Kate Alexander

In the romantic tradition of THE FLOWERS OF THE FIELD, an irresistible new novel of conflict and heartbreak, love and loss.

Rilla Grey would never have met Barney Wainwright if the outbreak of war in September 1939 hadn't seen him posted to her home town. Ill-matched in background and worldiness, Rilla is dazzled by the attractive, young officer until a hasty marriage based on necessity ends a charming interlude. Neither is prepared for the ravages of war, the equally intense battlefield of their fateful marriage nor the gnawing loneliness of long separation.

When they meet again, after the war, they are strangers with unshared memories and uncertain of their future together. But bearing the visible scars of hard won maturity they are to make a decision you will never forget.

Futura Publications
Fiction
0 7088 2154 5

MAGGIE

Lena Kennedy

From the East End of the 20s; through the London blitz; to the Australian outback, and back . . . every page simply brims over with life.

'MAGGIE is more than just a novel . . . it is the most intensely warm and human document I have read for a long time. I was sorry to have finished it and rather lonely too.'
THE SUNDAY PRESS (DUBLIN)

'A remarkable story and a remarkable book.'
DAILY EXPRESS

'It is a novel, and a good one, and one that doesn't let you forget for a single line that it is so . . . such are Maggie's adventures, tribulations and even victories that the what-happens-next quality never lets up.'
ALAN SILLITOE

'A rare and unusual book . . . a great delight to read.'
HOWARD FAST

Futura Publication
Fiction
0 7088 1747 5